Kate Johnson was born in the 19⸻  in Essex, where she belongs to a ⸻ second cousin who made the G⸻ brewing the world's strongest beer and she also once ran over herself with a Segway scooter. These two things are not related.

Kate has worked in an airport, a lab, and various shops, but much prefers writing because mornings are definitely not her best friend. In 2017 she won Paranormal Romantic Novel of the Year from the Romantic Novelists' Association with her novel *Max Seventeen*.

katejohnson.co.uk

x.com/K8JohnsonAuthor
tiktok.com/k8johnsonauthor
facebook.com/catmarsters

ALSO BY KATE JOHNSON

HEX AND HEXABILITY

KATE JOHNSON

One More Chapter
a division of HarperCollins*Publishers* Ltd
1 London Bridge Street
London SE1 9GF
www.harpercollins.co.uk
HarperCollins*Publishers*
Macken House, 39/40 Mayor Street Upper,
Dublin 1, D01 C9W8, Ireland

This paperback edition 2024
4
First published in Great Britain in ebook format
by HarperCollins*Publishers* 2024
Copyright © Kate Johnson 2024
Kate Johnson asserts the moral right to be identified
as the author of this work

A catalogue record of this book is available from the British Library

ISBN: 978-0-00-867143-3

Printed and bound in the United States

To all the Tiffanies. You're not alone now.

CHAPTER 1

*M*ost young ladies were expected to feel nervous upon attending their first ball, but this was probably not because they feared they would accidentally make the paintings on the walls come to life.

Lady Theophania Worthington, however, feared this exact thing, and so when she was announced at Lady Russell's grand ball, she froze at the top of the stairs for what felt like an hour and a half before her panicked, darting gaze landed on her sister-in-law's expression of tight fury. Elinor had been drilling her on this for weeks. Everything had to be perfect. She must not do anything wrong at all. Her *entire future* depended upon this *very moment.*

Fear thrummed through her, made her palms sweat inside her gloves, made the chalked patterns on the ballroom floor begin to swirl and move...

No! Not now! Please not now!

1

She tried desperately to make them stop moving, lost her footing, grabbed for a handrail she hadn't a hope of reaching, skidded for a terrible, heart-stopping moment, and fetched up in the arms of a pirate.

'Are you all right?' His eyes were the colour of rich dark chocolate and he had a scar on one cheek. 'Miss?' His hair was black as night and curled wildly. 'Are you hurt? Miss...?'

'Tiffany,' whispered Tiffany, who had always hated being called Theophania because it was surely the name of a dusty old bluestocking or querulous maiden aunt.

'*Lady* Tiffany,' hissed her sister-in-law, and then hurriedly corrected herself, 'Lady Theophania. We are not in the school-room any longer, are we, my dear?'

The pirate raised an eyebrow as he straightened Tiffany, who felt her face heat up. Of course it was of more concern to Elinor that Tiffany was addressed correctly than that she was unhurt. Must she be so obvious about it in front of this handsome stranger?

'Thank you, Mr...?'

He looked very amused. 'Santiago, *Lady* Tiffany,' he said, and gave an elaborate bow. The sort of bow that had gone out of fashion a generation ago—as had wearing green velvet to an evening event, Tiffany thought as she took in more of his appearance. And a brocade waistcoat. And a neckcloth tied so loosely he looked like a labourer.

A very handsome labourer with twinkling eyes and lips that looked like he was trying very hard not to smile.

'You have our thanks, Mr Santiago,' said Elinor, with tightly restrained disdain for the sheer foreignness of his name and demeanour. She was already shepherding Tiffany away. 'Come along, Theophania. There are people I want you to meet. They say the Lost Duke of St James has returned, and wouldn't it be a coup for you to become a duchess...'

Tiffany glanced over her shoulder as she was led away from the pirate. As he grinned at her, a hint of gold twinkled in his ear. One eyelid flickered in a wink that made heat blossom inside her.

It was at this point that the chalked arabesques on the floor came to life.

~

As he escaped out of the window, Santiago reflected that he had been greatly misled about English Society.

Nobody had told him it was quite so boring, or that the Ton was so very cold towards anyone who didn't look exactly like everyone else, or that the chalk drawings on the floor would come to life.

Santiago had seen purple fire play along the mast of a ship, had seen lava that burned blue and plants that ate small rodents, but had never seen chalk drawings move and start tripping people up.

Had it been an illusion? Some trick played on the guests? After all, nothing here was as it seemed. Including him.

He could still hear people screaming and bellowing as he stepped into a flowerbed and looked around. None of that was entirely necessary, he thought. Really, only a few people had been tripped up and the rest had just been a sort of ripple effect.

Only one lady hadn't fainted or screamed, and that had been the vision in silver who had already taken a tumble into his arms. She had simply bolted.

Her hair was pale, like moonlight, her cheeks flushed the palest dawn pink, her eyes like a storm-tossed sea. Her dress was of some silver gossamer, like pearls or shimmering starlight. A mermaid. A siren.

He shook himself. She was merely a human woman, and part of this absurd merry-go-round to boot. She was a lady. Lady

Tiffany. It had a soft, silken sound to it. A shame her chaperone appeared to be some kind of harpy.

Once, in Singapore, he had been chased by thieves down an alley, and had escaped by shinning up a decorated pillar as if it was the ratlines of a ship. But there were precious few ratlines in Lady Whatsherface's garden, and besides, he didn't suppose Lady Tiffany had spent much time on a ship.

He made his way towards the arrangement of hedges and arbours that appeared to have been designed to hide trysting lovers, considered whistling, and rakishly decided not to. The crunch of his boots on the gravel was probably enough to alert anybody to his presence.

Anybody, at least, who wasn't running with her silver skirts bunched up in both hands and her head quite foolishly turned to look behind her.

'Lady Tiffany,' he said, as she collided—not unpleasantly—with him. Her wide blue eyes stared up in panic. Her hairstyle had lost its neat curls and half its pins, and was slowly collapsing down the side of her head. Her white bosom heaved in a gown cut so low one slightly deeper breath would expose all her charms to him.

Santiago reluctantly reminded himself that he was trying to be a gentleman tonight, and dragged his eyes up to her face.

He gestured to a small alcove in the hedge. 'I think we're alone now,' he said.

~

THE PIRATE LED her to an alcove with a bench tucked into it. A stone lion gazed out despondently at the early roses. 'Sit down. Are you all right?'

Tiffany stared up at him. In the darkness she couldn't make out very much of his features, but the moonlight showed his white teeth and the gleam of gold in one ear. Perhaps he really was a pirate, the kind who kidnapped innocent travellers and sold them on the Barbary Coast. He had an accent Tiffany couldn't work out, but that was probably because Tiffany never met anyone who didn't have the exact same accent she did. But why would he be at this ball? How had he got in?

'Why are you wearing green?' she blurted.

He shrugged. 'I like green. Why are you wearing grey?'

Tiffany bristled. 'It's not grey; it's silver.'

A flash of white teeth in the darkness. He was laughing at her! 'My mistake,' said the pirate gravely.

'Gentlemen don't wear green in the evening,' Tiffany told him.

'I noticed,' he said. 'Don't you find it dull?'

Tiffany blinked at him. Yes, she did, but she'd never allowed herself to think it before. Gentlemen wore black in the evening, with snowy white linen, and that was simply how things worked. Nobody questioned it.

'That's just ... how things work,' she said, frowning.

'What happened in there?' he asked. 'With the ... chalk? It seemed to become...'—he waved his hand elegantly—'animated.'

Tiffany wanted to hunch over and curl into a ball with her feet pulled up on the bench, but that was not a very ladylike thing to do and besides, thanks to her benighted bosom she was wearing long stays with a busk that made even sitting down an exercise to be practised. It was chilly out here, and her skin was damp from exertion. She carefully arranged her skirt over her slippers.

'The chalk,' he persisted. 'Is that ... usual?'

'Usual?' Was he simple-minded? 'Do you think it is *usual* for chalk drawings to come to life at Society balls?'

He shrugged. 'I have never attended one before.'

'Have you ever attended any event where a chalk drawing has come to life?'

'No.' He considered this. 'But I have tried opium a few times and the things I saw were stranger than that.'

Tiffany began eyeing escape routes. 'Have you taken opium now?'

'No. Alas.' He grinned again. 'Perhaps it would have made the evening more entertaining.'

'You don't find balls entertaining?'

'You ask a lot of questions, you know?'

'So do you,' Tiffany said sulkily.

He sighed and sat down beside her, leaning back against the stone bench and stretching out long legs. He at least wore dark knee breeches and stockings, although the buckles on his shoes were frankly vulgar.

She watched as he fetched a slim case from his hideous coat and opened it to reveal a selection of cigars. He offered it to her, and she stared for a second before mutely shaking her head. He shrugged and lit one for himself.

'Are these parties all like this? A list of people attending, some skipping up and down, nobody speaking to anyone they don't already know, everyone wearing the same thing? The ladies at least have some variation,' he conceded, 'but why is everyone in this country allergic to colour?'

TIFFANY SMOOTHED her silver skirts over her ivory slippers once again and tucked a strand of pale hair behind her white ear. She'd seen a lovely deep blue dress at the modiste's, but apparently that sort of shade was vulgar. She'd only managed to get the silver dress because Elinor had left her unsupervised. That wasn't likely to happen again.

'The officers are in their regimentals,' she pointed out. Plenty had cashed out after peace was declared a year ago, but there were still enough of them in scarlet and blue to make the place look decorative.

'And every other man?'

'Everyone wears black and white in the evening.' Surely this was well-known?

'But why?'

Tiffany blinked. 'My sister-in-law says bright colours are vulgar,' she said.

'Do you agree?'

No. But while she lived in Elinor's house she had to follow Elinor's rules, and since Elinor believed every single word she read in *La Belle Assemblée* there was no point in arguing with her about it.

'All those gentlemen in black,' he sighed. 'It looks like a funeral.' He added, 'I suppose I had better get used to it. My dock foreman said nobby people wear black for years when someone dies.'

Tiffany choked a little, and said, 'What ... sort of people, did you say?'

'Nobby.' He glanced at her, and laughed. 'Ah. I see that is another word which is unacceptable. There seem to be so many of them. Perhaps,' he mused, 'it was an error to take etiquette advice from a Limehouse docker.'

Tiffany laughed incredulously. Who on earth was this man? 'Have you no one else to ask?' she said.

Mr Santiago shrugged. 'No. My father is dead; my mother is in a convent and my grandfather is both hundreds of miles away and dead.'

He said it as if he was describing his grandfather's hair colour or height. *My grandfather is from Yorkshire; he is of average height and quite dead.* 'I am so sorry—'

'Why? We have never met and were never likely to.' He sighed when he saw her expression. 'You think I am cold. But he— he was not a part of my life,' he said with a careless shrug, and Tiffany wondered what he had been about to say. 'And I have no attachment to him. I am only in town to hear what his solicitors have to say, and then I shall probably be on my way.'

'Your way to where?' Tiffany asked politely.

He gave an expansive hand gesture, the glowing cigar transcribing an arc in the air. 'I do not know. Perhaps I shall return to the Americas. Perhaps Europe.' As an afterthought, he asked, 'Do you enjoy travel, my lady?'

Tiffany had been raised in her brother's house in Hertfordshire, travelled to London occasionally, and once been taken to Brighton, because it was terribly fashionable now with the Pavilion. But the seagulls upset Elinor and so they had not repeated the experience.

But...

'I would like to travel more,' she said diplomatically. 'Paris, Venice, Florence.'

Mr Santiago looked bored. 'Ah, the haunts of every young Englishman,' he said.

Tiffany looked him over in the moonlight. His velvet coat was dark, but still recognisably velvet, his neckcloth was a shambles, and his hair was a tumbled mess. A gold ring gleamed in his ear, and the cigar end glowed as he puffed on it.

'Suddenly you know the exact habits of young Englishmen,' she said.

He acknowledged the blow with a smile. 'I listened,' he said, tilting his head in the direction of the ballroom. The music had restarted, and the sounds of people milling on the terrace had faded. 'And yet I notice it was only the men boasting of their travels.'

'Yes,' said Tiffany shortly. She rested her hand on the cool stone of the lion's head.

'English women do not travel?'

'No,' said Tiffany, even more shortly.

One dark eyebrow rose. 'I see,' he said.

No, thought Tiffany, suddenly furious, *you don't see, and you'll never see, because you are wearing a green velvet coat to a ball and you just used the word 'nobby' to describe the Ton, and however you got in here you will never be a part of this world.*

The lion's stone fur began to soften beneath her hand.

Abruptly, she got to her feet. 'I should go,' she said.

'I have upset you?' said the strange man with the pirate earring. He did not stand.

'Upset me? Mr Santiago, you don't have the faintest idea...' She tried to calm herself. There was no point in shouting at this stranger. She'd probably never see him again.

Although on the other hand, she'd probably never see him again...

'You truly don't know anything about Society, do you?' she said. 'And worse, you don't seem to care. You don't even seem to realise how dangerous it is for us to be out here alone like this. But let me explain one thing to you, and if it is the only thing you do learn about English Society, I hope you take it to heart.'

'I am all ears,' he said mildly.

'Good. Then learn this: you might find a ball such as this to be pointless and trivial, but I assure you it is of deadly importance to every woman in that room. And that is because every woman in that room is looking for a husband, either for herself or her daughter, and that is because without a husband even the daughter of an earl'—she gestured to herself—'has nothing. No money. No home. No power of any kind in the world. The reason I have not travelled, Mr Santiago, is because I had the misfortune to be born a daughter and not a son. My brothers all went on a Grand Tour of Europe. I have been to Brighton. Once. I have but one purpose in life, and that is to become somebody's wife. And bear him children. And then marry them off, and then die.'

'That is four purposes,' he said, looking vastly entertained, and that made Tiffany want to kick him in the shins.

'That is the life of a farmyard animal,' she hissed. 'You might get to swan in here in your green velvet coat with your earring, and use stevedore words to describe all the people in that room, but your future does not depend upon them.'

'I assure you,' he said, face much straighter, 'it does.'

'Then take it seriously, Mr Santiago. Find a proper tailor. Find a valet. Learn the rules. This all seems entertaining to you, but it is very serious to me.'

She turned to go, feeling somewhat haughty and magnificent, but his voice stopped her.

'Do you want to become somebody's wife?'

No. The answer in her head was immediate and vehement. She did not want to become like Elinor, whose only interests in life were clothes and gossip and who to befriend and who to avoid, because her only purpose was to marry off her children so that they could live in immaculate, cold marriages and raise children whose only purpose was to be married…

She didn't want to be a wife, a woman who only existed in relation to her husband, who didn't even get to keep her own name. She didn't want to spend hours achieving the correct hairstyle or chatter about music she didn't like, or gossip about who might have broken one of the million self-imposed dashed stupid rules the Ton lived by. She didn't want any of it.

Wouldn't it be a coup for you to become a duchess?

The stone lion's mane quivered. Tiffany glared at it, and it was still.

'Not even if he is a duke,' she said.

She had walked several steps before his voice followed her again. 'How did you do it?' he said. 'Make the chalk come to life?'

Tiffany felt herself go very still, and then she turned back and said deliberately and clearly, 'I don't know what you're talking about.'

~

'MORNING,' said the newspaper at the head of the table. 'There's post for you, Tiff— Theophania.'

Tiffany murmured a greeting to the newspaper in the assumption that her eldest brother was behind it, and helped herself to eggs from the sideboard. Coffee, too, since Elinor was still abed—with a 'stomach complaint' apparently, which was in no way related to the glasses of Madeira she had partaken of last night—and not here to tell her that chocolate was more fashionable.

'Anything from last night?' asked Cornforth, in a tone so neutral she couldn't tell what he wanted the answer to be. He seemed neither inclined nor disinclined to help her find a husband, and Tiffany was under no illusions that this was because he valued her company so much that he couldn't bear to lose her. Quite often, she thought he forgot she wasn't one of his own many children, and it was only since her hems had been let down that he recalled that she was actually his sister.

'A few cards,' she said. 'And a letter.' It was not a masculine hand, for which she was grateful. Tiffany was in no mood for suitors. She might have hoped that falling down the stairs last night had put paid to her chances, but it seemed that everyone else had taken a mysterious tumble shortly afterwards, and so nobody recalled her misdemeanour at all. She'd even had to dance a few times.

'Ah?'

'From…' Tiffany opened the letter and scanned to the end. 'A Great Aunt Esmerelda, apparently.'

'Ah.'

His tone did not reveal whether he had heard of her or not, which didn't help Tiffany very much. She knew every member of her family to the fourth degree of removal, and had most of the Peerage memorised besides, but she had never heard of any Esmerelda. It was definitely the sort of name that stuck in one's mind. Rather like Theophania.

'*My dear Tiffany,*' the letter began, which had Tiffany sitting up a bit straighter in her seat.

> *Please do forgive the intrusion over your breakfast. I regret very much that we were not able to speak last night at the Russell ball, but I greatly admired your extraordinary accomplishments.*

Accomplishments. Tiffany's neck prickled.

> *I would be delighted to receive you at your earliest convenience. Please do call upon me. I believe we have much in common and foresee us spending much of our future together. Yours, Esmerelda Blackmantle.*

Tiffany glanced up furtively to see if Cornforth was watching her, but he appeared absorbed in the newspaper.

This was surely the strangest letter she had ever received. The address given was a very smart one in Mayfair, and the quality of both paper and penmanship were excellent.

Thoughtfully, she returned her attention to her eggs, which had gone somewhat cold, but the letter by her plate kept drawing her attention. *Extraordinary accomplishments.* What could that mean? Had Great Aunt Esmerelda seen her dancing and been moved to write her a letter about it? Tiffany could dance in a tolerable enough fashion, but absolutely nobody would consider it worth writing about. What else? She had demonstrated no other accomplishments last night, such as singing or playing the pianoforte—which was just as well as she was terrible at both. And as for her drawing and watercolour painting…

Viscount Cornforth, heir to the Earl of Chalkdown, had married when Tiffany was a mere babe, and as such her nieces and nephews were close to her in age. This meant that she had been raised in the same nursery and taught by the same governess, dancing master and music master. The story of the drawing masters, however, was something that nobody in the household could account for.

Except for Tiffany.

It wasn't that she couldn't draw. She could: very well, in fact. So well that her drawings appeared lifelike. So lifelike that they … well, that they came to life.

Which had caused more than one drawing master to quit the household. Sometimes at speed. Occasionally screaming.

Elinor, of course, believed none of this nonsense and eventually decided that drawing masters were simply too highly strung to bother with. It was probably the only time Tiffany had been grateful to her sister-in-law for her dogged adherence to conformity.

Extraordinary accomplishments.

She put down her fork, and glanced at the letter as it lay beside her plate. Then she excused herself from the table and said to the footman, 'Send Morris up to me, will you? I'm going for a walk.'

LIMEHOUSE WAS the sort of area you got in every large city— squalid, heaving, constantly falling down and being built over. Santiago had spent half his life in places like this. He thrived in places like this. He'd learned to pick pockets and dodge fights in places like this, learned to beg and lie and sell anything he could, including himself. He'd learned to be charming, and devious, and he'd expected that would stand him in good stead when he began commanding his own ship. He hadn't expected it to be quite so useful now he owned a whole fleet of ships, and got to attend nobby parties with girls in silver dresses.

Nobby. Hah! Santiago had learned Spanish from the cradle, and a smattering of other languages since, but it seemed the English his father had reluctantly passed on was going to need some updating—and not from dock foremen.

He stepped out of the way as a private carriage rattled past, bearing the crest of some lord or another. There was a carriage like that waiting in the mews behind his grandfather's house. Santiago felt a terrible fear that if he set foot in it, he'd never come back to Limehouse the same man.

That kind of wealth and privilege had turned his grandfather into a cold, unfeeling man, and his father into a monster who cared for nothing but himself. And Santiago had spent far too long striving not to become his father to risk that happening to him.

He approached the high walls surrounding de Groot's compound on foot. All the warehouses here had massive security fences around them, surrounded by men carrying muskets they'd brought home from Cuidad Rodrigo and Seringapatam. Santiago, who carried an interesting variety of semi-lethal weapons about his person, had made a point of befriending as many of them as possible.

'Morning, *Señor,*' said one of them, a cheerful fellow with powder burns on his face from Salamanca. He gestured at the corresponding scar on Santiago's cheek. 'Tangled with any more pirate queens, have you?' He grinned at his own joke.

Santiago smiled back. 'If I ever cross Madam Zheng again, you'll come to my funeral, won't you?' he said, and the old soldier laughed and waved him through.

When Santiago closed his eyes, he could smell the jasmine tea that had been brewing as the knife cut into his face. She'd offered him a cup afterwards. He couldn't drink it now, the sense memory spoiled by the coppery taste of blood in his mind.

'Ah, *mijn vriend* Santiago! *Hoe gaat het vandaag met jou?*'

'*Estoy muy bien, gracias*,' Santiago replied, turning to greet de Groot. The man was well-named, a huge blond giant with a massive beard. He dwarfed Santiago in a hug, and gestured expansively at the yard where cartloads of goods were being unloaded.

'Look! The *Marijntje* came in, bringing jasmine tea and opium. I sell this to the teahouses down the road. They carry it themselves, on their backs!'

'I thought it smelled familiar,' said Santiago. When he smiled, his cheek felt tight.

'I don't care for it much myself,' said de Groot. 'I like the African tea we had in Swellendam, hey?' He grinned, and added in a terrible approximation of an East London accent, 'You fancy a cuppa?'

'You've gone native, *mi amigo*,' said Santiago, following the big man into the shady interior of the offices.

'It is my special skill,' said de Groot. He waved at an underling, who rushed off to do his bidding. 'Now, what can I do for you, *mijn vriend?*'

Santiago took a seat. De Groot's office was much better established than his own, and as a consequence much more cluttered. A plate of crumbs sat on his desk, and there was a child's wooden horse on the floor.

He'd made a home here, started a family, done all those things Santiago had put off thinking about. The Dutchman even looked like a business owner, in his fancy waistcoat and gleaming pocketwatch. Santiago wasn't so sure about the wisdom of that. Time was, he'd have robbed a man looking like de Groot.

How did I get from robbing rich men to being friends with them?

You worked on ships, and then you ran ships, and then you bought a ship. And then you bought more, and suddenly you had a business and the Revenue wanted to check inside your brandy barrels and then a neat little man turned up and told you your grandfather had died and—

His father had always told him this day would come, but Santiago had never fully believed it. Partly because he hadn't wanted to, and partly because his father was barely able to remember the truth most of the time, let alone tell it.

He could leave London at any time, could leave his business affairs in the hands of men who would be happy to get rich from managing them. He did not have to settle, and fill his office with children's toys. He could go back to the sea, get his hands dirty, and tangle with wild women. Maybe even with wild men. Nobody would know and nobody would care.

Thinking only of himself. Just like his father.

'Tea,' said de Groot, handing him an earthenware mug. 'Just like we had in Swellendam.'

'It didn't do much for my hangover then, either,' said Santiago.

He'd met de Groot in a fly-infested compound in South Africa, where Santiago had been carefully constructing blanket boxes to conceal packets of tea and de Groot had been mixing diamonds into clay to be fired into pots. Each others' ingenuity having been duly admired, they proceeded to get roaring drunk on Santiago's smuggled brandy, and had woken the next day with matching chicken tattoos and earth-shattering hangovers.

'Sometimes I tell people about my friend with a cock on his ankle,' said de Groot, eyes twinkling.

'And I tell them of my friend with a cock on his back,' replied Santiago. 'Did you ever remember what the joke was that made us get them?'

'*Nee*. I don't think I understood it in the first place,' de Groot lamented.

'The *Marijntje*,' Santiago said. 'She came in on time?'

De Groot shrugged. 'On time for China. Storms around the Cape, but there are always storms around the Cape.'

'The *Epunamun* hasn't been seen since Marseilles,' he said. 'Last month the *Sirena* never made it to Porto. And the *Pincoya* was last seen from a place called Foulness, but hasn't come in yet.' He squinted at the map behind de Groot. 'This must be a made-up name, yes?'

De Groot laughed. 'It is real, *mijn vriend*. The English have a strange sense of humour.'

Santiago shook his head in wonder. 'Have you had any ships coming in late? Or nor at all?' It had better not just be his own vessels.

De Groot frowned deeply for a moment, then said, 'The *Linneke* and *Anneloes* never came in either. I haven't lost this many ships since your people attacked us at Celebes.'

'Not my people,' Santiago reminded him, trying not to think of that liveried carriage and the house it came with.

'Hah! People are curious about you, my friend. The Spaniard who is not Spanish?'

'I'm not Spanish,' Santiago agreed.

'They say your mother was an Aztec princess.'

'Incan,' said Santiago, 'and you can believe that if you like.' He'd heard every variation of the rumour. His father had enjoyed spreading them.

His father had enjoyed many things Santiago did not agree with.

'But your father'—de Groot leaned forward—'was an Englishman. And not just any Englishman.'

'An exiled Englishman,' said Santiago, warning in his voice. 'Disgraced. And we were talking about ships.'

De Groot didn't look as if he was convinced by the change of subject, but he said, 'We were. You have lost three? So have I. And a few others—*Pernice, Damsgaard, Muller en Zonen*—have been waiting long waits. The Company—' by this Santiago knew he meant the East India Company '—have posted losses but they haven't given names. Price of brandy has gone up.'

'Price of brandy always goes up,' said Santiago vaguely. 'What about the French importer in St Katherine's? The one people say they buy their wine from.'

'When really they buy it from you, *mijn vriend*,' said de Groot, winking. He got up and pointed to sections of the Atlantic on the big map behind his desk. 'I heard of a Portuguese ship sighted off Tangier that never came in. But these things happen.'

'These things used to happen,' said Santiago, getting to his feet and coming over to the map. 'The corsairs were supposed to have been outlawed.'

The Dutchman, about whom there were rumours of Caribbean piracy, said nothing.

Santiago peered at the map, trying to make sense of it. 'Do you have the dates of when they were last seen?'

'Mine, yes. The others, you'd have to ask around,' said de Groot. 'Why? You think this smells bad?'

Santiago's gaze slid up the English coast, past Dover, past Broadstairs, past the mouth of the Thames, to the marshland of south Essex where the *Pincoya* had last been seen. To the large island with the strange name. 'Yes,' he said. 'It smells of foulness.'

She had walked past the house four times now. Eight if you counted return trips.

It was a perfectly nice house on a very respectable street. The front steps were neatly kept with little topiaries either side of the door, the railings painted a smart blue, and there was a small garden square opposite where the spring flowers were beginning to bloom.

She had dispatched Morris to the shops, knowing full well that the head housemaid had a young man who worked on New Bond Street and would be gone for hours. 'I shall just sit on this bench here in the garden for a while,' Tiffany had said, that first morning when she'd ventured towards Mayfair, 'and read my book while you run those errands.'

They both knew the errands did not exist. But they also both knew that Morris was not about to tattle on Tiffany, if Tiffany did not tattle on her.

Now she was out in Society, Tiffany had wondered if she might have a maid of her own, but Elinor had declared that taking on a second woman 'just to do your hair, Theophania,' was profligate.

Tiffany privately suspected that when Harriet, her eldest niece, made her come-out, a maid would be hired in an instant.

She had intended to approach the house and make herself known to this Great-Aunt Esmerelda. She really had. And yet she had found herself walking speedily past the house, eyes down, and only stopped on the corner to pretend to tie her shoelace.

So far, she had pretended to tie her shoelace on the same corner three days running.

But today would be different. Today, Morris had explained that she had to run to the apothecary and the lending library and there was always a terrific wait at both, which Tiffany took to mean her young man had the afternoon off. Morris was certain to return with her hair ruffled and her lips swollen from kissing, far later than usual. Tiffany had time to knock on the door of Great-Aunt Esmerelda's house.

She definitely had time.

Any minute now she'd go up there and do it.

The house was perfectly pleasant, with stucco walls and elegantly arched windows. Tiffany had visited dozens of houses just like this in London. Possibly, given her attention on carriage rides was always commanded by Elinor and her many lists of things not to say and do, on this very street.

If Elinor had been here, quite assuredly she would disapprove of Tiffany stooping to tie her lace again. But if she just made it to the corner of the square, she would be out of sight of the house and—

'Perhaps you need this?'

Tiffany turned, startled, to see a lady holding a bootlace. She felt her face begin to heat.

'I have observed that you frequently need to stop and fasten your lace by the end of the street,' said the lady. 'I cannot imagine why it should always break precisely as you walk past my house. Perhaps Nora cast a curse here and subsequently forgot about it.'

Tiffany couldn't think of a single word to say.

The lady addressing her was of average height, although Tiffany would always think of her as much taller, and elegantly dressed in deep blue. Her bone structure was impeccable, her age undetectable, and her complexion darker than any Tiffany had seen in the fashionable drawing rooms of the Ton.

'You are Lady Tiffany Worthington, are you not? You look so like your mother.'

The words were out before Tiffany could stop them. 'You know my mother?'

There was a slight tightness in the lady's face as she said, 'Of course, my dear. I know everyone. Now. Perhaps a cup of tea?'

With that, she swept away across the street, towards the very house Tiffany had been trying to find the courage to approach.

She called me Tiffany.

The possibility of not following her didn't seem to be an option, and so she found herself stepping past the blue railings and the topiaries and the smart red door, and into a hallway painted a fashionable green, with a handsome stone staircase.

'Do come and sit down,' said the lady in blue, who could not possibly be Great-Aunt Esmerelda. Great-aunts were surely elderly people, querulous and frail. Tiffany vaguely recalled her grandmother, the dowager countess, as a papery old lady who required assistance to stand, and always shouted at people because she was quite deaf.

The morning room to which Tiffany was led had striped wall-paper and comfortable sofas. An upright pianoforte stood against one wall, and the occasional tables were inlaid with fine marquetry. Upon one of them stood a tea set, with steam curling from the pot.

'Were you expecting...' Tiffany began, and faltered. The tea must have been made while she was standing outside. And the water boiled and the leaves steeped and the milk brought up and the sugar placed in the bowl—

'I expected you. Now, lemon?'

The lemon was freshly sliced. Tiffany could smell it from here. She nodded and watched as steaming tea was poured into a cup. She had absolutely no idea what the etiquette was for being invited into the home of a stranger you'd been waiting outside of for three days.

'You have the advantage of me, ma'am,' she tried.

'Do I?' The elegant lady smiled slightly. 'You did receive my letter? I assumed that's why you came.'

'Your— But you're—'

You're too young to be my great-aunt, and besides I don't even think I have a great-aunt, and how can we be related when you look like that and I look like this and I've never even heard of you before!

'Esmerelda Blackmantle. You can call me Aunt Esme.'

'And you may— But how did you know I prefer to be called Tiffany? Lady Cornforth—'

'Lady Cornforth', said Aunt Esme, her nostrils flaring, 'is your sister-in-law, not the Queen. If you prefer Tiffany, then Tiffany it is.'

Tiffany felt a smile break out. She purely hated being called Theophania. But how did this Great-Aunt Esme know that?

When Tiffany didn't take the teacup that was offered, Aunt Esme put it down on the table beside the sofa Tiffany didn't remember sitting on.

'I intended to make your acquaintance at the Russell ball, but unfortunately I was called away. Not, however, before I saw your distinctive accomplishments. Making the chalk come to life: that's a neat trick, I thought.'

'I don't know what you mean,' said Tiffany automatically, ice flushing away her smile. 'Chalk doesn't come to life.'

Everyone knew that, and 'everyone' included Tiffany. Chalk did not come to life, and neither did watercolors or sketches or the contents of the Royal Academy. Tiffany was very firm about this. Perhaps, occasionally, out of the corner of her eye, a painting might appear to move. Maybe sometimes she might imagine that a statue had winked at her. And as for that time she had idly doodled a daisy in the margin of a notebook and then found one lying on the table ... why, surely all that had happened was that she had swept it up on her hem and someone had picked it up.

Yes. It was all perfectly explicable. There was probably a clever fellow at Oxford or Cambridge who could explain it all to her in a scientific manner.

Esme raised one neat eyebrow. 'Half the ballroom simply tripped at the same time, is that the case? How fascinating.'

'I was out of the room,' said Tiffany, her heart hammering. 'My hem.'

'That's what you told that bulldog of a chaperone, is it? I mislike her, you know. Father made a fortune in sugarcane, and we all know what that entails,' she said darkly. 'I spent five minutes in her company at Lady Russell's and that was quite enough, I assure you. You, however, Lady Tiffany, I am quite interested in.'

Tiffany felt herself doing it. Becoming unnoticeable. She'd been doing it since she was a child when her governess wanted to teach her something boring or the drawing master had run off to tell Elinor his charge was possessed of the devil. She'd done it at the Russell ball. It was like a hedgehog curling into a ball, or one of those lizards her brother Phileas went on about that could change their colour.

'Now now, none of that,' said Aunt Esme. 'It might work on ordinary people, but you and I aren't ordinary.' She gestured at a painting on the wall, a rather dramatic scene of crashing waves and a coastline like rocks with teeth. 'Do you know, when you walked past, the waves began moving?'

'I'm so sorry,' whispered Tiffany. She worked so hard to control it, and now she was so rattled, and—

'Why? It's marvellous. To make a glamour is a wonderful skill. Even more so to manifest it into a physical object. What about your own illustrations?' she said.

'I don't draw,' said Tiffany, tightly.

Esme's brows rose. 'Come now. The daughter of an earl and you were not taught this basic accomplishment?'

The screaming drawing masters. She complied with almost everything else Elinor demanded of her, no matter how much she hated it, but drawing and painting, those were her lines in the sand. They had to be. For her own protection.

Nobody could know about her ... peculiarities. Especially not Elinor. She'd be packed off to an asylum for the rest of her natural days, and never spoken of again. Elinor had made it clear, so very many times, that there was no room for Tiffany to have any notions about herself.

'I don't mean to,' she whispered, once more a frightened child in the nursery, so afraid of her own power.

'But what if you did?' Esme's eyes were bright with excitement. 'Have you— No, it's all right. I don't mean to frighten you,' she said as Tiffany shrank back against the sofa. 'I won't force you into anything. I'm simply fascinated. Look.' She waved her hand at the fireplace, where a fire had been laid but not lit.

Esme narrowed her eyes at it, and the coals burst into flame.

Tiffany nearly spilled her tea. 'How— That's not— How did you—'

Esme simply smiled at her. It wasn't a knowing smile or a cruel smile or a smug smile. It seemed infused with genuine enthusiasm, like Tiffany's brother Phileas when he met someone else who got as excited about colour-changing lizards as he did.

'It's witchcraft,' said Aunt Esme. 'I'm a witch, Tiffany. And so are you.'

THE MORNING MIST hung low and eerie across the marshland. It clung to Santiago's clothes, his hair, his skin, clammy and unpleasant. The inn where he'd reluctantly spent the night had been dank and inhospitable, the locals seeming to resent his presence entirely. He didn't know if it was his accent or if they just hated everyone. Maybe it was both.

Nobody had any information on the *Pincoya*. There had been no storms. No wrecks. The sandbank was marked by the lightship—it was visible now, just off the coast. Someone recalled that the tide had been higher than expected, but that was about it.

Foulness lived up to its name. The locals pronounced it, somewhat pointedly, with the emphasis on the second syllable, but that didn't stop it being any less cold, damp and treacherously marshy.

The morning mist made travelling slow, not helped much by

the lack of proper roads and tracks in this godforsaken place. With no more horses available to hire, he plodded miserably on foot along a slimy, seaweed-coated path. The locals called it the Broomway, since it was marked out by broom-like sticks that were only visible when the tide was out. The whole path, it seemed, was only visible when the tide was out—and the tide was known to come in extremely quickly—but despite its utter impracticality it appeared to be the only method of accessing the whole of Foulness Island.

Santiago had been counting the hours carefully, since nobody at the inn would give him any indication of when it was safe, and he calculated he had perhaps an hour to get off the path before the incoming tide made it too treacherous.

'Oi, mister!'

It was a boy, scrawny and scruffy, appearing out of the mist. Santiago wouldn't have been surprised to discover he was the ghost of some poor child who had drowned out here when the tide came in too fast. Until he spoke again.

'I heard you was after hearing about a boat what went missing?'

'Yes?' said Santiago, wondering how much coin he had left. Everybody he'd spoken to wanted money even when they had nothing to tell him.

'Only I found summink in the mud this morning and it might be from a boat.'

'Yes?'

'It's too big to carry. Here, look, down this headway.' The boy led him down a path of questionable stability, and Santiago followed cautiously. You heard tales of wreckers, people who led ships onto rocky shores to murder the crew and plunder their goods. Did they exist on land, too? Was this boy luring him to a boggy, watery death in the endless mudflats of this godforsaken place?

Just when he was about to stop, the boy gestured to something pale sticking out of the mud. 'Here, mister. It's one of them ladies you get on boats.'

His blood ran cold at the sight of the pale face. 'Ladies—'

It was the remains of the ship's figurehead, carved into the likeness of a beautiful young woman with her arms upraised in dance. Only now her arms had broken off and there were vicious deep gouges on her torso.

Claws? Teeth? What on earth swam the Thames that could take a bite that size from the ship? Santiago gazed around, but all he saw was mud and mist.

'But they said there had been no wrecks,' he said, running his hands over the cold, dead wood. La Pincoya's carved face stared back unseeingly.

'That's the funny thing. I didn't see nuffink. Or hear it. Nobody did. Cos they ring a bell and that for people to help if there's a wreck, yeah? But I didn't hear it. Just saw the wave and then stuff started turning up in the mud.'

'What kind of stuff?'

The boy looked shifty. He was grubby and skinny, his clothes ragged and muddy. Despite the chill, he wore no shoes. Santiago had seen children like him further upriver, foraging in the muddy banks of the Thames for bits and pieces washed in on the tide. Mudlarks, they were called, as if they were wading birds hunting for fish, and not children hunting for the means to feed and clothe themselves.

For a while, on the Rio de la Plata, he'd done something very similar.

'Show me,' he said, 'and there's a guinea in it for you.'

'A guinea?' The boy looked disbelieving. 'Nah. What'd I do with a guinea?'

Santiago gave him a questioning look. A guinea was quite a lot of money. He'd have to unpick one from the lining of his coat.

'Nobody'd take it off me,' the boy explained. 'Nobody round here got change for a whole bean. Someone'd nick it off me.' He gave Santiago a calculating look. 'How many shillings you got? Shilling coins, I mean.'

'Er,' said Santiago. He tried to remember how much he'd spent at the inn and what he had left. English money was stupid, with its pennies and crowns and groats and bobs and guineas. There seemed to be a coin or a word or both for every conceivable amount of money. He had half a mind to miss the simplicity of the dollar. Even the French had worked out a decimal system.

'I'll do it for ten bob,' said the boy, to whom this—less than half a guinea—was probably enough to live on for weeks. Maybe months. 'Ten actual single bob. I don't want no crowns or coach wheels.'

'Done,' said Santiago. He looked around at the chilly grey sea mist, the mud and the marshes, the eerie shapes of sea birds and the distant, ghostly clang of ship's bells. He really had to get off this terrible, treacherous path and back onto terra firma. 'After you've shown me what you found.'

The boy looked sceptical. 'Half a crown now?'

'I thought you didn't—fine. But if you trick me into drowning in a bog, I will come back and haunt you,' Santiago warned.

'Mister, if I tricked you into drowning in a bog, I wouldn't get my ten bob,' reasoned the boy, and Santiago couldn't fault that logic. He handed over the coin, and off they set.

'I DO PREFER my house in Cornwall,' said Esmerelda Blackmantle, who insisted Tiffany call her Aunt Esme. 'There is good, honest work to be done there, and it makes the film-flam of Society seem somehow so … tawdry. That said,' she added, glancing at a pile of invitations on a silver tray, 'the parties are fun.'

'Have you lived there long?' asked Tiffany, for want of anything else. Her great-aunt had fetched a decanter and poured Tiffany a small measure of something strong and sweet.

'Not long. That is, since...' Esme faltered, which already seemed to Tiffany to be a rare occurrence. 'Since before you were born,' she finished.

'I have never been to Cornwall,' said Tiffany. She had never been anywhere.

'It is a wild and beautiful place,' said Esme. 'Untouched by the revolutions of the modern world. A much better place to grow witches than Mayfair.' She gave a delicate shudder. 'I always think a witch ought to be in communion with the earth, and that's rather difficult when one is surrounded by paving stones and gravel. But then you did not grow up in Town, did you?'

'No, ma'am,' said Tiffany, as if all this talk of witches was completely normal. 'My brother's house is in Hertfordshire.'

Esme's face suggested she might as well have grown up in a chicken coop. 'I did hear as much. Dreadful place. The very ground rejects us. Do you know what they build into their houses? Hagstones,' she said, making a shape with her hands. 'Lumps of flint and bits of grit all mixed into a giant pudding by nature, said to guard against witches. I mean, it doesn't, not in the slightest, because it's just some bits of rock. But the belief is there. People will do terrible things to avoid us.'

'Us?' said Tiffany warily. Esme was uncovering dishes on the sideboard and taking nibbles of whatever she found there.

'Witches.' She tilted her head. 'You must have known? Suspected? That you are not like other people?'

Tiffany felt her face heat. She'd gone to such pains to hide it!

'But of course, in Hertfordshire—and with that gorgon of a guardian—permit me to guess, my dear, that strong emphasis was placed upon conforming to the rules, and not being any different from anyone else?'

Tiffany nodded, unable to speak. Those were almost exactly Elinor's words. Tiffany had a position as an earl's daughter and Cornforth's sister, and she must always act accordingly. There were no exceptions for her: she was not special, and must behave just as all the other young ladies did.

The very worst crime Tiffany could ever commit in Elinor's eyes would be to embarrass the family.

'Ah,' said Esme, and in that syllable was a world of understanding. 'It is a pity you did not have other witches around to guide you, but— No, it could not be helped.'

'There are others?' Tiffany said weakly.

'Oh, yes. Just Gwen and I in residence right now, but Nora and Madhu are on their way. And plenty more, all over the country. I don't suppose you go much to Essex? No? Don't worry, Tiffany, we will teach you what you need to know. How to guide and control your magic. How to use it safely and responsibly.'

'Are there rules?' asked Tiffany. Everything had rules, even if no one said them out loud.

'Rules? Hmm. Not really. Promise a thing three times and it becomes binding; if you make a bargain you may find yourself bound to it; what you do comes back to you sevenfold; that sort of thing, so use it for misdeeds at your own peril. But all of that thrice widdershins by moonlight nonsense is bobbins.'

She leaned in, her eyes dancing, and said, 'What magic is, my dear, is possibility. Don't think about what you can't do. Think about what you could do.'

Tiffany smiled weakly, fighting a sudden urge to cry. Because what was Society except an endless of things one couldn't do?

Perhaps Esme was simply very eccentric, and liked to fancy herself a witch. After all, what evidence was there, really? Perhaps Tiffany had some disorder of the eyes that made her believe she was seeing paintings come to life. Yes, that was it. She ought to ask Elinor to find a doctor; although, any mention of eye disorders might raise the terrible prospect of spectacles, which Elinor believed to be a handicap worse than spots or freckles.

'Pippin!' called Aunt Esme. 'I found the cheddar.'

'Cheese! Mmm! I love cheese!'

Tiffany looked around, expecting to see a child, but Esme was leaning down to feed a grey cat.

'There you are. No, don't snatch. What have we said about manners?'

'Bugger manners,' said someone.

'There you go. No, no more, or you'll get fat and lazy and we'll be overrun with mice.'

'Sod the mice,' said the voice, and Tiffany stood up to look around for the speaker. There was nobody else in the room, apart from herself, Esme, and the cat.

'Oh, Tiffany, this is Pippin. Head mouser and greedy little so-and-so.' Esme gestured at the cat, who was sniffing around on the ground.

Pippin glanced at Tiffany, and she heard a childish voice say, 'Cheese?'

She stared. Pippin the cat hissed at her. 'Piss off!'

'They don't like it when you stare. It's an aggressive gesture to a cat. Blink slowly, and look away,' said Esme.

Tiffany, wondering if this was what it felt like to go mad, did so.

'Hmph.' Pippin sat down to wash his paws.

Tiffany moved past him to the sideboard, picked up the decanter, and poured herself a large glass of whatever was in it.

Esme waited until it was nearly to her lips before she said, 'How did he sound to you?'

Like a child. A young, extremely selfish, rude child. Who uses words I'm not supposed to know.

'Cats don't talk,' she said, and took a drink.

'No, but they do have thoughts and feelings, and we pick up on them.'

'We?' Tiffany said again, helplessly.

'Witches.'

'But witches aren't real,' wailed Tiffany, as the flowers on the wallpaper began to dance. 'They're just some silly story told to children!'

'That doesn't mean something isn't real,' said Esme sensibly. 'Besides, look at the evidence of your own senses. I've never met a witch who couldn't understand animals. Haven't you heard them before?'

Tiffany shrugged, and drank some more, the alcohol burning down her throat.

'I don't think I've ever been this close to one,' she said, and then realised that couldn't be true. There were cats everywhere. But Elinor did not approve of pets. 'I mean ... not inside a house.' She wasn't much of a rider, always having been too nervous and distracted by the chatter of the grooms—

She closed her eyes momentarily. It had been the grooms chattering, hadn't it? Not the horses themselves?

She peered around again, still half convinced it was a trick. 'How many fingers am I holding up?' she asked Pippin.

The cat went on washing his paws. 'Some,' he said. His mouth didn't move, but she heard the voice anyway.

'What colour is my dress?' she tried.

'Bored,' said the cat. 'Cheese.'

And right then Tiffany felt a peculiar sensation, as if something was terribly, awfully wrong with the world. Worse than drinking brandy at lunchtime with a talking cat. Much worse than that.

'I don't think he quite understands the concepts of numbers and colours the way we do,' began Esme, and then broke off, her head snapping towards the ceiling. Without a word, she bolted from the room, as Tiffany heard footsteps running above.

'I felt it,' Esme was saying as Tiffany followed her into the hall. 'What is it?'

'The beasty with them squirmers,' said a woman from the top of the stairs. 'In the sea, like.'

'The one you felt last week?' said Esme, rushing up the stairs in an unladylike manner.

'Aye. Pure nasty one. Not sated. Seeking another.'

'Another what?' said Esme. She was at the top of the stairs now, and Tiffany was halfway up before she realised it was an imposition. She craned her neck to see who Esme was talking to, and saw a woman with a shawl clutched about her shoulders, who appeared to be only wearing one shoe. Her greying hair streamed loose down her back.

'Can't be telling. It's hungry. So hungry.'

Esme nodded, and moved along the hallway. 'Where?'

'Can't be saying. But I can be showing.'

She and Esme disappeared along the landing, and then Esme's voice came back, sharply: 'Tiffany! Either come with us or leave now.'

'Come where?' said Tiffany, even more bewildered. At her feet, Pippin the cat twined around.

'Door thing,' he said boredly. 'Nothing to eat there.'

'Do you want to see what witches can do?' said Esme, and Tiffany's feet took her up the stairs before her brain could intervene.

THE HEADWAY the boy led him along was one of the rough paths that led from the Broomway back inland, towards farms or cottages. Santiago didn't really want to visit one of these, since by the time he made it back the Broomway would be covered with water and he'd have to wait for low tide again. Unless he could find someone with a boat to take him back. Perhaps he could steal one. He was getting very, very tired of this horrible place.

'Here, mister,' said the boy, gesturing to something half submerged in the water. 'Box of stuff. I tried opening it but it's all sunk in the mud.'

Santiago peered at it. A crate, the kind they packed textiles in. If he squinted, he could make out some letters stamped on the side: the lacemakers in Saint-Pierre-lès-Calais from whom he'd bought a large amount of lace, some of which he'd even declared to the Revenue.

There was a small fortune in that crate, now ruined and irre-trievable.

'There's some more bits of wood and that,' said the boy. 'And, a ... er...'

'A what?' said Santiago, wondering anew how a whole ship could simply vanish into the mist like this. 'Any survivors?'

'No, mister. That's what I was trying to say. There was some ... bits of people. Um. A hand, and bones that ... well, could've been from anything really, but I don't see as why no cows or horses or that'd be in the water.'

Santiago glanced back at the sea. 'We'll be in the water soon if we don't get off this path,' he said. 'It will be covered in less than an hour. Can we get to dry land by then?'

''Course,' said the boy. 'There's this ken where I kip up here. For cows and that, but it's out of the water and cows are nice and warm.'

'A ... ken?' said Santiago, following him. Sometimes English baffled him.

'Yeah. Where you kip,' said the boy, as if this cleared it up.

Figuring that the boy probably wouldn't risk his own life just to rob a stranger who'd promised him ten bob, Santiago followed

33

him, glancing back at the misty sea distrustfully. Which was why he saw it begin to boil before the boy did.

The ground beneath his feet seemed to shudder. His skin prickled. Something was very, very wrong—

'The tide,' he began, but that was like no tide he'd ever seen. And he'd witnessed the tidal bore of the Qiantang River and a monsoon in the Gulf of Khambhat. The water that had been lapping calmly at the land seemed to suddenly riot, the muddy shore rising up and forming into tentacled arms.

'What is that?' said the boy, horrified. He was backing away. 'I ain't never seen—'

'No,' said Santiago. 'Run, boy! *Vamonos!*'

He ran too, but the path was narrow and the tide was covering it now. The boy, ahead of Santiago, was reaching higher ground, and he just glanced back over his shoulder at the exact moment the water grabbed Santiago by the ankle and threw him up into the air.

ESMERELDA BLACKMANTLE STOPPED on the landing of her elegant house in Mayfair, between two semicircular tables with Queen Anne legs, and opposite an oil painting that looked—even from the corner of Tiffany's untutored eye—suspiciously like a Reynolds, and faced a door painted incongruously green.

'What—?' Tiffany began, but she was shh'd by the gray-haired woman, who placed her hand on the door.

Aunt Esme closed her eyes and pressed one finger of her left hand to the bridge of her nose. Her other hand fitted a heavy iron key into the lock of the door, and she said clearly, 'Take us to the site that Gwen has seen. Open the other side of my door painted green.'

Oh, this was nonsense. All of it was some silly trick. Surely the cat's voice had been provided by this Gwen, and now they were trying some stupid prank and—

'Oh holy God,' Tiffany gasped, as Esme turned the key and the cold, damp scent of rotting seaweed came in through the door. It was swiftly followed by a rolling mist, the sound of screams, and an extremely muddy child.

'Missus, missus! You got to— What is this? This ain't my ken!'

'No, child,' said Aunt Esme, striding through the door in her pleasant blue day dress. 'Who is screaming?'

'Er,' said the boy, staring around the hallway with its striped wallpaper and elegant side tables. 'It's, uh, this guv'nor, he's ... well you come see, I s'pose...'

Tiffany gaped. The door opened onto the outside, and not the outside of a Mayfair street or garden or anywhere in London. Through this door—this *upstairs* door—was a shoreline. Wet, muddy sand, bordered by a grey-green sea that heaved and swelled uneasily. A rocky jetty ran half-heartedly out into the sea, most of it covered with slime and seaweed. The smell was overpowering, rotten and sulphurous, borne in through the door on a breeze that blew her hair around her face and stirred the flowers on the table.

A seagull screamed. Tiffany could see them circling around something on the beach.

'Well? Come along-a-me,' said the grey-haired woman, Gwen, and stepped through after Esme and the muddy child.

'But it's a cowshed,' said the child, standing on the wet shore and peering uneasily into the pleasant hallway.

'It's a house in Mayfair,' said Tiffany distantly.

'No, miss, it's a cowshed on Foulness.'

They both looked at each other, the child on the muddy sand and the lady on the Axminster carpet. Tiffany had a split second of wondering if Esme had put something in her tea, but it was broken by Esme's sharp voice.

'Tiffany! Stop mithering and come here!'

So Tiffany stepped through the door into the cold, damp air that smelled of seaweed, onto a muddy shore. She glanced back, and there was a cowshed, on the edge of the dry land, with a door that opened onto the upstairs hallway of a Mayfair townhouse.

'I'm going mad,' she muttered. But last week she had made a chalk drawing come to life and today she had conversed with a cat, so why not walk through a door in Mayfair onto a beach?

There was a low wall, like the ha-has that bordered the park-land at Dyrehaven, separating the drier ground from the shore. Esme and Gwen had already gone over it, and were striding along the slimy jetty that disappeared into the mist.

'Fortune favours the brave,' said Tiffany, and picked up her skirts to follow them.

Ahead of her through the mist she could see Esme's blue dress as she knelt by something on the ground, and whatever it was, the gulls were very interested in it. Gwen was taking off her shawl and roughly wadding it up, and as Tiffany squelched across the sand in half-boots that had definitely not been designed for the purpose, she found that the object they were kneeling over was a person. A man.

He was unconscious; he didn't stir as Gwen put her shawl under his head. His clothes were torn and so sodden Tiffany didn't realise at first that they were wet with more than water. He was bleeding from a dozen wounds and breathing shallowly.

'He saved me,' the boy was babbling as Esme and Gwen began unfastening the man's clothing. 'The sea came up like … like this wave thing, and he saw it and if he hadn't told me to run it'd have got me.' He looked mystified. 'Why'd he care about me?'

'We are all God's children,' Esme said without looking up. 'What's your name?'

'Billy, miss.'

'Billy. And this gentleman is?'

The boy shrugged. 'Dunno, miss. Some swell asking around after a boat what sunk.'

'A shipwreck? Here?' The two older women exchanged glances. All around them the mud flats were ... well, flat. There was simply nowhere for a shipwreck to hide.

'No. Sort of. It just sort of ... vanished, like. There was this big wave, and ... not like the wave now, that was like... I ain't never seen nuffink like that.'

'Can you describe it?' said Esme. She still hadn't looked up. She and Gwen had got the man out of his coat and were working on his waistcoat, the buttons of which did not appear to wish to co-operate.

'The wave? It ... sorta...' The boy waved his hands for a bit, then said, 'Er, no.'

'Can you draw it?' said Gwen, and Tiffany backed away sharply.

'No,' she said. 'Please don't.' She did not feel in control of herself right now. If the boy drew something and she made it come to life—

Esme did look up at that, somewhat sharply, and nodded. 'Quite right. Cut these off, Gwen. Tiffany, go back into the house and fetch a blanket. Any one from any of the beds. And for heaven's sake don't let the door shut.'

Tiffany made herself look back at the door that shouldn't exist. In the rickety cowshed, *from which she could hear cows*, was carpet and wallpaper and Queen Anne tables.

She swallowed.

'Now, Tiffany,' said Esme, and her tone demanded such absolute obedience Tiffany found herself complying without even thinking about it.

She stepped back inside the house, and it smelled like furniture polish and cut flowers and the perfume Esme wore. When she turned to go towards the nearest door, she caught a glimpse through the hall window, of the Mayfair street outside.

None of this makes any sense.

She went into a bedroom, an ordinary, pleasant bedroom with calm blue curtains. There was a blanket folded on the bed. She picked it up, a nice ordinary thing from a nice ordinary room. Then she went back into the hallway where the door still opened onto a beach and her great-aunt was tending to an unconscious stranger.

An unconscious stranger who had now been divested of all but his shirt and was being thumped on the back until he coughed up water.

'Oh, there you are. Lay the blanket out here.'

His shirt was very fine and very wet and clung to his skin. It clung *everywhere*.

'Should I cut his shirt off?' said Gwen, brandishing a pair of scissors.

'No!' gulped Tiffany, who really wasn't sure if she could cope with much more masculinity on display.

Esme glanced at her face, smiled a little, and nodded. 'To preserve your modesty, then,' she said, as Tiffany's gaze glued itself to the dark hair on his legs.

Beneath the sand and the pallor was a scar on his cheek. Gold glinted in his ear. His hair was thick and dark and longer than the fashion.

'He's the pirate,' she said in surprise.

'Is he now?' said Esme disinterestedly. 'Help us get him onto the blanket. Take his arm. No, his arm not his hand, this is not a country dance.'

His arm was heavy, clothed in clammy linen, and unyielding. And his hand was bare. She had never touched a man's bare skin before.

Tiffany had to move into an unladylike squat in order to reach the blanket. It was virtually impossible to bend very much at the waist, thanks to the busk in the long stays that her benighted bosom required. She didn't think she was a lot of help in hefting him onto the blanket, and when she was instructed to pick up a corner of it she saw she was carrying less weight than the boy Billy.

'Come *along*. Into the house, before the door closes of its own accord.'

To Tiffany's alarm, the door did indeed seem to be slowly creaking shut. Would they be trapped out here on this godforsaken beach? She hurried across the sand, the low sea wall, and tried not to think about the heavy weight of the unconscious man she was carrying in a blanket that kept slipping from her hand.

'Hurry, hurry,' urged Esme, and Tiffany did, but as she tried to pick up her skirts she lost her grip on the blanket and the pirate began to slide off it.

'No!'

She stumbled, hauling her corner up, trying to push his leg back onto the makeshift stretcher, but it cost them precious seconds. The door banged as it closed, and all four of them froze.

'Um,' said Tiffany.

'Well, in that case, I'll have to—' began Esme.

The door fell off its hinges. A cow's pink nose poked through the gap.

Esme exhaled a juddery breath. 'Find another door,' she said.

'We can't just go through the opening?' Tiffany asked.

'No. It has to be a door. One that opens. Latch, hinge, that sort of thing. I've tried it with archways and openings. Doesn't work. We need hinges.'

The chalk arabesques tripping up the dancers. The daisy that left the page. The screaming drawing masters...

'Um,' said Tiffany. Her fingers twitched.

This strange peculiarity she had always denied. Had hidden

and covered up and run away from.

The talking cat, the fireplace coming to life, the impossible doorway...

'Yes?'

If Elinor heard about this, Tiffany would never see the light of day again.

Then we'd better hope she never does.

She squared her shoulders and took a decisive breath. 'If we just need hinges ... I might be able to help.'

Esme raised an eyebrow, then nodded at the door, as if granting permission.

Tiffany looked around her. She didn't carry drawing materials, as a rule—a hard and fast rule, since things always went wrong when she drew anything. The drawings writhed and came off the page. Flowers bloomed. She knew better than to draw animals.

But a door hinge...

Tiffany gently laid down her corner of the blanket, and the others did the same. 'Can you help me?' she asked the boy, who looked dubious, but helped her prop the damp, noisome door in place. 'I don't suppose you have any chalk, or charcoal...?'

He shook his head, and watched in consternation as Tiffany sighed and scooped up some mud with her hands. At least—given their proximity to the cow shed, she really hoped it was mud. The cowshed door was really just a few planks of wood nailed together, with very simple two-part hinges. A leaf of metal on each side, one with a pin and one with a hole. Tiffany remembered once watching a door being set into place on a barn or a stable or something when she was a child. The principle was simple.

Using one finger, she painted a crude replica of the pin hinges at the top and bottom of the door, and then turned to do the same on the door post. As she did she heard the boy gasp.

'How did you—'

There were rough hinges there, quite as if they'd been set by a blacksmith. They were brown and sort of smudgy, but they were physically real.

'Help me lift it,' she said, and in the end it took all four of them, but the door was slotted neatly onto its new hinge.

Aunt Esme laid her hand on it, murmuring, and Tiffany could swear she saw light flash across its surface.

'That will do,' she said, and opened the door into the Mayfair hallway. Tiffany felt her shoulders slump in relief, then hurriedly straightened, because a lady does not slump.

Esme pointedly wedged open the door with a rock, and then they went back to fetch the unconscious pirate, who was beginning to groan.

Tiffany thought she might collapse as her feet stepped onto the carpeted floor. A sudden scream had her dropping her corner of the blanket in shock, and then something flew at her face, and she screamed back at it.

'It'a seagull,' said Esme briskly, shutting the door a fraction too late. The gull had flown in, and in the chaos they all let go of the blanket, letting the pirate thump to the floor as the bird screamed madly around the hallway.

It knocked over the flowers and left a greasy smear on the painting that might be by Reynolds, and then Esme had the door open and was shooing it out.

'Bloody flying rats,' she snapped as she locked the door behind it, and the silence that followed was deafening.

Tiffany had never heard a woman swear before. She'd heard Cook mutter about the kitchen boy being a blimmin' thief, and she'd heard the maids giggling over 'clicketing' with a man, which certainly sounded like swearing even if she didn't actually know what it meant; but she'd never heard a lady swear. Not words she actually knew were swearing words.

'Come on then,' said Great-Aunt Esme, picking up her corner of the blanket. The pirate was beginning to stir. 'The blue room will do. One, two, three ... and up!'

Still shocked, Tiffany helped them get the pirate onto the bed in the room she'd taken the blanket from, and then Gwen was dispatched to the stillroom to fetch medicines and the boy Billy to heat water in the kitchen, and Tiffany was left standing with Esme, both of them muddy and wet and perspiring in a way ladies definitely weren't supposed to do.

'Well,' said Esme, as they regarded the nearly naked man sprawled on the bed. 'Nice work with the door, by the way. Those hinges just ... popped into life, as if they had been made by a blacksmith. Is it permanent?'

'The drawing? No. They don't last long. A few hours, maybe. I've never drawn with mud before.' Her hands were so filthy. She looked around for something to wipe them on, but her gaze kept being drawn back to the pirate as if he was magnetic.

His arms and legs had short dark hair on them. Did all men have that? Tiffany didn't allow herself to stare at artworks of naked men, because nobody at all needed them coming alive, so she had no idea if that was usually depicted. Surely she'd have noticed? It was so ... unmissable.

'I see. Useful nonetheless. Not exactly how I imagined our first meeting, but now I suppose you can't doubt the truth of the matter, can you?'

'The matter?' said Tiffany. The leg hair was damp and flat. Would it be soft when it dried?

'That you are a witch.'

Tiffany blinked at the pirate. The sleeve of his sodden shirt was torn and revealed a black mark inked into the brown skin of his arm, visible through the hair. Was he truly the man in the green coat she'd seen at the Russell ball?

'Well,' she said distantly. 'I believe you are. You have a magic door.'

'Bird?' chirped a childish voice behind her, and she looked around to see Pippin the cat sniffing around hopefully. 'Bird gone?'

'And I suppose I am too,' said Tiffany, her shoulders slumping. A lady's shoulders didn't slump, but maybe a witch's did. She could hear the cat's thoughts. It was madness. 'Why couldn't I hear what the bird was saying?'

Esme shrugged. 'Birds don't say much. Gulls mostly scream. Corvids are reasonably intelligent, though. On that note, if you ever need me, ask a raven.'

'Ask a raven what?'

Somewhere, a clock chimed, and a sudden panic rose in Tiffany.

'Oh no. My maid will be waiting. I must go—'

'Looking like that?' said Esme, and Tiffany looked down at herself. Her skirts were muddy to the knee, and sandy in a way she could never explain. Her boots were ruined. Her hair was falling down all over the place. She could feel the perspiration on her face and neck and her hands were unspeakable. She thought the seagull might have left its doings on her shoulder.

'Oh *no*,' she said again. She dashed to the window and looked out into the street. Yes, there was Morris, sitting neatly on the bench, a couple of packages beside her.

'Perhaps I can lend you something,' said Esme.

'And tell Morris what? She dressed me in this!'

'Ah,' said Esme. 'Yes. Well, perhaps you could say … you spilled something and…'

Tiffany went to rub her hands over her face, then stopped, because they were disgusting. 'There's no time. All right,' she said, and darted a glance at the pirate, who still appeared to be asleep. 'Just … don't, um, tell anyone about this.'

'Dear, I am a witch.'

This was a trick almost as useful as becoming invisible. It didn't last for long, unless she concentrated hard and gave herself a headache, but it was useful for balls and soirées and events where she wanted to look a little different. To curl her hair or flatten it, to hide a blemish or manufacture one, to make her gown more becoming or to fit somewhat worse. To make herself look more or less appealing, and nearly always the latter.

Now she concentrated on making herself look like she had that morning. The sand and mud on her skirts vanished, her hair wound itself back into its previous style, the bird doings disappeared. The mud from her hands disappeared, and her complexion evened out, although she could still feel the dirt and sweat, gritty and uncomfortable on her skin.

In a few moments, she was a neatly turned-out young lady who had simply been visiting her aunt.

'Now that is an excellent trick,' said Esme, walking around her.

'It won't last. I'll have to think of some excuse why everything is all dirty later,' said Tiffany. She glanced at herself in the glass over the dressing table. Yes. Perfectly presentable. 'I'm so sorry. I must go.'

'Siempre...' murmured a voice from the bed, and Tiffany whipped around to see the pirate's eyelids fluttering. He had ridiculously long lashes. 'Siempre huyendo,' he mumbled, and smiled sleepily at her before his eyes closed again.

'What did he say?' said Tiffany, her cheeks flushing.

'He said "always" and then... I think "always running away",' said Esme, her head tilted to one side. 'What do you suppose that means?'

'I cannot imagine,' said Tiffany, and all but sprinted for the door.

CHAPTER 2

SOME YEARS AGO

*T*he streets of Sao Paulo were never washed clean by the rain, no matter how much of it fell. The boy danced from one broken paving stone to another, leaping the puddles and the muddy sinkholes. His lip stung, and his ribs ached, but the loaf of bread was wrapped up safe and dry inside his leather jerkin. He and Mama would eat tonight!

But when he had darted through the warren of alleys and tiptoed over the narrow bridges and pushed aside the curtain that kept the draught out of their room, he found it empty.

'She left this for you,' said Senhora Calvo from the next room, holding out a grubby scrap of paper. 'You can read?'

Of course he could read. Mama had taught him, secretly, because Papa said he wanted to keep his ignorance intact. He grabbed the letter and scanned it anxiously.

'It says she has gone to the convent. But she goes there all the time,' he said. His mother was constantly praying, and she offered any service—cooking, washing, sweeping—to the nuns that they would allow her to perform.

His father said it was filthy papistry, but there weren't a lot of Anglican convents in South America.

'I don't think,' said Senhora Calvo gently, 'that she is coming back this time.'

His mother had written in Spanish, probably because no one else—especially his father—would be able to read it.

> I will not wait for that man any longer, and neither should you, Edo. You are old enough now, you do not need me any more. Go and see the world, and do not worry about me.

He stuffed the letter in his jerkin and raced off towards the convent, this time heedless of the puddles. The Senhora must have been wrong. Mama would be coming back for him. Papa left all the time, for weeks and months, but Mama wouldn't leave him. Would she?

But the nuns would not allow him admittance. It was the time of the Great Silence, and grubby little boys with eyes red from crying were not to be exempted from this.

'But I have brought her bread,' he said, holding out the loaf. 'I fought another boy for it. I broke his nose,' he added, because this was one of the few things his father had thought he should be proud of.

'Then this is the proceeds of violence,' said the nun severely, taking the bread from him, 'and your punishment will be to go hungry.'

'But—'

'Pray to the Virgin for deliverance from your sins,' she told him, but he would not, because Papa had said they were Church of England, even though he wasn't really sure where England was. 'Go and find honest work to support yourself. You are old enough now, Duarte.'

'That is not my name,' he told her. He would not have their version of it, not now they had stolen Mama. And he would never be Edo again, not now she had let them.

The nun looked unimpressed. 'Ed-ward, then,' she said, making a meal of the English syllables.

'No.' That was even worse. 'My name is Santiago,' he said. If he was going to be his own man, he did not need anyone else's name but the one he had made for himself. 'Tell her that,' he said, as the rain dripped off his chin and soaked through his shoes. 'And tell my father, if he ever comes back. My name is Santiago, and I am no longer their son.'

'OH DEAR,' said Elinor, peering at the jam pot and making a face. 'Strawberry, really. Nobody has strawberry any more. Raspberry is the only smart flavour.'

Tiffany gazed at the pattern of roses on the plates. Were they moving before her eyes or was she imagining it?

I'm a witch, Tiffany. And so are you.

She had spent all night tossing and turning, reliving those words in her head. The cat talking to her. The green door that opened onto a grey shore. The pirate.

I'm a witch.

When she remembered that she had demonstrated her peculiarities to Aunt Esme, a relative stranger, *twice*, she broke out in a cold sweat.

'Woolgathering again?' said Elinor. 'Really, Theophania. Did you even hear me?'

'Er,' said Tiffany. *I wonder if his skin is that golden shade all over?*

'No, you see? How else will you know what is *á la mode* if you do not listen to me?'

Tiffany wanted to say that she could read about what was fashionable in a magazine, if she cared, which she didn't. 'I cannot imagine,' she said.

'No. You would have merrily gone on eating strawberry jam as if it were 1810.' She laughed as if this would be an absurd, not to mention socially unforgivable, thing to do.

'But Cornforth likes strawberry,' said Tiffany. She glanced at her brother, who was frowning at his newspaper and not paying them any attention. She had a vague recollection of him visiting the nursery when she was small, and allowing her to serve him a sticky scone dripping with gloopy strawberry jam. He had gamely smiled and eaten it all, and not complained when she had got jammy fingers all over his coat.

'I don't think so,' said Elinor. 'James,' she said to the footman, 'tell Cook it is to be raspberry preserve from now on. Homemade, please. We are not in *trade*,' she added with a shiver of revulsion.

'But does it not take time to make raspberry preserve?' said Tiffany, who had never before had an opinion on flavours of jam and really wished she didn't have to fill her head with it now. 'Are raspberries even in season?'

'It is April,' said Cornforth, who apparently was listening.

'Are there not glasshouses? Really, I cannot bear all this mediocrity. Theophania, come, get dressed, we shall take a stroll around Hyde Park. Do try not to fall in the mud this time.'

'But I was going to go and see my … er, great-aunt,' said Tiffany, managing at the last moment to stop herself from saying 'the irresponsibly handsome half-naked pirate whose life I helped to save yesterday'. 'In Mayfair,' she added for good measure.

'I'm sure she can do without you for one day. All the time and effort we are putting into your Season, and you are spending it all with one dusty old relative I had never heard of until yesterday.' Which was when she had found the letter Tiffany had not been clever enough in hiding. 'Does she know any eligible young men?'

A flash of white teeth, a gold earring, the unexpected ink of a tattoo—

'I saw Lady Brimsey yesterday,' Elinor went on. 'Her daughter expects a proposal this week. And I hear Lord Rothchester has asked for permission to court the Atwood girl. The younger one, not the one with the annoying laugh.'

Tiffany had met the Misses Atwood, and whilst the older daughter did have a somewhat distinctive laugh, this was at least proof that she had a sense of humour. The younger one gave a clear impression of being a doll someone had bespelled to dance and smile.

I wonder if I could bespell a doll... No, that would be terrifying.

'Of course, the real catch of the Season would be the Duke of St James,' Elinor prattled.

'Isn't he about a hundred and twelve?' said Tiffany, wondering how she could manage to get to Aunt Esme's house again today. Not that it had to be today, but she hadn't been able to stop thinking about the pirate.

Because he might have died, obviously. Not because of the golden skin and the flash of white teeth and the gold earring—

'No, dear! The old duke died. His grandson inherited. The less said about the father the better,' said Elinor, with a glint in her eye. She mouthed, 'Duel. Exiled,' then added out loud, 'But nobody has seen hide nor hair of him. I happened to pass St James House the other day and there is still no knocker on the door. He has assumed the title, hasn't he, Cornforth? Cornforth! What could be so interesting in that wretched newspaper?'

Cornforth looked up at them and blinked. He was a sandy-haired man with a little chin, somewhat short in stature, and brown eyes that tended towards the serious even when he wasn't trying. He and Tiffany looked so little alike people rarely realised they were related.

'Well,' he said. 'Bonaparte has abolished the slave trade in France.'

'Anthony will be delighted,' said Tiffany, daring a glance at Elinor.

'It won't last,' sniffed her sister-in-law. 'I hear the French aren't supporting him in the slightest.'

'I thought ladies didn't discuss politics?' said Tiffany innocently, which earned her a poisonous look.

'Come, change for a promenade,' said Elinor, rising from her seat. 'It is time you strolled and were seen, Theophania. How else will you find a husband, if you simply hide away all the time? Oh, and dear, do darken your eyebrows, the way I showed you? You mustn't be too … colourless.'

Tiffany smiled tightly and allowed Morris to darken her eyebrows with a burnt clove. Apparently being colourless was only bad in one's hair and complexion, however, because the dress she was buttoned into was a miserable sprigged muslin with barely any colour to it at all. Still, it was frilly and fashionable, which was all Elinor cared about. She would have to alter it slightly, the way she had yesterday, and do her trick of fading into the background, which…

Hah! Yes. That would be the trick to get her out of Elinor's sight. But would it last long enough to get away properly?

You are contemplating acts of witchcraft, she told herself. *You know this to be both impossible and illegal.*

But since it was impossible, that probably meant it couldn't be illegal. Yes. Who could prove such a thing?

She dutifully followed Elinor into the landau, both hoods let down so that they could see and be seen. The horses tossed their heads and trotted on calmly. Tiffany tried to see if she could hear their thoughts, but all she heard was the chatter of the street.

Maybe the horses' thoughts were lost in that. Or maybe she could only hear cats.

Or maybe you can't hear animals at all, because what happened yesterday was a fever dream or a figment of your imagination. She simply had to return to Aunt Esme's house to find out.

As she looked about her, Tiffany was sure there were more crows about than usual.

The drive to the park was interminable because Elinor insisted on stopping to greet every acquaintance personally. It was very important to Elinor to have a great many friends and to be held in high esteem by all of them. It was almost as important that she found their taste and connections to be inferior to her own as much as possible. With Mrs Belmont, whose daughters were of a similar age to Tiffany, she exchanged pleasantries, and then innocently enquired if they would all be attending Mrs Wildingham's recital tomorrow.

Mrs Belmont stammered that they had another invitation, and Elinor smiled triumphantly.

'I wager they have not been invited. Ah, Sir Henry, Lady Brougham…'

Miss Brougham was wearing a cheerful shade of blue, the sort Tiffany longed to wear. Her brother Percy exchanged a few words about a theatrical performance he had recently seen. They were a pleasant pair, affable and unbothered by their lack of what Elinor would call 'physical charms'. As they drove away, Tiffany thought she would perhaps try to cultivate them as better friends.

'My dear,' whispered Elinor, not very discreetly. 'Did you see those spots? So terribly vulgar.'

'I hardly think he does it on purpose,' said Tiffany.

'Pfft,' said Elinor. 'And that terrible shade of blue on Miss Brougham, as if she were still a child. One could probably see her in the dark. Why do people feel the need to show off like that? Ah, Lady Greensword'—she raised her voice necessarily—'how pleasant to see you! Now wasn't that a wonderful musicale at Her Grace's salon?'

It was astonishing, Tiffany thought. There was absolutely no trace of irony in Elinor's speech. None whatsoever.

The crows were still watching her. There were two of them now.

Bird thoughts rarely make any sense. Tiffany still found herself staring intently at them.

'Theophania! I *said*, won't it be wonderful to see Kean's Richard II? His Romeo made me swoon, I don't mind declaring it.' Elinor clasped a hand to her bosom, for it was fashionable to adore tragic heroes. 'There! I am a hopeless romantic.'

'Why is it romantic to commit suicide?' said Tiffany, and the two older ladies gasped.

'Have you no sensibility?' said Lady Greensword.

'But the Church tells us—'

Elinor's laugh was a little too sharp. 'It is a *play*, Theophania. It isn't real. Now, come along, a little further and we shall alight for a promenade. I don't want to get there too late.'

Too late for what? Elinor saw the same people in the same places on the same days of each week. They exchanged the same gossip about the same things. It was all so unspeakably boring, and yet it was something Elinor looked forward to so eagerly she was sitting forward in her seat, eyes darting around like a child in a sweet shop.

Tiffany followed her from the carriage and allowed herself to be promenaded around, pretending to listen to Elinor's prattling about who was wearing unflattering outfits or marrying someone unsuitable.

She kept her responses to murmurs. She nodded and curt-seyed with the barest of effort. She willed herself to become unmemorable, to fade from people's sight. For the flowers on her skirt to blend with the flowers on the ground. For the feather in her bonnet to be simply one falling from a bird. For the crunch of her footsteps on the gravel to be merely background noise.

When Elinor paused to greet an acquaintance in an unforgivably boring hat, Tiffany hung back a little, and Elinor made no move to introduce her. The acquaintance glanced in her direction and then looked on at the rest of the crowd, her gaze simply bouncing off Tiffany as if she were a servant.

Tiffany slowed her pace. Stepped to one side. Held her breath as Elinor stopped to greet a closer friend who would definitely recognise her.

And let it out as the lady seemed not to even see her.

'By yourself today, Lady Cornforth? Not brought that young sister-in-law with you?'

'Oh no, Theophania is...' Elinor turned her head a little and frowned ever so slightly. 'She... Ah yes, she was visiting her aunt, I believe.' Her expression cleared as she mentally rewrote the world around her.

'How charitable.'

'Yes. Well, I have tried to teach her how to go about in Society...'

They moved off, and Tiffany slipped away through the crowd, as unseen as a breeze, triumph roaring through her.

HIS DREAMS WERE full of nightmares, terrible tentacled beasts spinning themselves out of nothing and tearing him limb from limb. He dreamed of ships being dragged beneath the waves, of a child screaming, of a door between worlds.

He dreamed of a mermaid.

His mother had told him stories of the *cuero*, a terrifying creature that lived in the water and looked like a cowhide, but had suckers and tentacles that could squeeze a person to death and consume him. Were they real? Had a *cuero* emerged from the sea on the Essex coast and tried to kill him?

'It seems unlikely,' said a female voice. 'Most probably the tide simply came in very quickly.'

His whole face felt like it had been filled with sand. Blinking hurt. Everything hurt. Santiago croaked, 'The tide came alive.'

'Yes, it can certainly seem like that sometimes, can't it?'

She gave him something to drink, and then he fell asleep again, and it was only later he realised she'd been speaking Spanish to him.

What had actually happened? Santiago was never quite sure how much of his recollection was real and how much was a fever dream. The sea had seemed to suddenly boil and grow limbs, great muscular tentacles that were made of water somehow. In the fragment of memory he could recall, the sea had become a living thing. It had grabbed him, like a cat grabbing at a mouse, and tossed him up in the air.

He'd heard the boy shouting from the shore, and then the sea—

—the sea—

—the sea flailed and spat him out.

He wasn't really sure about that last part. It must have been something he'd dreamt, that awful swooping feeling of flying through the air, propelled by some watery limb, arcing through the cold mist towards the muddy beach.

What followed was hard to recall. Dark, terrifying nightmares jumbled together with nausea and pain. The occasional cool hand upon his brow, the blessed relief of cold water between his lips, a quiet voice reassuring him.

He made a few attempts at waking up, but it didn't seem to be a very pleasant experience, so he lapsed back into what was probably a drugged sleep. It was a pleasant place to be, now the fever dreams had dispersed, but it appeared he wasn't to be allowed to dwell there for long.

'No, it is fine. I used to sit up with my nieces and nephews when they were ill.'

A woman's voice, followed by another. 'Does your family know you are here?'

'In a manner of speaking.'

He heard a door close, and then footsteps came closer. Someone leaned over him; a woman, her clothes and her person sweetly scented. For a moment he thought he felt her fingers against his cheek, and then they were gone.

What he definitely did feel was her bosom, pressing against his arm. It was a very splendid bosom, full and firm, and he sighed happily at its proximity.

She, however, exhaled sharply, and sat back.

'Mr Santiago?' she said, in a hesitant sort of voice, as if she didn't really want him to hear her.

'You know me?' he managed. He tried to blink open his dry eyes.

'I believe we have met,' she said.

Santiago didn't know who she was. He barely knew who *he* was. 'We have?' he croaked. He tried to peer at her, but everything was dark.

She leaned forward and held a sort of cup with a spout to his lips. He fancied it was the sort of thing one used to feed invalids with. Ah, wonderful, he was an invalid now.

'Yes,' she said, as the miracle of cold water passed his lips. 'At the Russell ball. You wore a green velvet coat.'

A green velvet coat. Yes, he had worn such a thing, during his sole venture into polite society. And now... Now he didn't seem to be wearing much at all. Which was sometimes exactly the right thing to be wearing in the presence of a young lady and a bed— and sometimes very much not. He strongly suspected this was one of the latter times, not least because absolutely every part of him hurt.

He blinked, but his vision was bleary. And the room was quite dimly lit. If he'd met this woman, clearly she hadn't made an impression. All he remembered from that evening was the silver dress girl, and how she'd made the chalk come to—

Wait.

'Mr Santiago? You are breathing rapidly.'

Her cool fingers touched his brow, but that didn't help. Mr Santiago. Who else had he met at that ball who would address him in such a fashion?

'It was you,' he croaked. He peered at her in the dim light. She glowed somehow, luminescent, her skin and hair pale and ethereal.

'What do you mean?'

'You made the chalk come to life! I saw it.'

She exhaled rapidly. 'I'm sure I don't know what you mean,' she said.

Santiago struggled to sit up, but she pressed him back down again. He protested this as violently as he was able, which wasn't very much. He had all the strength of a day-old kitten.

'Please lie still. You have been quite ill.'

'I know what I saw. You made the chalk come to life—'

'Chalk cannot come to life, Mr Santiago, everybody knows that. Even the great Mr Turner—'

'—and you made the sea come to life!'

At that, she paused for a moment, and then her voice sounded quite different as she said, 'The sea came to life? What do you mean?'

'It— It boiled, and it grew … arms,' he said, flailing his own limbs. The swooping, violent terror of it rose in his gullet, robbing him of speech.

'I don't think the sea can grow arms,' she said, matter-of-factly. 'Perhaps it was seaweed.'

'Seaweed?' he gasped, outraged.

'Or a … squid,' she suggested. 'My brother Phileas told me about a sort of jellyfish he saw on his travels. It had these huge, long tentacles, twice the length of this room. The locals said it had a sting that could kill a man. Perhaps such a thing happened to you? The tentacles might look as if they had come to life, and I imagine a nasty enough sting would cause a sort of delirium.'

Her voice was helpful, as if explaining to a small child why his flight of fantasy was charming but absurd.

'I know what I saw,' Santiago snarled. 'And what I felt.' He rubbed his ribs, where he could still feel the pressure of that immense tentacle that had grabbed and squeezed him. But that could not be real. Not in these waters.

'I am afraid you did take a bump to the head,' said the woman, who he was now convinced was some kind of *bruja* or *kitsunetsuki*, a malevolent spirit. A sorceress! What was the English word?

'You made the sea come to life,' he said, succeeding this time in sitting up, and glaring at her. He could see more of her now, her pale face and silvery hair and that bosom which had obviously been made to tempt a man beyond all reason.

'Nobody can make the sea come to life,' she explained, so patiently it was patronising.

'Nobody can make chalk come to life,' he snapped back, 'and yet you did.'

'I really think you should rest,' she said, standing. 'Perhaps after some sleep you will be able to think more clearly.'

'I know what I saw,' said Santiago, his head pounding. 'You made the chalk come to life. You made the water come to life. You took my ships!'

Perhaps she was a siren, like in the myths of old. Luring

sailors to their deaths. That would explain the silveriness. And the bosom.

She frowned. 'You mean the ship that vanished off Foulness? Your boy told us about it.'

What boy? 'The other ships!'

'What other ships? Mr Santiago, please do not over exert yourself—'

'My ships,' he said, as calmly as he could through gritted teeth, 'which you sank using the same wicked hoodoo as you used on the chalk!'

'No other ship has sunk in the Thames for quite some time, I assure you,' she said.

'What about in the Mediterranean, hmm? The Bay of Biscay? The English Channel!'

'All over the world? Mr Santiago, I have never even left England. The furthest I've ever been from London is Brighton.'

'That is on the English Channel—'

'Mr Santiago,' she said, clearly vexed with him, but right then the door opened and the light that spilled in blinded him.

'What is all this shouting?' said another female voice, perhaps a little older. Perhaps the one that had spoken to him when he first awoke. He realised now that the mermaid girl had been speaking English.

'Guv'nor! Guv'nor!' That was a boy, rushing past the woman silhouetted in the doorway. 'You're alive!'

'I told you he was alive,' said the siren, as the boy hurled himself at Santiago's bed.

Santiago tried to find a smile, but he was somewhat bemused. Who was this boy?

'Yeah, but he wasn't hardly moving. There was this cove called Bonko in this ken I kipped in once, took a bump to the head, fell asleep and never woke up again. We didn't know he was dead 'til he started stinking.'

'A charming tale,' said the older woman, as the boy sniffed at Santiago. He was quite sure he smelled less than savoury, although hopefully, not dead yet.

'You may need to remind me of your name,' Santiago said to the boy.

'Billy, guv. Remember, you said you was gonna give me ten bob for showing you the stuff what washed up on the beach, yeah?'

The child looked hopeful, and Santiago nodded as a vague memory emerged. He had promised such a thing. He looked around, as if expecting to see a purse of money sitting on the nightstand, but none of his possessions were in attendance. This seemed fitting, since most of his wits seemed to be absent, too.

'And I certainly will, once I have access to my belongings,' he said. 'And some more besides.' He regarded the boy, whose age was somewhat impossible to guess. The world's cities were full of children like him: skinny, shifty creatures, like foxes. They belonged to no one. They were invisible to most. Santiago knew this, because he'd been one, once. 'Were you injured? Are you well?'

'Nah guv, they've been feeding me. I had a right wolf in the stomach, but the grub's good, and loads of it. That lady in the kitchen makes it all fancy, like sometimes it smells at the lascars' ken.'

Santiago was too tired to try to work out what that all meant, but the new lady, the older one, moved forward and said, 'Madhu is from Mysore, and she often makes the food of her homeland for us. Well, as close as she can get with the ingredients available.'

'She does? This is excellent. I have not had a good curry in England. I ship spices out of Mangalore, and rice of course.' Santiago shook his head, and regretted it as little bursts of light appeared behind his eyes. 'That is not the point. You,'—he turned to the girl who had worn the silver tissue dress—'you made the sea come to life.'

Now there was more light in the room he could see she might not, perhaps, actually be a mermaid or siren, but that she was an ordinary human woman. Well, an ordinary human woman with silvery blonde hair and a magnificent bosom. She wore some shade of sea green that did nothing to help matters.

She rolled her eyes at the older woman. 'He has clearly taken a blow to the head. I did not make the sea come to life. Nobody can.'

'Well,' began the older woman, then cleared her throat and said, 'Of course not. You must rest, Mr Santiago.'

'How do you know my name?' he said suspiciously. 'Witchcraft!'

'You met Tiffany a fortnight ago,' she said patiently.

Santiago nodded, exhaling slowly. Tiffany, yes, that was the name she had given him. Lady Tiffany, if he remembered correctly—not that remembering things correctly was much of a given right now.

'I think perhaps you should get some rest,' said the older woman. 'Is there anyone you would like us to contact? Your family? A business associate?'

'I have no family.' He rested his arm over his eyes. Even the low light in this room was too much. 'And my … my business associates can manage without me.' Not that he exactly had any. He had clerks, and foremen, and captains.

'That sounds lonely,' said Tiffany, quietly.

Lonely? No, he wasn't lonely. He was independent, and that was totally different.

'I am not lonely,' he said. 'You cannot trap me with your siren's words.'

She inhaled, as if about to speak, but then stopped. The other woman said, 'You must rest, Mr Santiago. I am sure you are feeling very tired.'

Yes, he was feeling tired, now she mentioned it. Very tired indeed.

'Just rest, and we will take care of you.'

The last thing he saw before merciful sleep took him was Lady Tiffany, watching him.

CHAPTER 3

'*H*e had a purse of money in each coat pocket, coins sewn into his hems and even a banknote in a pocket of his smallclothes,' said Esme, as she poured Tiffany a glass of wine. And it looked like proper wine, too, not the over-sweetened ratafia she was usually offered.

'He's not short of a few bob,' said Nora, who wore an apron over her serviceable dress like a servant, and her hair cut short like a Frenchwoman, and yet did not behave as if she was either of those things. She had shoulders like a stevedore and a vocabulary to match. She and Madhu had simply appeared in the house, quite as if they'd always been there.

'But he is not a gentleman,' said Tiffany. 'His hair—his *hands*, Aunt Esme, did you see?' Tiffany had only seen the bare hands of a gentleman up close at dinner, but they were usually as soft and manicured as her own. Perhaps a splotch of ink if he was bookish. But Mr Santiago had thick calluses on his fingers and palms, and scars both old and new on the backs of his hands. *And as for that black ink...*

63

'Oh, yes. The hands of a sailor. He might have wealth now, but he has known hard work, and plenty of it.'

'I think he is well-travelled. When I spoke to him in Kannada I think he understood a little,' said Madhu, who appeared to be the cook but also might not be. She wore a drape of deep pink and gold over her gown, and had a golden ring in her nose. Her *nose*.

The women of the house—and it seemed to be just women—moved freely between upstairs and downstairs. Were they servants? Did they have servants? Were they all witches? Tiffany didn't know how to ask. She still wasn't sure she wasn't imagining it all.

''Twas the beasty with them squirmers,' said Gwen firmly. She had paintbrushes stuck in her hair and a great many pockets, all full of notebooks. Tiffany had no idea what she scribbled in them. 'I seen it three weeks Tuesday.'

There was a pause. 'Dear,' said Esme crisply, but not unkindly, 'three weeks Tuesday last? Or three weeks Tuesday hence?'

Tiffany drank some wine.

'Depends,' said Gwen after some thought. 'It still be to come. And it has been.' She frowned at something nobody else could see. 'There be a great light,' she added, helpfully.

'Oh, well, hallelujah,' said Nora. She threw herself down on the settee in a most unladylike manner, but nobody reprimanded her. Perhaps all witches were like this. 'How long's he going to be here?'

'Until he is well enough to leave,' said Esme. She refilled her own glass, glanced at Tiffany's and refilled that too. 'Gwen?'

'He will escape from Elba, mark my words,' said Gwen.

'That was last month,' said Tiffany nervously. She wasn't supposed to know about politics, but really, the return of Bonaparte far transcended that, surely? The man could be planning an invasion of these isles at any moment!

'Well, it's good to know when she is at the current time,' said

Esme. 'Now. I mislike having a man about the house as much as the rest of you—'

'Hah!' snorted Nora.

'—but he is our guest and so is the boy Billy.'

There was a short pause as they all tried not to look around themselves too noticeably.

'The silverware in the pantry is the most expensive,' Esme called loudly. 'Do not accept less than ten guineas for the set.'

After a moment, Billy's curly head appeared around the edge of the door. 'I ain't a thief,' he said.

'Really? Then how do you survive?'

Billy's gaze darted between the five women. 'Uh, you know,' he said. 'This and that.'

'Hmm. Well, you have my blessing on the silverware—to the left of the kitchen, we don't lock it—but if you steal anything from me personally I shall cut off your fingers and feed them to you.'

'Take my pocket-watch and I'll crush all your bones to flour,' added Nora, as she took out a knife and cleaned her nails with it.

'Once I knew a man who was turned into a fish because he stole a chicken,' said Madhu. 'Then the fish was caught and the man was eaten.'

'He'll put it back by tomorrow,' said Gwen, and as she spoke, the fire in the grate roared.

Billy's eyes, which had grown wider with every statement, landed on Tiffany.

'I shall,' she began, and tried to think what one did when one was robbed. 'I shall call the magistrates,' she said, and they all scoffed and rolled their eyes.

'Tiffany, you are a witch,' complained Esme. 'I am sure you can come up with a better threat than that.'

I am a witch. Esme said it so casually. 'If he is found guilty, he could be hanged,' said Tiffany, of the skinny boy who was gazing at the bowl of fruit on the sideboard as if it was all made of gold. 'And—and I am not accustomed to threatening people!'

'Oh dear. I recommend you learn. It is most satisfying. Now then, Billy. You indicated that you had not become acquainted with Mr Santiago before the events that transpired upon the shore?'

The boy's eyes slid in the direction of Nora, who translated, 'You didn't meet him until yesterday?'

'Oh. No. He said he'd give me ten bob for showing him what washed up in the mud,' said Billy.

'And what had washed up in the mud?'

'I dunno. Boxes. I had a look but it was all ruined. Bottles smashed and that. I was gonna get some of the fabric for a blanket but it was all this thin stuff and I ain't got no use for that.'

'Lace?'

Billy shrugged. He had just seen the plate of biscuits Madhu had laid out on the table. 'Nah. That slippery stuff.'

'Silk?' said Tiffany, and tried to ignore Nora's snort.

'Yeah. Maybe.'

'They say silk can stop a musket ball,' said Tiffany, who had read it somewhere.

'Well, next time someone shoots one at you, your ladyship, you can tell us,' said Nora.

'June,' said Gwen. They waited, but nothing more was forthcoming.

'Yes. Now, what can you tell us of the gentleman?' said Esme.

Billy shrugged. He sidled further into the room, and at Esme's urging snatched a biscuit off the table and shoved it whole into his mouth. He moaned a little, and shoved another one in.

'He said he'd give me ten bob,' he repeated, spraying crumbs. 'And you said he had money.'

'I shall make sure the ten bob is forthcoming,' said Esme.

'Fanks miss, you're a toff.'

'Perhaps I shall fetch more biscuits,' murmured Madhu, and glided from the room.

'Anything else? About Mr Santiago?'

The boy shoved the last of the biscuits in. 'He saved my life,' he said.

'Yes, you have said. Most chivalrous. Do you know anything else about him? Where he is from? His place of business? The nature of his business?'

Tiffany watched, fascinated, as Billy swallowed what had to be six biscuits all at once. 'If he chokes,' said Nora, 'I ain't helping.'

'That will not be necessary. Billy?'

Billy began licking his fingers. 'He told me to run. When that... 'ere, what was that thing?'

'Thing?'

'Like a sort of...' He made tentacled motions with his fingers.

'Beasty with squirmers?' said Gwen.

'Yeah. Made out of water. I ain't never seen nuffink like that before. But I seen all them boxes smashed up on the shore and some bits what used to be people, and Mr Santiago saved me from that, so I ain't telling you anyfink.'

'Why not?' asked Tiffany, curious.

''Cos you're witches, innit. You made the beasty with the squirmers.'

'I assure you we did not,' said Esme firmly, then darted a quick glance at the others, who all shook their heads.

Tiffany looked away. She probably hadn't made the beasty. Probably. She certainly had not drawn a tentacled beast or looked at a picture of one recently.

She had dreamed of squirming monsters and crashing waves, but if she could make her dreams come to life then the world would likely be an absolutely terrifying place.

'And we, I should like to point out, saved his life,' said Esme. 'And yours, I should wager, if you were sleeping in a cowshed and in need of stealing a blanket. Ah, Madhu. With some parathas for our young friend, too, I see.'

Billy's eyes got bigger as the smell of the parathas filled the room. Tiffany didn't know what they were—some kind of unleavened dough?—but the smell was making her stomach rumble. They smelled of melted cheese and spices and deliciousness.

She watched the boy sit at the table and begin stuffing hot, doughy goodness into his face, grease running over his chin. She had never been allowed to eat like that. Her nurses and governesses had impressed upon her the importance of ladylike manners when she was barely old enough to feed herself. Tiny bites, never finish the plateful, never eat anything that might make a mess of one's hands or face. Never eat anything that might make one's breath smell.

She would never have been allowed a paratha.

Aunt Esme sat down in one of the other chairs, leaning on her hand and watching Billy. 'They are good, aren't they? We know a wonderful merchant who stocks all sorts of spices. Terribly difficult to get them shipped down to Cornwall but one can't have everything.'

'One can if one has a magic door,' said Nora idly, and was ignored by Esme.

'Although sometimes it is quite shockingly hard to get hold of nutmeg. I wonder,' said that lady, 'if perhaps the merchant buys his spices from your Mr Santiago?'

Billy merely shrugged and carried on eating. The food, it seemed, was its own kind of magic.

'If that were so, perhaps we could ask if he ships nutmeg. Or knows someone who does.'

'Woss nutmeg?' asked the boy, through his food.

'A spice, quite delicious and versatile. From the Banda Isles of Dutch Indonesia. One would need shipping concerns in the

South Pacific to bring it here, I should imagine. I wonder, Billy—could you find out for us? Perhaps supply the name of his shipping concern?'

Billy's eyes darted from her face to the food, and then back again. 'I didn't understand half what you just said,' he admitted.

Esme smiled. From nowhere she produced a handful of shillings.

'I reckon,' she said conversationally, 'there's a pound here, in change.'

Billy's brown eyes got very big.

'Would a pound help your understanding?'

He nodded vigorously.

'Good lad.' The coins tipped from Esme's hand into two neat columns on the table. 'Tell me by luncheon and it'll magically become a guinea.'

It was a cargo of porcelain that did it.

Santiago had been on board a Dutch vessel, innocently—well, mostly innocently—shipping the stuff from Canton to Penang when they were set upon by pirates. From whom he managed to escape, only to be captured by their leader, a woman half his size and ten times his deadliness.

She had interrogated him about the cargo, about his ties to the Netherlands and to Spain and to Britain, and when he had tried to charm her she had laughed and slid the blade of her curved sword down his cheek.

'A reminder,' she had said, or something similar to that. It had been in Cantonese and Santiago wasn't really all that fluent. He'd probably not been that much older than Billy at the time.

Her questioning had been subtle. The British authorities in

Penang had been slightly less polite. And the less said about the time he'd been suspected of smuggling in Manila the better.

None of them held a candle to Billy, whose idea of subtle was to drink his cold tea and announce, 'The ladies downstairs want to know if you sell nutmeg. What's nutmeg?'

'A spice. And yes, sometimes.' He tried to remember if he had any. The *Epunamun* might have been bringing some. But she was lost somewhere beneath the briny waves, just like the *Pincoya*. 'Why?'

'I dunno.' He picked at a biscuit left on the table by the bed. 'The lassy what cooks makes these bread things, right, like … kind of pies with cheese in them, and spices and stuff. Like the lascars eat.'

'You know lascars?' Those were the sailors from Southeast Asia, who had been settling in the docklands of London for decades, but Santiago didn't know how many of them had made it to Foulness Island.

'Yeah. When I was in… Before I left town.' He said it casually, as if London had become such a bore for a young lad. 'Down the docks. Funny I never met you. The ladies said you was in shipping.'

Ladies. At least one of them was a lady, the daughter of an earl no less. The imperious Mistress Blackmantle would also fall into that category, although he wasn't sure about the other three. And ladies surely couldn't be witches, could they?

Now that his head felt clearer, Santiago found his mind recoiling less and less from the idea. In Brazil he had encountered a *bruja*, a wise woman who had communed with her spirit gods. She had sung and danced in the firelight, seeming unearthly, and yet she had been kind to a small boy whose mother spent all her time praying, and whose father had run away from his debts yet again.

In South Africa he had encountered the *sangoma*, who interceded between the living and the dead by means of divination, in order to heal and comfort the sick. In the South Pacific he had met sorcerers who passed down their powers from father to son and mother to daughter. None of them had harmed him, although he did recall one ritual whose intent seemed to be to cause the death of a man whose wife was coveted by another. Santiago remembered that, because the lady in question had preferred him to both men.

Why should there not be witches in England? Perhaps they were everywhere, and all those bizarre rituals he had witnessed at the ball were simply another form of arcane belief. What had Mistress Blackmantle and her women done to him, after all? Taken him in and healed his wounds?

Yes, but who called down the cuero *in the first place?* asked a dark little corner of his soul.

He cleared his throat, aware Billy was awaiting an answer. 'It's a busy place. And I am only recently in town.'

'Yeah? Down Wapping, are you?'

It was almost sweet, the way the boy thought he was being so guileless. 'Limehouse,' said Santiago, trying not to smile. 'Are you angling for a job, Billy?'

'A job?' Billy paused with a biscuit halfway to his mouth. 'I … dunno. I ain't never had one.'

'Well,' said Santiago, 'I could always use somebody to run errands for me. Carry messages. Fetch food. Such a valuable member of my company would be well remunerated, of course.'

Billy's gaze darted from side to side.

'Paid,' Santiago clarified. He sat up and stretched. The bed was comfortable, but he had spent too much time in it, and he ached as if he had been in a tavern brawl. 'In fact, you could begin right now, if you like.'

'I could?'

'Yes. I should like you to take a message to my office in Limehouse.'

'How much'd I be paid?'

Santiago smiled. He thought about how much he paid his dockers, and they usually had families to support. 'Threepence a day,' he said. 'Food included.'

Billy's eyes were huge. 'I get me grub included?'

'As much as you can eat.' Which would almost certainly cost him more than threepence a day at the rate Billy was going.

'Cor.' Billy stuffed another biscuit in, apparently without thinking, and said, 'What's the message?'

'WHAT ON EARTH are you doing, wandering off like that?' scolded Elinor. She fiddled with her parasol and handed it to her footman in irritation. 'Lady Dandridge asked after you—of course, her son is worth two thousand a year for all he is so terribly short—and for a moment I thought today was the day you went to visit your aunt.'

Tiffany, who was somewhat out of breath from almost-but-not-quite running back from Aunt Esme's, smiled and tried to look as if she'd been doing no more than strolling.

'Today? No, of course not. I was merely chatting with some friends.'

'Friends?' Elinor laughed. 'I don't recall you ever having friends, Theophania!'

No.

No, she didn't.

There had been Henry, the boot boy. Tiffany knew she wasn't supposed to be friends with him, because Elinor had not considered such a child suitable, but she had turned herself unseen and sneaked out of the house to play with him in the fields and the ruins on the hill. But Henry had gone away to fight Bonaparte, and she had heard nothing from his family for months.

There had been no other children near her age in the families whose estates abutted Dyrehaven. Tiffany had tried to befriend the village children, but they'd been frightened of her—or perhaps of Elinor—and Tiffany herself hadn't really known how to talk to them anyway. That left her nieces and nephews, the oldest of whom was three years Tiffany's junior and the youngest still in short trousers.

Coming to London hadn't helped, because every other young lady here seemed to be entirely comfortable with the social whirl, all of them sophisticated and polished and trilling with inane laughter at every silly joke a gentleman made.

But none of them had recently rescued a man from drowning and slipped unseen through a crowded park and had a conversation *with a cat*.

Because none of them were witches, but Aunt Esme and Gwen and Madhu and Nora were, and they didn't care in the slightest whether Tiffany's gown was fashionable or her posture correct or her conversation bland.

None of them were defined solely as daughters or sisters or wives or mothers. They were women, whole and complete with no men in sight.

'I—' Elinor seemed to mistake her expression. 'I didn't mean it like that. I am sure you will make friends once you've attended a few more events. Why, it's simply that at a ball, there is no time to talk.' She began walking again, taking her parasol from the footman and nodding to an acquaintance. 'Perhaps we should attend a … a few more At Homes, and then perhaps a gallery. Yes, you can make friends at a gallery.'

'No' said Tiffany sharply.

'No?' Elinor stopped. 'My dear, you must have friends. It is positively abnormal to be alone as much as you are. People will begin to think you are strange, and nobody wants to marry a strange girl.'

Then I shall become a witch, and have my own friends, and never have to marry anyone. Tiffany lifted her chin, and as she did, remembered the pirate smile and the gold earring and the black ink. Hah! *Perhaps I shall marry a pirate.* That would show Elinor!

If Elinor noticed her strange mood, she did not show it. They went home, and ate a cold luncheon while Elinor decided upon whom they would pay calls later.

And as Tiffany followed her from the house, dressed once more in an insipid gown that made her look like a vanilla slice, a raven cawed overhead and a pale rectangle dropped from the sky.

'Take it,' said the raven's voice, a harsh croak inside her head, and she darted to pick it up before she'd even realised what she was doing. She skipped after Elinor into the carriage, the card tucked into her palm, and didn't look at it until Elinor had turned to her maid to fix a curl of hair that kept unravelling.

Tiffany smiled to herself, because she had been gazing at it and willing it to unravel the whole time. Was this magic? Simply willing things to happen, and therefore making it so? Was this what she had been suppressing her whole life? It suddenly seemed as easy and natural as breathing.

She turned her attention to the card hidden in her palm. It was a trade card, engraved with flourishes and an illustration of a fine three-masted ship. SANTIAGO PACIFIC AND EURASIAN TRADING CO., it read. OPP. BELL INN, NEXT TO DE GROOT'S, CNR COMMERCIAL RD, LIMEHOUSE BASIN. WHOLESALE FINE SILKS, TEA, COFFEE, LIQUORS, TOBACCO...

The list of goods boasted of went on into quite small print. But that wasn't important. What was important was that thanks to Aunt Esme's ravens, Tiffany now had Mr Santiago's direction.

Now all she had to do was find out what Limehouse Basin was.

CHAPTER 4

*I*t was three days before Santiago saw the siren again.

Three boring, frustrating days, when the women of the house—and there seemed only to be women—fussed over his wounds and fed him broth and muttered in corners. He still wasn't sure whether to trust them, because something had sent that monstrous water creature to destroy his ships and try to drown him, but on the other hand...

On the other hand, he had felt like he'd been thrown about and half-drowned by some sort of giant squid made out of mud, and now he felt ... fine. No more than a bruise or two. A little tired sometimes.

He kept watching for signs of witchcraft from the ladies of the house, but all he could really lay at their door was that they made marvellous poultices and delicious curries. The most senior lady of the house had introduced herself as Mistress Blackmantle, the sort of title even Santiago thought somewhat old-fashioned. She spoke to him in Spanish, Miss Madhu exercised his patchy Tamil and even patchier Kannada, and Nora translated some of Billy's more confusing cant terms.

Gwen played card games with him, and usually won, mostly because she already seemed to know what the outcome of the game would be. Madhu served him food that seemed to soothe whatever ache or discomfort he was currently feeling. Nora, when she thought he wasn't watching, managed to lift the clothes press all by herself in order to sweep beneath it.

These women were not natural. Did that mean they were evil? And did that mean the bewitching Lady Tiffany was, too?

Clothes were procured for him, and he was permitted to sit in the parlour and play dice with Billy, who won an outrageous amount of money from him, mostly by cheating. The boy seemed to have decided he belonged to Santiago now, which was fine, he supposed. Billy did at least know London, or at least the rougher parts of it, and he'd managed to obtain a packet of cigars for Santiago, which had the effect of endearing him more than it should have.

'And that's when I ses, if you're gonna hang around Seven Dials in a dress that's what's gonna happen,' said Billy, and when Santiago laughed he casually flipped one of the dice over.

'Billy, Billy. You'll have to get better at cheating than that,' said Santiago. 'Look. Let me show you…'

''Ow's a fine gent like you know about cheating?' said Billy, with not a trace of embarrassment at being caught.

It was a skill my father taught me.

'Yes, that is a good question,' said a voice that made Santiago's pulse race. He looked up, and there was the siren, neat as a pin in a dreadful shade of peach with an equally appalling bonnet.

'No, please don't stand up,' she added drily, when neither of them made a move to.

Billy shot Santiago a questioning look.

'My lady,' said Santiago, endeavouring to nod to her in a manner that might be acceptable.

'Mr Santiago. Billy. How pleasant to see you again. I trust your health has been improving?'

'Yes.' Santiago gestured to himself, as fully dressed as he could be bothered when doing little more than playing dice by the fire. He wore a waistcoat, mostly unbuttoned, and a loose neckcloth, and had allowed Mistress Blackmantle to drape a blanket across his lap despite the mildness of the day.

Not that Lady Tiffany would have noticed, as her gaze did not seem capable of dipping below his chin. 'Your aunt has been most kind,' he said. 'I will shortly be returning home.'

'Oh? Does Aunt Esme know that?' asked Tiffany, taking an elegantly uncomfortable-looking seat on an elegantly uncomfortable-looking sofa.

Santiago lounged in his wingback chair. 'I will not trespass on her hospitality any longer,' he said, a phrase which seemed to impress Billy.

'Cor, you don't half talk all fancy,' he said. 'Is that what nobs sound like?'

A faint smile touched Lady Tiffany's lips, and Santiago smiled too, as he was transported to that evening outside the ball when she had made the chalk come to life...

'I can assure you that they don't,' she said, 'and also beg you to never use that word again.'

'What? Nobs? But you are. Well nobby,' said Billy.

Her smile began to look a little fixed. 'My father is an earl,' she said. 'I am an aristocrat. Mr Santiago, on the other hand, is of the merchant class. Two quite different things.'

He felt his eyebrows go up. 'I am a merchant? How do you know this?'

'I—' Her cheeks coloured.

'You talk in your sleep, guv,' said Billy, and her blush grew deeper. Santiago grinned. It suited her to have some colour in her face.

He reached for his cigars, cut one and lit it, which did not seem to meet with her approval.

'I came across your trade card,' she said stiffly, withdrawing it from her reticule. Ah yes, the little cards Penderghast had told him would aid business. He'd been along to an engravers tucked behind Oxford Street and asked for something suitable. The resulting tall ship and flowery lettering had been a little over the top for his tastes, but he'd been assured by all that it was the very thing.

'There could be more than one Santiago,' he said.

'There could. But Spanish names are not that common in London and when one takes into account that you are clearly a seafaring man, it would make the coincidence somewhat … unrealistic?'

Santiago cocked his head. 'How do you know I am a seafaring man?'

Her gaze darted, for the first time, below his collar, and Santiago felt himself smile even wider. She had seen his tattoos. Which ones? The dragon, the swallow, the ship? Maybe even … his shellback turtle?

'What are you smiling at?' snapped Lady Tiffany, her cheeks very red now.

'Nothing at all, my lady.' But he let his gaze slide over her, because turnabout was fair play. She was fully clothed, from the toes of her neat boots to the tips of her gloves; she hadn't even taken her bonnet off. For her to have seen his tattoos, he must have been naked, or near enough.

He drew hard on his cigar. The tip glowed orange.

Her clothing was doing its best to disguise her figure, but he'd seen it the night she'd worn the silver tissue dress. Curves. Lots of curves. Curves that were going up and down right now under her high-necked pelisse.

Lady Tiffany cleared her throat. 'Aunt Esme,' she called, a slight break in her voice.

'Yes, dear?'

Aunt Esme must have been right outside the door.

'Can I come and help you with some tea?' Tiffany's voice was a little desperate.

'No need, dear. I'll bring it. Very remiss of me not to.'

'I don't—' Tiffany began, her voice rising, but Esme's neat footsteps were already clipping away down the hall.

She swallowed. Clutched at her reticule. Looked around, her gaze avoiding the paintings on the walls. Billy, unconcerned with what was going on between them, was playing a game of dice all by himself.

'No butler,' Lady Tiffany commented, in the direction of the curtains. 'No footman.'

'No men at all,' Santiago said. 'This must please you, my lady.'

Her eyebrows went up questioningly. But it happened a fraction too late.

'My head may be a little disordered,' he said, 'but I do recall our conversation at the ball.'

Her cheeks pinkened. 'I beg you to forget it—'

'But how could I? You were so very clear. You wish to never marry. Not even,' he prodded, 'if he is a duke.'

'I...' she began, and licked her lips nervously. 'It is unlikely to happen in any case,' she said.

'But even if a duke—a young, handsome, wealthy duke—proposed marriage to you, you would turn him down?' he said, entertained.

'Even the Prince Regent himself,' she said with a tight little smile that turned to acid in her eyes. 'As you see, my aunt and her ladies have little use for husbands.'

He relented. 'Is this usual in English households?'

'No,' admitted Lady Tiffany. 'Not really. No.' She sighed. 'Not in this sort of household.'

'This sort?'

'The... The genteel sort.'

'Ah,' said Santiago, nodding. 'The nobby sort.'

'Please don't—' Realising he was teasing her, she cut herself off and glared. 'What were you doing at the Russell ball, Mr Santiago?'

He shrugged. 'I was invited.'

She did not look as if she believed this. 'By whom?'

'Lady Russell.'

'I did not know you were among her acquaintance.'

He puffed on his cigar. 'Why else would she invite me?'

It wasn't a lie. He had never actually met Lady Russell before the night of the ball, and in fact didn't expect to ever again. He had turned up at the appointed time, which seemed to appall her as absolutely nobody else had bothered, and after a stunned introduction excused himself for a walk around the grounds until more guests arrived. In this manner he had avoided being announced, which was a relief. Given how many things he'd got wrong, it was probably just as well virtually nobody knew who he was.

As for the invitation ... well, that itself wasn't a direct lie. Not exactly.

Nothing here is as it seems. Hadn't he thought that at the time? He'd had simply no idea how much stranger it could get.

'And yet you do not seem to know how to go about in Society,' said Lady Tiffany.

Santiago blew out some smoke and watched through it as Mistress Blackmantle brought in a tea tray and set it down.

'It occurs to me I should probably be supervising you,' she said. 'Billy doesn't appear to be much of a chaperone.'

Billy glanced up from his game. 'Whassat?'

'Quite.' She poured the tea into delicate cups and made a production of asking if either of them would like milk, lemon, or sugar.

'I don't suppose there is any brandy?' asked Santiago, just to annoy Lady Tiffany.

Her nostrils flared.

'I am afraid not. But the tincture is alcoholic, if that helps,' Mistress Blackmantle added, manifesting a tiny bottle from nowhere and adding a couple of drops to his tea.

'What tincture?' asked Santiago, suspicious.

'It is for your health.'

'What is in it?'

'Oh, herbs,' said Mistress Blackmantle, with a wave of her hand.

'Hemlock is a herb,' Santiago said.

'Why on earth would I give you hemlock? I wish to strengthen our acquaintance, not end it.'

'You do?' asked Santiago and Tiffany at the same time.

Mistress Blackmantle shrugged. 'We may have some business together, Mr Santiago. Trade. I understand you ship nutmeg?'

'I ship many things,' said Santiago, trying to recall if he had any in the warehouse or if it had all been sold on.

'Then perhaps we shall do business. Do try not to be so shocked, Tiffany.'

'But,' said Lady Tiffany, daughter of an earl, self-proclaimed aristocrat, 'you ... you are a lady, Aunt Esme.'

'I am many things. As is Mr Santiago, I am sure.'

She said it so mildly, while handing around a delicate little plate of cakes, that Santiago wondered if he'd imagined the inference in her voice.

'But—trade, Aunt Esme!'

'Trade in goods, Tiffany. Why—there are those at the top of Society who have got there by trading people. What is a little brandy and silk compared to human life?' She fixed Santiago with a sudden look that had him pinned to his seat.

Literally pinned. He found he could not move. Beside him, Billy knelt on the floor, entirely unconcerned, playing with the cat and stuffing cake into his mouth.

'You do not traffic in human life, Mr Santiago?' Mistress Blackmantle said, still neatly arranging cakes on a plate.

'I do not,' he said. 'And I have never.'

He could suddenly move again.

'Glad to hear,' said Mistress Blackmantle. 'But you do wish to move at the top of Society?'

'Well,' began Santiago, wondering if he had imagined his momentary paralysis.

'You said you were leaving Town,' Tiffany said.

He shrugged. 'Perhaps I shall stay a while longer.' His grandfather's lawyers seemed to have decided to approve of him, and Santiago was becoming aware that simply leaving the country again at this point would be somewhat irresponsible. Not to mention, there was a rather fine pair of arctic blue eyes flashing at him now, and he thought he might miss those.

'But—'

'Do you know anyone in Town?' asked Mistress Blackmantle.

'He appears to be acquainted with Lady Russell,' said Tiffany, frowning.

'A most redoubtable lady,' said Mistress Blackmantle tonelessly.

'But he came to her ball wearing a green coat.'

'Goodness. That must have been the most exciting thing to happen at one of Lady Russell's balls since the Prince Regent went face-first into the punch,' said Mistress Blackmantle. She took a delicate bite of cake. 'These are very good.'

'Well, perhaps the second most exciting thing,' said Santiago, raising an eyebrow at Tiffany.

Her gaze skittered away to the cat. 'I don't know what you mean.'

'The chalk on the floor came to life all by itself, did it?'

That was a test. Mistress Blackmantle did not turn a hair, which was interesting. But Lady Tiffany looked away, her cheeks going pinker.

'I'm sure I don't know what you're talking about.'

'You are a witch,' he said.

'You are no gentleman,' she replied.

He spread his hands. 'Evidently.' He cocked his head at her, an idea occurring. 'Much less evidently than you,' he mused.

Tiffany looked wary. 'What do you mean?'

'Well … does anybody outside this house know you are a witch? I have not been much in Society but I feel I would have heard about it.'

'No,' said Tiffany, cheeks colouring again. 'And I would thank you to—' She glanced at her aunt, and amended, 'That is, nobody would believe you if you told them.'

'No? You think so?'

Lady Tiffany's eyes narrowed. In this light they were the grey-green of a storm-tossed sea. They had been blue a moment ago. Perhaps witches could change their eyes as other ladies changed their dresses. 'Are you attempting to blackmail me, Mr Santiago?'

'No, not at all!' He puffed on his cigar and held her gaze. 'Not at all.'

She raised her chin and glared at him.

'But you may have something that is of use to me. I could pay you,' he said, knowing full well she would refuse.

'Mr Santiago! No gentleman ever offers to pay a lady for anything!'

'And that is the problem,' he said, leaning forward. 'I do not know how to be a gentleman. Nobody in this town will take me seriously. I wear the wrong clothes and say the wrong things and know nobody but a street urchin,' he nodded at Billy, who was too busy eating cake to notice. 'But you know. You know all the secret rules.'

'They're not a secret,' she said, and faltered, honesty getting the better of her. 'I just suppose we don't ever share them.'

'Share them with me,' he urged, leaning forward. 'Teach me to be a gentleman. You are bored, Lady Tiffany. Or you would not be making chalk drawings come to life. Teach me.'

When she wasn't trying to be the bland doll Society evidently expected her to be, Tiffany had a very expressive face. Her pale brow creased in the centre as she looked from him to her aunt and back.

'The *illusion* of gentility?' said Mistress Blackmantle, with an emphasis he didn't quite understand the significance of.

'You wish me to … make you appear to be a gentleman?' asked Lady Tiffany, doubtfully. She frowned at her aunt.

'Appear, yes … in dress, in manner.' He glanced off to the side and admitted, 'I do not wish to make a fool of myself again.'

'Well, I can't promise miracles, Mr Santiago!'

He laughed. 'You make chalk come to life! You healed me of my wounds in a fraction of the time it should have taken.'

'Actually, that was my aunt, and Madhu and Gwen—'

'Lady Tiffany was of great assistance,' said Mistress Blackmantle smoothly. 'She is a very *accomplished* young lady.'

Tiffany's cheeks coloured. 'And you will tell nobody about the … um,' she waved her hand vaguely, then added sharply, 'No, Pippin! We do not bite people, do we?'

To his astonishment, the cat retracted its claws from where it had been about to capture Billy's fingers, and sat back to wash its paws.

'I will tell nobody about this,' Santiago promised faintly. After all, nobody would believe him.

'Then we have a deal.' She held out one gloved hand, and he reached forward to take it.

'Wait—' began Mistress Blackmantle, but their hands were already touching.

Her kid leather glove was buttery soft against his bare fingers. Her fingers were long and elegant. And her gaze held his for a moment as her fingers briefly squeezed his.

Something like a spark leapt between them.

Santiago was suddenly very grateful for the blanket across his lap.

'Ah,' said Mistress Blackmantle. She put down her plate. 'Did I not warn you about making bargains, Tiffany?'

Tiffany's eyes grew wide with horror.

'What do you mean?'

Mistress Blackmantle smiled, and Santiago couldn't quite shake the feeling that she had intended this outcome all along.

'That you're stuck with each other until the bargain is fulfilled.'

'I DECLARE,' said Elinor at breakfast, 'it quite captured the voluptuous splendours of the East. It was little less than magical.' She observed her raspberry jam on toast with satisfaction. 'Lady Greensword kept muttering on and on about political parallels, but I say she simply cannot appreciate a good melodrama the way I do. She has not the sensibilities.'

Tiffany, who was sure her sister-in-law was quoting her review of last night's theatrical performance directly from the *Morning Chronicle*, said, 'I preferred the farce.'

'The farce? Really, Theophania. No man will marry you if you laugh too much. The melodrama was the thing, was it not, Cornforth?'

If I laugh too much? Tiffany could only blink in disbelief at such a statement.

'Cornforth! The melodrama! Last night!'

'Hmm?' He twitched his paper. 'Oh. Yes. A fine commentary on the French tyrant. We must all do as the hero said, and set our faces against it.'

Elinor's face took on the pinched expression it did when she wanted to frown but daren't because she feared wrinkles.

'Must you read that paper all through breakfast?' she said instead. 'There are papers at your club, I am sure.'

Tiffany kept her eyes on her plate, so as to avoid meeting her brother's gaze. She was fairly sure by now that he read the papers at breakfast purely to avoid his wife.

This is the life Elinor wants for me. Marriage to a man who avoided her as much as possible. A life where she was a mere accessory to a man, whose only power was over the petty and mundane. The correct shade of eveningwear. The most fashionable kind of jam. Exercising control over her sister-in-law. She didn't seem to even be aware of the restrictions her life imposed upon her. She relished them. She seemed to sincerely believe that Tiffany, and indeed everyone else in the world, envied her.

Tiffany looked at the raspberry jam on her toast and considered that if she ever ended up like Elinor she would go stark raving mad. Well, more mad than a person who could talk to cats and make drawings come to life already was.

'The Prussians,' said Cornforth, eyes back on the paper, 'have begun arresting those they suspect to be in sympathy with the Frenchman.'

'Really?' said Tiffany. That was a worrying development, surely? A word in the wrong place and one could end up in jail!

Elinor rolled her eyes. 'Nobody wishes to hear about the activities of the Russians.'

'Prussians,' murmured Cornforth.

'Exactly. Such a dull subject for discourse. Theophania, you must remember to talk about the melodrama last night.'

'The voluptuous splendours?' said Tiffany innocently.

'Yes! I declare it little less than magical,' said Elinor, adjusting the angle of her plate and therefore unable to see Tiffany mouthing the words along with her. She had definitely read them in the *Morning Chronicle*.

'I will remember that,' said Tiffany, 'when I visit my aunt.'

'Your aunt?' said Elinor. 'Again? No. We must go to the modiste, for I heard she has some marvellous new French silks and there is time to have a new gown made up before Mrs Garbet-Smithe's rout.'

'I don't think I need a new gown,' said Tiffany, and saw by the flare of Elinor's nostrils that she hadn't been thinking about Tiffany. 'And your taste is so excellent, Elinor, I am sure you don't need me there. But I did promise my aunt. And what is a lady's honour, if she breaks a promise?'

That line made her smile all the way to Aunt Esme's house. She and Morris had come to a new understanding whereby the maid could go off and do as she pleased, no questions asked, and then when she wished to return home Tiffany would send a note —delivered by Billy, usually, for the outrageous sum of a ha'penny—to the shop on New Bond Street, where, mysteriously, she could be found, usually surreptitiously straightening her hair.

Elinor was not happy with this arrangement, of course, as Morris had housemaid duties to attend to. Tiffany was absolutely sure the household finances could stretch to another ladies' maid, or a promotion for Morris, but she was also absolutely sure this wasn't the point Elinor was trying to make.

Your threats don't frighten me, Mr Santiago. I have survived a lifetime of Elinor Cornforth.

Nora let her in. 'Get Esme to show you how to open doors, will you?' was her greeting.

'It is very nice to see you too,' said Tiffany, and Nora scowled at her. 'Will she show me how to operate the green door?'

Nora looked slightly surprised. 'The anywhere door?' she said. 'No. Esme's the only one who can do it.'

'But I drew the door that got us home—' Tiffany said.

'You fixed the door she'd already used. Different thing. It's her magic. Believe me, love, we've all tried.'

Love. Tiffany had heard tradespeople call women this casually, but only women of their own class. She was a Miss to a stranger, and a My Lady to anyone who knew her. She'd never been a Love to anyone.

'But how does the door work?' she said. 'How does any of it work? The—' She lowered her voice. 'The *magic?*'

'You concentrate on what you want, and you make it happen. Like—I want that fire to be lit. So it lights. I dunno how else to describe it.'

'But are there rules?' Apart from not making bargains, she thought bitterly. 'Limitations? Where does it come from?'

Nora rolled her eyes. 'Don't go poking at it,' she said. 'Think about it too much and it's all a house of cards.'

She stomped off below stairs before Tiffany could ask what that even was.

She found Mr Santiago in the drawing room, slightly more appropriately dressed than usual in a blue wool coat and an appallingly tied neckcloth. Glimpses of that golden skin were visible around his collar, and it made her breath catch.

Somebody—Billy? Esme? Nora? Surely not himself—had shaved him, and the sight of his bare throat made Tiffany feel somewhat peculiar. Gentlemen didn't go around baring their throats. And probably for good reason, if they made ladies feel this warm and fluttery.

He was studying a thick, thick book, frowning at it as if trying to read ancient Greek. 'This is ridiculous,' he said.

A curl of dark hair fell over his forehead. It looked very, very soft. Tiffany found herself wondering if it would be soft to touch, if it would yield against her fingers when she pushed it back out of his eyes—

'I am supposed to memorise all of this?' He flipped the book closed with what she was fairly sure was a swear word in Spanish. 'Impossible!'

Tiffany smiled. It was the Peerage, of course. She had suggested it might be an educational primer. 'That is merely volume one,' she said. 'Of this year.'

He looked aghast. 'How many are there?'

'Only two,' she said, setting down her reticule on the table. The door was open and she could hear Aunt Esme and Gwen in the parlour. 'And little changes from year to year. That is—obviously much changes but you will hear about it from gossip.'

'I will?'

'Oh yes. There is little Society adores more than gossip,' Tiffany told him, and failed to entirely keep the sourness from her voice.

'You do not care for it?'

Cornforth and Elinor's behaviour was, of course, absolutely above reproach, but those with long memories might wonder why Tiffany's mother was not in London to launch her daughter into Society. She had seen the sideways glances, the whispers behind fans. Elinor was quite sharp at quelling the speculation, and of course, it became just another reason to act with absolutely perfect propriety at all times.

'No. It is frequently mean-spirited,' she began, and then attempted to sound careless, so he wouldn't suspect anything. 'But above all it commits the sin of being very boring. But you must never say so.'

'You must not? I mean, I must not?'

'No. To be bored is the height of rudeness,' Tiffany sighed. 'Even though almost everything on offer is unspeakably dull.'

'Does no one say anything? If it is all so dull?'

'Of course not. When pressed, I say a boring thing was "most invigorating."' She saw him mouth the words in consternation, clearly unsure whether to believe her or not. 'Unfortunately, even the *Peerage* cannot be described thus. You would do well to read it all though.'

'Have you?'

'Oh yes.' Tiffany tried not to sigh again and failed. 'Every year.'

'But there are'—he looked at the book in despair—'hundreds of entries. Hundreds. Thousands. And all so detailed.'

'That's why it is such a thick volume.'

'Are you in here?'

Tiffany sighed. 'In a manner of speaking.' When he appeared to require more detail, she reluctantly added, 'Page 132.'

He flipped to it eagerly, and scanned the text. '*Henry Worthington, Earl of Chalkdown*—your father?' At her nod, he continued to read. '*Viscount Cornforth, Baron Warlington, a General in the army, and Colonel of the 75ᵗʰ regiment of foot; born— succeeded— married, first, 29 May 1773, Sarah Anne*—your mother?'

'No,' said Tiffany shortly. 'You'll have to read on down if you're looking for me. Quite a long way down.'

He looked surprised, but continued murmuring names as he read them. '*Robert, Viscount Cornforth— Sir Anthony, Dr Phileas, Mr Cornelius*— Your brothers are somewhat older than you?'

'Yes.' She managed to make the syllable as short as she could. Cornforth had been married by the time Tiffany was born.

'Ah! *And secondly— 30ᵗʰ June 1792, Miss Amelia Davenport, by whom a daughter.*' He looked up at her, then back at the page. His brow creased. 'It then… It talks about the family history.'

'*Of this family there have been persons of great note and eminence for several ages,*' recited Tiffany from memory. She knew the whole entry. Could picture the layout on the page from the first edition that had thudded onto the nursery table in front of her when she was about five. 'The first Earl was created in 1524. His name was Thomas. Fell out of favour, that name, for a surprisingly long time, following Cromwell. They were Henrys after that. Currying royal favour.'

'The book doesn't list your name,' said Santiago, looking again as if he'd missed it.

'No. Well. They'd run out of ink, wouldn't they? Theophania Penelope Ameliana Worthington. What a mouthful.' And if they'd listed her date of birth, it would have been painfully obvious that her parents had anticipated the marriage.

'It lists your brothers' accomplishments, but you—'

Tiffany drew herself up and looked squarely at him. 'Are only distinguished by the father I was born to and the man I will marry and the sons I will have, so my name is less than relevant, isn't it? I will soon relinquish it for my husband's title. Now. Perhaps it is time to move on from that, and we will discuss correct forms of address.'

He looked up at her for a long moment, and Tiffany, who had made a career out of not being noticed by anyone, suddenly felt terribly, terribly seen.

'I think you are very relevant,' he said, 'Lady Tiffany.' But he closed the book, and stood, and allowed her to lecture him on the ways to address married granddaughters of dukes.

CHAPTER 5

She'd threatened him with dancing next. Santiago could dance, at least in the manner that suggested he was thinking of entirely more horizontal activities, but he hadn't a clue where to start with all the holding hands and skipping about he'd witnessed at the Russell ball. Some of the sets seemed to go on for half an hour or more.

For a moment he thought wistfully of the tango he had learned in Buenos Aires. Too few girls, too many men, and so they had twined around each other in the sultry heat. But there would be none of that here in England.

You could just leave, he thought as he climbed the rickety wooden steps to his office. He could find someone to run the London office for him. Simply slip onto one of his own ships and sail away, be just another sailor, a smuggler, a pirate, with no responsibilities except to his own pocket. He could forget that mausoleum of a house, and the liveried carriage, and all the gold-edged invitations, and nobody would know who he was ever again.

Be Santiago for the rest of his life. Not even Mr. Just Santiago.

Or he could face up to his responsibilities, stop running away like a child, and be the man his father had never been. It couldn't be hard. All he had to do was not be a dreadful human being and he was already ahead.

He thumped the two heavy volumes of the Peerage down on his desk and shoved them to one side to get some actual work done. Somebody around here had a shipping empire to run and he didn't see anyone else doing it.

And yet…

His fingers drummed on the desk. The entries were not in alphabetical order, Tiffany had explained, but in order of precedence, which was ancient and intricate and, he suspected, completely made up. But there was an index, alphabetical by title.

Dammit. He'd already drawn the first volume towards him and was flipping through the index. There. Page 27.

His grandfather's styles, achievements and titles were listed at length. His father's, less so. Merely his name, and dates of birth and death, the latter being somewhat approximate.

Santiago's own birth had been recorded too, with a neat list of names borrowed from his father. There were no further details. What would the Peerage know of a street rat, a guttersnipe, a pirate and a smuggler?

'One day, son,' his exiled father had told Santiago, 'you'll go back to England, and the old man can see what he's got for an heir. A grubby little urchin the colour of mud.' He'd cackled into his tankard. 'And he can't pretend you're not his heir, because I've sent all the proof of legitimacy. He's stuck with you. With a little street rat who doesn't even know what pounds, shilling and pence are.'

'Then tell me,' said Santiago, who had been very small and hadn't yet learned what a snake his father truly was.

'Tell you? And spoil it? You'll be the downfall of that whole lineage, my boy—the ruin of everything he's worked for! He'll spin in his grave! Now, go and tell your mother to stop praying. If she wants to spend so much time on her knees, I've got something else she can do…'

A knock on the door brought him back to Limehouse, and his dusty, bare office. 'Guv?' It was Penderghast, the dock foreman, ambling in with the post. 'Your boy's cheating at dice. The lads think it's funny now, but they might change their minds.'

'Duly noted.' It all looked fairly routine, until he reached a letter on fine paper written in a delicate hand. Was there a faint scent coming off it?

'And that cove's hanging around again. Shall I tell him to piss off?'

'Ask him if he wants a job managing a boisterous and overpaid messenger boy,' Santiago murmured, not looking up.

'Guv?'

'Nothing. Let me know when the Revenue men arrive, yes?'

'Are we expecting them?'

'There's a ship in the dock half full of coffee, of course we're expecting them.'

He waited until his foreman had lumbered off again, impatient to open Tiffany's missive. What sweet nothings had the siren inscribed to him?

Dancing lessons with M. Lemaigre, Jermyn St, above Granet & Chapelle tailors. After luncheon at two today. TW. PS you will also need a tailor but do not patronise said, no availability, Nora might know someone. PPS This cannot be your address. Move somewhere fashionable.

Well. Hardly a love letter. He wondered whether to cry off the dancing lessons, then figured it meant he might get to see Lady Tiffany's bosom in motion, and decided it was probably worth it.

~

ON MONDAY, Tiffany attended an At Home at Lady Greensword's townhouse, where she pretended not to be bored silly by the boasts of the lady's two nephews as they related the excitements of their Grand Tour. Behind them hung a painting of Venice. Tiffany amused herself by making the little boats bob about, one at a time, while no one was watching. Well, Aunt Esme had told her that she needed to practice control, and it was almost certainly the closest she'd ever get to seeing real boats in Venice.

At the same time, Mr Santiago had been sent to dancing lessons, the outcome of which she itched to hear. But Tuesday was taken up with a visit to the modiste, during which Elinor spent a full hour choosing between two equally dull shades of peach cambric, and Tiffany barely managed to slip out unseen in order to hand a hastily scribbled note to a street urchin who promised to run to Limehouse with it.

On Wednesday the reply to her note came back that Mr Santiago had attended his dancing lessons and found them most invigorating—these last two words underlined. He had been listening to her!

Thursday morning involved a promenade on Rotten Row, during which Elinor kept up a lamentable habit of including her in the conversation so that she couldn't fade into the background. She had smuggled out a note to Mr Santiago that he must—as an absolute imperative—find a decent tailor and pay him very well before he could even think of appearing in Society. She added that he must also find an excellent valet, because a gentleman could not possibly dress himself, and that no, Billy would not be an acceptable substitute. The boy hardly even wore shoes most of the time.

PS. I may not be able to respond as I am to attend the theatre and such an event is always followed by tiresome visits from gentlemen I was not able to repel. Last time the house positively reeked of lilies.

His reply came on Friday, attached to an arrangement of daisies.

My dear Lady Tiffany, One cannot possibly imagine your repelling any gentleman at all. Unless some sort of mythical tentacled animal is involved, in which case I find such an event entirely plausible.

'Well!' she said, as Elinor physically strained towards her in her eagerness to read it.

Had he just complimented or insulted her? Did he mean he was repelled by her? The thought wounded her, which was ridiculous because she had no attachment to the man. He was a tradesman with pretensions, and he was blackmailing her.

'Theophania?' insisted Elinor, and Tiffany made the words on the page become completely illegible. It was easy to do, now she wasn't trying to suppress it. Aunt Esme called it a glamour, and said some witches couldn't do them at all. She said Tiffany had a natural affinity for illusion and manifestation, and all she really had to do was allow herself to explore it.

'It's from Aunt Esme,' she said, laying the note down beside the daisies. 'Merely thanking me for my help choosing embroidery colours.'

'You spend too much time tending to that old woman,' scolded Elinor. 'Does she even know anyone in Society? You must cultivate friendships with suitable young ladies of your own age. You don't want to be a sad old maid, do you?'

Aunt Esme isn't sad. Neither is Gwen, or Madhu or Nora. But Tiffany couldn't say that out loud.

Later, in her room, she composed and burned half a dozen replies to Mr Santiago. Eventually she wrote to her aunt to tell her that Mr Santiago was unconscionably rude and that perhaps she could do no more for him.

Do not forget the bargain you have contracted

Came the reply that a raven dropped on the floor as it flew through Tiffany's bedroom the next morning.

No. How could she? If she did not teach him how to go about in Society, then he would tell everyone she was a witch. And if that sort of rumour spread, then it didn't matter if no one believed in witches anymore. The scandal of having *any* kind of rumour attached to the family would have Elinor packing her off back to Dyrehaven—or worse. It was not out of the realms of possibility that she might be sent to Bedlam.

Mr Santiago might be blackmailing her, but of the two threats, Tiffany found Elinor by far the most terrifying.

And... *You are bored, Lady Tiffany.* Damn the man for being right! Teaching him how to be a gentleman was much more fun than being a lady.

Esme's note went on.

I have found a tailor who may also be willing to act as valet. He was not born a gentleman either so he will be a perfect fit I think. Do come on Monday.

Tiffany had no idea what that meant. She spent the next two days alternately deciding not to go to her aunt's on Monday and then deciding to attend, just to spite Mr Santiago.

Sunday's church sermon was all about doing one's duty.

Tiffany wouldn't have put it past her aunt to have influenced the vicar, but she conceded the point, and told a thin-lipped Elinor that she had promised to visit her aunt the following day.

'Who is this aunt?' said Elinor, who was always grumpy on Sundays because the servants only undertook light duties. 'I have never heard of her.'

'She is most elegant,' said Tiffany. 'I believe she attended Lady Russell's ball earlier in the year.'

'She did?' This appeared to mollify Elinor. 'It is strange we did not meet her there.'

'I am sure you were simply too in demand,' Tiffany replied, wondering if she was laying it on a bit thick.

On Monday, she marched forth with Morris to the townhouse in Mayfair, and entered to find the carpets in the drawing room rolled back and the furniture pushed against the walls. Nora, Gwen and Madhu stood on one side of it, with Santiago—in another disreputable coat, because evidently this tailor had not attended him just yet—and a somewhat mute and terrified Billy on the other.

'Ah, Tiffany! Capital. Do take off that spencer, my dear, and perhaps change out of your half boots. It is time to practice dancing properly.'

'But I have been practising with Monseiur Lemaigre,' said Santiago. His hair looked ruffled, as if he had been running his hands through it. She did not know another gentleman who would do such a thing.

'And does Monsieur Lemaigre offer clever conversation at the same time?' said Aunt Esme. 'When one dances at a ball, one does not do so in silence. One converses pleasantly and wittily with one's partner.'

Santiago ran one hand through his hair, and Tiffany couldn't help her sigh of annoyance. He glared at her. 'My exhaustion amuses you?' he demanded.

'Ex— I don't know what you mean,' she said. She had been avoiding looking at him directly, but now she did, she could see the tiredness around his eyes. The loose cloth around his neck looked as if it had been pulled at in exasperation half a dozen times and his waistcoat was quite wrinkled. *He really must acquire a valet.*

His dark brows rose. 'Really, my lady? You don't think that your lessons might be in the slightest bit tiring?'

'Well, I managed them, and I am but a weak and feeble woman,' she replied.

'You are neither of those things, but also, you are not running an international shipping business from the other side of the city.'

'Limehouse is not even *in* the city, and if it's such a tedious journey, perhaps it is time to look into that fashionable address I suggested to you?'

'I have a fashionable address!' he snapped.

Tiffany laughed. She couldn't help it. 'Limehouse is not fashionable,' she said. 'Limehouse is not anywhere.'

'I—' Suddenly realising he'd said too much, Santiago cleared his throat. 'I was not speaking of Limehouse,' he muttered.

'Oh?'

There was a slight silence, during which Tiffany realised everyone else, the witches and Billy, had been watching them back and forth. Billy's eyes were wide. Madhu looked like she wanted to smile. Gwen and Esme shared a lightning-quick glance.

'I ... inherited a property,' Santiago said reluctantly. 'It is ... in one of your "fashionable areas".'

Tiffany felt her mouth drop open. 'And yet you continue to live above your warehouse, like a ... a tradesman?'

'I *am* a tradesman,' Santiago fired back. His eyes flashed darkly.

'I thought that was the problem!' Tiffany threw up her hands.

A sudden trill of music made them both jump. Aunt Esme had seated herself at the pianoforte and played the opening chords of a quadrille.

'If you are going to converse, you may as well dance,' she said. She played the first bar, and looked at them expectantly. 'Form up.'

To Tiffany's surprise, the three witches did as she asked, Nora taking the gentlemen's side. Billy hesitantly stood next to her and said, 'I dunno all the steps.'

'Have you not been in attendance when Mr Santiago has his lessons?' said Esme. 'Madhu, please partner Billy. Everybody?'

She played the opening chord again and the three 'gentlemen' bowed, with varying degrees of success. Grudgingly, Tiffany had to admit Santiago's was actually not bad. She curtseyed in response, and as they were at the head of the set, accepted his hand.

He was not wearing gloves. Hers were very fine. She felt the heat of his fingers through them.

'I do not understand why trade is so unacceptable in Society,' he said, as they began to dance.

'Then you understand nothing of Society.'

'I understand that there are a hundred things I may be sneered at for,' he said.

'We do not sneer.'

'You are sneering now!'

'I am dancing, Mr Santiago,' said Tiffany, allowing herself a smile as she circled away from him, and wiping it back off as she turned back.

'Many aristocrats make money from trade,' said Santiago.

'No. Many aristocrats make money from business interests.'

'It is the same thing—'

'It is *not* the same thing.' How to explain it? 'We employ people to take care of business for us. We do not sully our hands with it ourselves.'

'You think my hands are sullied?' They briefly squeezed hers before he let her go again and Tiffany felt herself flush.

'I—'

'If I employed someone to take care of my business for me, this would be acceptable?'

'I— Well, yes. I mean...' He would have still come from trade, but it would be *more* acceptable if he didn't manage it himself. 'I mean, Mr Santiago, that members of the aristocracy do not live above the shop, as it were. They never attend the shop.'

'But I thought the aristocracy made its money from vast estates in the countryside?'

'Yes, of course.' She was on surer ground here. 'My family owns several.'

'And the tithes from the people who work the land pay for your family to live in luxury?'

He was making it sound exploitative now. 'Mr Santiago, you are sounding positively French.'

He grinned at her. His teeth were very white. They made his skin look even more golden.

She reminded herself that the men of Society did not have golden skin. *No, they have skin like uncooked dough.* No! That wasn't the point.

'We take care of the people who work for us,' she explained, before he could start singing the Marseillaise and running off to support Bonaparte. 'And we take care of the land.'

'I see. The land surrounding your country house? Dyrehaven, is it not? I looked it up,' he added, before she could ask how he knew. Well, she had been the one to give him a copy of the Peerage after all.

'That is my brother's house, yes. And yes, of course, he supervises the estate manager and—' Too late she realised his trap. He was cleverer than Elinor at manipulating her!

His dark, dark eyes glinted and he smiled a pirate smile at her. 'Then he does not live above the shop so much as right in the centre of it?' he said.

'All right, you have made your point.'

'Have I?' he murmured, and at that point they peeled away from each other to walk around the rest of the set. Tiffany didn't know if the others had been conversing as she and Santiago had. She had almost forgotten they were there. The pianoforte itself seemed to fade away as they walked the length of the drawing room, eyes on each other even as the other dancers moved between them.

His lashes were so thick and dark it looked as if he had lined his eyes with black paint, the way actors did. And his eyes themselves, like the darkest pot of chocolate before the milk was added. They held hers as she returned to him, and then he took her hands.

She wanted to rip off her gloves and feel his hands. Would they be as rough as they looked? Would they be strong and capable? Would they be warm? What would they feel like against her skin?

His lips were parted as he gazed down at her. One lock of hair fell over his eyes, that lock she had wanted to brush away before. Her fingers twitched to do that now. She was so close she could see the tiny imperfections in his skin, the darkness at his jaw, the pink indent of the scar on his cheek. She suddenly, shockingly wanted to know how it tasted.

'Tiffany?' said someone, from a great distance.

His breath stirred the curls at her temple. She could feel the rise and fall of his chest when she leaned forward. His eyes were so deep and dark she could drown in them…

'Oi! Lady Tiffany! Have you gone deaf?'

Nora's foghorn voice had Tiffany leaping backwards and stumbling. What had she been doing? Shamelessly pressing herself up against Mr Santiago, practically purring like a kitten, seconds from licking him all over?

'Are you all right?' That was Madhu, taking her arm and leading her to a chair.

'I know what's wrong with her,' said Nora, somewhat slyly.

'Please excuse me,' said Santiago, bowing briefly and leaving the room with unseemly haste.

'And him,' cackled Nora.

'Nora, please,' said Esme.

''Tis pleasant to see young newlyweds,' said Gwen and there was an embarrassed silence.

'I am quite well, thank you,' said Tiffany, who felt as if she'd been melted from the inside. 'Nothing that a cup of tea won't fix.'

'I will go and put the kettle on,' said Madhu, and the dancing lesson appeared to be over.

~

SANTIAGO PACED THE KITCHEN CORRIDOR, trying to think of bilge-water and suppurating wounds and all the times he'd nearly died in terrifying storms at sea. Anything to take his mind off the heaving of Lady Tiffany's bosom, the pinkness of her parted lips, the yearning in her eyes.

He'd seen how tightly fashionable evening breeches were worn. If he'd been wearing those now, absolutely everyone would have seen his reaction to her.

Dear God. Did she go around looking at every man she danced with like that? No wonder she was supervised so heavily by her sister-in-law. There must be a crowd of desperate suitors beating at her door day and night!

He slapped his own cheeks to try to regain control, but every time he blinked he saw the heave of that soft white flesh, the tremble of each white-gold curl, the plumpness of her lips...

Someone cleared their throat. 'Mr Santiago? If you will excuse me...'

It was Madhu, making her way past him with her gaze averted. He stepped back, and waited until he could put the table between them before he followed her into the kitchen.

'Is everything all right?' he said, as she filled the kettle from the jug and set it on its hook over the fire.

'Yes, of course. Everyone needed a rest. Your dancing lessons are coming along well,' she added politely.

'Are they? There are so many steps. I don't know how I'm supposed to learn them all.'

Madhu shrugged. 'Just follow everyone else. That's what I do.' She ran her hand over the tea caddy and closed her eyes briefly, and did Santiago imagine it or did something change in the room?

Of course. She was a witch. They were all witches. That was why he'd had such a ridiculous reaction to Lady Tiffany. She looked like a siren, with all that white-gold hair and her bloody heaving bosom. She was probably casting a spell on him!

A scratch at the back door interrupted his budding righteousness, and they both turned to see a young man standing there. He was impeccably dressed and carried a stack of large boxes.

'Good afternoon,' he said, in a voice that sounded even younger than he looked. 'I am Robinson.' He gave a small bow. 'I believe I am expected?'

Madhu gave him a lightning glance and said, 'The tailor?'

'Yes, ma'am. I have brought samples of my work.'

'You are very young,' said Santiago. The boy was beardless as a girl.

'I am skilled enough, sir. Is the gentleman in residence? Nora

—that is, Miss Leatherheart said I should come today to meet him.'

Madhu deliberately let her gaze stray to Santiago, who straightened. Clearly he didn't resemble a gentleman yet.

'I assume I am the gentleman in question?' he said.

'Well, unless it's Billy…'

Robinson looked him over, assessing Santiago in a manner that suggested he could see every sinew and the bones they connected. 'My apologies, sir,' he said, as if he wasn't assessing Santiago like a piece of horseflesh. 'I did not expect to find you in the kitchen.'

'I came for tea,' said Santiago, as if that was an excuse. 'Mr Robinson, perhaps we should go upstairs.'

'Yes, sir.'

Santiago led the way, because Madhu was still making tea, and found the others where he had left them. He avoided the gaze of Tiffany, who was fiddling with her reticule and not looking at him either.

Nora was playing cards with Billy. 'Oh, there you are,' she said to Robinson. 'You found the place all right then?'

Robinson gave a small bow. 'Yes, thank you, Miss Leatherheart.'

She laughed. 'It's Nora to you.'

Robinson gave a polite smile. 'Above stairs, ma'am, it is Miss Leatherheart.'

'Quite right too,' said Mistress Blackmantle, looking over Robinson in much the same way he had looked over Santiago. 'Nora says your tailoring is excellent.'

'It is, ma'am. I have brought some samples. I can have them altered for the gentleman tonight if he wishes.'

'There is no rush,' said Mistress Blackmantle, before Santiago could say the same. 'I had in mind a small soirée here in a week or so. Mr Santiago, would that suit you?' Again, before he could answer she went on. 'Evening dress, then, as the priority, but he will definitely need outfits for daytime. Strolls in the park, afternoon calls, and so on. I expect that after my event you will be the talk of the town.'

'Is that a good thing?' said Santiago.

'It depends,' murmured Tiffany.

'Shall we say ten days' time? A week Thursday?'

Robinson had put down the boxes and taken out a notepad and pen. 'Thursday the eleventh. Yes, ma'am. I have some pieces I can make up for morning and afternoon wear too. Two of each?'

'Yes, and linen.'

Santiago might as well not even be here. He found his gaze straying to Tiffany, and made himself stop. She was a witch. She had bewitched him!

'Would you also be willing to act as Mr Santiago's valet for the evening affair?'

'Ye-es,' said Robinson, glancing with a very practised eye at Santiago's clothes. Which had looked perfectly fine when he'd put them on, and indeed were some of his favourites that he flattered himself made him look quite smart. Not that he'd been trying to impress Tiffany, because she was a witch and she was bewitching him and he was wise to it. That wasn't the point.

Not the point at all.

'I can,' said Robinson, 'but sir will require a valet for the daywear too.'

'What? Is "sir" me?' said Santiago. 'I assure you I can dress myself.'

Mistress Blackmantle laughed. Lady Tiffany laughed. Even Robinson permitted himself a small smile.

'No,' said Tiffany, somewhat patronisingly. 'If you wish to enter Society at the highest level, then no, you cannot dress yourself.'

'Everyone would know,' said Mistress Blackmantle.

'It would be a physical impossibility,' said Robinson.

Santiago sent him a questioning glance. The boy was surely just trying to get himself a job?

'These clothes are not designed for a gentleman to dress himself in,' said Robinson. 'That is their very point. Servants dress themselves, sir. Shopkeepers dress themselves. Gentlemen do not.'

'So...' Santiago frowned. 'The fact that I can't dress myself in these things is the point?'

'Exactly,' said Tiffany.

'Stupid, innit,' said Nora. 'That's gin rummy, kid, pay attention.'

Billy uttered a word that Santiago would wager had never been heard in a polite lady's drawing room. Only Tiffany looked surprised, and even she less than he would have expected.

'Now,' said Mistress Blackmantle. 'You will require a valet, Mr Santiago. How about taking on Robinson on a trial basis? To ready you for my soirée and perhaps some daytime events following on from it?'

Santiago only had the vaguest idea of what a valet actually did. Helped him dress, cleaned his clothes?

Can he make me look like a gentleman? Or even with all this fine tailoring and a man to help me into it, will I still look like a pirate and a smuggler, a guttersnipe from the worst stews of South America?

I wonder if it will ever stop feeling like I am pretending?

'Do you not have other employment, Mr Robinson? As a fine tailor'—whose wares they still hadn't seen—'and valet, why are you not in demand?'

There was a delicate pause. From the corner of his eye, he could see Nora's face screwing itself up.

'I'm afraid my face didn't fit, sir,' said Robinson blandly. 'I have been doing piecemeal work, sir, and therefore have no employer to give notice to.'

'Shall we say a trial period of a fortnight?' said Mistress Black-mantle, as if Santiago wasn't there.

'That would suit me, ma'am. Sir?'

'I ... yes?' said Santiago helplessly.

'Half a crown a week?' said Mistress Blackmantle.

Robinson's flawless brow creased a little. 'Were it just valeting I should say yes, ma'am, but I shall also be tailoring. Would ten bob a week be acceptable?'

'For the owner of Santiago Pacific Trading, I should think so,' said Mistress Blackmantle, then as an afterthought glanced at Santiago.

Ten shillings a week was a lot of money. He could see Billy's eyes getting wider and wider from across the room.

But if he was to look the part...

He glanced quickly at Tiffany. She gave a very quick, very decisive nod.

'That would be acceptable,' said Santiago, and then he was a gentleman with a valet.

CHAPTER 6

*W*hat followed were ten days of hurried preparations for Mr Santiago's debut in Society. Tiffany went to bed every night convinced it would be a disaster; after all, had she not trained her whole life for this? Santiago had a few weeks of lessons, in between running what seemed to be a busy shipping empire.

'And of course, he is busy with the house,' said Aunt Esme, with that small smile Tiffany did not have the courage to ask about. 'Now, I believe I shall invite the Misses Brockhurst. One an artist, one a renowned translator of German folklore. She's fascinating so long as you don't get her started on the Brothers Grimm.'

Tiffany dutifully added them to the list of invitees to Esme's soirée. It was quite short, and mostly consisted of artists and bohemians: the sort of people who would not be too shocked if Mr Santiago made a terrible faux pas. Not to mention they would have no other plans at such short notice. Tiffany knew Lord and Lady Selby were to hold a ball that evening and she still hadn't come up with an excuse not to go. She was currently working on some sort of plan to attend both, using her increasingly useful witchcraft to persuade Elinor that she was in her chambers getting ready for the ball whilst actually attending Aunt Esme's soirée, then racing home to join them in the dining room before attending the Selby ball.

It was either that or pretend she had a headache. The headache would probably be simpler. But on the other hand...

She was a witch. There seemed little point in denying it now. At Esme's house she practised her craft, learning how to light the fire by an effort of will, or conjure a light with her hands. And she was positively encouraged to draw all she could, in any media Esme could find for her. The more she drew, the better at it she became, until her drawings looked so realistic they could quite literally be picked up off the page. Every day she left Esme vases of flowers, their petals velvety and their scent delightful, quite indistinguishable from the real thing.

'What is it like?' she asked, as idly as she could.

'Oh, you know, full of hobgoblins and the like. Miss Camelia Brockhurst is incensed that the Brothers Grimm did not choose the far more prevalent myth of Snow White falling in with thieves. Apparently there is a Scottish version involving cats. She does tend to go on slightly too long about it.'

Tiffany blinked at the inkwell. 'Uh, no, I meant Mr Santiago's house. Is it suitable for a gentleman?'

Aunt Esme laughed as if Tiffany had said something very funny. 'Oh, I should say so! But not at all ready for receiving guests. I am told,' she added quickly. 'I have not visited, of course.'

Tiffany gave her a sidelong glance, scribbling idly with her pen on the edge of the paper. She ought to remind Mr Santiago to have some visiting cards made. His trade cards would send entirely the wrong impression.

And then, of course, she would know his address. She

wondered what sort of person he had inherited it from. 'Has Nora visited? Or Madhu?'

'Single ladies visiting the home of a bachelor? Of course not.'

Tiffany was about to say that neither of them seemed to consider themselves ladies, when something ruffled the page she had been doodling on. A tiny black feather fluttered as she moved her hand.

'A raven, then?' she guessed, as Esme picked up the feather and inspected its gleaming iridescence. 'Did you send one of those?'

'This is quite marvellous, you know. Do you think you could draw an entire raven and have it come to life?'

Tiffany shook her head. 'I can't do it with living things. They just don't animate. Plants and things, yes, but not animals and people. Besides, they only last a few hours and then they fade away. That would be quite awful with a person.'

'It would indeed,' said Esme, setting down the raven feather. 'Is it only with things you have drawn yourself?'

'No. Well ... I don't know. Paintings sometimes move, like that one did,' Tiffany said, pointing to the seascape she'd noted on her first visit. 'People move, wave, that sort of thing. It's more like ... like when you see something out of the corner of your eye and you're not sure if it moved or not. Except I am sure it moved,' she added, with feeling.

'Could you make a painting come to life, do you think? With practice?'

Tiffany found herself screwing up her face as she thought about it, then stopped, because Elinor said that caused wrinkles. 'I don't know. Would I want to? To make a painted person speak?'

The thought suddenly came to her that she could enchant the portrait of her father that hung in the library at Dyrehaven. Ask him why he never came home. Ask him where her mother was. But would he answer? And would she want to hear his answer? What if asking the portrait questions meant her father would hear them—and know she was a witch? He could condemn her. He could certainly have her sent to the madhouse.

She shuddered. 'Would it not be eerie?' she said.

'Dear, we are witches,' said Esme, 'we *are* eerie.' But she took the hint and changed the subject. 'How about Sir Isembold Button for the soirée? A most entertaining gentleman and current favourite of the Regent.'

'But Mr Santiago is not going to move in the same circles as the Regent,' laughed Tiffany.

Esme merely arched an eyebrow. 'Well, my dear, nothing would surprise me. Now. I believe I was going to show you how to do a finding spell. It's quite simple, and you can use it on people as well as objects. Take a candle, thus...'

HIS GRANDFATHER'S house was a huge edifice that formed most of one side of the square. Smoke and dirt had darkened the stonework, turning a plain building into a glowering one. The last time Santiago had seen a building this big it had housed the tomb of the Mughal emperor, and that had been a damn sight prettier.

Currently, he occupied precisely one and a half rooms of it, a bedroom overlooking the street and the dressing area accompanying it. The dressing area was almost the size of the bedroom, and currently lined with racks showcasing the frankly jaw-dropping amount of clothing Robinson had managed to assemble for him in just over a sennight.

'That don't look very comfortable, guv,' said Billy. He sat on a large chest, drumming his heels.

Santiago tugged at the high collar Robinson had fastened around his neck. It was so high and so heavily starched he thought it would add to the scar on his cheek. 'It isn't.'

'It fits as it should, sir,' said Robinson. 'Would you like me to tie your neckcloth?'

Tiffany had told him he should defer to his valet in all matters sartorial. And to be fair, the young man's work was excellent, and the style of dress Santiago was being stitched into was exactly the sort of thing everyone at the Russell ball had been wearing. He saw rowdy young men spilling out of fashionable clubs in such outfits on the streets around this mausoleum of a house.

It was just all so … plain.

He allowed Robinson to fuss and fuss with the stack of cloths he had brought, each one carefully folded and starched and placed with reverence upon a dressing table. The wretched thing was wrapped carefully around his neck and tied with great precision, studied, undone and replaced. This happened twice.

'Robinson?' he said pleasantly, as Billy got bored and started wandering around, opening drawers and poking at the contents.

'Sir?'

'The next cloth will be the final one.'

'But if it isn't right, sir—'

Santiago fixed him with the sort of look he had given one of Madam Zheng's pirates when the man had tried to take his purse. 'The final one.'

Robinson sighed as if tortured. 'Yes, sir,' he said mournfully.

The process of dressing went on. 'What time is it, Billy?' Santiago called, unable to turn his head because of the muslin noose around his neck.

'I dunno.'

'Can you see the clock?'

'Yeah.'

'Then what time is it?'

'I dunno,' Billy repeated, as if Santiago was the one being stupid.

'You cannot read a clock?'

'Whassa point, guv? What've I got to be on time for?'

Santiago supposed he had a point.

'You gonna teach me, guv?' asked the boy, as Santiago had his coat taken off and fussed with for the third time.

'In my plentiful spare time, why not,' he murmured.

'Miss Gwen, she said she'd teach me how to read and that. But she forgot, I think. Or she said'—Billy's face appeared in his field of vision, all screwed up with recollection—'that I already knew. Or would already know. I like Miss Gwen, guv, but she don't make no sense half the time.'

'No. I would not ask her to teach you about clocks,' Santiago said.

Some time later—maybe half an hour, maybe three weeks—Robinson gave him one last critical look, and stepped back.

'There, sir,' he said, and Santiago risked a look in the mirror.

The person looking back at him was … a gentleman.

He was dressed in severe black and immaculate white, and he couldn't move his head very much, nor his shoulders, and his breeches were so tight he feared for his modesty, but he looked, from the neck down at least, like a gentleman.

Robinson had offered him a shave and a haircut. Santiago had undertaken the former himself and turned down the latter. The fashionable young men he saw around the place cut their hair like they hated it; and besides, he wanted to be able to take off this ridiculous gear and just be Santiago again. If he cut his hair like a young buck, Penderghast and de Groot would wet themselves laughing at him.

'Mr Robinson,' he said, 'you have outdone yourself.'

Robinson nodded, and gave a small smile. 'It's just Robinson, sir. No Mr.'

Ah yes. Santiago had been instructed as much by Tiffany. He glanced at his valet through the mirror. 'How come a talented young man like yourself isn't already in someone's employ?'

Robinson shrugged and began gathering up discarded items. 'Like I said, sir, my face doesn't fit.'

Santiago leaned in and inspected the scar Madam Zheng had given him. 'Neither does mine, I think.' He straightened up and looked himself over. 'Still, you have endeavoured to make me look the part. Do you think they will look at me and think, "He was born a gentleman"?'

'If I can carry it off, you can, sir,' said Robinson. 'Shall I tell the coachman to bring the horses round, sir?'

'Yes. Thank you.' The coachman was already in situ, because the horses were a permanent feature of the house, regardless of whether the owner was in residence. The butler and housekeeper were hiring new maids and footmen, and dust sheets were being removed whether Santiago liked it or not.

He was a gentleman now. He had a gentleman's house and a gentleman's clothing.

He felt like an actor on a stage.

It only remained to see whether he could play the part.

TIFFANY HAD DECIDED upon a plan to go to Aunt Esme's for a 'card party' earlier in the evening, promising to be back in time for the Selby ball, and then decided she would see how things went. Either she would return in time for the ball as promised, or feign some kind of illness. She wasn't sure she would have the stamina to fade into the background and pretend not to be there, or maintain a glamour over her appearance all evening.

Because she already knew she would be casting a glamour. To look nice for Mr Santiago. Even though she knew there was absolutely no reason to.

The man was blackmailing her. Probably. At the very least he was using her.

Tiffany had to keep telling herself this, because the alternative was admitting how attractive she found him, and then that would lead to getting her hopes up, or—even worse—him reciprocating her feelings … and then she might end up marrying him. A tradesman! Elinor would probably die of shame, so at least there was a silver lining.

But now she had seen the freedom Esme and the others had, the idea of marrying anyone seemed twice as repulsive as it had before. She couldn't bear the idea of shackling herself to a husband who barely seemed to tolerate her, like Cornforth and Elinor, or who drove her away as conclusively as Tiffany's father had to her mother. No. She would go and live with Esme, and be a witch, and never be beholden to a man again.

All she had to do was see Mr Santiago successfully attend a few events, and then her freedom would be close enough to taste—

'You cannot go,' Elinor said.

Tiffany looked up from the gloves that were being buttoned by Morris. 'I beg your pardon?'

'To your aunt's again. I forbid it. You spend every waking hour there. Cornforth and I have gone to the trouble and considerable expense of arranging a Season for you and you refuse to take part. Your selfishness knows no bounds.'

Elinor had mentioned the expense? She must be angry. Usually she considered such things vulgar.

'I will be back in time for the ball—'

'I have invited people for supper! Mrs Barrowes and her daughters, who are also having their first season. They are looking forward to meeting you. And Lord Felbourne is bringing his sister.'

'But I promised my aunt—'

'And you wonder at having no friends! You simply cannot assume you are above all this, Theophania.'

My name is Tiffany.

Oblivious to the curling of Tiffany's hands into fists, Elinor rattled on. 'I see the superior little looks you give the other girls. You are not better than any of them.'

I am a witch.

'They are all the daughters of peers—of dukes and marquesses! Confidantes of the Prince Regent! You need to find a husband just as much as they, and they have a better chance—'

'Why?'

The word spilled out of Tiffany before she could stop it. Boiled out of her. Hot and unstoppable.

Morris, who had frozen when Elinor began speaking, quietly scurried from the room.

'Why? Their chances are better than yours, young lady, because they smile and make conversation and do not enter every social occasion as if they were doing it a favour.'

'Not why are their chances better. Why do I need to find a husband?'

Elinor simply stared at her, cheeks pink with anger, her decorously small bosom heaving.

'Do you think yourself special?' she asked after a long moment. 'That you alone need not marry? Will you support yourself, run your own household, on your pin allowance?'

'I have funds in trust from my father,' said Tiffany, who had never really needed to think about that money before.

'For your dowry! But I see, you will not be needing that, hmm?' Elinor's foot tapped. 'Perhaps if you live quietly in the country with one maid and no footmen? Rusticating?' She spat the word as if it was a terrible punishment, when to Tiffany it actually sounded quite nice. 'And who will pay her when your funds run out? Who will care for you in your old age, with no husband and no children?'

'I will have friends,' Tiffany said, because Aunt Esme and the others were her friends. Sort of.

Elinor openly snorted. 'Well, that will be a first, child!' She looked over Tiffany's elegant blue dress, which was unadorned and flattering and might impress Santiago, and shook her head. 'Morris! The pink satin with the frills.'

Tiffany hated that dress. It made her look like a milkmaid.

'Perhaps the blue—'

'The pink,' said Elinor viciously, turning on her heel. 'And dress her hair properly. We expect company.'

Mistress Blackmantle had told Santiago this would be a relaxed gathering of artistically inclined friends who would not look down upon him for being in trade. He had hoped this meant nobody would have, or use, a title, but the first person he was introduced to was a Lord Hornwood.

Now. A lord with a first name was likely the son of a Duke; a lord who was a peer in his own right would be introduced as Lord Hornwood, Earl of Somewhere That Sounded Made Up In This Stupid Country, and a lord with just a surname was probably a baron.

This meant a small bow, little more than a nod. Lord Hornwood did not seem displeased.

'Pleasure, sir.' Hornwood looked him over approvingly. 'Where did you find this one, Esme?'

'On a beach, in Essex,' she replied, and they both laughed. Santiago laughed too, just for the look of it.

'Dark, delicious, dangerous. I predict a hit.' Hornwood winked and sauntered off.

'I think you have an admirer,' said Esme Blackmantle.

Santiago's brows went up. 'I did not think such things were spoken of here.'

She laughed. 'Oh no, not spoken of. That doesn't mean they don't happen.'

She hesitated. 'I may have misread you, my dear—I had thought your interests lay with my niece.'

Was it that obvious? Not that it mattered because she had made it achingly clear she did not want to marry and that she found him far beneath her besides. It did not matter that she had fine pale skin and white gold hair and a bosom that haunted his dreams. It didn't matter at all.

'They don't,' he said. 'Lie anywhere. Not with Lady Tiffany. I would never presume,' he babbled, trying not to think about lying with Lady Tiffany.

'Of course not,' said Esme smoothly. 'I should warn you, however, Hornwood is devoted to his valet, so don't go looking there. I could introduce you to some select gentlemen if you would like.'

Santiago had recovered enough composure by now to say, 'Mistress Blackmantle, you are incorrigible.'

She smiled. 'I am. Now, who shall I introduce you to? Mistress Winterscale?' She gestured at a lady all in red, who caught her eye and came over, looking Santiago up and down in a manner he did not like.

The introduction made, she said, 'I had been hoping to meet you. Tell me, are you yet married?'

That was alarmingly direct. Santiago tried not to splutter. 'No, and I am not expecting to be—for some time,' he said hurriedly. 'I have only recently arrived here in London, and I have many affairs to set in order—'

She smiled and laughed throatily. 'I am sure you do, Your Grace. Rest assured I am not baiting my hook for you. It is Lady Tiffany, is it not?'

Why did everyone think he was after Lady Tiffany? She didn't even like him.

'I am acquainted with the lady,' he allowed, 'but not well.'

'Well, give it time. Now please do excuse me, I have an appointment at the Admiralty.'

'This late?' said Mistress Blackmantle, as if the hour was the only thing strange about a woman having an appointment at the Admiralty.

'Ah, yes. You know how it is,' she said knowingly. She curtsied, and sailed off.

'A singular lady,' said Mistress Blackmantle. 'Mark well her words, for she always knows what is to transpire.'

'She cannot know who I will marry,' said Santiago.

'Can she not? Ah, Miss Brockhurst,' she waved at a lady wearing a grey dress and what was most obviously a wig. 'Do come over and tell us all about your latest translation.'

Miss Brockhurst was undoubtedly very intelligent and passionate about her subject; so much so that all Santiago had to do was nod and look interested. Indeed, he was somewhat relieved when Mistress Blackmantle interrupted to introduce him to someone else, an African gentleman wearing a much more exciting waistcoat than Santiago had been permitted.

Mr Noakes was well-travelled, and the two of them were deep in discussion about the perils of Barbary pirates when he became aware of a presence at his shoulder.

'The beasty with the squirmers,' said Gwen without preamble. 'You have faced it.'

'Miss Gwen, do you know Mr— wait, the *cuero*?' He stared wildly between Gwen's slightly unfocused gaze and Mr Noakes's surprised face.

'I don't know if that is how it is called,' said that gentleman, 'but I have seen a beast of great—immense—power, seemingly made of waves.'

Santiago goggled at him. 'I have seen it too! It seemed to come from nowhere, in shallow water, and it grabbed and threw me into the air! I still have its marks on my— er, my skin,' he finished, realising that rolling up his sleeve would be both frowned upon and, thanks to Robinson's precise tailoring, probably impossible.

'The creature touched you? And you live?' Mr Noakes was astonished. 'I saw it take a whole ship. As if the sea itself had grown arms and engulfed the vessel.' He shook his head. 'No one else saw it. I was on middle watch. The witching hour.'

''Twas not witches,' said Gwen indignantly. 'Witches will not bring forth such a beast! 'Tis evil.'

'Are not witches evil?' asked Mr Noakes.

'Witches are people,' said Esme Blackmantle smoothly, appearing from nowhere. 'Some are good and some are evil and most are somewhere in between.' To Santiago, she said, 'Might I have a private word?'

He glanced back at Mr Noakes, eager to learn more about the creature that had nearly killed him and had probably sunk his ships. But Mistress Blackmantle was clearly not in a mood to be disobeyed, and had already taken him by the arm to draw him out of the room.

'Tiffany is not coming,' she said.

He should not be so disappointed. He had little interest in Lady Tiffany beyond her help in conforming to this blasted Society. In fact he had many reasons to be actively disinterested in her. She was a witch. She might have brought forth that tentacled beast. She did not want to marry.

It should not matter to him that she was not here.

And yet.

'Why not? Is she ill? Did she send word?'

'No, but she should have been here by now. So I sent a raven.'

'A ... raven?' He knew that the younger footmen on the backs of carriages were called tigers. Was a raven another kind of servant?

'Yes. The Cornforth carriage has just left, and it isn't heading here.'

Mistress Blackmantle was still walking. She continued along the hallway and into the kitchen, where Madhu and Nora were leaning over a dish of water and a candle.

'Have you found her? Gwen's message was rather garbled, and then she started talking about tentacled beasts,' said Esme.

Nora nodded. 'Gone to a ball, by the looks of it. Loads of fancy nobs dressed up like magpies.'

'Magpies have colour on their wings,' grouched Santiago.

'Is it the Selby ball?' asked Esme. She had produced a cloak out of nowhere and was swirling it onto her shoulders.

'I dunno, how would I know?'

Esme peered at the bowl, which looked to Santiago to simply contain plain, clear water. 'Hmm. Yes. She— Ah yes, there is a frieze with the Selby crest in the lobby, you see? Now, you will make my excuses, please. Send up more wine and nobody will realise I am gone.' To Santiago, she added, 'Here,' and threw him something.

His own evening cloak, carefully tied around his shoulders by Robinson earlier in the evening and removed by an extremely unimpressed Nora on his arrival here.

'Come,' Esme Blackmantle commanded, already halfway down the hall.

He glanced back helplessly at the two women leaning over the table. They were whispering to each other and giggling. Was that witchcraft? Had they just been doing witchcraft?

'Now,' said Mistress Blackmantle, striding up the stairs. Santiago hurried to follow her. 'What is about to occur is something I shall ask you to forget. I have no carriage ready and a journey in a hackney is simply not to be borne under these circumstances. Besides which I did not receive an invitation. Stand there and let me look at you,' she said, taking him by the shoulders opposite a lamp.

She peered at his face, as one might peer at a horse for sale. 'Not too mussed. Not perspiring. Are you drunk?'

'Er—'

'No matter, you don't seem it, and there's a reason "drunk as a lord" is a saying. On which matter, *Mr* Santiago,'—here she dealt him a wicked look—'have you any of your cards? Not the trade ones, the proper ones.'

He blinked at her, then nodded and indicated his breast pocket. Tiffany had instructed him to bring cards to the soirée, and the thought of her inspecting them filled him with dread.

'Good. Now, did you receive an invitation for the Selby ball?'

'Yes, but I declined because of this event.' Not to mention the thought of a ball terrified him, now that he knew how much he'd got wrong the first time.

'No matter. They will be thrilled to see you. Now, shh a moment and let me concentrate.'

Santiago had very little idea what was going on. He watched as his hostess placed a hand upon a green door which bore the sign of a compass, and murmured some words to it. Where was she taking him? Surely they should be going downstairs and outside? Should he be sending someone to fetch the carriage from his own mews?

'Now, take my arm and pretend you've been there all along,' said Mistress Blackmantle, upon which she opened the green door and swept him into another world.

THE PORTRAITS on the walls were watching them.

Tiffany wondered if she could make them do anything in

particular. Cross their eyes, blow raspberries, stick their tongues out. All the things she wanted to do to Elinor, and would the moment they were out of company. She didn't need to give Elinor any more ammunition against her. Her silence so far had already been condemned as sulking, when in truth it was simply the only way Tiffany could keep herself from snarling at her like an angry cat.

She nodded along to the conversation of every gentleman she was introduced to, gave smiles that did not reach her eyes, and replied in monosyllables. Infuriatingly, this only served to make them talk to her more.

If I married you, she thought as one man waxed lyrical about the prize pigs on his estate in Gloucestershire, *you would do nothing but talk at me and I would do nothing but disappear.*

And yet she would end up married, probably to someone just like this man, unless she had the courage to leave. Could she do it? Could she go and live with Aunt Esme? Perhaps even before the end of the Season?

Elinor would never speak to her again, which was a definite upside, but she would probably prevent Tiffany from seeing much of Cornforth and the children. And whilst Tiffany was grateful her years of shepherding them around like an unpaid nursemaid were over, that didn't mean she never wanted to see them again.

People were still arriving, and the announcements had become interminable. Tiffany was listening with half an ear to see if anyone she could actually stand had arrived. The Belmont sisters, perhaps, or the Broughams. It was too much to hope that—

'Mistress Esmerelda Blackmantle!'

Tiffany blinked, and turned, and stared. And yes, there was her aunt, resplendent in crimson, descending the short flight of steps into the ballroom. Her lips curved in a positively feline smile as she saw Tiffany, and nodded.

What was Aunt Esme doing here? Had she been invited? Surely not, or she would not have organised her soirée for the same evening. Was it over? How had she—

'His Grace the Duke of St James!'

A sudden hush fell over the ballroom, or at least the human voices in it. The orchestra played on, and so it seemed that the gentleman standing at the top of the steps was entering to music of his own, like a character in an opera.

He stood tall and straight, broader in the shoulders than many gentlemen, immaculate in black and white. His gaze as he surveyed the room was calm and assured, his demeanour that of unquestioned confidence. In the brilliant warmth of the ball-room's many candles, he was breathtakingly handsome.

Below the music there was an excited hum of whispering female voices.

'Did he say St James?' hissed Elinor, jabbing Tiffany in her ribs. She did not turn to reply. She could not move.

Gold glinted in his ear as he turned his head. The light caught the scar on his cheek. The man who had just been announced as the Duke of St James was Santiago.

CHAPTER 7

*T*here were so many things to remember. No wonder most men of the aristocracy assumed an air of detached disinterest; they were probably frantically trying to remember what to say and do, and more importantly, what *not* to say and do.

You have commanded ships through storms and faced down a pirate queen, Santiago reminded himself. *This is child's play.*

This should *be child's play…*

'Your Grace,' said Mistress Blackmantle as Santiago reached the bottom of the stairs. Behind her, half the ballroom appeared to be crowding in, gawking at him. Panic filled him—was his outfit correct? Should he have allowed Robinson to cut his hair? Did he have something in his teeth or on his face? 'How delightful to see you again.'

We saw each other thirty seconds ago when you brought me through some kind of magic door. Santiago smiled and nodded. 'Mistress Blackmantle. The delight is all mine.'

He was aware of a murmur spreading out after he spoke. Perhaps they had expected him to speak in the same accents as

129

themselves. And whilst Santiago could—he had, of course, learned from a man who spoke just as these people did—he did not see why he should.

He might wear the clothes and learn the dances and accept the invitations, but he had to keep some things for himself.

Mistress Blackmantle said, 'May I be permitted the honour of introducing a few acquaintances? After we have greeted our hostess, of course.'

'Of course.'

He offered his arm and they strolled away, quite as if this was all entirely normal and he wasn't instantly terrified that offering her his arm had been a massive faux pas.

'Remember, you are a duke, and therefore everything you do is correct,' murmured Esme Blackmantle, before saying much more loudly, 'My dear Lady Selby. How well you look, and what a splendid occasion this is.'

A woman of middling years turned and smiled, her split-second surprise almost unnoticeable. Before she could speak, Esme powered on.

'Lady Selby, it is my honour to introduce to you His Grace the Duke of St James.'

He wanted to bow, because Tiffany had told him a Mr should bow to practically everybody, but he wasn't a Mr, and she was going to be so furious when she found out. He managed a nod instead, which was beginning to present a problem in the form of his ludicrously high collar. He would not escape this occasion without a chafed face.

'Your Grace,' murmured Lady Selby, curtseying deeply. To him. Because he was a duke. He was a duke and now everyone knew.

He didn't think he had been this afraid since he faced three days of storms in the Bay of Biscay.

'It is indeed a beautiful occasion,' he said, and then completely ran out of words in English. And in Spanish. And in any of the other languages he'd picked up along the way.

Well ... not completely run out of words. A few came to mind, but Tiffany would have him horsewhipped if he used them in this kind of company.

Tiffany...

Mistress Blackmantle made some small talk about the company, and the music, and the flowers, and he smiled and agreed with her, trying all the while not to appear as if he was looking around for someone else. Which he was. Because Tiffany was going to be incandescent with fury and he had better get it over with.

What would she do, he wondered, as Lady Selby took it upon herself to introduce him to a horde of people the names of whom he hadn't a chance of remembering. Lady this and Sir that and Miss whoever. There were a lot of misses. Fresh-faced, eager, some of them practically vibrating with nerves.

Yes, he agreed, the occasion was splendid. No, this was not his first ball—he and Tiffany had decided that pretending he hadn't been at Lady Russell's would be construed as a snub—but he had not met many people last time. Yes, his accent was delightfully exotic and no, he did not think everybody should be speaking like it soon. Dear God, he hoped not.

He realised after an interminable conversation about the weather that Mistress Blackmantle had disappeared. He was left with his hostess, who seemed perfectly pleasant but kept regarding him as if he was a tiger on a leash.

And all the while he kept wondering where Tiffany was and what she had planned. If she was planning to use her infernal magic to set off some monstrous event, or if she'd already used it to ... to...

He realised he didn't really understand what she could actually do. Make chalk drawings come to life, and ... well, that was it.

He didn't seriously believe she'd made the water attack him. Tiffany was many things, but experimentally cruel was not one of them. Besides, Mr Noakes had seen the same phenomenon, and how could she have possibly been anywhere near his ship at the time?

'Ah, Lord Cornforth, Lady Cornforth...' wittered Lady Selby, and Santiago thought that sounded familiar. He turned with a bland smile that froze in the next instant.

'... and Lady Theophania, it is my honour to introduce to you His Grace the Duke of St James.'

There were people with Tiffany and they were bowing and curtseying. Lady Tiffany herself was demonstrating the precise and exact degree to which one ought to curtsey to a duke, her eyes decorously lowered.

Her face was pale, almost as pale as her moonlit hair. There was no colour in her cheeks. Her gown was a washed-out pink with far too many frills. And when she raised her head, her face had all the expression of a china doll.

This isn't really me, he wanted to tell her. *I'm still Santiago, the ruffian you dragged off a beach, the vagabond with the tattoos, the tradesman you keep trying to despise. The Duke is just a ... a character I'm playing. A charade. A suit of clothes.*

If only he could discard it so easily!

'Your Grace,' said the woman beside her eagerly. She was perhaps twenty years older than Tiffany, and appeared in every respect to have aimed to look as much like everyone else present as possible. He doubted he would recognise her again. 'We were so sorry to hear of the passing of your grandfather. He was such a great man and will be so sorely missed.'

From what Santiago could gather, his grandfather had been a miserable old recluse who had barely left the family estate in Yorkshire for years and had declined every invitation that arrived at his mausoleum of a house in Mayfair. Despite this, people kept sending them—and they were simply addressed to the Duke of St James, so Santiago was perfectly within his rights to, for instance, attend Lady Russell's ball, where a siren with a glorious bosom had shouted at him in the garden.

Said siren was doing a very good impression of a statue now. Santiago kept smiling at her, but she barely met his gaze.

'I had the honour of meeting him occasionally on parliamentary matters,' said Cornforth, who must be Tiffany's oldest brother. He looked very little like her, and had the air of a much older man weary of being trapped in a younger body. 'I understand Your Grace has not been long in London?'

'No,' Santiago agreed. 'A few months only.' Tiffany had told him not to talk about his business, but that was when she'd thought he was a mere tradesman.

Of course, he *was* a mere tradesman. He was just also one who happened to have inherited a dukedom.

'Your Grace, please excuse me,' said Lady Selby, as a footman appeared at her elbow. 'My lord, my ladies.' She curtsied and hurried away.

Lady Cornforth appeared quite extraordinarily pleased that she had been left in custody of the ball's star attraction. 'I hear Castle Aymers is quite an extraordinary estate,' she said. 'Dating back to the twelfth century!'

'Indeed,' said Santiago, who wasn't even entirely sure where Yorkshire was, let alone which bit of it he owned. Probably all of it, he decided gloomily. He'd have to visit at some point. Exchanging letters with a steward wasn't really good enough. He had responsibilities now.

He didn't want responsibilities. He wanted to sail and smuggle and barter, and he wanted to make Lady Tiffany's eyes flash like sunlight on ice.

But Lady Tiffany wasn't even looking at him.

'Our own estate in Hertfordshire is not so grand, of course,'

Lady Cornforth demurred. 'Although it is perfectly charming. Parts of it date back to the Restoration. We usually hold a house party there in May for Cornforth's birthday. You simply must come, Your Grace.'

A house party? Was that one of those affairs that went on for days? With this woman in her own house? Santiago smiled politely and murmured a nothingness. But she still wasn't done.

'I must confess I mislike all these new styles of architecture, don't you, Your Grace? There is no character in them.'

'Perhaps it is up to us to put character in them,' said Santiago, who had no particular feelings on the matter at all.

'I quite agree,' she said immediately. How did Tiffany live with this woman? 'But Carlton House! Constantly under refurbishment. We attended the celebration of the Duke of Wellington last year, of course, and we were struck by the ... the gaudiness of it. So much colour!'

Carlton House was the residence of the somewhat unpopular Prince Regent. Santiago knew that; he suspected even Billy knew that. He had seen prints of its opulence and colour. It looked a great deal more fun than this slightly insipid ballroom, lined with portraits that seemed to be looking down at him with disapproval.

'And of course that dreadful man is remodelling the Marine Pavilion in Brighton. In some kind of oriental style!'

'Oriental style?' said Santiago. 'I have travelled in the Orient. I should perhaps like to see it.'

'Well, it will be nothing like the real Orient, I'm sure,' sniffed Lady Cornforth. Somewhat belatedly, she added, 'Are you acquainted with His Highness, Your Grace?'

'The Prince Regent?' Santiago paused before answering, just to make her squirm. 'I regret I have not had the honour.'

'A presentation at court is perhaps the thing,' said Cornforth. 'Now that you have assumed the title.'

That sounded appalling. He had enough people staring at him here. He could feel the weight of their collective gaze coming from every direction.

'We had Lady Theophania presented at court in March,' Lady Cornforth went on. 'Such a dreadful crush, and those ludicrous gowns. You gentlemen must be very grateful you do not have to wear the hoops. Of course, Theophania did not enjoy it, did you? Dear? You are very quiet this evening.'

There was something pointed in those last few words. Something barbed.

'Merely taking in the occasion,' said Tiffany, raising her gaze to the level of her sister-in-law's chin for the merest fraction of a second, before letting it drop.

'She's a very shy girl,' Lady Cornforth said, of the young lady who had harangued Santiago mere minutes after their first meeting. 'Very sheltered. Fresh, one might say.'

Fresh? She radiated more chill than an iceberg. Santiago worried for his extremities.

'But very thoughtful and charitable. Indeed, she spends much of her time with her great-aunt. I am sure your presence is a great comfort to the dear old lady, Theophania.'

Dear old lady? The woman in the crimson gown who had dragged him through a magical door?

At this, Tiffany's eyes slid sideways towards Lady Cornforth. 'Indeed,' she said, and her voice was like the blade of a knife.

'However, she is also very lively, especially when dancing,' said Lady Cornforth, which was so blatant a segue Santiago could barely keep his eyes from rolling.

'Perhaps Lady Tiffany would do me the honour of a dance?' he said, and realised his mistake a fraction too late.

She had been introduced to him as Lady Theophania. And it was clear from her demeanour that she was pretending they were strangers.

Lady Cornforth's eyes flashed, and red spots appeared on her cheeks, but she didn't seem to know how to respond to that. Her husband's face went very blank.

'Please, I beg your forgiveness,' Santiago covered. 'It is only that Mistress Blackmantle was telling me so fondly of her great-niece, whom she calls Lady Tiffany. It was a slip of the tongue. Please, permit my apology for the over-familiarity.'

Lady Tiffany herself gave a colourless sort of nod. Her sister-in-law gave a strangled sort of smile that said he wouldn't have got away with that if he wasn't a duke.

A mere title, a single word, and suddenly he could get away with anything.

Was this how his father had felt?

Santiago felt the hands of the past reaching forward for him, and tried not to flinch. *I will never become my father.*

'Mistress Blackmantle?' Lady Cornforth said. 'The lady announced shortly before you?'

'Yes. She has been very kind to me since I arrived in London.'

He could see Lady Cornforth trying to fit the elegant and fashionable lady into the box she had clearly already marked 'doddering old fool'. 'I see,' she said slowly.

The orchestra began to play the opening chords of a dance, and hope stirred in Santiago because he thought he recognised the music from his lessons.

'I have no partner for this dance,' said Lady Tiffany suddenly.

'It would be my honour to partner you,' he said. Everything seemed to be his honour this evening. He'd never heard a more meaningless phrase in his life.

He offered her his arm, and she took it and he felt the steel tension in her body. She was not subdued. She was enraged.

She curtseyed. He bowed. The couple at the head of the figure began to dance, and Santiago kept his eyes on Tiffany.

She stood still and quiet, poised, elegant; but Santiago had felt the rage vibrating through her. He braced himself.

She said nothing as he took her hand and stepped towards her. He said, 'It is a splendid occasion, is it not?'

'Most splendid,' she agreed tonelessly. She did not look at him. Her eyes were blazing in the direction of their hands.

'Certainly livelier than the event at your aunt's,' he said.

'I am sorry to have missed it.'

'Are you?'

She looked up at him then, and he almost wished she hadn't. Her blue eyes burned like ice.

'It was not my choice,' she hissed. 'Your Grace.'

Here it was then. 'You are angry with me—'

But the dance moved them apart, and he took the hand of the young lady closest to him instead.

'Your Grace,' she said breathlessly, and seemed to be trying to curtsey mid-dance.

'It is a splendid occasion,' he murmured, trying to keep an eye on Tiffany.

'Your Grace, it is such an honour,' she said, and Santiago realised he was beginning to hate that damn word.

'Indeed,' he replied, and then Tiffany was back, her polite smile for her partner vanishing the moment she saw Santiago.

'I can explain,' he promised rashly.

'Explain what, Your Grace?'

'You don't have to keep calling me that.'

'It is the correct form of address for a duke,' she reminded him, eyes flashing.

'Yes, but—'

'But?' she said politely. 'You are the Lost Duke of St James, are you not? Fraud is a terrible crime, you know.'

'I am the duke,' he said through gritted teeth. 'But it is just a title.'

That was the wrong thing to say. Again. 'There is no such thing', Lady Tiffany told him coldly, 'as "just a title".'

'I mean...' he began, and ran out of steam again.

'Your title comes with lands. People live upon those lands and it is your duty to take care of them. To know whose roof needs patching and whose child is sick.'

'I have stewards—'

'But it is not their land and those people are not their people. You have the responsibility.'

Santiago sighed. 'And I will take it, but—'

'Not to mention your seat in the House of Lords,' she added sharply, just as the dance separated them again.

Yes. Oh God. The House of Lords. Not so much the cut and thrust of politics but the dull shuffling of old men who cared only for their own interests. He'd rather be back in that foetid jail in Penang.

He exchanged polite nothings with his new partner, and then Tiffany was back.

'Where is my aunt now?'

He shook his head. 'I don't know. She slipped away. Probably to her own event. I had hoped to see you there,' he added, but she didn't respond.

'She came here solely to introduce you to our hostess and then left?'

Santiago sighed. 'She used a ... I don't even know.' He lowered his voice. 'A magic door?' He felt foolish even saying it.

But Tiffany seemed astonished. 'She showed you that?'

'More than showed,' he said with feeling. 'She brought me through it.' The sensation had not been unpleasant in a physical sense, but there was still a profound wrongness to it. They had crossed Mayfair and half of Belgravia in a single step.

'But ... why? She said that was for emergencies.'

He gave her his most piratical smile. 'Perhaps she thought this was an emergency.'

Tiffany rolled her eyes. 'An emergency? You not being in attendance at this ball?'

'You were not in attendance at her soirée.'

'I had no choice,' she hissed. 'I would have been there.'

'But you were not, and so she brought me to you.'

'Why?' She seemed baffled. 'Because of the bargain we struck?'

'What other answer can there be?'

Right then their hands touched, and a desperate tug of attraction pulled at him.

'Please tell me my aunt is not matchmaking too,' Tiffany groaned.

He snorted. 'It will fall on deaf ears. I am not attracted to you.' Her cheeks were pink with exertion and her silvery hair was flying and her bosom was—dear God, the way it bounced—

Her eyes flashed. 'And you are a liar.'

'I did not lie to you.' Apart from the part about not being attracted to her.

'And a blackmailer,' she added.

'I have never blackmailed!'

'You're blackmailing me over being a witch,' Tiffany hissed.

'I never threatened that.'

'Well, it definitely sounded like it to me!' Tiffany stepped back and he went to follow her, but the dance was ending, and everyone was bowing and curtseying again.

Santiago followed suit, aware all eyes were on him. 'Thank you for the dance, my lady,' he said.

'Indeed,' she replied, and with a catlike smile, added, 'It was most invigorating.'

He opened his mouth to reply to that particular little insult, but then a sort of shudder ran through him.

It ran through Tiffany too. He saw the shock on her face. But no one else seemed affected.

'Your Grace, I think I should perhaps like to sit down,' Tiffany said quickly, and he nodded and gave her his arm. But as he began leading her towards the seating areas at the edges of the room, her fingers tensed on his arm and she turned him towards the French windows that had been opened to the night air.

'What was that?' he murmured.

'I don't know. But it felt...'

'Magical?'

She nodded tersely. 'But you are not a witch, Mr— Your Grace.'

He wanted to make some quip there, but they were accosted by Mistress Blackmantle, suddenly hurrying towards them. She had a distinctly windswept look about her.

'Lady Tiffany, I require your presence most urgently,' she said.

'What was that?' demanded Santiago. 'I felt a ... shudder. Like the earth shaking.'

She looked surprised. 'You felt it? Did anyone else...?' She looked around at the milling company, who seemed utterly unaware of whatever was going on. 'Then Gwen was correct. The creature that attacked you is back, Your Grace, and this time it appears to be in the Thames.'

CHAPTER 8

'*D*o you mean,' began Tiffany, and lowered her voice, 'the beasty with the squirmers?'

'The *cuero*?' said Mr Santiago. No, he wasn't Mr Santiago any more, and he never had been. He was a duke. He was The Duke.

The illusion of gentility. How he must have laughed at her! She should have simply put a glamour on him to change the appearance of his clothes, and let it wear off so that people could laugh at him in his terrible shabby coat and appalling neck cloth.

Only they wouldn't dare laugh at him, because he was the Duke of … of *bloody* St James! He was higher in precedence than everyone else in the room! He could wear sackcloth and ashes and it would probably become the newest style.

Tiffany was working up a decent righteous anger when another sort of shock ran through the three of them. It was some kind of magic, and it felt all wrong.

'The creature, whatever we call it,' said Aunt Esme. 'Yes. Come along.'

She began moving away through the press of people. 'Where?'

said Tiffany, because they seemed to be heading towards the French windows and she had no idea how a giant tentacled beast was meant to be inhabiting Lady Selby's garden with no one noticing. 'To the river?'

'Well, it's not going to be in Hyde Park, is it?' Aunt Esme, uncharacteristically rattled. She opened her mouth to say something else, then uttered something under her breath that looked very much like a word ladies weren't supposed to know.

Behind her, Tiffany could see Elinor approaching. She considered muttering the same word.

Esme turned to face Tiffany and spoke in a low, fierce undertone.

'Tiffany, listen to me. I need your help right now but I will not force you into it. You can stay here, and dance and talk, and find a husband like your sister-in-law wants you to. Get married. Have babies.'

Something low thrummed in the air, and it wasn't the magical creature. It was Tiffany's own future.

'Or?' said Tiffany.

Esme glanced sideways hurriedly. 'Or you can come with me, save the city, and be whoever you want to be.'

Tiffany was terribly conscious of Sant— of the Duke standing right beside her. She recalled the still, clammy paleness of him when they'd found him on the shore. The livid red and purple marks the creature had left on his skin. The wide-eyed terror of the boy Billy as he'd begged for their help.

The sea boiled and came to life...

Some parts of him might be a huge lie, but that had been real.

The Thames was constantly choked with boats both large and small, and on both sides buildings came right onto the shore. If the water of the river boiled and came to life—

'Tiffany?' said Aunt Esme, her dark eyes intent on Tiffany's face.

'Theophania?' said Elinor.

And Tiffany grimaced and said, 'Oh dear, I have such a headache. Aunt Esme has agreed to take me home. I am most terribly sorry.'

'But—' Elinor said, looking from her to Esme to the Duke and back.

'I will escort the ladies to their carriage,' said the Duke, bowing. 'It will be my honour.'

'I— But— I thank you, Your Grace,' stammered Elinor, as they swept past her, Tiffany trying to do her best to look terribly ill.

'Is it just us?' she whispered.

'Gwen had a bit of a funny turn about this beasty. Madhu is staying with her. No one makes a soothing tea like Madhu. And Nora is … ah. Here.'

To Tiffany's astonishment, Nora stood in the curve of the main stairs, wearing a maid's cap and carrying several cloaks. To her even greater astonishment, she curtsied. 'This way, ma'am,' she muttered, and led them to an unobtrusive servants' door hidden by the stairs. They went through it into a drab and ill-lit corridor and Esme said, 'Cloaks, now. It is best we are not recognised.'

'And then?' Tiffany tried to unfold the bundle of cloth. Nora had hers on and was helping Esme; the Duke seemed to have no trouble swirling his about his shoulders like some sort of swashbuckler.

Esme indicated the door. 'The same way we arrived.'

'Marvellous. The magic door again,' he said sourly.

'You don't have to come,' said Tiffany.

He snorted. 'My lady, I have faced this beast once and it has left its mark on me. I will not let it wreak havoc in this city.'

That was annoyingly attractive. Tiffany tried to ignore that and shook out her cloak as she said, 'And what will you do when we get there?'

He shrugged. 'I know water. Rivers, oceans. I know tides and depths. What can you do?'

Draw a picture. That was all she could do. Draw things that came to life. What good was that? What would subdue this creature?

'I said we didn't need her,' Nora said, standing patiently without offering Tiffany any help.

'I can be useful,' Tiffany said firmly, fumbling with the fabric. 'Er ... what is the plan?' she asked hopefully.

Esme shrugged with unconvincing nonchalance. 'Oh, we find out the nature of the beast and work out how to subdue it as we go.'

'But it is not a beast; it is water,' said the Duke.

'You said it had tentacles. You have the marks of tentacles on your ... er, on you,' said Tiffany, her face going hot. She tried to find the top of her cloak. It seemed to be all hem.

'Mr Noakes also said it was made of water,' said the Duke. 'You must subdue the ... er, angry water,' he added, running out of steam.

'And how do we do that? Pour a large amount of oil on it?'

'And where is your expertise in sailing?' the Duke said, throwing up his hands.

'Would you two stop it?' hissed Aunt Esme.

The Duke gave a peaceable nod, and took Tiffany's cloak from her. He shook it out, swirled it around her shoulders and efficiently fastened it.

His fingers were directly under her chin. His bare fingers. Only maidservants had ever touched her like this. The heat in her cheeks spread rapidly all over her body, and she stepped back against the wall to finish fastening it herself.

His dark, dark eyes were amused.

'Perhaps we can appeal to the genius loci,' Aunt Esme was saying.

'The...?'

'The spirit of the river,' Nora explained. 'You may have heard of Father Thames?'

'Nobody learns Latin these days,' lamented Esme.

'Father Thames is the spirit of the river?' Tiffany's mind raced. 'If he was real, which I'm not sure he is, but if he was, and if we could talk to him, and I've no idea if...' She trailed off, trying to think.

The others exchanged glances. 'Try that again?'

Tiffany tried to organise her thoughts. She wasn't entirely sure she believed in the spirit of the Thames, but then she also didn't really believe the sea could boil and come to life, and yet. 'If you could talk to Father Thames, would it help? I mean ... to a representation of him?'

'It would help enormously,' said Esme, leaning in.

'You can do that?' said Nora, with something like a grudging respect.

'She can make chalk drawings come to life,' said the Duke.

And she could make paintings move. But she'd never tried it with statues, had never dared. Would it move? Speak? 'If I could bring the statue to life—I mean, the one at Somerset House—' she said, 'do you think it would help?'

Esme nodded. 'Yes. Yes, I do.'

'And it's by the river anyway so if this all cocks up we can try plan B,' said Nora.

'What's plan B?' said the Duke.

Nora shrugged.

'Excellent.'

Esme put her hand on the door, closed her eyes and murmured a few words. And when it clicked open, a cool breeze wafted in at them, bringing with it the stink of the river and another tremor.

'Quickly, before anyone comes,' Esme said, and the four of

them hurried through the door into the courtyard of Somerset House.

Tiffany had been dragged here for exhibitions, of course, but mostly she'd been concentrating far too hard on not allowing the paintings to come to life to actually take much in. Now, at night, the courtyard seemed vast, the pillared wings of the building rearing huge and dark around them. None of the windows were lit, but it was past midnight and Tiffany supposed even the Admiralty Board had to sleep at some point.

Aunt Esme shaped her hand around the air, and a light appeared in her cupped hand. It spread gently until it was as if someone had placed several candelabra around them. Tiffany had been learning how to do this, but the lights she could conjure were nowhere near as impressive as this.

'*Madre de dios*,' whispered the Duke, crossing himself in a way Tiffany would think more about later.

'It's just a witch light,' said Esme. 'A bit of the moon, aimed where we want it. If you find that impressive, wait and see what happens next.'

He smiled faintly.

'This statue?' said Nora, striding out into the courtyard.

The statue of George III and Father Thames was huge, and set facing the entrance from the Strand so that everyone could see and admire it. Tiffany hadn't really looked closely at it before, but now, in the magical light Esme had conjured, she saw it was in the classical style, with the king draped in robes and standing above the river god—of course, because the king commanded even nature—who reclined on what might have been a cornucopia and who wore—

Well, it was more about what he *didn't* wear.

'Oh my goodness.'

The Duke chuckled softly in the darkness. 'Perhaps the Thames is not so mighty after all.'

Tiffany's face got even hotter.

'We'll have none of that, thank you, Your Grace,' said Esme briskly. 'These spirits can be enormously difficult, so we must tread with care and quite some good amount of flattery. I shall do most of the talking. Tiffany, if you wouldn't mind?'

The four of them stood facing the enormous statue. It was on a plinth in a sort of sunken stairwell, surrounded by a stone balustrade. She couldn't reach it, which was probably just as well. But did that mean it couldn't reach her?

She shook that thought and stepped forward. Never having actually made a painting come to life on purpose, or a statue at all, she wasn't entirely sure how to proceed. But she was being watched by two proper witches and a duke, so she supposed she ought to do something.

She tried to picture the enormous statue simply moving and getting up off his plinth.

Esme usually said things in rhyme when she was using the door, but Tiffany had never actually had to use words before. Should she try to think of a rhyme?

'Just Father Thames, dear, not the king,' Esme called. 'I don't think we need to deal with His Majesty right now.'

'Yes, of course,' Tiffany said, and tried once more to concentrate. But now all she could think of was the statue of King George coming to life, and if the reports in the papers had any truth in them, the poor man was out of his wits. That would be a disaster.

Behind her, someone cleared their throat.

Fine. 'Oh, statue of Thames before me, come to life, I implore thee,' she said, and made a gesture to sort of throw her will at it.

The statue moved.

Tiffany startled, and behind her someone swore. She thought it was Nora.

The statue rolled its shoulders as if it had been asleep in an uncomfortable position. The ground trembled again. No, it wasn't the ground. It was a sort of shudder that ran through Tiffany.

'Good Father Thames,' began Esme, in a clear, loud voice. 'We do most humbly—'

Father Thames glared at them and grumbled something in a language the like of which Tiffany had never heard before. His voice was uncomfortably metallic, like the grinding of gears, but then she supposed he was made of bronze.

She couldn't understand a word he said. His tone of voice was, however, very clearly, 'Ugh, what do you want?'

She glanced at the others, who all looked mystified—even the Duke, with his extensive travelling experience.

Esme's face froze. 'Any ideas?' she murmured.

'Well, he's pre-Roman, innee?' said Nora. 'But maybe...' She stepped forward. '*Salve, Pater Tamesis*,' she said. '*Supplices te rogamus tuum auxilium*.'

'*Ach*,' grumbled the statue. '*Rómánach*.'

'*Non sumus Romani! Britannia sumus*.'

'*Britannia*?' said the statue doubtfully.

'*Romanos odimus. Nos eos conspuimus*,' said Nora, and spat on the ground.

'What is she doing?' murmured Tiffany, edging closer to the others.

'It is Latin,' said Esme. 'I read it well enough but I don't speak it much. I think she's telling him we're not Romans, we're British.'

'But—'

At that point the magic made them all shudder again. Tiffany was somewhat curious as to why it was affecting the Duke, but mostly she was interested in the way the statue's head turned towards the river.

He spoke again, and so did Nora, and Tiffany frowned. She could make drawings and statues come to life, and she could draw things and make them real, and she could alter her own appearance, and make other people believe she wasn't there. Would it be possible to alter what she heard in the same way?

She tried to draw on the same feeling she had when she made herself invisible, or when she had fixed the door on Billy's cowshed. As if all of her body, her breath, her muscles and bones, and most of all her will, were concentrated together.

Power rose within her.

And with a sort of pop in her ears, she heard Nora and the statue speaking English.

'—tribe are you from? That terrible Iceni woman burned the city to the ground. I was choked with ash and timbers and bodies for days.'

'We are not Iceni,' said Nora firmly.

'We need your help,' said Tiffany, and the statue of Father Thames turned its metallic head and regarded her.

He had been made with a beard and long hair, on top of which sat a wreath of leaves and flowers. He wore nothing else, and as he swung himself to sit upon the plinth with his legs dangling down, Tiffany found herself eye to eye with a metal appendage that, no matter the Duke's sniggering, very much drew the attention.

She forced her gaze up.

'There is something in the river,' she said. 'Some kind of creature.'

'There are many creatures in me,' said Father Thames good-naturedly. He plucked a piece of fruit from the metal cornucopia behind him, and crunched on it. The sound sent Tiffany's teeth on edge.

'This one isn't natural. It's made of—'

Father Thames abruptly sat up, as the shudder ran through Tiffany again.

'Magic,' he said. His great head turned to look over his shoulder, but the plinth supporting the statue of the king was in his way.

'It is made of magic?' she said, turning to the others when the statue didn't respond.

'Is that what he said?' said Aunt Esme, as Nora nodded. 'I didn't know you could understand Latin, Tiffany.' She looked impressed. So did the Duke.

'I—' For a moment Tiffany thought about saying yes. But she had been raised in the belief that telling lies was wrong, and anyway, she was sure to get caught out in it. 'Not exactly. I did a ... a spell?'

Now Esme looked even more impressed, but before she could speak, Father Thames did.

'A spell?' He rounded on her suddenly, and the gap between the balustrade and the plinth inside it didn't seem like very much at all. 'You put this ... thing in me?'

'No! No. I am trying to stop it,' she said.

His metal eyes narrowed. 'Why?'

'If it is powerful enough to throw a man from the water, think of the damage it could do to small crafts and bridges,' said Tiffany.

'It is more powerful than that,' said the Duke, stepping forward. 'It has swallowed ships whole. It grows tentacles made of water and drags the ship down.'

The river god glowered at him. 'I do not understand his heathen tongue. Is he Roman?'

'No, he's from Chile. The point is, sir, that this thing in the water has enormous destructive power. You said you didn't like what the Iceni woman did to your city? This creature would be ten times worse.'

She didn't know if that was actually true, but if it got him on their side then she was fine with exaggerating.

Father Thames simply slipped off his pedestal to the ground a whole storey below. The ground shuddered beneath his feet, and Tiffany stumbled.

Hands grasped her shoulders. 'Are you all right?' murmured the Duke.

'Perfectly fine,' Tiffany stammered, although she couldn't help shrinking back against him as the ground shook further. Tiffany knew there were water gates from the river that allowed one to access Somerset House at basement level, but she had never been down there. What was he doing? Smashing through doorways? Though walls?

Lights were beginning to illuminate the upper windows, and a few shouts rang out.

'Not being funny or anything, but somebody's gonna come after us,' said Nora. She was already moving towards the south wing.

'Should we follow?' said the Duke, his body still pressed against Tiffany's. *Don't let go of me,* she wanted to say, but she quite sensibly straightened away from him instead. But then his hand slipped down her arm to her hand, and she didn't move from that.

'Yes, good plan,' said Esme, and then all four of them were running, and Tiffany was still holding the Duke's hand.

By unspoken agreement they did not try to follow the statue down to the basement level, but ran to the south wing entrance. It was of course locked, but that didn't seem to be much of a problem for Esme, who simply whispered to the door and it opened. Tiffany had no time to wonder at this before they were running through the gallery, the floor shaking beneath them.

'Whose idea was it to bring the statue to life?' Tiffany joked lamely as Esme opened the door to the terrace. She was shaking.

Santiago squeezed her hand and smiled, and then they were running again.

The terrace of Somerset House was lapped by the river, with

water gates beneath it. From one of these strode the bronze statue of Father Thames, the dark water of the river rippling around him at waist height.

But that wasn't even the thing that drew her attention. The water was ... boiling. There were small craft on it even at this time of night, being rowed at high speed away from the statue. The water fizzed and flailed as if it had arms.

Beside her, Santiago muttered in Spanish and crossed himself again. Nora swore. Esme's hands gripped the terrace balustrade until her knuckles were white.

'Still think water can't come to life?' said Santiago.

'No. Still think I did it?' said Tiffany, staring at the river as it came to life.

'No.'

He was still holding her hand.

Behind them, people had begun moving around in Somerset House. Esme muttered a few words and the terrace door slammed shut, locks clicking.

Father Thames raised his arms and shouted at the water in a sonorous, deafening voice. It was somewhere between thunder and the ringing of a bell, if one happened to be right in the middle of the thunderstorm and right next to the bell.

'What's he saying?' said Esme.

'It's not Latin anymore,' said Nora.

Tiffany cleared her throat. 'He's commanding the water to obey him. He says... He says it is water of his water. That they are the same ... body? He commands the invader to leave. No, not invader...'

The language he was using was so ancient Tiffany didn't expect anyone could understand it. The words were arriving in her head in English, but some of them were muffled, as if they didn't have an exact translation.

'Infection!' she said. 'That's what he sees it as. Whatever is in the water is infecting his river. He is commanding it to leave.'

'Water's infected enough as it is,' Nora said. 'Half the sewers in London empty into it.'

'Only half?' murmured Santiago.

'If it is an infection, perhaps we need Madhu to brew a cure,' mused Esme.

'For the whole River Thames?' said Tiffany. 'It flows for miles. All the way from—' She broke off suddenly as her gaze followed the direction of her own thoughts.

'What is it?' said Santiago.

'It flows past the Houses of Parliament,' Tiffany said.

'Yes?'

'I mean, right past it. Up to the walls. And the Tower.'

'And all the tributaries,' said Santiago in dawning horror. 'Every river has tributaries.'

'Dear God,' breathed Esme. 'The Tyburn. It runs beneath Buckingham Palace.'

'Beneath it?'

She nodded, face pale. 'Covered over and forgotten years ago, but it's there. And it still reaches the Thames. Via Westminster.'

'But no one will be sitting in Parliament this late,' Tiffany said, trying not to think that Cornforth often worked very late nights at the Home Office and the Commons was probably no different.

'Do we really wish it to be destroyed anyway? And as for the Queen's house at Buckingham—'

They watched the river writhing around the statue as he fought and bellowed.

'What do we do?' asked Tiffany.

Esme straightened her spine. 'We drive away the infection and ward the river. Can you draw without a canvas?"

'I—I don't know.'

'Use the floor?' suggested Santiago, and Tiffany was about to say she didn't have a pencil when she realised she did, because her dance card was still hanging from her wrist.

She nodded, and went to kneel on the ground, which necessitated letting go of his hand. She felt a little bereft without it, but the river was boiling so she should probably focus on that.

Don't think about what you can't do. Think about what you could do.

'What am I to draw?'

'A cauldron. As large as you like, then some ingredients. Draw it full of water.'

Tiffany knew what a cauldron looked like. There were several in the kitchen at Dyrehaven, where she had spent much of her childhood trying to get out of people's way.

She began to draw. 'Larger,' said Esme. 'The size of a carriage.'

Tiffany didn't know what they were going to do if anyone saw them. Then she realised they didn't have to worry about that, either.

'Everyone give me your hands,' she said, and they all did, without question. 'Now, think invisible thoughts.'

'You what?' said Nora, but Esme shushed her, and Tiffany concentrated hard on making them unnoticeable.

'Did it work?' she said a moment later.

'I can still see you,' Santiago said.

'Nobody is shouting at us, that'll do,' said Esme. 'Now, the cauldron? And make the water hot, if you can.'

Tiffany began drawing a large pot, and since it was a terribly crude sketch she added a little perspective and some lapping water, with steam rising gently from it. Then, not quite knowing how to proceed, she reached down to the ground and tried to will it to come to life.

Her hand touched wetness.

'Capital!' exclaimed Esme.

She was speaking as if all this was perfectly normal. Tiffany had just drawn a cauldron the size of a carriage, and now it was standing in front of them, tall enough so she could barely see over it. One moment it had been flat, and now, as if she had simply moved and seen it from a different perspective, it was upright, three-dimensional, and warm to the touch.

'Impossible,' breathed Santiago.

'No, just improbable. Now, draw these for me, please. Nora, Your Grace, please throw them in. We shall start with lavender.'

Tiffany drew everything she was asked to, her hand cramping, her gloves filthy from the ground, the cold evening air creeping into her bones. She didn't realise a headache was creeping up on her until a hand touched her shoulder and a voice murmured, 'Are you all right?'

Tiffany shrugged off Santiago's hand. She needed to concentrate. 'Yes, of course, thank you. A honeycomb, Aunt? Yes.'

'You are ... grimacing.'

'I am concentrating.'

He got the hint, and took the honeycomb when she handed it to him.

'There, that should do it. Nora, if you would?'

Nora sized up the cauldron, and said, 'You could've given it handles.'

Tiffany stood up and drew a handle. She lifted it, and it held.

She raised an eyebrow at Nora.

'All right,' Nora laughed. 'Another one ... here?'

Then she put her back to the cauldron and her hands through the handles, and took a deep breath.

'What are you doing?' said Santiago, alarmed. 'It will crush you—'

'No, it won't,' said Nora, and lifted the cauldron as if it was a bundle she was taking to market.

Astonished, Tiffany watched Nora carry the cauldron to the balustrade, brace herself, and then somehow hurl the whole thing over her head. It flew several yards into the dark, swirling water, and began to sink.

'Sisters,' said Esme, and took Tiffany's and Nora's hands. 'Let infection from this river be cleansed, and our protection settle on the great Father Thames. Let our will add strength to his mettle; and when this is done, return him to metal. Repeat it with me.'

Was this a spell? It certainly felt like one. Tiffany repeated the words, and as she did she felt the power grow between them. And after the third repetition, Esme and Nora shouted, 'As I will this, so will it be!' and Tiffany added her voice a second later.

The power seemed to release from her, and she could almost feel it bursting out across the river, pouring into the flailing, shouting statue, and filling him with light.

I am a witch.

The river god roared, the sound making the buildings quake.

'Be gone!' he bellowed, and the water gave one last, desperate flail before it subsided almost immediately. Something within it seemed to flow against the tide, out towards the sea, swelling the river as it went and then passing out of sight beneath Blackfriars Bridge.

Calm descended over the Thames, the only ripples emanating from Father Thames as he waded back out of the water. Tiffany saw that much before she crumpled.

CHAPTER 9

'*A* good evening, *mijn vriend?*' De Groot's eyes were sparkling as he strode into Santiago's office. 'You look like shit run over twice!'

Santiago stifled a yawn. 'The aristocracy party until the sun comes up,' he muttered, which was true, but not the reason he was so tired.

Last night's escapade at Somerset House had left him reeling in more ways than one. Tiffany had brought a statue to life and then a massive cauldron—but more importantly, she had held his hand and she had smiled at him.

And then she had fainted and he'd had to carry her home.

Granted, this had been made easier by Mistress Blackmantle and her door magic. Santiago had wanted to carry Tiffany personally to her chambers and see her safely tucked up in bed, but even with his shaky grasp of acceptable behaviour he knew that would not be possible. So he had made his bow and said his goodbyes and walked halfway to Limehouse before he remembered his grandfather's house on Grosvenor Square.

'I don't know why you want to be part of all that,' said de Groot. 'A lot of expensive fuss and nonsense. Now, did you hear about the disturbance in the river last night?'

'No?' said Santiago, with the level of innocence he usually reserved for customs officials. 'What happened? The men said there was some minor damage to the boats—was there a storm?'

De Groot shrugged. 'Could be, could be. But it didn't affect anywhere else in the city! No wind or rain. Just the river.'

'Some large creature out of place?' Santiago suggested, yawning again. 'A whale, or…'

'A whale?' De Groot laughed heartily. '*Mijn vriend*, what an imagination you have!'

When Santiago closed his eyes, he saw the river god standing in the water. 'You have no idea.'

'Guv!' That was Billy, rushing in at ten times the speed anyone needed. He was even faster now he was getting three squares a day and had proper boots on his feet. Santiago was fairly sure he'd grown an inch. 'I mean … Your Grace.'

He bowed, giggling to himself, and de Groot raised an eyebrow.

'Grace?'

'Long story. Yes, Billy?'

'There's this fella wants to see you. Did the whole title thing too.'

'Revenue?' He was running through a mental list of anything he needed to hide.

'Don't fink so. He— Oi! I said wait out there!'

The man standing in the doorway certainly didn't look like Revenue. He wore a brown coat and good boots, and he was clean-shaven and tall.

But none of that was what made Santiago clutch the arms of his chair and swear.

'Aye,' said the man. 'I thought it might take you like that. Your Grace,' he added.

De Groot got to his feet. He towered over everyone, this man included. 'Is there a problem, *mijn vriend*?'

Santiago scanned the stranger's face and saw there features he hadn't seen for decades. The eyes were bluer, the hair sandier, and the jawline narrower. But for all that, this man could have been his father, back from the dead.

He is dead. The Governor of Penang told me personally. The Peerage listed the date. He is dead.

'De Groot,' he said, rising and trying to recover his wits. 'Thank you for your visit. But I must deal with this. Thank you, Billy, please show *Señor* de Groot out.'

Billy looked unconvinced by this, but he read Santiago's expression, rolled his eyes and ushered the Dutchman from the room.

'I will call again later,' said de Groot, looking between Santiago and the stranger with an odd expression on his face.

'Yes, yes.' Santiago waved him away. 'Shut the door, Billy.' He knew the boy would be waiting outside with his ear pressed to the keyhole, but it was worth a try.

To the stranger, he offered the chair de Groot had just vacated. A silence fell.

Eventually, the stranger said in a slow, measured accent, 'Your grandfather, he preferred to speak first.'

'I am not my grandfather.'

'No,' agreed the stranger. He was looking around the office with great interest.

'You knew him?'

The stranger gave him a very knowing look. 'I did. He was kind to me, in his way. I owe him my education and position, and I'm very grateful for that.'

Santiago knew what he had to ask; he just couldn't bring himself to.

'Your mother?' he said, a lame sidestep.

The stranger shifted in his chair. 'Hannah Nettleship. Her father was Squire Nettleship. Well thought of in these—that is, in those parts.'

'And those parts are?'

'Yorkshire. East Riding. God's own country,' said the stranger with some satisfaction, as if he had personally made it so. 'His lands ran alongside His Grace's—that is, your grandfather.' He paused. 'Our grandfather.'

And there it was. The family resemblance was no coincidence.

Santiago did not think he much resembled his father, thank God. He took after his mother more strongly, which had always amused his father. 'Wait until you sally in to claim the Dukedom,' he'd say. 'Brown as a heathen, and all that hair. It ain't English, you know.'

But this man... Well, they said the firstborn resembled the father the most, and that was what this man was, after all. His father's firstborn, Santiago's older brother, and the reason the Marquess of Shorevale, heir to the Duke of St James, had been forced to flee the country all those years ago.

And if he hadn't, then Santiago wouldn't be here. Legitimately claiming the dukedom. Was that what this man wanted? To lay his own claim?

Did Santiago want him to?

He stood up abruptly. 'We cannot have this conversation here. I need ale.'

His brother—his *brother*!—shrugged in a laconic sort of way, and followed Santiago out of the warehouse, along the road, and into a tavern where the pies were at least edible. He ordered a couple of flagons of ale, and the first one went down so fast it didn't touch the sides.

'Perhaps some brandy,' he added to the serving man, whose eyebrows went up. 'I know you have some; I sold it to you. Bring the bottle.'

'Is that wise, Your Grace?' said the man he'd better get used to thinking of as his brother.

'Probably not,' said Santiago. 'And don't do the grace thing. I'm Mr Santiago around here.'

He nodded. 'All right, Mr Santiago.'

Having got himself on the outside of a glass of brandy, Santiago felt more inclined to talk. 'Your mother. Is she still with us?'

'I'm afraid she died at my birth. I was raised by my grand-parents.'

'I am sorry to hear that.'

'Don't be, they were lovely people.'

That startled a smile out of Santiago. 'And you never knew my —our—father?'

'No. He was long gone before my birth.' He cocked his head. 'My grandfather said His Grace could probably have sorted it all out, if it had just been the duel. Leniency for high spirits and all that. But there were enough other … er, misdemeanours to be take into account.'

Santiago sighed. 'I can believe that.' He drank some ale. 'I haven't asked your name.'

'So you haven't.'

Santiago raised his eyebrows, and the other man smiled slightly. 'William. William Nettleship.'

'Santiago.'

William nodded in a considered manner. 'Spanish for St James. I heard you were named after your father.'

'I was.' Santiago did not elaborate, and William did not press him.

The rain in Sao Paulo. The bread he never got to eat. And his name, the only thing that was his at all.

'They say you're from Peru or somewhere,' said the man with his father's face.

'Chile.'

'I thought it was hot.' But William seemed to know he was joking. 'And now you're back to claim the inheritance.'

Ah. 'I am the legal heir,' said Santiago. He had the documents to prove it. His father had taken a twisted pleasure in sending notarised copies of them back to England, so that the old duke would know his heir was utterly out of his reach.

William nodded. 'Aye. Aye. Whereas your father disclaimed all knowledge of my mother, killed her brother in a duel, and fled the country before my birth. There's little legitimacy in that.'

He said it without rancour. Santiago still had to ask.

It wasn't that he'd wanted to be the duke in the first place. He'd always known it was coming, especially since that day he'd heard of his father's death. He'd known one day he'd have to go home to a country he'd never seen, and take responsibility for a needlessly huge estate, complete with crumbling castle and hundreds, if not thousands of tenants. The properties all over England. The lands in Ireland and in the West Indies, neither of which he was comfortable with. The many and varied business interests, from canals to factories.

He just wanted to sail ships and smuggle goods and get away with it.

But smugglers did not get to dance with mermaid-eyed sirens.

He asked his brother, 'Do you wish to challenge me over it?' and found he was actually tense for the answer. Not that William *could* challenge him. But...

William snorted into his ale. 'Challenge thee? Nay, lad.' He slapped his thigh. 'I wouldn't be duke for all the tea in China.'

Santiago tried to hide his relief. 'Actually Indian exports of tea are more— never mind. You have no desire to be the duke?'

'None at all. Made a misery of your grandfather. Mind you, that's because he insisted on overseeing everything personally, himself. Too much for one man, my Grandpa Nettleship always said. Other men delegate. And I'm glad they do, for I had a nice position of it with the Earl of Ackermouth.'

'What was your position?'

'I was his steward. A considerable estate, although nothing to yours.'

'But you have left that position?'

William nodded, and poured them both a brandy. 'I did. And your next question, Mr Santiago, will be for why?'

Santiago allowed that this was so.

'I admit I was chancing my hand. I am not a gambling man by habit, sir, but this was a risk. I heard that you had come to claim your title and decided to present myself to you, both as your brother and as a man who knows how to handle a large estate in Yorkshire.'

This was unexpected. And possibly the answer to his prayers. 'You wish me to employ you as my steward?'

William considered this. 'I wish to enquire if you are happy with your current stewardship and offer my services.'

'And if I am happy with my current stewardship?'

William said drily, 'Then my opinion of you goes down, sir, because you shouldn't be. Fellow was only good for following His Grace's orders. Can't stand on his own two feet. If you don't wish to oversee him every day, you'll regret keeping him on.'

Santiago sat back on the wooden settle, the brandy making itself known to his system. It was warm in the tavern, and the variety of fragrances verged on the less pleasant, but he liked taverns. He liked the honesty of them. People went about much the same business here as they did in Lady Tiffany's ballrooms, but they did it with a lot less pretence.

He glanced over at the whores in their rouge and scanty dresses, pouting at all comers. Did Tiffany feel like that, when she was trussed up in some frilled abomination and sent off to dance with a sweaty nobleman twice her age? At least these women only had to deal with their culls for half an hour or so at a time. Tiffany would be sold to the highest bidder for the rest of her life.

The thought made him cold with rage.

'If they see you ordering brandy, they'll charge you twice as much,' said William mildly, following his gaze, and Santiago realised he'd been gazing at the wenches without even seeing them. By now, his father would undoubtedly have ordered a couple of them over, even—especially—if he had company. Even if that company was his own son.

But Santiago was not his father.

He reached into his jacket and brought out his cigar case. William declined the one he was offered, but didn't seem to mind Santiago lighting up.

'How do I know you aren't going to swindle me?' he said. 'Run down the estate and try to stage a coup?'

'You don't.' William took a sip of ale. 'But the coup would be pointless. Even if you were dead in your grave, sir, I'd not inherit a single square foot of the estate, and as for the title, it'd have to go to the nearest legitimate male relative.'

Santiago nodded. 'I looked him up,' he said around his cigar. 'A cousin many times removed, known for his gambling debts.'

'And I've no desire to work for one of those. I've proper references, should you wish to see them.'

Santiago would like to see them. He would be derelict in his duty not to. And Tiffany's words about his responsibilities rang in his ears. *There is no such thing as 'just a title'.*

'I shall have to give notice to the current steward,' he warned. 'And I will be checking your references.'

'As is right and proper.' A smile played around William's mouth. 'And if I am not a scoundrel and I know how to do my job?'

'Then I believe you will have a new position managing Castle Aymers.' He frowned. 'Is the village really called Aymers Chevres?'

'I'm afraid so.' William checked the ale tankard and waved for another. 'Aymers being from the Anglo-Saxon, meaning a swamp island—which it's easy to believe, the house being on a hill and the land requiring careful drainage—and Chevres from the Normans, there being a goat featuring prominently on the ancient arms.'

'A goat?' said Santiago. He'd thought the creature—now squashed into the corner of a crowded shield—was a deformed unicorn.

'Aye. Means persistence and strength. I don't know about you, sir, but I could murder a pie. My shout.'

'Nonsense, I have more money than I know what to do with. Landlord! Drinks for everyone.'

As a cheer went up, William said, 'Well, that's one way to get them to like you.'

'It's never failed me yet,' agreed Santiago. 'To your health, my brother!'

TIFFANY WOKE LATE, feeling as if she had suffered the headache she'd feigned. For a moment she thought she'd had an exceptionally vivid dream about Father Thames, and then she stretched and felt the ache in her back and her knees as she'd knelt on the ground to draw the cauldron. *I drew a cauldron the size of a carriage. In front of everyone.*

Well, not everyone, but the Duke had been there. The Duke, who she had known as Mr Santiago. He might not have outright lied to her, but lying by omission was still a terrible thing to do! Why wouldn't he have told her? Did he think she'd be angling for his hand in marriage?

'Hah!' she said out loud, trying not to remember the imprint of said hand in hers as they ran.

A scratch at the door heralded Morris. 'My lady? Are you awake?'

She was offered tea and toast, but was still sitting by the fire in her wrapper when Elinor burst in.

'Theophania! What a triumph!'

Tiffany chewed an unwisely large bite of toast and gave her sister-in-law an enquiring look.

'The Duke! Smaller bites, dear. Chewing is unladylike. He seemed quite taken with you. Did you see him, Morris, when he brought Lady Theophania home last night?'

'Yes, my lady. Only from a distance though.'

'Is he not a well-made man? Rather darker in the complexion than I should prefer but one can't have everything, and your colouring should cancel that out.'

'Cancel it out?' said Tiffany. She had been told her whole life that she was a colourless little thing, with her pale hair and insipid eyes. Was Elinor finally discovering a purpose for it?

'With the children. Your son will be the next duke! Think of that.'

The future closed in around Tiffany like a hand on her throat. Marriage to a member of the Ton, bundled off to some country estate to have babies, and then a lifetime of getting them all married off.

Last night I brought a statue to life and helped heal an entire waterway and warded the whole River Thames.

Tiffany pressed a hand to her face. What would he do with that information now? He'd already threatened to blackmail her if she didn't help him. Now he had a whole display of witchcraft to tell people about! What else was he going to ask of her?

Her hand in marriage?

No.

Aunt Esme didn't have a husband. Neither did Nora. And the two of them strode about the place doing precisely as they liked. Nora cut her hair short and swore like a sailor. Aunt Esme wore crimson gowns and spoke to dukes as if she was their equal.

What could Tiffany do, if she had that freedom?

'I have sent an invitation to the house party. We shall have the very best suite prepared for him. Did he perhaps mention if he enjoys fishing?'

'Fishing?' said Tiffany, baffled. A country house party, with Santiago. The Duke. Him. Striding around the place doing sporting and hunting things with the other men, getting all dishevelled in that way he had that she should not enjoy, making all the other grown men look like little boys.

This would be torture. Could she feign a headache for the whole week? Not that she didn't long to leave London, and she did want to get back to Churlish Green to enquire after her childhood friend Henry and his family, but at what price? Four whole days of the Duke occupying not just her thoughts, but her house?

'The sprigged muslin with the peach flounces, I think, Morris,' Elinor was saying. 'It is the newest and most à la mode.'

'For what occasion?' said Tiffany, who didn't really like that dress much.

'Why, for afternoon calls! Everyone will want to speak to you today, Theophania. The duke himself will no doubt be calling, and everyone else will be green with envy that you are the only one he danced with. And he brought you home!'

'Properly chaperoned,' Tiffany added quickly, before this turned into the sort of rumour that ended with her walking down the aisle. Receiving visitors after a ball was always a tedious task, and she didn't need to add extra gossip to the mill. 'Aunt Esme and … and her maid were also with us.'

'Yes, yes, of course. Strange looking creature, her maid. Has she had lice?'

'Er, I don't think so,' said Tiffany. Given the efficiency with which they had cured Mr San— the Duke's wounds after he was attacked on that beach, she didn't think health issues were something that plagued the household. Why, it seemed Madhu could cure somebody with the correct blend of tea. 'I think it looks chic. Like a Frenchwoman.'

Elinor sniffed. 'Why anyone would want to appear French is beyond me. Come on, up you get. There is not much time to waste and your hair was not put in rags last night.'

'I am sure you have your preparations to make,' Tiffany said, and thankfully Elinor was excited enough about hosting the Duke that she bustled off to harass someone else.

Tiffany turned immediately to Morris. 'Not the sprigged muslin,' she said firmly. 'I can't stand it.'

'But Lady Cornforth said…' Morris began, peering at the door to make sure it was definitely closed. 'It isn't my favourite either,' she admitted.

Tiffany stood up, and tried to ignore the soreness in her feet. Her dancing slippers had not been intended for racing about after river gods. There had been blood on her stockings when Morris had peeled them off her last night.

She hobbled to the clothes press and said, 'Where is the sprigged muslin?'

Morris located it quickly in a drawer. Tiffany shook it out, and as the maid was explaining that it would need to be ironed, Tiffany put her foot on one of the horrible flounces and yanked the dress upwards. There was a loud rip.

'Oh dear, what a shame,' she said.

'I could sew—'

Tiffany grinned and tore the skirt in half up to the knee.

Morris gasped and giggled behind her hand. 'My lady!'

'Such a shame. Perhaps you can do something with it, Morris. For yourself.' The maid could get a few bob for a dress like this if she mended it carefully. 'Or give it to the poor. Meanwhile, alas, I cannot wear it and so...' She hunted through the drawers for something more to her liking, and came up with a duck-egg blue dress that she had always felt flattered her eyes. Elinor didn't like the dress, and if Tiffany thought about why she remembered that she'd chosen the fabric herself.

'This will have to do, I suppose,' she said theatrically, and Morris giggled again. 'Now, could you possibly fetch me something for my feet, please? And while you're at it, I do think I would feel an awful lot better for something medicinal in my tea. Possibly brandy.'

Morris was smiling as she went away, and Tiffany thought that perhaps, today might not be a bad day after all.

A FEW PINTS of ale and a pie turned into several more pints of ale and half a bottle of brandy, and by the time Santiago suggested to his now dearly beloved half-brother that he had some claret in the warehouse, they were both listing quite badly to starboard. And to port. And in all directions, really. The street was swaying like the deck of a ship.

'Perhaps we shouldn't have that claret,' said William, slapping himself on the cheek.

'You want more brandy instead?' said Santiago. 'Good plan.'

He slung his arm about his brother's shoulders and they stumbled in the vague direction of Santiago's yard. The afternoon had disappeared somehow, sped up like an overwound watch, and now most of the street was in shadow.

'Thing is though... The thing is,' Santiago said, 'I never had a brother, 'cos my parents hated each other. Hated. My mother went into a convent. That's how much they hated each other.'

'Amazing they had you, then,' said William.

'Sí, but that, *lo que pasa es que*, is that they did it to spite my grandfather. Your grand— *Our* grandfather. Because, I mean. Look at me.'

He spread his hands, nearly falling over in the process.

'You are a very handsome man,' said William.

'Is not what I meant, but thanks. I mean I'm all ... *Soy todo Español. Sí?*'

'You said, right,' William said, 'you said you weren't Spanish. You're from, whassit. Chilly place. That's not chilly.'

'Some of it's very chilly. Icebergs and...' Santiago tried to think of the word for the big slabs of ice on the mountains. '...the like. But no, thing is, actually, my mother's like this Incan princess. No. Other one. Mapuche.'

'Is she?'

'S'what they say. S'nonsense obviously, cos her father was *el Conde de Mozzarella de ... Tango.*' No, that wasn't quite right. 'I will remember soon. Why's the aristocristicity have such long names?'

'I suppose it's summat to do on cold nights,' said William, and the two of them burst out laughing.

'Your ... Grace?' said a hesitant voice, and he swung his head around muzzily to see a blurred figure addressing him. Slight, neat—probably, under all that blurring—polite.

'Robinson? What the devil you doing here?'

'I came to see if Your Grace wished to be dressed for the theatre. I see ... that is perhaps not the case?'

'Theatre? I don't... Do I have a ticket?'

'You have a box, sir. By long-standing tradition. There is a farce, and then a tragedy, and I believe some country dancing.'

Santiago shook his head, and the street shook with it. 'No. Can't stand a farce. No. English humour. S'weird.'

'As you say, Your Grace. Shall I have the carriage sent round, sir?'

'What? No. I c'n walk.'

'Not sure you can,' murmured William.

'Robinson! Have you met my brother? I have a brother! William, *este es mi ayuda de cámara*, Robinson.' He'd probably messed up that introduction somehow. Tiffany's lessons blurred in his head.

'Sir.' Robinson gave a neat bow. William gave a sort of salute.

'Robinson. You're the one who makes him look like a gentleman?'

'Yes, sir.'

'I'm not a sir, lad. Just a common or garden mister.'

'I wish I was a common or garden mister,' said Santiago wistfully.

'Will you be requiring my help to get back to the warehouse, Your Grace?' said Robinson, who was probably a foot or two shorter than Santiago and surely weighed about as much as a cat.

'No no no,' said Santiago, waving a hand airily. 'No, you go on home, my lad. Take the evening off! Go to the theatre. I have a box, you know.'

'Thank you, Your Grace,' said Robinson, and watched them weave past down the narrow street.

'He's a good lad, that Robinson,' Santiago said, as they strolled —well, perhaps stumbled a little—along.

'Certainly seems it,' said William.

'Can't understand why he'd not got a better position.'

'You are a duke,' pointed out his brother.

'Weeeellll,' said Santiago expansively. 'Only just. I'd've, I'd've, I'd've thought a fellow of his accomplissiments—' That was a hard word to say. Santiago tried out a couple of variations, and none of them seemed right.

'It's a mystery,' agreed William, and then frowned. 'Whassat?'

'Whass what?'

William turned, which meant Santiago turned too, and there was a group of men, stevedores by the look of it, approaching a smaller figure. The smaller figure was backing away, holding up its hands in an appeasing manner.

'Is that Robinson?' Santiago said, squinting.

One of the stevedores let out a nasty chuckle.

'He's got no money,' Santiago called. 'Not a penny. Have you, lad?'

'That's no lad,' said one of the stevedores, leering unpleasantly.

'Eh? No, you're right, he's not a lad; he's my valet.'

'Your Grace,' murmured William urgently.

'No, not to you, I'm Santiago, *sí*? He's my valet,' said Santiago, straightening himself up and trying not to sway. It had been ages since he'd punched anyone. Months at least. It was always very satisfying when they deserved it.

'Oh, is that so?' said the stevedores, who presumably weren't ones who worked for him, at least not often. He hoped not anyway. He was probably going to have to beat them up and that was bad when it came to hiring journeymen.

'*Sí*. Yes. It is.' He was already moving closer. His mind seemed to sharpen up a bit at the prospect of violence.

Dukes didn't brawl. But Santiago, who had grown up on mean streets and rough harbours and smuggling ships—he bloody well brawled.

'Then this little lad has been lying to you!' roared one of the big men, grabbing Robinson by his impeccable waistcoat and lifting him off the floor.

'Oh, bugger,' sighed William. He was already rolling up his sleeves. Santiago beamed and took off his coat. He attempted to hang it on a stack of crates. He failed.

'Please, I don't want to cause any trouble,' said Robinson.

'Then you shouldn't be walking around dressed like a—'

The man who'd been speaking got cut off by Santiago's fist. He let go of Robinson, swore, and swung at Santiago, who ducked and wove probably a bit more than he intended to.

'*Vamos!*' he shouted. 'Come on!'

Then someone smacked him facedown into the dirt.

CHAPTER 10

The day turned dull and overcast. Callers made it through the drizzle to leave cards and bring flowers for Tiffany, most of them bursting at the seams to ask about the Duke.

'Oh yes, he seems very pleasant,' she repeated. 'Though we did not have much conversation.' Then she turned the subject to something else. If she had nothing else to thank Elinor for, it was the ability to direct a conversation.

Until someone said, 'Indeed, I have found him to be a very pleasant and interesting young man,' and she looked up to see Aunt Esme dropping an elegant curtsey to the room.

'Can we be totally sure,' said a young man who had presented Tiffany with a posy of violets, 'that he really is the Duke?'

This sent a flurry around the room. Ladies looking shocked. Gentlemen looking somewhat smug. She supposed a young handsome duke with a piratical scar and a mysterious backstory would rather outshine any other young man on the marriage mart.

Not that he was so very handsome. He was merely ... different.

'What proof,' asked Mistress Blackmantle, taking a seat, 'would you require?'

'Well,' blustered the young man, whose name Tiffany had already forgotten. 'The, er, was he, er, his parents' marriage! Was it valid?'

'I believe a notarised copy of the register was sent to His Grace the late Duke,' said Aunt Esme mildly.

'And he was born within— That is, er, do excuse me, ladies, but he was born ... after the marriage?'

'So the second notarised copy says,' said Aunt Esme, smiling pleasantly.

'But how do we know he is the person mentioned in those records?' persisted the gentleman, who clearly didn't know when to give up. Tiffany wondered how he was at the gaming tables.

'How do we know any of us are the people mentioned in our records? You could have been swapped at birth and nobody could prove it.'

A few people laughed nervously at this. Aunt Esme sat there, utterly composed whilst her opponent spluttered.

'Well, I look like my father!' he said. 'And I have the family signet ring.'

'So does His Grace,' said Aunt Esme, and added more slyly, 'and so does His Grace. Now, Tiffany dearest. We hardly had the chance to talk last night, and I have been quite desperate to invite you to supper.'

Reeling from this conversational segue—although not quite as much as the young man Esme had just so efficiently rebuffed— Tiffany said, 'Oh, yes, I'd love to.'

'Capital! Shall we say seven tonight?'

'Tonight?' said Elinor, and Tiffany tried not to wince. Elinor always found some way to crimp her plans.

'Yes, of course. No time like the present.'

'Well, Theophania did have a somewhat tiring night last night—'

Esme laughed in a patronising manner. 'My dear, only the dreadfully unfashionable go to bed early! I shall expect you at seven, Tiffany. Not too late, because I wish to compare some embroidery silks with you. Lovely shades of green and blue, just the thing for your complexion.'

'I do like green and blue,' said Tiffany gratefully. Elinor was obsessed with pink and peach and they were terrible with Tiffany's colouring.

'Then it is sealed. I shall see you then. Do bring your sketchbook, dear. Goodness, look at the time. I have hardly paid a call on Lady Selby to thank her for such a lovely evening.'

And she was gone, in a whirl of silken skirts and subtly expensive perfume.

Into the small silence that followed, the gentleman beside Tiffany—who had brought her peonies, but whose name she had no recollection of—asked, 'Is she your aunt on your mother's or your father's side?'

'Father's,' Tiffany said quickly, because any hint that Esme might be related to her mother would result in Elinor forbidding all contact with her. 'But not a direct aunt. I forget the degree of relation. Have you tried the honey cake? It is very good.'

Later, after the guests had all gone, Tiffany went to the library and checked the Peerage again, just in case she'd missed it the first time. Of course, Blackmantle could be her married name, only ... Mistress Blackmantle did not dress as a widow. She dressed as ... well, Tiffany hardly knew. As a woman who was not told what to do by anyone else.

The family bible stood on its own stand. Tiffany checked that too. But of course, she could be a more distant relative, and 'great-aunt' was simply the easiest thing to say.

Either that, or she'd been crossed out of a previous edition for some misdemeanour and never added to subsequent bibles. That could be it. Yes, probably.

She could tell Elinor didn't want her to go to Esme's this evening. She was fussing around, making excuses to come by Tiffany's room or interrupt her reading or ask when she had begun sketching, but she never quite managed to voice a reason as to why Tiffany couldn't go. She might not know Aunt Esme, but it was clear she was a lady of consequence who was received in all the best ballrooms and was on close acquaintance with a certain young, handsome duke.

Not that he was so very handsome. He was just … a degree more agreeable than some of the other gentlemen. That was all.

I wonder if he will be at supper…

Not that she wanted him to be. No. Of course not. He was a liar, for starters, or at least he had lied by omission, and he was probably making fun of her, and also he was forcing her to help him because of that stupid bargain. Blackmailing her. Or at least threatening to. Yes. He was a terrible man, and it didn't matter in the slightest how golden his skin was or how dark his eyes, or the way his mouth curved at one corner when he was amused, or how fascinating that black ink on his arms was…

Tiffany cleared her throat, even though there was no one else in the room, and went to get changed for supper.

Perhaps into the green evening gown that was a particular favourite. Purely for herself, of course.

But when she arrived at Aunt Esme's, it was clear the house was in some uproar. Delicious scents wafted from the area of the kitchen, but everyone was standing in the hallway, facing a somewhat frantic Billy.

'Miss, miss!' he cried when he saw her. 'You got to help, miss! I mean … er, your ladyshipness.'

'Help with what?' she said. 'Has something happened?' Her

stomach tightened uncomfortably. Was Santiago hurt? Was he in trouble?

'It appears our esteemed friend is in gaol,' said Aunt Esme very drily. She was pulling on gloves as she spoke, and Nora was kneeling to change her footwear.

'Sant— the Duke is in gaol?' said Tiffany, just in case she had misheard. How on earth was he in gaol? He was a duke!

'It appears so. Billy wisely came here to ask for help—'

'I didn't know no one else,' Billy said bluntly.

'Thank you, Billy.'

'Well, I mean I do, but they're the coves from when I ended up in Seven Dials and you don't wanna owe them favours, ma'am, no you bloody don't.'

Nobody told him off for his language. Tiffany said, 'I thought you were from Foulness, Billy?'

'Nah, s'just where I ended up when I ran away from Seven Dials. Which is where I ended up when I ran away from the workhouse. I like living with the guv'nor,' he said fervently. 'I don't wanna see him hang!'

'I'm sure it won't come to that,' said Esme briskly.

'Hanged with a silken rope, ain't it, Your Ladyship?' said Nora.

'I am sure the Duke hasn't committed a hanging offence,' said Esme. 'Madhu, dear, I'm so sorry about supper. Will it keep warm?'

'Of course,' said Madhu. 'Do you want me to fetch a sleeping draught? For the guards?'

'Hmm,' said Esme, pausing as she shrugged into her cloak. 'I had thought to simply talk to them, but if it comes to that, I will send Billy back for some. Tiffany, you're with me.'

'Me?' said Tiffany. 'But—'

'Yes. It will be good for you. Also, you have a few tricks up your sleeve we might use.'

'What tricks?' said Tiffany as they left the house into what was now a steady downpour. A hackney cab very nearly screeched to a halt at Esme's raised hand. 'Nora could bend the bars of the gaol. Madhu could make a … a sleeping draught for the gaolers!'

'Dear me, how dramatic. I simply meant that you can make yourself unseen, which may prove useful. Billy, what was the charge?'

'Brawling, miss.'

'Brawling. Well, one cannot brawl alone. Was he acting by himself?'

'No miss. He was with this other fella. And his valet.'

'Robinson brawls?' said Tiffany, agog.

'I dunno, miss. I heard all the shouting, but when I went to see they was being loaded up into the hurry-up wagon and then I ran to the gaol to see and the guv'nor, he told me to come get you. Through the bars, like.'

Bars. Oh dear God in heaven. They were going to visit a gaol. Tiffany was so preoccupied with worrying about what Elinor would say that she paid no attention where they were going until she realised it was very dark outside, and not just because of the rain.

'I would counsel you to keep your wits about you,' said Esme as they descended from the cab, 'as the denizens of the area are somewhat desperate, and I have not taught you how to curse people yet. Stay close to me. You too, Billy.'

The gaol was a wretched building, or perhaps it was part of a collection of wretched buildings. Everything looked so ramshackle she was astonished anyone managed to be held there at all. The rain made gulleys in the street, which appeared to be made of mud and other things she didn't want to think about, and here and there were bundles of rags in the darkness that might have even been people.

Esme rapped on the door and demanded entrance, which was granted without question. Tiffany didn't know if that was a witch thing or if the gaol would let anyone in, and only controlled who was allowed to leave.

Inside was a courtyard, just as dark and filthy as the street outside. A smell arose that Tiffany didn't think she'd ever be rid of. In the darkness, something whined and howled.

'Down there,' said Billy, pointing to a grill set low in the wall, barely above the ground. Rain poured into it. 'That's where I saw 'im.'

Tiffany tried to peer in, but it was so dark she saw nothing. Surely the boy was mistaken and it was a drain?

Then something looked up at her from the running water. Not from the grate, but from the water itself, and it wasn't moving with the flow but staying still. An eye, round and unblinking, with an oblong pupil. It seemed to come closer to the surface of the water—and then vanished, in a flurry of tentacles.

Tentacles…

'Tiffany, stay with us,' called Aunt Esme.

Tiffany shook her head and blinked. The running water was just running water. No doubt it had simply been something disgusting and her mind had played tricks with it. She hurried after her aunt.

The gaoler escorting them was a cadaverous man who leered at Tiffany in a way that made her feel as if something was crawling on her skin. He took them into a dimly lit room where the only relief was to be out of the rain, and said, 'Who was it you was after?'

'I believe he will have identified himself to you as Mr Santiago,' Esme said.

'Oh yeah. The Spaniard.'

'He's not Spanish,' all three of them said at the same time.

'And his valet also,' said Tiffany, who was trying not to breathe through her nose. 'Mr Robinson.'

'And the other fella with the funny accent,' piped up Billy.

The gaoler grunted and indicated that they should follow him. 'Watch your step,' he said, leading them down a set of creaking wooden stairs to a dark, low tunnel lit only by the occasional dish of burning fat set into niches on the wall. They stank like rancid bacon, and the flicker of the flames on the walls had Tiffany wishing she was anywhere else at all.

Why had Esme brought her, and not one of the others?

'It is very dark,' Esme said.

'You want a candle, that's tuppence.'

She sighed.

'It ain't a serious charge, if you get my drift,' the gaoler said as he rapped on a door they passed, apparently just to hear the inmate howl. Tiffany flinched.

'I believe I do,' said Esme. 'A fine, perhaps?'

'Five guineas.'

'Five guineas?' said Tiffany and Billy at the same time. It was an outrageous sum.

'Each.' The gaoler smiled, revealing blackened teeth.

'But that's—'

'Something you may need to help me with, my dear,' said Esme to Tiffany, and was it a trick of the light or did her eyelid flicker in a wink?

Tiffany felt in her reticule for a pencil.

They were led to a grated opening in the curved tunnel wall, and the gaoler said, 'They're in there.'

'May we have a candle?'

'Threepence.'

'It was tuppence back there!' said Tiffany.

'And now it's threepence.'

Esme fished out her reticule and tossed him a thrupenny bit. The gaoler grinned to himself and sauntered back the way he'd come.

'Oh well,' said Esme, and shaped her hand around the air,

which came to light, just as she had on the Somerset House terrace. *And to think I was frightened then!*

'Holy mother of God,' said a voice from the gloom.

'What is that?' came another.

A glint of gold, a flash of white teeth, and then Santiago was grinning at them through the bars. His face was bruised and bloody and his coat was torn. He looked more like a pirate than ever.

He bowed. 'Mistress Blackmantle,' he said. 'Lady Tiffany. Billy. How kind of you to come.'

TIFFANY LOOKED SHOCKED, and he couldn't blame her. This place was dreadful, even compared to some of the gaols Santiago had been in. He'd considered trying to break out, but he was still half-cut, and he didn't really fancy being set upon by whatever rabid mutts the gaoler kept.

'This is who you went to fetch?' said William in disbelief. 'Ladies?'

'Not just any ladies,' Billy informed him eagerly. 'See what she did with the light there?'

'All right,' said Esme Blackmantle, with a quelling hand in his direction. 'We don't want to end up behind bars too.' She kept glancing back along the passage, but the gaoler was taking his time with their candle. 'The gaoler appears to be open to bribery.'

'Then you must feel right at home, Your Grace,' said Lady Tiffany. 'Bribery is after all, simply the cousin to blackmail.'

'I have never blackmailed anyone,' said Santiago. Did she really think so little of him?

She spluttered. 'Then why am I giving you etiquette lessons?'

'That was not bribery. That was a bargain.'

'A bargain dependent on you not telling anyone about the witchcraft,' Tiffany said hotly.

'I remember it differently—'

'Children, please,' said Mistress Blackmantle, and Tiffany's mouth snapped shut, her eyes continuing to glare daggers at him. 'Have you paid the gaoler anything already?'

Santiago sighed. 'We gave him a few pence for a blanket and some water. And I feel we will catch something from either.'

'Dear me, what lessons could we possibly learn from this?' said Tiffany crisply, and he realised that she wasn't just afraid.

She was furious.

And that made him weirdly happy. If she didn't care about him, she wouldn't be angry at all. Disappointed, perhaps. But not furious.

'I fear your friend has the advantage of us,' she said, her words like cut glass.

'My apologies. My brother, William Nettleship.'

'Mr Nettleship.' She nodded coolly. Her hand appeared to be tracing something on the wall outside the cell, and more of her attention was on it than him. 'I see His Grace has managed to lead you astray.'

'How do you know it was me?' protested Santiago.

'Well, it wasn't Robinson. Are you all right, Robinson?' Tiffany asked, with much more kindness in her voice.

The valet nodded, his eyes wide.

'You have not asked if I am all right,' said Santiago, trying not to sound as plaintive as he felt.

'Have I not?' She did not correct this. He heard a clink and saw Billy's eyes go wide.

'Ah, good,' said Mistress Blackmantle. 'If you will excuse me, I must go to give succour to those poor souls in the cells we passed.'

She nodded at them and left, leaving the pale bobbing light just hanging there in the air.

'What's succour?' said Billy, somehow making it sound obscene.

'Spiritual aid. Something I imagine His Grace will be seeking the moment he leaves this place.'

The only thing Santiago would be seeking when he got out of here was clean water. And maybe whiskey. 'Lady Tiffany. Why are you here?'

'I came to see if it was true. His Grace the Duke of St James in a common or garden gaol. I only wish I'd brought my sketchbook.'

The eerie glow of the witch light turned her pale skin into marble, her hair into silver. She sounded like a lady but she was eerie, unearthly. 'You should not be here.'

'I,' she informed him icily, 'am on the right side of the bars.'

'This is no place for a lady!'

Tiffany was barely even looking at him. 'It's no place for a duke either, and yet here you are. Remind me of the charge again?'

Santiago set his jaw and muttered it.

She didn't look up from whatever her hand was doing on that foetid wall. As politely as if they were at a ball and she'd misheard him, she said, 'Your Grace?'

He sighed. 'Brawling, my lady.'

'Brawling,' she repeated thoughtfully. 'Ah yes. Remind me which of our lessons covered that?'

He glowered at her from beneath his hair. 'They covered honour and defending the helpless. Should I have stood aside and let those thugs beat Robinson to death?'

That surprised her! 'Thugs?' she said. 'Robinson?' For the first time she moved her gaze from whatever on the wall was so fascinating. 'Who would want to beat up Robinson?'

There was a sticky silence. Santiago considered trying to explain it to her, and decided it wasn't his secret to tell. 'Some stevedores. Who will get no work at my docks,' he added drily.

'Let me see if I have this right,' she said, peering into their disgusting cell. 'Some large, burly dockworkers simply decided to beat your polite and unobtrusive valet to death, and you chivalrously decided to step in and save him?'

'That's about the size of it, ma'am, yes,' said William, who had been largely silent thus far.

'But why?' said Tiffany.

'Because good valets are hard to find,' snapped Santiago.

'I meant—'

He knew exactly what she meant. But right then the pale witch light went out, and hurrying footsteps brought Mistress Blackmantle, followed more slowly by the gaoler with the promised candle.

After the much brighter witch light, it seemed sickly and dull, and his eyes took a moment to adjust.

'Look what I have managed to find,' Tiffany said to her aunt. 'Fifteen guineas. In my reticule,' she added, her smile bright.

There was a clink of coins. Santiago narrowed his eyes. Her reticule was hanging from one wrist, and she hadn't touched it this whole time.

'Fifteen guineas and a little extra for yourself,' said Mistress Blackmantle, as if the gaoler had done them any favours.

The money was a magic of its own. The gaoler had their cell door unlocked in a trice, and Santiago gestured the others out first. He could hardly wait to get out. There was barely a noxious substance in the world not contained within that hideous cell, not to mention the rats. The rainwater had been a delightful refreshment.

He stepped into the corridor, which was hardly better, and stood looking at the gaoler's outstretched hand.

'You have had all my coin,' he said.

'All of it, sir? With friends like these fine ladies who carry so many guineas, have you nothing for the poor gaoler who did so much for your comfort?'

'You brought a flea-infested blanket and water dirtier than what washes in off the street,' Santiago said.

'It's more than most get,' whined the gaoler.

'I believe it,' said Santiago. He started to walk, then paused. The cell door further up appeared to be missing its lock. And so, if he squinted, did the one next to it.

Give succour, indeed.

He turned back to the gaoler. 'If I had been wearing fine clothes and bearing a title, and sent my boy to fetch money, how would I have been treated?'

'Like a king, sir,' said the gaoler. He looked over Santiago's work clothes, which were not of poor quality, but were certainly not ducal in style, and were now in such a parlous state he thought Robinson might have to burn them. 'But you'd have a hard time persuading me you was a titled lord, sir.'

He laughed at his own joke. Tiffany's lips twitched.

'This is very true,' said Santiago solemnly. He felt in a pocket and pulled out his card case. 'Here,' he said, and tossed one of his ducal calling cards to the man. 'So that you know where to send the bill for the doctor.'

He started walking again, the others following him.

'What doctor?' said the gaoler, bewildered.

Santiago gave the nearest cell door a shove. It opened easily, and a ferocious face peered out.

'The one you'll be needing,' said Santiago, and walked out.

CHAPTER 11

*S*he didn't see the Duke for several days.

But every night she dreamed of the beasty with the squirmers.

Sometimes it was the tiny thing she'd seen in the filthy puddle at the gaol. And sometimes it was the huge monster that had attacked the Thames. And sometimes Tiffany thought she saw a woman's face, pale and distressed.

She longed to ask Aunt Esme about it, but after the supper that never was, Elinor had kept her too busy. She insisted on taking Tiffany walking every day in Hyde Park, which was terribly busy with other people who would not admit they were there for a glimpse of the Duke too. They attended card parties and supper parties and musicales, and after a while people began to speculate that the Duke had left town for some reason.

'You should have danced with him again,' Elinor told Tiffany.

'You think he left because we only danced once?' she said.

'Don't be ridiculous,' said Elinor, although her face disagreed. 'I meant you should have taken your chance. I have invited him to our house party for Cornforth's birthday.'

'Has he replied?'

'No.' Her face said this was not acceptable. 'But he is a duke. I am sure he is very busy,' she allowed.

Tiffany assumed it was because he was waiting for his bruises to heal. She had only caught a glimpse or two at the gaol before Aunt Esme whisked her away in a hackney, but all three of the men had looked somewhat worse for wear.

And then one day there he was, striding along Rotten Row as if he hadn't a care in the world. The bruises on his face were faded, but visible enough to provoke whispers from everyone he passed. His eye was blackened, his lip cut. It should have made him look like a thug, and yet it only made him look like the more poetic kind of pirate.

He greeted Tiffany and Elinor quite elegantly, and conversed with them about the weather as if everything was completely normal. Tiffany could feel Elinor straining like a dog on a leash, desperate to ask what had happened but too bound by politeness.

'I was considering going to Vauxhall Gardens tonight,' he said. 'I hear they have the most impressive gas lighting and I should like to see it. Will you be there?'

Elinor loathed Vauxhall Gardens. It wasn't just that it was gaudy and a little dangerous, it was that anybody who could pay a few shillings was allowed to enter, no matter their class or refinement.

Tiffany had always wanted to go.

'Oh, we adore Vauxhall, don't we, Theophania?' Elinor said.

'We do?' said Tiffany. 'I mean, we do. Adore it. Yes. We might have supper there,' she said, twisting the knife. 'In one of the boxes.'

The supper boxes were notoriously expensive and while the Cornforths could easily afford it, Elinor objected strongly to the idea of being put on display for the hoi polloi to gawp at.

'That sounds very exciting,' said the Duke, his eyes on Tiffany. 'If I take a box, will you join me?'

And then Elinor had to say yes. She bragged about it to everyone else they met that morning, and spent most of the afternoon criticising Tiffany's wardrobe.

'He is taken with you. He might offer for you!' she trilled.

'Wonderful,' muttered Tiffany. All her plans to be a failure this Season being derailed by one piratical duke. One lying, manipulative duke, she corrected herself. The fact that he looked like an illustration for one of the more excitable kinds of novel was neither here nor there.

'You will be a duchess! A *duchess*, Theophania! No, no, none of those bold colours, she must have something delicate and innocent,' she snapped to Morris.

Morris put away the blue dress Tiffany liked and brought out a pink one she hated.

'Much better. You must be on your best behaviour, Theophania. None of your strange moods and answering back. Gentlemen don't like it when you answer back. Do try to be agreeable.'

The instructions went on throughout the evening as they travelled to Vauxhall Gardens, which in itself was quite the trip. Tiffany had never travelled south of the river, or been on any watercraft larger than a punt on a boating lake, so the ferry crossing the Thames came as something of a shock.

Elinor clutched at Cornforth's arm, her eyes tightly shut, the whole way.

Tiffany gazed in wonder at the panorama of London set out before her. The half-built Regent Bridge on her right, the many wharves of Mill Bank on her left, the grandeur of Parliament rising in the distance.

Parliament. Had that creature—she couldn't help thinking of it as the beasty with the squirmers, *thank you, Gwen*—really been intending to threaten the government? The river seemed quite peaceful now, with ferries and boats going about their business. Had Tiffany simply imagined everything that had happened that night at Somerset House?

When she closed her eyes, she remembered Father Thames standing waist-deep in the water, and the thrum of power that had been raised in her when she and the other witches had helped him ward the river. Father Thames held them safe in his hands.

The other witches. I am a witch.

She opened her eyes and looked at Elinor, huddled fearfully against Cornforth as the boat rocked gently with the river. *I am a witch and I am not afraid.*

Tiffany concentrated on her favourite colours and styles to wear. As the sun set over the river, she imagined herself gowned in the sparkle of the light on the water.

And when they handed their cloaks to an attendant in Vauxhall Gardens, Elinor gasped, because Tiffany's gown had been transformed into a shimmering confection of mermaid green and blue.

'But—you were wearing the pink—'

'I changed my mind. Oh look, there is Miss Brougham. I shall go and say hello.'

Indeed, rather than mingling with the sort of people Elinor was terrified of, the Gardens were full of people they knew. Tiffany strolled past the circular Gothic Orchestra with Miss Brougham, and paused to speak to Lady Selby by the Turkish Tent. Set in a wide arc around the central garden were the famous supper boxes, open to the evening air, where anybody might watch you eating supper. Waiters bustled by with tiny plates of servings so small even Elinor would find it hard to leave a ladylike amount.

And everywhere, there was light. Strings of glass bowls filled with pale, wondrous gas light, the warm glow of oil lamps by the supper boxes, the candles being brought by busy waiters. Light danced and glowed on the faces of the revellers, bounced off the clinking glassware, and glittered on the gown Tiffany had projected onto herself.

It would only last a few hours. But for those few hours she could wear what she wanted to, for herself.

'Lady Tiffany! Won't you join us for supper?'

Of course. The real reason so many people of quality were here this evening. The main attraction himself, the Lost Duke.

Tiffany turned and smiled politely. The Duke had a supper box, probably the one with the best view of the festivities, and he was lounging on the seating like a large tomcat, scarred face and all.

She allowed her expression to turn insincerely regretful. 'Good evening, Your Grace. I am quite afraid I have plans with my family. I regret—'

'Your Grace!'

Tiffany said one of Nora's rude words inside her head as Elinor rushed up with unseemly haste.

'How kind of you to invite us! We should be delighted, shouldn't we, Cornforth?'

'As you say,' he murmured, and gestured Tiffany and Elinor ahead of him. Elinor, who so hated the idea of being watched by *all sorts of people* as she ate, was now giggling girlishly as she shuffled around the booth.

The box held a few other people, who moved aside to let them in. Tiffany, with grim inevitability, found herself sitting next to the Duke. There were no chairs, merely benches to be shared, which seemed very improper to Tiffany. She could feel the Duke's leg against her own. His leg!

The Duke made introductions to the rest of his party: an artistic-looking woman and her glamorous kinswoman, a dark complected gentleman in an exciting waistcoat, and a beautiful lady he warmly introduced as Miss Nayak.

Tiffany smiled and nodded at them all until she got to Miss Nayak, who gave her a knowing smile. It was Madhu. She wore a gown of deep, beautiful pink that made her complexion glow, and an elegant striped turban with an ostrich feather. Around her neck was a jewel that could have bought half of Mayfair, and the gold ring still glinted in her nostril.

Tiffany forced herself not to look if the Duke was still wearing the gold ring in his ear.

'How very wonderful to see you here,' Madhu said. 'Would you care for some ham? It is very good, although sliced so thinly I think you could see a candle through it.'

'Have you seen what they consider to be a chicken?' said the African gentleman, Mr Noakes, gesturing to a small roasted bird on the table. 'I have seen bigger pigeons.'

'The wine could come in larger bottles too,' said the artistic Mrs Carrington, and she and her kinswoman Miss Ross giggled together, their cheeks pink.

'I will take that hint,' said the Duke, and gestured imperiously. *Some things he did not need to be taught*, Tiffany thought. 'The red champagne, was it not? And two more of the Burgundy,' he said to the waiter who hurried to his summons. 'And ... perhaps some Madeira?' He turned to Lady Cornforth, who nodded, wide-eyed at the profligacy. Burgundy did not come cheap at all these days, after the French war.

Tiffany smiled and nodded along, trying not to be too obvious as she watched Madhu. She seemed entirely at home in the elevated company, a world away from her kitchen in Aunt Esme's house. When the wine came, she casually tipped three precise drops from a small phial into the Duke's glass.

'What on earth— Is this some ritual from the Orient?' laughed Elinor nervously.

Tiffany watched the Duke's throat move as he swallowed. Did all men have beautiful throats or was it just something she'd never noticed before?

Madhu replaced the phial in her reticule. 'No, it is merely something from my stillroom to help heal the Duke's bruises. How is Mr Robinson getting along?' she asked.

'Much better now, after your tonic. I thank you. Miss Nayak has quite the knack for herbal remedies,' said the Duke, smiling warmly at Madhu.

I bet she does. Tiffany eyed the painting hung behind him. It was of a horse and rider. She wondered what would happen if she made it come to life and kick him in the head.

'Every woman should be mistress of her stillroom,' said Madhu. 'Don't you agree, Lady Cornforth?'

Elinor hurriedly swallowed the mouthful of ham she'd just taken. 'Really? No. I prefer the apothecary. I am far too busy to go concocting potions like some sort of … of…'

Say it, willed Tiffany.

'…of witch!' said Elinor, and laughed at her own audacity. 'Lady Theophania, of course, knows how to make basic household remedies, don't you, dear? She is quite skilled in all household matters.'

Tiffany nearly choked on her Madeira.

'Yes,' said the Duke thoughtfully, taking a cigar from his pocket and clipping the end off it. Tiffany could feel Elinor's disapproval coming off her in waves. 'I have witnessed her accomplishments.'

He smiled at her wolfishly, then winced as a tiny painted hoof kicked the back of his head.

'What a shame you are so injured, Your Grace,' she said. 'However did it happen? Falling from your horse, was it? Did you have an embarrassing tumble?'

Elinor glared daggers at her from Cornforth's other side.

Cornforth himself merely went on eating cheese and ham and drinking Burgundy.

The Duke lit his cigar from a candle, which made Elinor whimper in distress. 'I am not an accomplished horseman, I will admit,' he said. 'I prefer sailing. But these bruises were not obtained in so noble a manner.' He sighed. 'I must inform you that there are quarters of this city where it is quite unsafe to walk alone.'

'Then no man of sense would go there,' said Tiffany.

'Then I must be a man of little sense, my lady. And it is a good job I did go there, because otherwise who would have been there to defend my loyal manservant? For he was set upon—set upon, I tell you!'

Elinor nearly swooned. The impropriety of the cigar forgotten, her hand clasped to her bosom, she gasped, 'So noble, your Grace!'

At that point Tiffany realised something. The Duke's behaviour was outrageous, and he knew it. So did everyone else. The way he lounged like a cat and smoked cigars at dinner and the frankly obscene loucheness of his neckcloth—none of this would be acceptable in any person of lesser ranking. But because Santiago was a duke, and dukes could get away with anything, the rules of polite behaviour were being rewritten to include whatever he did.

Icy fury rose inside her. Of course he got to do whatever he wanted to. Of course! But if she, a mere earl's daughter, wore an incorrect shade of pink, then Elinor's head would explode.

Oblivious to her anger, the Duke shrugged modestly and blew out a smoke ring. Tiffany said, 'Yes, yes, so noble, very chivalrous. I wonder that your heart can even be contained in your chest.'

'Theophania!' hissed Elinor. Madhu looked like she was trying not to laugh.

'I would have done it for anyone,' he said, and the look he gave the company was one so very smouldering she half expected his cigar to burst into flame. Even Cornforth looked impressed.

'I am sure you would, Your Grace,' said Tiffany. 'A lesser man would have stepped back. Walked on by. Simply gone to the nearest tavern and drowned himself in drink,' she added pointedly.

'Alcohol excess is a plague on our society,' he agreed, sipping his Burgundy. 'Waiter! A quart of arrack, if you please.'

'I have observed that many gentlemen consider it manly to drink to excess,' said Mr Noakes, somewhat bravely.

'It is not so manly when their behaviour becomes no better than that of a common brawler,' said Tiffany, and wafted away some of the Duke's smoke.

'A gentleman who cannot hold his drink is no gentleman,' said Cornforth, in that way of his that made you feel slightly guilty for assuming he wasn't listening at all.

'I quite agree with you, sir,' said the Duke. He puffed on his cigar, and remarked idly, 'Have you been to the new exhibition of art at Somerset House, Lady Tiffany?'

Her nostrils flared. Tiffany was seconds from making the horse kick him again when Madhu said, 'Goodness, isn't it warm in this box! I should like to take a turn about the grounds.'

'I will come with you,' Tiffany said quickly, and ignored Elinor's hissed and whispered jibes as she scrambled from the box.

'Perhaps I could escort you,' the Duke said lazily from behind her, and Tiffany knew if he tried then she might murder him, so she pretended not to hear him and marched away with Madhu.

She didn't pause until they were around the other side of the Gothic Orchestra, out of view, and then she took a deep breath and said, somewhat stiffly, 'Thank you.'

'It's no problem. I thought if the two of you argued any more the whole box would go up in flames.'

'But you're the one he was flirting with,' Tiffany said, and didn't quite succeed in keeping the sulkiness out of her voice.

Madhu laughed. 'Only to annoy you.' She reached into her reticule and glanced at Tiffany. 'Here,' she said, and passed her a little bottle.

'I don't have any bruises.'

'It's not for bruises. Although it might cause them. It's brandy.'

'Brandy?'

'Yes. I thought that was best for you right now.' Madhu gave her a calculating look. 'Perhaps a cigarette also?'

'Madhu!'

'They are very relaxing. No? Very well, then. Let us stroll into the gardens and let the brandy do its work.'

Tiffany didn't dare take a sip until they were past the last of the supper boxes, because while she might be prepared for some levels of outrageousness, she was not about to start openly drinking from a bottle in public.

Further away from the central courtyards, with their brightly coloured and lit pavilions, there were long walks between tall hedges. Lights burned here and there, but the overall air was one of secrecy.

Tiffany suddenly realised the woods would be full of trysting couples, and blushed. She took a swig of brandy.

It burned down her throat, far stronger than the ratafia she was usually allowed, and without any of the sugary flavour. She shuddered a little, and drank some more.

'Feeling better?' said Madhu.

'A little, yes.' She took Madhu's arm and they began strolling. The sounds of the orchestra and the pleasure gardens faded behind them. For a long, lovely moment, there was silence, and she didn't have to think about the Duke, or being a witch, or the Duke, or Elinor, or the Duke...

'He just irritates me so much!' Tiffany burst out.

'Yes, he's very good at it.'

'It's as if he does it on purpose!'

Madhu shrugged. 'He does.'

Tiffany blinked at the dark walk. 'What do you mean, he does?'

'You do it too. Come along, Tiffany, admit it. You enjoy needling him.'

Tiffany drank a bit more brandy. It was fun to annoy him. She couldn't lie to herself about that. 'He lied to me,' she said, as if that was an excuse.

'Only by omission. Look at it this way. If he had told you who he was, would you have believed him?'

'I—' Tiffany knew she wouldn't have. 'Well, what about that brawl?' she said, emboldened by the brandy. 'He keeps saying it was to defend his valet, but I could smell the alcohol on him.' She whispered the last part, despite having a bottle of brandy in her hand.

'Yes, and I suspect the alcohol is why he didn't dodge all the blows,' Madhu said. 'Tiffany, you should probably ask him a little about how he grew up. About why he took in the boy Billy, and why he defended Robinson.'

'What do you mean? I don't care about how he grew up.' But she did, secretly. She longed to know where he had been and what he had seen, all those ships and voyages and new lands. She wanted to know what it was like to be a child in Chile. What his mother was like. If his father was a scandalous as they all said. 'And why would anyone pick on Robinson? That's the part I don't understand.'

Madhu was silent for a few steps. 'Robinson,' she said. 'Nora has known him a long time. He is a very talented tailor.'

'Yes, I see that.' It was probably best that she didn't think about how neatly the Duke's coat emphasised his broad shoulders and narrow waist, how lovingly his breeches clung to his legs, how the white of his linen gleamed against his golden skin...

'But he...' Madhu was choosing her words carefully. 'He was not born a gentleman.'

'I don't suppose many valets are.'

'No, Tiffany. He was not born a gentleman.'

There was an emphasis there that took a moment to get through to Tiffany, and when it did, she stumbled.

Robinson, who was small and neat and spoke in a voice pitched slightly above what one might expect. Robinson, who was almost supernaturally unobtrusive. Robinson, who had said *my face didn't fit*. 'He— You mean, sh—'

Madhu kept on calmly walking, bringing Tiffany along with her. 'He. Yes.'

'But ... that means...' Her mind whirled. How had she not seen it? 'Does he know? Does Santiago know?'

Too late she realised she shouldn't have referred to him by that name. But Madhu didn't seem to have noticed.

'I would imagine so. He is an observant man. An observant man in need of a good valet,' Madhu added gently. 'And Robinson is a good valet. Why should it matter what else he is?'

Tiffany opened and closed her mouth a few times. It ought to matter, because it went against the order of everything she'd been raised to understand. But then how many of those things had she discarded since she had met Aunt Esme and become a witch?

How many other new ideas would reveal themselves to her?

She drank some more brandy. It did not appear to be about to run out. 'Well then,' she said.

Madhu was watching her carefully. 'You understand?'

'I ... think so. Those men attacked Robinson because they ... well, they saw what I had missed?'

'One assumes as much. There is a certain type of person who very much objects to another living his life in the way he sees fit,' said Madhu, on a sigh. 'You will likely encounter many of them, as a witch.'

'The former, or the latter?'

'Both. We do our best to help the latter, of course. And as for the former... Well, healing and understanding are not the only things I can infuse a drink with.'

'So ... Santiago was really just trying to help his valet?' Tiffany said, in a small voice. *I shouted at him.*

'Yes. As he helped Billy. And I strongly suspect he has given his half-brother a job, too. The man might look like a pirate, but he has the heart of a small fluffy animal.'

Tiffany sighed irritably, and drank some more of the brandy.

'There is always a place for you in our household, you know. Esme may be our senior, but we are all equals.'

For a moment Tiffany allowed herself to imagine it. A household where she could wear whatever she wished, and never go to another ball again if she didn't want to, and never have to make polite conversation with another crashing bore. It would be blissful.

'Elinor would never let me,' she sighed.

Madhu made a thoughtful sound. 'I could always give her some special brandy,' she said, and Tiffany suddenly laughed.

HE HEARD her laughter before he saw her, but that shimmering mermaid dress was hard to miss even in the darkness. Tiffany glowed, her white gold hair and her porcelain skin lit up from within as she laughed with Madhu.

Madre de dios, but she was beautiful.

Had he gone too far earlier? Was she truly annoyed with him? He'd flirted a little with Madhu, partly out of habit because she looked like a princess in her pink gown, and partly to see if it upset Tiffany. And it had. Which had to mean...

Was it possible that he occupied her thoughts as she did his?

She whirled around at the sound of his footsteps, and her eyes widened as if she'd been caught out doing something she shouldn't.

'Sant— Your Grace!'

'Lady Tiffany. I— Miss Nayak. I apologise for startling you.' He couldn't stop looking at Tiffany.

'Not at all,' said Madhu. She smoothly released Tiffany from her arm and stepped back. 'If you will excuse me, I did promise the receipt for my paratha to Mr Noakes.'

And she was gone, like a whisper, leaving him alone with Tiffany. Alone on a dark walk, where few other people passed and their only audience was the trees.

'You escaped the supper table?'

He nodded. 'The orchestra began to play a favourite of Mrs Carrington and so we strolled out and I...' He shrugged helplessly. 'I wanted to make sure you were all right.'

'I am perfectly fine, as you see. Madhu was an excellent chaperone. I suspect if anybody displeased her, she'd turn them into a frog.'

He laughed nervously. Could they do that? Could Tiffany do that?

Lady Tiffany scuffed her feet in the dirt. She looked at the ground, at the hedges, at anything but him. Finally, she said, 'Madhu told me about Robinson.'

His heart skipped. Would she disapprove? 'She did?'

'Yes. About why ... those men attacked him. And I...' She straightened and nodded, as if she'd come to a decision. 'I must apologise to you, Your Grace.'

He blinked. 'Why?'

'Because I had … assumed,' she spoke carefully, 'that you had been brawling for … your own reasons.'

'Because I was drunk?' Santiago said.

She shrugged uncomfortably.

'Well, I was. But I would have done it if I had been sober. Robinson is vulnerable to men like those stevedores. I will not let him come near the docks again.'

'Ever? Don't you live there?'

'Haha, Lady Tiffany, you know full well I live on Grosvenor Square.' At least he did when he was duking.

'That does sound unrealistic,' she said, tapping her lip thoughtfully. She seemed to have forgotten she was holding a small bottle. 'Perhaps Aunt Esme can help. Or Madhu. She makes potions, you know.'

'I do know.' Santiago smiled, because he rather thought Tiffany was a little bit tipsy. 'Robinson, William and I have all healed quite well because of them. Without Madhu's excellent work, I would not be here tonight.'

Her forehead creased. 'Were you very badly hurt?'

Concern! She was concerned for him! 'Nothing I have not suffered before,' Santiago dismissed, as if his ribs didn't still ache and his shoulder wasn't yellow with bruising. 'But Billy is not much of a valet. Should you be telling me about Madhu's potions?'

'Probably not.' She drank almost idly from her bottle, and Santiago knew she must be drunk, because she had explained to him that a lady was never to be seen eating and drinking in the street. 'Is Mr Nettleship really your half-brother?'

He felt his eyebrows go up. 'Yes.' He wondered how to explain the circumstance to her.

'They said there was some scandal about your father and why he had to leave the country,' Tiffany said, 'but I have never been told what it was.'

'Ah,' said Santiago. 'Yes. Well … William would be that scandal.'

Her eyes flew wide. 'Truly? Oh, my goodness.' He saw her eyes darting about as she took it in. She glanced up at him a couple of times, as if she wanted to ask him for the details, and he realised he wanted to tell her. To tell her that his father had told him one story and it had taken years to realise he was lying, and that it had only been William himself who could fill in the gaps and make it all make sense.

Tiffany stood there in the shadows, glowing as if she was made of moonlight. He wondered if that was a thing witches could do, like Esme had made that light, or if it was just Tiffany being so luminous.

How was she not overrun with suitors? Why was every man in this city not madly in love with her? Was everybody in England blind?

He wanted to tell her that he'd never seen a lovelier creature, that her eyes and lips enchanted him, that her skin was made of pearls and her hair of stardust, and that her bosom—well, he should probably not be telling her what he thought about her bosom.

But what he said was, 'Your dress is very beautiful.'

She looked up at him, and smiled. 'You know a gentleman should never compliment a lady's dress,' she said, and smoothed the shimmering skirts with her fingers. Skirts Santiago was instantly jealous of. 'But I thank you.' She bit her lip, and confided, 'Elinor had a fit when she saw it.'

'Her taste is not to be recommended,' Santiago said, and she smiled up at him as if he had said the most enlightening thing.

'No, it is not. And I think I should not let her bully me anymore,' she said. 'I don't like pink. I shall not wear it anymore.'

'I am pleased to hear it,' said Santiago.

'Or frills. Or flounces. They make me look like an iced cake.'

He laughed, and after a shocked second when her ears seemed to catch up with her mouth, she laughed too. She clapped a hand to her bosom, and as she did, her glove caught on her necklace and it came loose. They heard it tinkle and hit the ground.

'Let me,' he said, quickly bending to the ground to look for it. But the necklace was a flimsy thing, a thin ribbon and cameo pendant, and it was pretty dark now, away from all the spectacular gas lighting.

'Wait a moment,' said Tiffany, and whispered to herself for a moment before a light appeared, floating gently downwards.

Santiago stared up from her feet. 'You made that?'

'It's quite simple,' she said, but she sounded quite pleased with herself.

The pale light was enough to see the necklace by, and he stood with it in one hand, wondering if he dared try to fasten it around her neck. But then he heard footsteps. 'Quick, put the light out!'

'Er—' She gestured at the light, which moved closer to her hand, but didn't go out. 'Um—'

'This way!' Santiago said, taking her arm and pulling her through a gap in the hedge. The light, thank God, came with her, and then they were in a small grove, lit only by that pale light.

'I can't remember how to make it go,' she whispered frantically, making shooing gestures.

'Then leave it. For now, leave it, and you can use it to see this by,' he said, holding out the necklace.

Tiffany looked down at his palm, his rough sailor's palm, in which her delicate cameo lay so incongruously. Robinson was always on at him to rub lotion into his hands, or at least wear gloves when he went out as the Duke, but some of those calluses were old friends to Santiago.

The delicate shell of the cameo was warm from her skin.

'Will you do it for me?' she said, and his heart leapt. And— well, not just his heart. Santiago couldn't deny that at this point he would rather be taking things off Tiffany, not putting them on her.

But she was a nicely brought-up lady, and he was a duke, and Santiago knew from William what happened when nicely brought-up young ladies were found alone with men. Especially when said ladies had made it plain that they did not wish to marry. Not even a duke.

He moved behind her, and very gently, taking care not to touch her bare skin with his fingertips, brushed aside the curls that clung to the back of her neck.

He failed. Her skin was warm, and damp with perspiration. Just as it would be after he'd spent the night making love to her...

She exhaled, and he swallowed roughly. *Stop thinking about making love to Lady Tiffany!*

'My apologies,' he whispered, and it came out hoarsely.

She nodded, and it made another wisp of hair fall loose.

He wondered what her hair would smell like. How it would feel to stroke his fingers along it, to take the mass of it in his hands. How it would look cascading loose over her shoulders.

He shook himself. 'My hands are rough,' he said. 'Sailor's hands.'

He saw her throat move as she swallowed. 'You have travelled very far?'

'Across the Pacific,' said Santiago. 'Across Asia.' He carefully placed the ribbon around her neck and her fingers came up to hold the pendant in place. 'Around Africa. I have only been to Europe for the first time this year.'

'How are you finding it?' she asked politely.

'Cold,' he replied, although maybe that was wishful thinking. He was on fire. His hands trembled. Her skin smelled so delicious.

'But it is summer now,' she said.

'Yes. But it is nothing compared to the heat of India, of Mexico, of Egypt.'

'You have been to Egypt?' Her voice was full of longing. 'Did you see the pyramids?'

'I did.'

She sighed, and from this angle he could see the magnificent things it did to her bosom.

'I wish—' she began, and stopped. Her chin went up. 'Perhaps I will travel. Now that I am a witch.'

Right, yes. A witch. Not an ordinary young lady he could consider marrying.

Marrying? Where had that thought come from?

Santiago exhaled sharply and made himself tie the ribbon on her necklace into a secure reef knot. Let unfastening it be her maid's problem.

'You are so lucky that you could travel,' she said.

'It did not feel so at the time,' he muttered.

'No? Why?'

He wanted to put his hands on her shoulders. To turn her to face him and kiss her. Take her in his arms, feel all that warmth and softness against his aching body, and kiss her until neither of them could remember their names.

Instead he let his hands drop and said, 'Because usually we were being chased.'

She half turned then. 'Chased?'

'Yes. Whatever scandal you think my father committed, what followed once he left England was even worse. I say I am from Chile, but I remember little of it. We moved constantly, all over the continent. Chasing one scheme after another. Always in debt, in trouble with the wrong person, always gambling and drinking and losing—'

'That sounds terrible,' she said.

'It wasn't so bad.' He laughed bitterly. 'That's a lie. It was.'

She turned fully then, and looked up at him with her eyes like the ocean tides. 'Would it help you to know I have never met my father?'

He stared at her. 'Never?'

'No. He left before I was born. Wellington—Wellesley, as he was—was very busy in India and my father...' Her gaze darted away for a moment, then came back. 'I think my father wanted an excuse to leave the woman he regretted marrying,' she said, lifting her chin defiantly.

'We have this in common,' Santiago whispered.

'He has barely been back to England since—once to claim the earldom after his father died, and once last year when Wellington returned home. He made no attempt to see me either time, and whenever I tried to find him I was rebuffed.'

Her eyelashes trembled. He wanted to take her in his arms for an entirely different reason now. To hug her close and tell her that such a father was not a man worth missing.

Not that such knowledge helped. He had told himself over and over that he owed his father nothing, that to stay in Sao Paulo and wait for him, to continue to follow him from country to country, to allow himself to be dragged down to his level would all be madness. That he owed nothing to the man who couldn't even remember his name.

That had not helped the guilt when he did, eventually, board a ship bound for Manila and left his father behind for good.

'But perhaps that is better,' she said.

'Better?' That the man had missed out on knowing his extraordinary daughter?

'Yes. Better than knowing him and being continually disappointed.'

'Being disappointed? In... him?' There was simply no way he could be disappointed in her.

Tiffany nodded. Her moonlit ringlets bounced.

Santiago shook his head. 'How do you— You are the only person I know who understands any of this.'

She smiled ruefully. 'I wish I did not.'

'And your mother?' he asked. From such a lack of information about her, he had to assume she had died.

Tiffany sucked in a sharp breath. 'We don't talk about her,' she said.

'But— Is she—?'

'I have no idea,' Tiffany said, and inhaled rather too raggedly for his liking. 'I stopped asking a long time ago. I assume she is still living but I know nothing else. I am told I cannot know. What use is that to anyone?'

'Tiffany…' He wanted to take her into his arms. She looked so lost and alone—abandoned by her mother and her father, and left in the care of a sister-in-law who clearly saw her as a burden.

I don't think you are a burden. I think you are extraordinary.

He watched her compose herself, patting at her hair and her cameo pendant, and bestowing upon him a bright smile that was almost convincing. 'Perhaps we understand each other better than we realise,' she said, and something tore within him.

Santiago shoved at his hair, but dammit, he was wearing a stupid hat. He took it off and ran his hand through his hair anyway.

'I am a duke! But I have no idea how to be.' The words spilled out of him. 'My father not only failed to prepare me for this, he *wanted* me to fail. He refused to tell me a thing that would be useful. He wanted to destroy his father's legacy by sending back a South American street rat to flail around and drag the family name down into the dirt.'

'You are not a street rat,' she said. 'You are a successful trader! How many ships do you own?'

'Thirty-one, but that is not the point—'

'Isn't it? I know I said trade isn't respected here but money is, and you appear to have made an awful lot of that.'

He put his hands on his hips, hat dangling from a finger. 'I thought talking about money was vulgar.'

'It is, but that's not my point.' She came closer and he couldn't help breathing her in again. 'Santiago, if you were a street rat and now you're a successful businessman, then you're clearly capable of making a success of yourself. Of improving yourself and becoming very impressive—' She broke off.

'You think I am impressive?'

In the darkness, he could see her white bosom rising and falling. Her eyes flashed with passion. *Say yes. Say you think I am impressive.*

'Yes,' she whispered.

It would be so easy to kiss her right now. Sweep her into his arms, plunder her mouth, drag her to the nearest bench and have his wicked way with her. He wanted to, so badly it made him a little insane.

'*Mi amor,*' he breathed. He had never called anyone that before. 'Tiffany!'

Both their heads whipped around at the loud whisper.

'Tiffany! Your family is looking for you!'

Tiffany stepped back from him hurriedly, and ran her hands over her hair, her dress, her bosom, quite as if they had been kissing and she had to check she was in order.

He nearly stepped after her. Nearly.

'Madhu?' she called, and that woman stepped through the gap in the hedge.

She took them both in with a glance, nodded briskly, and said, 'Come. You have been with me all evening. Good evening, Your Grace.'

She held out her arm for Tiffany to take, and she did, but not before she'd turned back to Santiago and said, 'Good evening,

Your Grace. I hope to see you at our house party.' She pressed something into his hand.

It was her necklace.

And then she was gone, taking the witch light with her, and he was alone in the darkness.

CHAPTER 12

*I*n the tower, a woman cried. She was made of silver and tears, tears that flooded an ocean and swelled into tentacled arms—

Tiffany awoke with a gasp, and fought the tentacles that turned out to be simply bedsheets, damp with sweat and twisted around her. Heart pounding, she stared wildly around the unfamiliar room.

Right. She was at Dyrehaven, and this was the room she'd been assigned for the house party. Before this she had been preparing for her come-out from the nursery, because Elinor didn't see the point in preparing a separate room for her before they left for London.

It wasn't the best room in the house, because those were for the guests. Tiffany's room overlooked the stables, and had an awkward narrow passageway from the main landing. Still, it was private, and that was the main thing.

She sat up in bed, reached for the candle and then remembered she didn't need to. She shaped her hand around the air the way Aunt Esme had told her to, wished for light, and a small, pale light appeared.

She had learned how to douse them too, now. On the same day Aunt Esme told her she wouldn't be coming to Dyrehaven.

'I'm afraid I have a previous engagement,' she said, as Tiffany perfected the finding spell she'd been learning. 'In Kent, of all places.' She looked harassed, and Tiffany decided not to argue.

'I will miss you,' she said. 'Elinor has only invited people whose sons she thinks I could marry. There are hardly any young ladies at all.'

'But there is a duke?' said Esme, a knowing smile on her lips.

Had Madhu told her? When Tiffany thought about that evening at Vauxhall—about how Santiago had looked at her like he was about to ravish her, and *she'd wanted him to*—she realised how close they'd come to ruin. If they'd been found like that, alone and unwatched, by her family, they'd be forced to marry. And Tiffany knew that she never wanted to marry.

She just ... really looked forward to seeing Santiago when he arrived.

Once dressed she slipped down the back stairs with Morris and darted away towards the village. Elinor had always considered it inappropriate for Tiffany to spend time playing with the village children, but she hadn't been able to keep an eye on her all day, and so when Tiffany befriended the boot boy there had been nothing her sister-in-law could do about it.

Henry had always intended to become a footman, and he'd just been accepted as an under-footman when Bonaparte escaped from Elba and the call to arms had raced around the country. Tiffany's childhood friend had gone off to fight, and she intended to see if there was word of him. His sister had married fairly recently, she thought, and by now there might be children. It would be entirely appropriate to call upon them.

Besides, Elinor's preparations for the guests were absolutely driving her insane.

The village of Churlish Green was an easy walk from Dyrehaven, and a pretty one too. It ran down an ancient sunken lane alongside the brook and skirted a hill, upon which stood the old ruins of what Tiffany had been told by her governess was once a monastery. Skeletal and forbidding, the windowless arches rose above the treetops and were sometimes cut off if the brook flooded.

She crossed the ancient stone bridge over the brook and made her way along the pretty village street lined with half-timbered cottages and shops.

Tiffany greeted the grocer and the butcher and the postmistress, and made her way to Ivy Cottage. It was set back a little from the road, with a long garden Tiffany recalled as always full of flowers. Now it was full of weeds, and the whole cottage had a sad, neglected look about it. A handcart lay in the long grass, one wheel broken.

Henry's father had died many years ago, and his mother in the last few years, after which Henry's sister had married. Tiffany had not seen her since; every attempt to visit had been curtailed by Elinor. She frowned as she reached the front door; the paint was peeling and the wood splintered as if it had been kicked.

'Hello? It's Lady Tiffany. I came hoping to see Miss Proudbody, as was? Amy?'

The woman who eventually opened the door a sliver was not, at first glance, the Amy Proudbody Tiffany remembered. She had been a healthy young lady with pink cheeks and round hips. The woman before her now looked as if she had hardly eaten all week, her hair straggling from its cap, a crying baby at her hip.

'It's Cotton now,' she said, her tone colourless. 'You'll have to excuse me, my lady. We're not fit for visitors.'

'Miss— Mrs Cotton! What happened?' Tiffany thought she saw bruises on the woman's arms.

Amy Cotton shrugged tiredly. 'I got married, my lady. If you're here asking after Henry, I had a letter Tuesday last. He says the food's terrible, but he's all right.'

Another baby screamed inside the house.

'If you'll excuse me, my lady,' said Mrs Cotton, and wedged the door shut.

Tiffany stared at the peeling paint for a moment. Then she nodded and walked back through the unweeded garden to the main street.

'That is not a happy house,' she said.

'No, my lady,' Morris whispered.

'We should do something.' Why hadn't Elinor done something? As the lady of the house, it was her duty to take care of the residents of the village.

'What, my lady?'

As a witch, you will encounter a great many people like this. Hadn't Madhu said it was their duty to help people? Surely there must be a way.

She made her way slowly back along the high street, and after a moment she turned into Mr Sandyman's haberdashery shop. His wife was behind the counter, a cheerful woman with a riot of curly hair.

'Lady Tiffany! How well you look. London must suit you!'

Tiffany thanked her for the compliment, and wondered how to broach the next subject. Mrs Sandyman had always been a terrible gossip.

'I came to hear if there was any news of Henry Proudbody,' she said, and Mrs Sandyman's face darkened at the mention. 'His sister says he has sent a letter.'

'Yes, and well he seems to be doing. At least someone in the family is.'

And that was all it took. Within five minutes, Tiffany had the story of how Henry's sister had married the first man to ask, shortly after her mother had died, to try to keep house and home together. Only he was a rotter and a wastrel, Mrs Sandyman confided. Got a couple of brats on her and spent every penny she made taking in laundry on cheap gin. Probably already at the tavern now. Cast out poor Henry, who might not have followed the drum had he not been beaten by his brother-in-law and looking for a way to escape.

'He beat Henry?' Sweet Henry, who had run and played with her among the ruins?

'I believe so,' said Mrs Sandyman darkly. 'Everybody knows he beats her. But she will not report him or leave him, on account of the children.'

'There must be something we can do,' said Tiffany.

Mrs Sandyman shrugged. 'I remember my father telling me of the rough music when a man behaved as he has.'

'Rough music?'

'Aye. The skimmington ride, he called it. Pots and pans outside his house, dragged through the streets and shamed. Burned in effigy. That man was so ashamed he left and was never seen again,' she said in satisfaction.

'Well, that sounds effective,' Tiffany said.

'Aye. But we live in different times now, my lady.'

'More's the pity,' muttered Tiffany.

Mrs Sandyman rolled her eyes and lowered her voice as customers came in. 'I know it is un-Christian of me, but I pray his next drink of gin will have him in a ditch.'

'From your mouth to God's ears,' murmured Tiffany, and took her leave.

All the way back to the house she fumed. How dare such a brute beat Henry's sweet sister? And Henry himself! The poor boy might go off to war and never come back, and it would all be the fault of this Mr Cotton.

Aunt Esme thought she needed to work on threatening people, did she?

The sky darkened as she walked, as if matching her mood.

'My lady? We really must get back before the heavens open,' said Morris, and Tiffany wondered how going home to greet guests could ever be important right now. But she went back to the house, and allowed herself to be washed and dressed as she tried to work out what Aunt Esme would do.

The first guests arrived after luncheon, all of them dashing into the house to avoid the drizzle that had begun to fall. Lady Greensword, of course, with her two insufferable nephews. Immediately upon arrival, they started comparing Dyrehaven to the classical palaces they had seen in Italy.

Santiago never goes on about his travels like that. Tiffany suddenly realised she was thinking of him as Santiago again, and not the Duke. She should stop that, or she might slip up and then Elinor would have them down the aisle before she could blink.

And she didn't want to marry him. She didn't want to marry anyone. She wanted to be an independent woman, like Aunt Esme. Once the Season was over, perhaps she could see what funds had been settled on her for her dowry and how she might access them for herself.

The thought cheered her through the rest of the arrivals, nearly all of them couples with sons or nephews, or single gentlemen of Cornforth's acquaintance. Tiffany was quite sure Elinor's dinner table would be unbalanced, especially as Esme was not in attendance, but she had thought of that and invited Mrs Belmont with her two plain, shy daughters. No competition at all for Tiffany—at least, no competition if Tiffany actually wanted to find a husband. Which she didn't.

She was in the saloon—Elinor preferring this appellation to the unpatriotically French-sounding salon—being talked at by the Greensword nephews when something towards the back of the house drew her attention.

Tiffany, who had a view of the front drive from here, hadn't seen any carriages or riders coming along the drive. Not that she'd been looking out for the Duke. Not at all.

But she felt him coming.

Over the fields, it seemed. The pendant she'd tucked into his hand on a whim she couldn't explain—he was carrying it. She could feel it coming closer.

There were voices in the hall. The saloon fell quiet as people pretended they weren't listening. And then Underhill, the butler, was announcing, 'His Grace the Duke of St James.'

The room fell quite silent as Santiago strode in, and stood framed in the doorway. One of the Greensword nephews murmured something, but Tiffany didn't hear him.

The reason she hadn't seen his carriage arrive was that he'd evidently ridden here, and not just from the nearest coaching inn but all the way from London. His boots were coated in mud, his breeches spattered with the same, and the tails of his many-caped greatcoat were heavy with rain. As he removed his hat, he pushed his other hand through his hair. Sweat and dirt mingled on his face. His neckcloth was so loose he might as well have not been wearing it.

He was filthy. He was sodden. He was terribly inappropriately dressed.

Tiffany suddenly, shockingly, wanted to lick his neck.

'My apologies for the hour,' he said into the silence. 'There was an accident at the wharf. I could not leave when I had planned.'

'Was anyone hurt?' Tiffany asked, searching him for signs of injury. But he looked well. He looked better than well.

The butler looked ready to escort him away, but Santiago's gaze found Tiffany. Those dark, melting chocolate eyes met hers for a second that stretched out into hours. 'One man was hurt,' he said. 'I left him in good care.'

She nodded, unable to speak. Her knees felt weak. Her bosom was heaving all of its own accord.

'Your Grace?' murmured Underhill, and Santiago nodded and left.

Immediately the noise level of the room rose. Tiffany could hear the shocked whispers.

'I say,' said one of the Greensword nephews. 'If he wasn't a duke, he wouldn't have got away with that.'

'Filthy as a labourer,' agreed the other.

'Wouldn't look out of place digging a ditch,' said the first, and Tiffany got lost for a moment in a fantasy of Santiago in shirt-sleeves, damp linen clinging as it had when she first saw him, muscles straining. Like a labourer. A common, filthy labourer.

'If you will excuse me,' she murmured, and made her way to the sideboard, wishing like hell she could pour herself a brandy. She had to keep her wits about her or all the paintings in the room would come to life, and that would be a disaster because they were mostly of disapproving ancestors.

'What a dreadful apparition,' Lady Greensword said nearby, making Tiffany's heart clutch. 'I had heard he was raised *abroad*.' She whispered the last word as if it was a synonym for a circle of hell. 'But one had assumed breeding would come to the fore!'

'And that he would magically know how to behave?' Tiffany found herself saying. 'That simply because his grandfather was a duke, he would know the correct dress for arriving at a house party?'

'Well … I mean …'

'He must have ridden pell mell to get here,' Tiffany said. 'And all because he would not leave an injured man at the wharf.'

'I'm sure he has *employees*,' said Lady Greensword, and apparently that was a dirty word too.

'And should a man of breeding leave such a thing to his employees? Is it not the responsibility of a duke to take care of those under him—which is practically everybody? What kind of man would see another injured and simply say, "Well, got to be off, I have a house party to attend!" He—'

'Theophania,' said Elinor, quietly and furiously, and Tiffany realised her voice had been raised.

'I believe it may be time to dress for dinner,' said Elinor frostily, and Tiffany knew she'd be punished for this.

~

DYREHAVEN, the country seat of the Earl of Chalkdown, currently occupied by his son and family, was a house approximately the size of a small country.

Santiago had expected a large house. He had seen the royal palaces in London, and of course his grandfather's house took up one whole side of Grosvenor Square. But out here, barely thirty miles from London in leafy Hertfordshire, there was room for a lot more.

A *lot* more.

The thought of what awaited him at Castle Aymers was genuinely terrifying.

He had been given a suite of rooms that included a sitting room and bathroom, of all things, with a tub big enough to almost lie in.

'It would take every servant in the place to fill that,' he said in wonder. There were stacks of linen towels and a variety of scented soaps. It was barely comprehensible for a man who had spent most of his life either in filthy streets or on filthy ships, where cleanliness tended to come with saltwater.

'Only a few, sir, and those quite well practised, I should imagine,' said Robinson, who had been instructed quite firmly that too much Your Gracing would not be kindly met. 'I can ring for them if you would like?'

'Good God, no. The basin and ewer will be perfectly fine.' He strode in that direction, then paused, sniffed himself, and said, 'Won't it?'

'Yes, sir. I have brought your own soap and cologne.'

'I have my own soap?' said Santiago, who had been subjected to a visit by a perfumer a few weeks ago, after which he was presented with his own signature scent. It smelled … fine, he supposed. Quite nice. But what about it was worth the extortionate fee, he had no idea.

'Yes, sir. One never knows what one will find. Will it be straight into evening clothes, sir? I believe I heard the bell just now.'

Santiago allowed Robinson to go on setting out his things, fussing over waistcoats and neckcloths, while he washed. The distance hadn't looked too far when he'd set out, but his backside was protesting the hours spent on horseback.

Still, at least Robinson had arrived safely, having set out at the crack of dawn with the luggage in order to make sure every ducal need was catered for. He would surely have fretted if he'd had to wait for Santiago to see to the poor fellow who had been bitten by something hidden in the depths of a water barrel.

He'd rushed the man straight to Esme's house, watching his hand turn purple and his lips turn blue, and panicked when Miss Gwen answered the door and said everyone else was away.

'But I knows what treats them nasty beasty bites, you see if I don't.'

She'd given the docker some violently green liquid to drink, and almost immediately his colour had begun to return.

'What bit him?' she asked. 'Some sea beasty?'

Santiago shrugged, his heart hammering. 'I don't know. When we emptied the barrel there was nothing but a few dead bugs.'

Gwen made a face. 'I don't know no bug turns a man like that,' she said.

'You should see the spiders we have in South America,' Santiago told her.

'Them think me hopeless, you know,' Gwen said, patting the hapless docker's hand. 'But I knows what's what. You've just enough time so you can change for dinner,' she added. 'The duchess looks resplendent in blue.'

'Duchess?' said Santiago. 'I wasn't aware of a duchess attending.'

Gwen blinked. 'What? No. Off you go and enjoy yourself. Tell Billy we've ham for dinner.'

And now here he was, washed and perfumed and dressed in his finest, descending the grand staircase and following a couple of young bucks into a drawing room.

In his pocket was Tiffany's necklace, the one she'd inexplicably handed him at Vauxhall. What did she mean by it? Was it a token of her affection? Was there a deeper meaning to it? Had she cast a spell on him?

The drawing room, like the rest of the house, was blandly decorated. He detected the hand of his hostess in this; Lady Cornforth seemed allergic to bright colours or patterns. The whole house looked like someone had forgotten to paint most of it.

'What an elegant room,' he remarked to her, after apologising again for his earlier appearance.

Tiffany didn't seem to mind it, he remembered. She had gazed at him as if he'd been made of chocolate. It had taken all of his composure to leave the room and not rush over and yank her into his filthy, sweaty arms.

He looked around for her as Lady Cornforth prattled on, but she was nowhere to be seen. After a few polite minutes, he asked, 'And where is the delightful Lady Tiffany?'

'Alas,' said Lady Cornforth. 'She has a headache. Such a shame. I am sure she will join us tomorrow.'

He frowned. 'She seemed perfectly well this afternoon.'

Elinor's smile was tight. 'Yes, well, it came on suddenly. Tomorrow I am sure she will be right as, well, rain.' She gestured with a small laugh to the drizzle that kept falling.

Santiago smiled politely, and asked her to introduce him to people, which she was only too happy to do. The company did not seem overly enthused by his presence, and he realised that nearly everyone here was a young man looking to marry, or the parent of such. Elinor was clearly desperate to get Tiffany married off.

At dinner, he was seated between a Lady Greensword, who was forthright and incorrect about nearly everything, and a Miss Belmont who was so shy and nervous she barely ate anything and spoke only in an inaudible whisper.

One of the young bucks at the table started droning on about his travels, and Santiago realised half the table was enraptured. Mostly the female half. What had Tiffany said, that first night, that ladies didn't travel?

Apart from Tiffany's mother, who from all he could gather had gone abroad shortly after her child was born, and never returned. And for this, she had been vilified. Nobody spoke of her. Barely a line in the Peerage.

There were not even any portraits. He had asked Cornforth, who had simply looked awkward and mumbled something about her not having been here long enough.

He wondered if Tiffany even knew what she looked like.

'Truly,' one of the Greensword nephews was droning on. 'The most spectacular sight. The awe of the ancient world.'

'It is so exciting to hear of your travels, my dear,' said Lady Greensword indulgently. To Santiago, she said, 'Jeremy has travelled quite extensively. Venice, Naples, Rome—'

'So, Italy?' said Santiago.

'—Florence ... why ... yes, but also... Dear, did you not travel to ... er, Flanders, was it?'

The nephew in question looked over at her. 'What? Oh. Yes. Ghent, Bruges. Lovely, lovely. But nothing compares to Italy. I have never been somewhere so ... remote. So ... so very different from everything we have here.'

Santiago thought about the mist over the Yangtze river, the gleaming domes of the Taj Mahal, the man-eating lizards of the South Pacific. 'What makes it so very different?' he asked.

'Oh!' Clearly delighted to have an audience, and quite neglecting the lady to his left, Jeremy launched into an account of the food—so spicy!—and the architecture—so ancient!—and the culture—so very, very foreign!

Eventually, after a monologue explaining how he overcame seasickness in the Venice Lagoon, he slowed enough for his brother to get a word in edgeways.

'We did think of visiting Spain, of course, but it was so frightfully dangerous at the time. We were risking enough, travelling as we did.'

Around the table, murmurs went up about their bravery in having travelled whilst Bonaparte was still at large.

'But of course, you could tell us about Spain, Your Grace,' said Lady Greensword, and Santiago really really wished Tiffany was here so he could see her face at that comment.

'I am afraid I have not had the privilege of travelling there,' he said.

'But—' she said, and began to go a little pink. 'But you are Spa — Are you not Spa—?'

'I was born in Chile, my lady,' said Santiago patiently. 'Which is currently under Spanish rule, although the situation may have changed lately. I have not been there for many years.' Not since they were chased away by his father's debtors, and gone to Argentina, then Peru, then Brazil…

'Oh. So it's like Spain, then?'

He shrugged and swirled his wine in its glass. 'I have no idea. People speak Spanish, yes. But they also speak Mapuche and other local languages.'

'Do you speak … um, that?' asked the Belmont sister sitting opposite him.

'A little. My mother was fluent.'

'I had heard she was a Mayan princess!' broke in a man further down the table.

'No, they are from Mexico. I did travel there, but—'

'What's the other one? The one with all the gold?'

'Ah, you mean the Aztecs. Actually, she is descended from el Conde de Moctezuma de Tultengo, who is said to be a descendant of Moctezuma—the great ruler of the Aztec Empire,' he added, when they all looked at him blankly.

'So she's an Aztec princess!' breathed one of the Belmont sisters.

'If you like,' he said hopelessly. They might as well enjoy their fantasies.

'Where is she now? Is she coming to England?'

'I doubt it,' said Santiago. 'She entered a convent when I was eight.'

That silenced the chatter. Sensing some awkward questions about how and when his mother had converted to Anglicanism and then back to Catholicism again to enter the convent, he changed the subject. 'At which time I began travelling more extensively. I spent many years travelling the Pacific.'

'The Pacific?'

That turned out to be a mistake. He spent the rest of dinner regaling them with tales of his travels, while the Greensword nephews and their aunt became increasingly sullen. The stories were cleaned up, of course. Fewer cholera-ridden slums and druglords with machetes, and more beautiful islands and exotic foods.

He told the stories as if he was telling them to Tiffany, but most of his jokes fell flat.

After dinner, when the table was cleared and the ladies excused themselves, he knew he was supposed to stay for cigars and port with the gentlemen. But he noticed the glance that went between Lord and Lady Cornforth as she left the room, and he knew something was up.

Tiffany didn't have a headache. Tiffany was being confined to her room for some other reason, and he didn't think it had anything to do with her health.

His hand absently patted his pocket, where he slightly fancied her necklace was still warm from her skin.

He excused himself after knocking back one small, quick glass of port. The cigars on offer were flavourless things, so he left his in the ashtray and made vague mentions of having left something in his room.

Halfway up the grand staircase he heard voices. Voices that were somehow raised and hushed all at the same time. Lady Cornforth, berating someone.

'Well, if she's not going to even open the door then she can go to bed with no supper.' Someone else murmured, another female voice. 'No, Morris. You will not leave it outside the door. And you will tell the kitchen not to send anything up, and if she ventures down, to give her nothing. Do you understand me? If she is going to behave like a child, then she can be treated like one. You will leave her until the morning.'

Footsteps hurried down towards him and he ran downstairs too, grateful for once that his evening slippers were thin-soled and didn't clomp about like a pair of boots would. He ducked around the side of the staircase, and waited until Lady Cornforth had hurried past in the direction of the drawing room.

Well, that was pretty unequivocal. He hurried up the stairs and caught a maid heading towards the other end of the corridor, where presumably the servants' stair was. She looked vaguely familiar, probably from the time he'd carried Tiffany home.

'Excuse me,' he said softly, and she turned to bob a curtsey and nearly dropped her tray.

'Your Grace!'

'Yes,' he said impatiently. 'You are Lady Tiffany's maid, yes? Morris?' When she nodded, he continued, 'Is she unwell?'

'Er,' said Morris, who was clearly a terrible liar. 'Yes?'

'That is very sad to hear. Will she come down this evening?'

'I … er, I don't think so, Your Grace.'

'Oh dear. Perhaps you should leave that for her, in case she is hungry later?'

Morris looked terrified. She had just been told one thing by her uncompromising mistress, and now here he was telling her another.

'Er…'

'Look.' He smiled at her, the smile that had worked on everyone but the pirate queen of the South China Seas, and said, 'Perhaps I could speak with her? It would lay my mind at rest. I have travelled all this way to see Lady Tiffany…' he said, and let the implication hang there.

What are you doing? he screamed at himself. *Implying that you've come all this way to … ask for her hand? Once Morris gets that into her head, she'll tell all the other servants and then everyone will know!*

But he really did want to speak with her. And he had no way of knowing which was her chamber.

'If you accompany me then there can be no impropriety,' he added, and Morris looked very torn.

He kept smiling.

'Well, I suppose...' she said, and he smiled wider.

She led him towards what he thought was the side of the house, where the windows probably looked out onto the stables, and indicated a door quite firmly closed.

The necklace in his pocket was getting warmer. He wasn't imagining it.

'She has locked it,' Morris whispered.

Santiago nodded and tapped at it gently. 'Lady Tiffany?' He hesitated, then for the benefit of the maid, added an endearment. '*Mi amor*, are you all right?'

No answer.

'Tiffany? Can you hear me?'

'Perhaps she's asleep, sir,' said Morris, and he nodded.

'Thank you, Morris. I will perhaps see her tomorrow.'

He watched her go, and then he knocked harder on the door, knelt down and put his lips to the keyhole. 'Tiffany, open the door right now, before I break it down. You know I am capable.'

Nothing. She wasn't in there, and probably hadn't been for hours. Overlooked the stables, eh? Well, then.

It didn't take him long to escape the house by means of the servants' stair—startling a few footmen cadging a smoke as he did —and make his way around to the side of the house. The service wing was here, abutting the main house and shielded from the front and back lawns by a high hedge. This time of night, it blazed with light and activity as the servants cleared up after dinner, but everyone was inside, away from the rain.

If anyone saw or heard him scale the walls and climb over the roofs they didn't challenge him. This sort of thing probably happened all the time at house parties anyway. He'd noticed at least one couple at dinner eyeing each other up—and they were both married to other people.

Yes—there was an open window, approximately the distance from the front of the house he'd calculated. The room within was dark, but the pendant in his pocket was warm. He carefully crept across the slick, wet kitchen roof to the ledge beneath Tiffany's window, and took a deep breath.

'Tiffany?'

No response. She almost certainly wasn't in there. But just in case—

'Tiffany, it's me. Santiago. Are you all right? Answer me.'

Nothing.

'I'm going to come in now,' he warned, and raised his head to look inside the room.

There was a shape in the bed. He called again, but it didn't move, and when he finally swung into the room and crept closer, he saw that it was a bundle of clothes shoved into the approximate shape of a person under the covers.

He sighed. She had run away—but where? Where could she go from here? She had to know it wasn't safe for her to be on her own at night, even if this was the estate she'd grown up on and she knew it and the village nearby like the back of her hand...

He crossed to the dressing table, where a candle stood half burnt, and lit it to see better by. The room was neat, with an ugly mauve dress hung up as if to be changed into for dinner. But the dressing table itself was what intrigued him.

Written on a piece of paper was a name. MR COTTON, HUSBAND OF AMY COTTON NÉE PROUDBODY, OF IVY COTTAGE, CHURLISH GREEN. That was the village he'd ridden through on his way here. Beside it was a flower, a weed really, already withered and half dead. And beside that a single earring, a pale stone he couldn't identify in the gloom. When he brought the candle closer to them, it flared.

It flared green.

A spell. She had done some kind of spell on this Mr Cotton, and now... What, she had gone to find him? Why? Who was he?

The necklace in his pocket was warmer than before. He fished it out, afraid it might burn him, and stared at it. It was made of shell, a white cameo of an unknown woman on a pale blue background, strung from a green ribbon, and it was very faintly glowing.

Santiago had seen many strange things in his life, but a green candle and a glowing necklace were stranger than the rest put together.

'Where are you?' he whispered, and the cameo woman turned her head slightly to the left. He nearly dropped it. 'Tiffany?'

He let the pendant drop to the full length of its ribbon, and it strained, ever so slightly, towards the far wall of the room. Towards the back of the house. Towards the village.

'*Mierda*,' he muttered.

CHAPTER 13

*T*he rough music, the skimmington ride. Pots and pans and burning in effigy. Tiffany wasn't sure she could quite manage dragging anyone through the street, but she could very well do the rest.

She was righteous in her anger as she marched towards the village, which was just as well as she hadn't realised quite how dark it would be, or how frightened she would be in the hollow lane. She daren't conjure a witch light in case someone should see it, and she wasn't completely sure she could put it out again. She had put on her stoutest boots and plainest dress, and a dark cloak covered her satchel of supplies, but the rain had soaked her in minutes, and it only seemed to be getting harder.

Aunt Esme had said a finding spell worked best with a crystal or semi-precious stone of some kind. She had used a topaz earring, which now glowed warmly in her palm. There was a weed she had pulled from Mrs Cotton's garden as she passed by earlier. His name she didn't know, but she had described him as accurately as possible when she did the ritual. And now it had led her here, to the tavern, which was full of light and noise and merriment.

She had filched a box of chalks from the nursery, and used it to draw on the stones of the wall by the brook what she had planned after Elinor shut her in her room. A row of pots and pans, held together by string. A string she tied to the gatepost of Ivy Cottage—which stood dark and forlorn, a baby crying within.

Next she drew fearsome shapes in the dirt with a stick— monsters and ghouls with drooling fangs and huge claws. And finally, an effigy—although the only one she'd ever seen was Guy Fawkes, burnt on the village common in November, so she drew something like that, on a stake, with flames coming out of it, and then she waited.

And waited.

A couple of men left the tavern, staggering slightly, and went off in the opposite direction from Ivy Cottage. Tiffany really wished she'd got Morris to bring her up some food. She was cold out here, and being hungry only made it worse. And, she realised, while she had the earring pointing her towards the tavern, she had no idea what this Mr Cotton looked like.

Oh dear, had all this been terribly foolish?

She was about to turn for home when the door opened, and the earring in her hand pulsed hotly. A figure, silhouetted in the dark, portly and stumbling.

'Go home and sober up, Jeb Cotton,' called a voice from within.

He shouted something back into the tavern that Tiffany was sure would make even Nora blush, and belched loudly.

Tiffany squared her shoulders, and reached down to pick up the drawn piece of string from the ground. She wrapped it around her hand and yanked, and the pots and pans she'd drawn jangled noisily.

'What the bloody hell?' slurred Jeb Cotton.

She jangled them again, and then gestured to the ghouls and monsters. They rose from the dirt, not alive but flickering and pulsing in the rain. They were eerie, and even though Tiffany knew they weren't real and would disappear in an hour or two, they still made her shiver.

Now came a bit of a gamble. 'Monsters I have drawn, make to wail and groan,' she whispered, and a dreadful moaning wail rose from them.

'What? Who's there?' shouted Jeb Cotton. Behind him, people were starting to come to the tavern door. They stood around, looking confused.

'Jeb Cotton!' Tiffany shouted, trying to deepen her voice.

'Aye?'

'Wife beater!'

'I bloody never,' he protested, and stumbled in the road.

'You bloody do, Jeb Cotton,' said one of the men standing in the tavern doorway.

'Drunkard!'

'That one's right enough,' laughed another man.

'You neglect your wife and home! You spend all your coin on gin! Your wife starves while you grow fat!'

There was a general muttering of assent among the other men. Jeb stumbled closer, and Tiffany held her nerve.

'Who are you?' he shouted. 'This is all lies! Lies!'

'Do not come any closer,' Tiffany warned, panicking a little and waving a glamour over her face to make herself unnoticeable. She yanked on the string again, and the pots jangled.

'Yeah? Or what? You're a girl,' he sneered, 'and I know what to do with girls—'

She gestured the effigy into life, and up it blazed, sudden and blinding in the wet, dark night.

Jeb swore and stumbled backwards, losing his footing and sprawling in the mud.

The crowd at the tavern door had spilled out by now, and among the gasps and cries of fear, Tiffany heard someone say incredulously, 'It's the rough music. It's a skimmington ride.'

'This is the roughest of rough music, Jeb Cotton,' Tiffany intoned. 'It is a warning. You will cease your ill treatment of your wife. You will cease drinking. You will work hard and care for your family.'

'I will, I will!' gibbered Cotton.

'You never have before,' said one of the men from the tavern. They were beginning to move closer now.

'Aye, we've all told you!'

'That good woman will end up in the poor house because of you,' said another.

'And poor Henry run out of town to be shot at by the French!'

They had begun to pick up her pots and pans now, and Tiffany shrank further back into the shadows as the men began banging them together, making a rough music of their own. The flickering light from the effigy made the puddles dance.

'This is witchcraft!' Jeb spluttered, gazing up at the misshapen effigy and the wailing shadows.

'No, this is justice,' said one of the men.

Lights were beginning to show in windows, and doors were beginning to open. Out came more than one villager—people Tiffany had known for years—banging their own pots and pans together and advancing on Jeb Cotton as he lay sprawled in the mud.

Tiffany glanced up at Ivy Cottage. It remained dark, but she thought she saw a pale face at one window.

She made herself unseen, and crept that way while the villagers advanced on the terrified Jeb. Flitting down the weed-choked path, she tapped on the door.

'Open it,' she hissed. 'I'm a friend.'

But the door stayed closed, and barred from within. Tiffany

took from her satchel an envelope that contained a banknote and Aunt Esme's address in London, and slid it under the door.

When she turned to go back to the street, her path was blocked. By Jeb Cotton.

'You!' he gasped. 'Who are you?'

Tiffany looked into his face, lit by the flickering flames of the effigy, as the crowd closed in behind him. He was puffy and red-nosed, his breath stank—and not just his breath. She was sure if she had more light she'd see a wet stain on his trousers that had nothing to do with the rain.

'Do you beat your wife?' she demanded. 'Answer me!'

'I— I— Only when she deserves it!'

'If you are not honest with me, Jeb Cotton, I will—'

He gibbered and sank to his knees. Maybe that had been a bit too much.

'I'm sorry! I'm sorry! Them brats keep wailing and she— I— it makes me feel like a big man, I'm sorry, please don't hurt me!'

Tiffany had never tried to make herself look fearsome before, but whatever her features contorted into, it terrified Jeb Cotton, who sobbed and curled into a ball.

'You will never darken this door again if you know what's good for you,' she snarled. 'You do not deserve Amy Proudbody. You'll sleep in a ditch until you can become a better man!'

How's that *for a threat?*

Tiffany drew herself up and strode past him, out of the cottage gate, and all the villagers drew back from her in terror. In the darkness, the only light came from the burning effigy, a horrible misshapen lump with its face on fire. The shadow ghouls still wailed and groaned.

'Make him feel ashamed,' she said. 'Don't hurt him, but make him feel shame.'

She turned to walk out of the village, and the crowd parted as if afraid she would curse them next.

'Oh,' she said, slightly drunk on this new power. 'And if any other man behaves like this with his wife, or any other woman, I will be back to mete out the same justice.'

And she strode away, victory coursing through her.

The power was immense. She had made those ghouls speak! Well, moan. She had incited a group of timid villagers into publicly shaming one of their own. She had strode—stridden— she had walked with purpose, just like Aunt Esme did, and they had been terrified of her! She had made a threat surely even Nora would be impressed by!

She had helped Henry's sister.

The elation carried her out of the village and up the monastery hill. She didn't know why, but for some reason she needed to be up high, closer to the moon, to celebrate.

The ground was wet and muddy beneath her feet. Tiffany curved her hand in the air to conjure a witch light, concentrating on forming the white ball of light, and didn't see the tree root until it had already tripped her.

She fell, legs tangling in her skirts, and tumbled down the muddy, slippery hill, hands grabbing at nothing until darkness closed over her.

SANTIAGO HADN'T BROUGHT A HORSE, because his was exhausted and he really didn't need anyone asking questions about why he was borrowing one so late at night. But he had taken a lantern from the stables, and slipped back to his room for his cloak and boots.

The rain was really coming down now. What if he'd got this all wrong and Tiffany was tucked up somewhere nice and warm, perhaps simply in another bedroom where Elinor couldn't find her? Perhaps she was just visiting a friend.

Late at night. In a rainstorm. Via a window out of a locked room.

'Tiffany?' he called desperately. 'Tiffany?'

There was no answer. If it hadn't been for the pendant in his hand, straining to his left, he'd never have even noticed the little bobbing white light between the trees.

Like the one she'd conjured at Vauxhall, just before she'd given him this necklace. It had to be her.

'Tiffany!'

There was a hill here, ringed with tall trees and topped by the ruins of some ancient building. He crossed a drainage ditch that was already sloshing with water, and began climbing the hill. The will o'the wisp light bobbed around aimlessly, illuminating nothing, but the pendant in his hand grew warmer and strained towards the far side of the small hill.

He could hear running water now. The stream that ran through the village and along the edge of the Dyrehaven lands had clearly routed itself around one side of the hillock. Trees grew along its edge in what he was sure was a very picturesque manner on a bright sunny day, but right now only added to the nightmarish lack of vision. The moon shone through the remains of a rose window, darkening the ground like a spider's web.

'Tiffany?'

Then he saw her, and his heart stopped.

She was a crumpled heap of fabric, and if it hadn't been for her pale, moonlight hair spilling from her cloak he'd have never seen her. The edge of her cloak and her skirts trailed in the swollen waters of a brook that looked as if it should not be running half as high as it was.

She lay very still.

'Tiffany!'

There wasn't enough light. Santiago skidded down the slope towards her, and grabbed her around the shoulders, tugging her bodily from the water. Her frame wasn't large but her clothes were heavy, and it felt like an age before he'd got her anywhere near like safety. He collapsed on the muddy ground, clutching her to him, his heart beating like a drum.

'Tiffany, wake up. Can you hear me? Wake up!'

His fingers were at her throat, feeling for a pulse, when she stirred. *Gracias a Dios.* 'Tiffany? Wake up, *mi amor.*' The endearment slipped out without him really realising it. 'Can you hear me?'

Her skin was like ice. She wore a sturdy cloak, boots and gloves, but they were all soaked through. As he rubbed vigorously at her shoulders, she began to shiver violently.

Shivering was good, he told himself. It was when a person stopped shivering you needed to worry.

She struggled a little in his arms, her eyes barely opening. 'No. Lemme go.'

'Tiffany, *mi amor*, I think you have fallen and you're hurt. I will take you back home, yes? You need to get warm and dry.'

She blinked at him a few times, and then those pale, clear eyes came into focus. 'Santiago?'

To hear his name on her lips! 'Yes, *mi amor*! I am here. I have you safe. We will get back to the house…'

Staggering and slipping in the mud, he tried to get to his feet, but Tiffany fought him.

'I can walk!' she cried, which was an extremely preposterous lie.

'*Mi amor*, no. Let me carry you. At the very least lean on me!'

She fought him stubbornly, bringing both of them back down into the mud more than once before she finally conceded that she needed his help. Weak, her limbs trembling, she clung to him in a manner he was sure he would have enjoyed if he hadn't just found her unconscious and about to drown in a ditch.

Don't think about that now. Just get her home.

He walked her along the increasingly high banks of the brook, its waters gushing and frothing, back towards the trees and the lane. But it seemed twice as long this way. Where was the lane? The water was coming halfway up the trees now.

Then he saw the moon shining through the rose window, and his heart sank.

'We have come around in a circle,' he said.

'What? No. The lane is here somewhere.'

'The stream has burst its banks. Look.' He pointed through the copse, where younger and weaker trees were already leaning precariously under the force of the water.

'No, it can't. We're a mile from home. Henry and I played here for years.'

'Henry?'

But she wasn't listening. 'We need to get up higher and then we can see,' she said, and that was a sensible idea, so he helped her back up the slope, into the shadow of the ruins.

But all they saw was that the stream had indeed burst its banks and roared along what had once been a peaceful channel between fields towards the monastery hill. And instead of diverting around one side of the hill, where a small wall had been set to reinforce its course, it had smashed down the stones and was flowing around them in a full circle. Where the two channels met and thundered off down the lane was a whirlpool of branches, mud and treacherous currents that was evident even in the moonlight.

'But this can't...' Tiffany said, gazing around in confusion and dismay. 'It's... I've never seen...' She shivered in her cloak. 'Perhaps I could draw a bridge...'

Santiago squinted at the raging water. It had filled the lane now, turning their path home into a muddy river. Even if they could cross the moat that surrounded them, the sunken lane would carry them off.

'To where?' he said. 'Can you draw all the way back to the house? The lane is…'

They both stared at the torrent.

'Here,' he said, drawing her beneath his cloak. 'This might keep you … er, keep you from getting any wetter.'

She tried to keep a decorous distance from him, but it was impossible.

'What do we do?' she asked, in a very small voice that had begun to tremble.

A few minutes ago she had been unconscious and nearly drowning. He couldn't let her freeze to death up here.

'We… Ah, we find shelter,' he said, glancing at the ruins without much hope.

'Shelter? The monastery hasn't had a roof for centuries!'

But she led him to the sturdiest-looking corner, where the rain wasn't battering them so hard, and Santiago wondered if his cloak could keep them from getting any wetter. And if that would be enough when she was already soaked through.

But Tiffany was looking at the walls of the ruined monastery with a calculating expression, and fiddling in the satchel she had slung across her body, under her cloak.

'Shelter,' she muttered. Her gaze strayed to the rough stone walls. 'Santiago, you have travelled the world. Have you ever had to build a shelter in an emergency? Like… Like the fellow in the Daniel Defoe book?'

He had no idea what book she meant, but he had seen huts made out of everything from palm leaves to slabs of ice.

'Yes, but what do we have? You can't draw us a shelter.'

'No, but I can draw us materials. What do we need?'

'Well,' he said, looking at the stone corner they found themselves in, 'I suppose … some lengths of wood, strong branches or trunks, and … some smaller ones to cross them, and … something to make thatch from? But you can't—'

Tiffany took a deep breath, rainwater dripping down her face, and drew a packet of coloured chalks from her satchel. She turned to face the nearest wall and pushed her wet hair back from her face.

In the moonlight, she seemed made of liquid silver.

'Watch me,' she said.

And he did. For a few minutes he watched in astonishment as she drew sturdy trunks and branches growing out of the stone and loose lengths of wood—and then they came to life. What had been a chalk drawing on stone was suddenly a real piece of wood in his hand—albeit somewhat pastel-coloured, and smudged from the rain.

'Well?' she said, as he stared, dumbfounded, at her work. 'Build something!'

The rain and the mud were soon forgotten as he stacked and propped the wood to form walls, a roof, even a platform off the muddy ground. She drew thick branches of conifer that he used to cover the sloped roof, and to fill in the gaps at the front of the shelter.

She drew a fire pit to his directions, in front of the open entrance. Santiago was fairly sure she'd have drawn a brick chimney if he'd let her. Her eyes were bright and her cheeks pink with a little more than excitement.

She drew firewood. She drew kindling. She even drew a peg on the wall for his lantern.

When she knelt to draw a blanket, the chalk wobbled all over the wall.

'Are you all right?' he said, turning from lighting the fire.

'I am perfectly fine,' she said, and ten seconds later her eyes were closed.

~

For once, she didn't dream of the pale woman and the squid.

She awoke to warmth and security, and a sort of comfort she had never known before. It was a reassurance, as if everything was being taken care of, as if *she* was being taken care of. The remains of a dream, perhaps, gathered around her. She breathed in the scent of the fire—hmm, much more like woodsmoke than the usual coal—and of damp wool and leather, and of—

Of—

Cigars, and wine, and cologne, and something underneath it all, too. A scent she didn't recognise, but wanted to burrow her face into.

A scent that did *not* belong in her dream.

Something rough gently abraded her cheek. The mattress she lay upon rose and fell. It said, '*Mi amor?*'

She was being held in the arms of a man and he was almost entirely undressed.

Tiffany screamed.

'Tiffany, don't panic, it's me—'

'Get away from me! Take your hands off me! Unhand me, I say!'

Santiago had already raised his hands in surrender, but Tiffany was tangled up with him and too flustered to know what to do. He'd been holding her in his lap, his cloak wrapped around them both, and she caught herself in it as she scrambled backwards. Under her hands and knees the ground was rough, and only the flickering flames of a fire lit the room—

She stopped, panting, before she scrambled so fast she ended up in the fire. It burned cheerfully in the entrance of their little shelter, the one Santiago had made from the materials she'd created. A tiny room, not quite high enough to stand in, tucked into the corner of the monastery ruins.

Through the opening, she could see rain still falling. Everything else was darkness.

She forced herself to look back at him, kneeling there by the wall, hands raised.

'You were too cold,' he said carefully, eyeing her as if she was a wild animal. 'Your clothes were soaked through. I found you half in the stream, do you remember?'

Tiffany shuddered, and nodded. She'd thought that part had been a dream, too.

'You could not get warm if you were soaking wet. Wet is the enemy of warm.'

The cold wind blew around her bare calves. Her *bare* calves.

Dreading what she would see, Tiffany looked down at herself. She wore her shift, and nothing else.

'Oh no,' she whimpered. 'Oh no, no, no…'

Santiago still had his hands raised. 'I took your clothes off you because they were soaking wet,' he said, emphasising the words carefully. 'Only for that. I promise you—'

'I will be ruined,' she whispered numbly. No matter that she didn't want to get married. She would be an outcast. Women were sent to asylums for less. 'I am ruined.'

'No, you are not!' He seemed horrified at the suggestion. 'No impropriety occurred. I swear it to you on my own life. On Billy's life. Please, believe me, *mi amor*.'

Tiffany didn't know what '*mi amor*' meant, and she didn't want to. It sounded most improper. 'You were holding me!' she gasped. 'In a … in a very *improper* manner!' His body had been so warm, so firm, and the way he held her was so comforting…

'To warm you up! You were freezing! If I had not held you, you could have … you…'

To her shock, he looked as if he might be about to burst into tears.

'I have seen men die from the cold,' Santiago said, his dark eyes pleading with hers. 'I have seen them turn pale and cold, and stop shivering, and barely breathe. I have seen toes and fingers—

once a whole foot—turn black and crumble away. I cannot let it happen to you, Tiffany. *Por favor, no podía dejarte morir...*'

His hands trembled, and Tiffany faltered. He wore his shirt and breeches, and now she could tell they were eveningwear. She had never seen a man in just his shirt and breeches before. Even his feet were bare.

She looked around. Her clothes had been hung over frames he must have made from discarded pieces of wood. She could see the water puddling beneath them.

'I'm not going to lose any fingers or toes,' she said, betraying herself by shivering.

He held up his leather cloak. Unlike hers, it was not saturated with water from the stream, and it looked substantially thicker, too. 'Then come here and stay warm. Please. Please trust me.'

She hesitated. He *had* been warm. And here, with her back to the opening of their shelter, she felt the chill steal back over her.

But she had been trained from birth in propriety. The only people who ever touched her were trusted servants. Even her nieces and nephews didn't cuddle her anymore now she was a grown lady.

'It is so very improper,' she whispered, and Santiago looked exasperated.

'More improper than dying? Will they put that on your headstone, I wonder? Lady Tiffany: dead of a fever but thank God her virtue was intact!' He shoved a hand through his hair. 'I apologise. Your virtue is safe with me. I promise I will never touch you unless you ask me to. I promise. I promise.'

Too late, she felt the ripple of his promise wash over her. *Promise a thing three times and it becomes binding.*

'You have bound yourself to it now,' she whispered.

'I mean it,' he said, his gaze steady on her.

And she believed him. She believed that he wouldn't take

liberties with her being held so close to his body. But it was that body which concerned her.

Tiffany had spent her life avoiding works of art. She had glimpsed the odd classical statue or painting of a fellow wearing very little, but both modesty and her own uncontrolled witchcraft had kept her from any more than a passing glance. Occasionally, she had seen workers in the fields or on the estate, stripped to their shirtsleeves in the summer, and Elinor had always muttered that it was disgraceful and Tiffany shouldn't look.

The only man she had ever seen in a state of undress was Santiago, that day they had rescued him from the beach. The memory of his golden skin, dusted with dark hairs and imprinted with black ink, warmed her dreams.

I want to know what his skin tastes like.

The thought shocked her, as it had earlier in the day when he'd stood there all dishevelled and sweaty from his ride.

'Tiffany?'

She let herself look at his face, and with a sigh she allowed herself to acknowledge how extraordinarily handsome he was. His jaw so finely cut, his lips so perfectly made, and his eyes … she could lose herself in their dark depths.

What was wrong with her? Perhaps she did have a fever.

'Do you trust me?' he asked, and she nodded.

She knew it was a bad idea, and would haunt her dreams for months, and it was terribly, terribly improper, but she shuffled over to him and sat beside him. She in her shift, he in his shirt. She could feel the heat radiating off him even before he drew her into his arms and pulled his cloak over them like a blanket.

Did all men feel like this? Beneath their layers of careful tailoring, did they all have strong shoulders to lay your head on, and hard chests to wrap your arms around? She had never met a man whose skin she wanted to lick before, but Santiago's scent was making her light-headed.

He turned his head as he fiddled with the cloak, and the roughness of his jaw gently abraded her cheek. Tiffany had seen labourers with unshaven faces, but never a gentleman. She had never thought about what it would feel like against her skin.

'Better?' he murmured, and she nodded, unable to speak. 'Are your feet tucked in? Your boots were soaked, I thought it best to take them off...'

She really wished he'd stop reminding her how unclothed she was. 'I am perfectly ... fine.'

He stopped fussing with the cloak and hesitated. 'May I?' When Tiffany nodded, he put both his arms around her, his hand carefully placed on her shoulder. She was wrapped up in the warmth of him, the comfort, the security. This was what she'd been dreaming about just before she woke. It wasn't a childhood memory. It was Santiago, holding her with such care and tenderness it brought tears to her eyes.

'We should get some sleep,' she said, to distract him. 'If we rise at first light, we can probably get back to the house without anyone realising we've gone.'

She had to believe this, or her reputation would be more than tattered.

'They might realise I have gone,' said Santiago. 'I said I was returning to my room for something. Perhaps I can say I decided to go to the village tavern.'

Tiffany suddenly remembered the burning effigy and the ghouls and the angry villagers. 'That might not be the best idea,' she began, but she couldn't think of a better one. She was so tired.

'Why? Does it have a bad reputation? That doesn't seem to bother anybody. I have noticed,' he said heavily, 'that a gentleman can get away with behaviour ladies are not even supposed to know about.'

'I believe they're positively encouraged,' she said, smothering a yawn.

'Yes. You were right, of course.'

'Was I? About what?'

He rested his cheek against her hair. Tiffany's stomach turned over. 'That the life of a gentleman offers much more than the life of a lady. There is so little you are allowed to do. Or to be.'

He remembered that? 'But now I am a witch,' she said, as lightly as she could. 'And perhaps that means I do not need to marry and rely upon a man. Perhaps I can be like Aunt Esme, and live independently, and simply do and say and wear what I wish.'

He was silent for a moment. Tiffany felt her eyes closing.

'That is truly what you wish?' he said, and there was a tone to his voice she couldn't quite identify.

'It is,' she said firmly, and ignored the little voice inside her that said independent ladies did not get to lay their heads on strong shoulders and be held as they fell asleep.

'Then I wish you joy of it,' he whispered, and as Tiffany succumbed to sleep, she thought she felt his lips brush her forehead.

THE RAIN HAD STOPPED by the time they woke. Santiago knew this because their makeshift shelter had melted away overnight, and he was woken by a cool breeze and the sun in his eyes. It was a little past first light.

Tiffany slept in his arms, her pale head tucked into his shoulder. She had snuggled against him as if she had been made to fit there, her luscious curves a temptation he had spent most of the night resisting.

He rested his head back against the rough stone wall and idly fantasised about waking her with a kiss, laying her down on his cloak and baring her to the morning sun, caressing her pale skin with his hands and lips and making love to her until they were both boneless.

But he could not do that.

He could take her home, make some noise as they approached the house and cause her family to see them, and then that would mean he'd have to marry her. She would be upset, of course, but perhaps once he started making love to her...

No. He couldn't do that to her, either.

He could take her safely home, see her back into her room in secret and keep their night together from everyone else. And then, perhaps after another day or two at the party, he could go to her brother and ask if he would give his permission to propose to Tiffany...

He sighed, and closed his eyes. It didn't matter how he did it, Tiffany didn't want to get married and that was that. He would have to keep her at arms' length for the rest of his life. Perhaps an independent lady could have gentleman friends, or perhaps he would only see her at social events. Which he would attend in search of his own wife. He would find a suitable young lady, marry her and beget heirs, as was his duty, and maybe one day he would look back and remember the time he was infatuated with a witch who looked like a mermaid, and laugh at himself.

It didn't seem so very long ago he'd come to England intending to claim the dukedom, hand over responsibility to someone else, and then go on about his life exactly as before. And now here he was, contemplating marriage and heirs.

I don't want to marry some suitable young lady.

But had a duty to. The dukedom wasn't just a title. Tiffany had helped him see that, dammit.

He stared at the dawn as it rose over the fields. The monastery was no more than a pile of rocks, and they were sitting on wet, muddy grass. The cosiness of last night, the intimacy, was all gone.

He leaned down and allowed himself to brush his lips over Tiffany's hair, and then he squeezed her shoulder and said, 'Wake up, *mi amor.*' He had to stop calling her that. 'It is time to see if the waters have receded.'

She didn't fight him this time. She simply blushed a deep pink and scuttled away to check her clothing, which of course had now fallen to the ground.

'It is very damp,' she said, squeezing a fold of her dress, 'but it will have to do. It isn't far to the house.'

Santiago tried to keep his eyes off her as she bent over, tried not to gaze at the way her shift draped over her hips, at her pretty lower legs revealed by the shortness of the garment, at—

He turned away abruptly, before her maidenly innocence was corrupted by the sight of his desire for her in very thin silk evening breeches, and pulled on his boots.

'I will go and check the levels of the water,' he said, and she nodded, still without looking at him. Santiago strode away, letting the fresh morning air cool him down, and wondered if he could throw himself bodily into the stream.

The water had receded. He walked all the way around the hill, and saw that while the force of it had knocked down the retaining wall that was meant to divert it, the torrent had drained away and the lane was accessible, at least if one didn't mind getting one's feet wet. He waded through the puddles a few times, and it barely came up to mid-calf.

He glanced back towards the ruins, silhouetted from this angle against the rising sun. Would she be dressed yet? He had to get her back before the household began to wake. Or at least, before the upstairs part of it did. There would be maids rising already, but with any luck their attention would be focused on the inside of the house.

He made a meal of approaching Tiffany again, stamping about and coughing loudly so she knew where he was, and she approached after a moment, eyes still diverted from him.

Her dress was a plain affair, and it didn't look as if she'd been able to fasten it properly, but the plain dark blue suited her translucent complexion. Her pale hair fell in strands around her face, blanketing her shoulders with white gold. Her cheeks were pink, and her skirts muddy.

She was quite the most beautiful thing he'd ever seen.

'I have nothing to fasten my hair with,' she said abruptly. 'All the pins... I don't have time to put them back in and anyway... Do you have a piece of string, or something?'

He wanted to touch her hair, quite desperately. Wanted to lift it and feel its weight in his hands. Stroke it and see if it felt like moonlight.

He cleared his throat and patted his pockets. 'Ah, no. Wait, I have my neckcloth?' He held it out, limp and creased.

She frowned, but said, 'It will do,' and used it to tie her hair at the nape of her neck. 'We had better get going,' she added, and started down the hill past him.

He found her at the bottom, staring down at six inches of muddy water as if it held the mysteries of the cosmos.

'What is it?' he said, and she said, 'Nothing,' far too quickly.

She allowed him to help her through the puddles, and marched off down the lane, a woman on a mission. It was only a few minutes before the house came into view.

'When we get back,' he said, hurrying to keep up with her. 'Your room overlooks the stables, yes?'

'Yes— Wait, how did you know?'

Santiago cast about for an excuse. But he was cold, tired and aching, and he was madly in lust with Tiffany, and so he just said, 'I went looking for you. If we try to get back over the roof that way, there's a good chance someone will see you. Do any of your family go riding early?'

'Not usually,' she said, and her shoulders slumped a bit. 'But we have a household of guests.' She straightened. 'It's all right. I can make myself unnoticeable.'

'Un—'

'I am a witch,' she said impatiently. 'You don't need to worry about me. Just get yourself back, and make up whatever excuse you like. As you said, a gentleman can—'

She broke off abruptly and turned her head towards a sound. Then Santiago heard it too: hoofbeats, coming down the lane.

He swore, and looked around for cover. The sunken lane had high sides with little chance of an exit, unless they were to scramble up the exposed roots of a tree.

He glanced back at Tiffany. But she had vanished.

I can make myself unnoticeable.

Right. Well, that was disconcerting. He nodded, cleared his throat, and began to swagger. When the horses came around the corner, they were bearing the Greensword nephews.

'Good morning,' he called, reaching up to touch a hat he wasn't wearing. Shirt unfastened, neckcloth gone, riding boots with muddy evening breeches—he surely looked extremely dissolute. But on the other hand...

'Your Grace,' they both said, touching crops to hat brims.

... on the other hand, he was a duke.

'Frightfully early for a ride,' he yawned.

'Frightfully early to be out and about. You disappeared after dinner,' said one of the nephews.

'I did. Very rude of me. Must apologise to the host. I had some...'—he allowed a small smile to touch his lips—'pressing business to attend to.'

From the looks they gave each other, it was very clear what

they thought that business was, and he didn't disabuse them of the notion.

'I must get on,' he said, gesturing to the house. 'Is it too early for a stiff brandy?'

'Never,' laughed one of the nephews, and they trotted on.

Santiago breathed a sigh of relief and sauntered on, tense as he waited for the horses to pass out of earshot. The moment after they had, Tiffany said, 'You do a good impression of a dissolute young aristocrat.'

His pulse leapt. She was right beside him. 'It is all an act,' he reassured her.

'I am sure. But one wonders where you found your inspiration.'

He smiled. 'Oh, I have witnessed some sights,' he said.

'From very up close?' she asked innocently.

'Intimately so,' he teased her.

'It is a wonder you find the time, Your Grace,' she said, and his face fell a little at her use of the title, 'to interrupt your busy schedule of brawling...' She smiled a little, and added, 'And rescue maidens in distress.'

The imprint of her body seemed to still be pressed against his. 'Were you very distressed?' he asked softly.

Her expression was fierce. 'Distressed is perhaps not the right word. I had just been performing more powerful magic than I ever had before.'

'You had?' His mind reeled. 'Before you made the shelter?'

'You made the shelter,' she reminded him. 'I merely provided the materials.'

'An entirely ordinary thing for a young lady to do!' She shrugged. 'But before that, you were performing some other feat? Tiffany—why did you go to the village?'

She hesitated, so he stopped, and turned to face her.

'I...' she began, and her gaze darted away again. Then she

lifted her chin. 'I was helping someone who needed to be helped,' she said.

'Alone? In a rainstorm?'

She tilted her head defiantly. 'It was not a rainstorm when I left.'

Santiago felt his eyes widen. 'Did you make it a rainstorm?'

'No! I—' She broke off, as if suddenly considering that she might have.

She was looking upwards, her remarkable bright blue eyes filled with wonder and speculation and excitement, and the breeze lifted her hair and blew her cloak back away from her bosom, and Santiago could no more have stopped himself from moving closer to her than he could have changed the tides.

'You are so extraordinary,' he breathed, and she looked back at him in surprise.

'Me?'

'Yes, Tiffany. You.' He lifted a hand to brush the hair from her face, a gesture far less intimate than anything that had passed last night and yet somehow so much more. Her lips were pink and full. His need to taste them was almost overwhelming.

'I—I only did what you have done,' she whispered.

Dazed, he could only shake his head.

'Helping people. You are remarkable, Santiago,' she said, and as she swayed closer to him her breasts brushed his chest and he groaned, because he had to have her now, had to kiss her, and she was swaying towards him in search of a kiss too, and—

'Lady Tiffany Worthington!'

The fire in his veins turned to ice so quickly it hurt.

'Is this what you call a headache?' hissed Lady Greensword, and they both turned to see her standing in the lane with the Belmont sisters and Lady Cornforth. All of them staring at Santiago mere inches from kissing Lady Tiffany.

'*Mierda*,' he breathed.

CHAPTER 14

*U*nsurprisingly, Tiffany was confined to her room once more, and this time a sturdy footman was posted outside the door. Elinor shouted at her a lot, went away to find Cornforth, then came back and shouted at her again.

'Your brother is dressing for the day. Had I not risen early to walk with Lady Greensword we might never have known you were missing! What were you *thinking*, Theophania?'

Tiffany, who wanted a hot bath so badly it almost made her cry, sat on the bed and contemplated her future.

She would have to marry the Duke. If he would offer for her, at least. Because despite her best efforts he still did not know every rule of etiquette in this country, and perhaps he might think he could get away with it.

He probably could. He was a duke, after all. But she would be ruined forever. Denied entry to Society for the rest of her life. Oh, the balls and the parties she could do without, but being snubbed by absolutely everyone forever? Elinor would keep her locked up here at Dyrehaven—or worse. Tiffany was absolutely sure women had been confined to Bedlam for less.

And if he did offer for her? How could she possibly be a duchess? This was after all the man who had blackmailed her into helping him.

Although … he hadn't seemed all that upset about her using magic so far. He'd rather seemed quite impressed by it. But the fact remained, he'd blackmailed her. Or at the very least manipulated her.

She would escape and go to Aunt Esme's. As soon as Elinor left she would summon a raven and send word, and then she would climb out of the window again and go—somehow, although she was hazy on the details of coach travel—she would go to London, or to Kent. Tiffany wasn't completely sure where Kent was, but she was sure someone would have a Paterson's Roads she could consult. The stagecoach came through the village a few times a week. Perhaps Amy Proudbody could shelter her, and—

'Theophania! Are you even listening to me? I have never known a girl so rude.'

Tiffany looked up at Elinor, in her ostentatiously simple dress with her hair artfully styled to look effortless, at the red blotches on her cheeks and the white patches on her knuckles. And she realised she wasn't afraid.

'Please stop calling me Theophania,' she said.

Elinor looked nonplussed for a moment, then rallied. 'That is the name your parents gave you.'

'Well, it is the name my mother gave me,' said Tiffany. 'My father having avoided me all my life and my mother having abandoned me when I was too young to remember. Perhaps their choices are not the ones we should be honouring right now.'

Elinor gasped. 'It is a sin to not honour thy father and thy mother!'

A sin, Tiffany decided giddily, that could probably wait to be dealt with, after all the witchcraft.

'You are so ungrateful!' Elinor stormed on.

Tiffany took in a deep breath and let it out. 'I am very grateful to you,' she said, 'and Cornforth, for raising me and introducing me to Society.' That part wasn't entirely true, but she thought she ought to give Elinor something. 'But I should not have been left with you. It is not a sibling's duty to care for children. I don't see why I should be grateful to parents who clearly had no interest in my welfare from the moment I was born. And probably before that,' she added, considering her father had left long before her birth.

'Wicked girl!' Elinor gasped.

'Well then, isn't it well that you will soon be rid of me?' said Tiffany. She felt lightheaded, as if she could float away. The future she had dreamed of, leaving Elinor and becoming independent, was almost upon her. Aunt Esme would know what to do.

Santiago would know what to do, too, but she should probably keep her distance from him for now. Besides, he would want a proper wife soon enough, and Tiffany was to be ostracised from Society.

He might offer for you. But if he did, should she say yes? She didn't want to be married! The closeness they had shared last night would never translate into marriage and besides, being married meant being someone's property, and the prospect of that after the hope of independence was too much to bear.

She tried not to think about how perfect it had felt to fall asleep in his arms last night.

'Theophania,' said Elinor, a calculating look in her eyes. 'Did you plan this?'

'No,' said Tiffany wearily. 'Believe me, marrying the Duke is the last thing I want to do.'

~

It was the only thing Santiago wanted. And the one thing he couldn't do.

'... perhaps not your choice of bride, but you must understand there is no alternative,' said Lord Cornforth.

He was seated at his desk in his study, a neat room with estate maps on the walls. He seemed somewhat hastily dressed, and Santiago realised it was probably not even breakfast time for the gentlemen who had stayed up late playing billiards and drinking.

'Theophania is, of course, an earl's daughter, and has been raised in the expectation of running a large household. I am sure she will make a most acceptable wife. We can apply for a special licence; I am on friendly terms with the Bishop of Westminster, so we can simply announce it as a love match, cemented during a house party, and hold the wedding as soon as—'

'No,' said Santiago.

Cornforth blinked. His eyes were not the same blue as Tiffany's. They were somewhat insipid.

'No?'

Santiago took a deep breath. He was a duke, after all.

'Lady Tiffany has made it clear that she does not wish to marry. And therefore, I will not force her.'

Cornforth blinked a few more times, as if it would help him to understand. 'But, Your Grace—she has been compromised. Her honour has been compromised.'

Santiago thought about protesting that he had very carefully not compromised her honour in any way, and realised that even if he were believed, it wouldn't matter anyway. Hadn't Tiffany told him, that very first night, that simply being alone together was a risk?

This stupid goddamn country and their stupid *goddamn* rules.

'I must honour her wishes,' he said.

Cornforth looked down at his desk, and then out of the window. Then he said, 'Your Grace, you were seen by Lady

Greensword and the Misses Belmont and my own wife. We cannot pretend it didn't happen.'

In a somewhat detached manner, Santiago considered that they probably could, because he had met very few problems in his life that couldn't be fixed with enough money.

His fingers absently came up to stroke the scar on his face. That had been one of them. This was another.

'If you refuse my sister,' Cornforth said, his voice steady, 'then you understand I will have to meet you.'

'Meet me?'

'In a duel.'

Santiago exhaled sharply. 'Just like my father,' he said, and for some grim reason that made him laugh.

The hands of the past reached forward for him again, and this time they had him in their grasp. He was turning into his father. Dishonouring a woman and killing her brother in a duel—

But he had no intention of killing Lord Cornforth. He opened his mouth to say so, and then caught the other man's expression.

Cornforth had that very English complexion that stained red on the cheeks, and right now they were crimson. His nostrils flared. His lips were tight.

'You think this is a laughing matter?' he said.

Santiago held up a conciliatory hand. 'No. Of course not. I was only thinking—'

Cornforth stood abruptly. 'I advise you to name your second, Your Grace. I will be asking my brother to stand up with me. I will give you time to make the arrangements.'

'Arrangements?' Was the man serious?

Cornforth's eyes were cold. 'You have seriously maligned the honour of my sister, and as such I must challenge you. You will meet me in a duel, Your Grace.'

'And if I do not?'

Lord Cornforth looked down at him through centuries of breeding, and said, 'You will.'

~

BY DINT of drawing a raven feather and using it to summon a bird, Tiffany was able to send a message to Aunt Esme, but however fast ravens flew, it wasn't fast enough to get her there before a full day had passed, during which time Tiffany was confined to her room with only Morris bringing her the occasional meal.

'What is happening?' she asked each time, and Morris got that terrified look she had when Elinor shouted at her, and said she didn't know.

Had Santiago offered for her? Had Cornforth refused? She couldn't think of any reason why he would—Santiago was a duke, for heaven's sake, and a wealthy one at that, and there were no obvious stains on his character—at least, none that Society appeared to know about. Not that she wanted to marry him, of course, but ... but ... why hadn't he asked?

She spent the whole day, from dawn to dusk, fretting and planning. Her mind wouldn't settle. She would convince herself that everything would be all right, and she could go and live with Aunt Esme and be a witch, and then just as quickly despair that she would never be allowed to attain her dream, because what woman did? She would be forced to marry Santiago and spend the rest of her life bearing his children and marrying them off. She would become cold and manipulative, like Elinor, and Santiago would pay her less and less attention until they barely spoke.

Once or twice she considered making herself unseen and climbing out of the window, but she was too tired and too out of sorts to make it work, and besides, where would she go?

When she tried to sleep, her mind strayed to the feeling of Santiago's warm, hard body against hers. It *had* been pleasant. And the way he'd looked at her in the lane just before they were discovered had her feeling decidedly warm inside. Perhaps marrying him wouldn't be so bad. She still had his neckcloth. Maybe she could use it to find him.

Only ... if he were going to offer for her then surely he'd have done it by now? And someone would have come to tell her? Why was she being kept in isolation? Perhaps Elinor feared her moral decay was contagious.

And then, some time in the early morning, there was a commotion in the hall that came closer and closer to her room.

There was Elinor's voice, arguing and complaining, and then—

'Oh do be quiet, child, and get out of my way.'

Aunt Esme!

The door was unlocked and Esme stood there in what appeared to be a coachman's caped greatcoat and boots. 'Tiffany,' she said, her face full of hauteur. 'Have you been locked in here all this time?'

She nodded.

Esme turned to Elinor and for a moment Tiffany thought she would strike her. Instead she snapped, 'Dreadful woman,' and swept into the room, locking Elinor out of it.

Carefully placing the key on the dresser, she waved her hand and muttered something under her breath. 'There, now she can't hear us. Are you all right?'

Tiffany nodded. 'I'm bored more than anything. They won't tell me what's going on. Is Santiago all right?'

'I have no idea. They said he has gone,' said Esme.

Tiffany's stomach dropped. 'Gone?'

'Yes. They didn't say where. He is a resilient young man, I am sure he will be fine.'

Of course he would. But that wasn't the point. The point was that he had been out all night with her and ought to offer marriage and instead he had just ... gone.

I suppose it is a good job I did not want to marry him.

But she could not quiet the sick, dull feeling inside her.

Esme sat beside Tiffany on the bed. 'Your message was not detailed. Tell me what happened.'

Tiffany did, earning approval for her building of the shelter and frank admiration for the rough music.

'I see you have become better at threatening people,' Esme said.

'I told him he could sleep in a ditch. I do hope he didn't wash away,' Tiffany said, frowning.

'Good riddance to bad rubbish,' said Esme. 'Now. Is there any chance you could be with child?'

Tiffany felt herself go cold and then hot. 'I—I don't know,' she said. 'How would I know?'

Esme's eyebrows rose, and then she glanced at the door where, no doubt, Elinor was trying to listen in.

'She has not explained these facts to you?'

Tiffany shook her head, and then Esme proceeded to explain in brisk, mortifying detail precisely how a woman could get with child. It sounded... Well, it sounded terrifying, if she was honest.

She told herself this made it even better that the Duke didn't want to marry her.

'Nothing like that happened,' she said faintly, when it was over. 'Nothing at all.'

'Good. That makes things simpler. Madhu made you up a remedy just in case,' she added.

'Madhu? But ... what do you mean, just in case?' Tiffany said.

'I have seen the way you two look at each other,' said Esme. 'Frankly, it is only a matter of time. Now. Do you wish to marry him?'

'It doesn't appear to be my choice,' Tiffany said, despairing.

'There is always a choice,' said Esme. 'You could exit Society completely and come and live with me. I have a house in Cornwall. It is very pleasant.'

Cornwall. About as far from London as you could get. It wasn't quite the life of independence Tiffany had been imagining. It was a life in exile.

But if she married him, she'd be stuck with him forever. And he might seem handsome and charming now, but what if he, a well-travelled man, got bored of London Society and vanished to travel the world again? She would be left behind with the children, doomed to repeat her mother's mistakes. Marry in haste, repent at leisure.

Esme watched her face. 'We shall leave right away,' she said. 'What do you want to take with you?'

THE PRIVATE PARLOUR at the Pale Hound Inn was not particularly large or luxurious, but it was private, and it was the only one in Churlish Green. The village was all abuzz about some event that had happened the night before, and they had been fascinated to see a personage such as the Duke of St James stride in with his valet and demand a bedchamber.

'How many nights, Your Grace?' asked the innkeeper.

'Just one for now,' said Santiago bleakly. After all, he might not be here when dawn broke.

All those years he'd been determined not to turn into his father.

William had arrived that evening, and calmly instructed Santiago on the rituals of a duel. Billy, inevitably tagging along, was a mixture of excitement and fear.

'But you'll win, won't you, guv?' he said.

'I shall strive to,' said Santiago.

He was now, under William's quiet instruction, writing notes. To his solicitors, instructing them what to leave to William and to Billy and Robinson; to de Groot, asking him to keep an eye on the business until William could find a replacement; and to Tiffany, to...

To say what?

I know you don't want to marry me, but your family thinks you should, and for that reason your brother and I are going to shoot each other at dawn.

Lord Cornforth was an English gentleman. Tiffany had explained to him that such young men were educated by tutors and boarding schools, and not just in Greek and Latin but in how to shoot and fence, too.

Santiago had not. Oh, he knew how to handle a pistol, but the damn things were temperamental and inaccurate and whenever he'd needed to use one he generally hadn't had the time to stand quietly and take aim. He preferred fighting with his fists. You could take someone out without killing them, with fists. But a pistol? It really only had one purpose, and that was to kill.

'William, this is stupid,' he said, not for the first time.

'Yes, it is,' agreed his brother, who was drinking small beer and staring at the window, waiting for the sun to begin peeping over the horizon. They had, by mutual decision, lied to Billy and Robinson about when the duel was to take place, and so those two were both still asleep upstairs.

'And it doesn't solve anything! Look at our father.'

'Every time I look in the mirror,' murmured William.

Santiago stared down at the letter, which so far only bore a salutation. And not the one he wanted to write anyway.

My dearest, Tiffany.
I want very much to marry you, but you do not want to marry

*me, and so I will not force you. I hope you can find the independence
you crave and that you will live your glorious life in the best way
possible. And I hope you see the pyramids.*

With all my heart, your Santiago.

But he didn't write that. He simply wrote '*I'm sorry,*' and folded
the paper.

'We should go,' he said. 'Before it gets light. We mustn't be
late.'

The site of the duel had been set, with incredible irony, as the
monastery hill that was to blame for their situation in the first
place. Perhaps then, if Cornforth shot him, his last memory
would be of holding Tiffany in his arms.

Santiago had faced the prospect of death several times—at sea,
on desperate streets, by the blade of a pirate queen. But he had
never been offered an appointment for it.

Quietly, they left the inn. The monastery hill rose over the
village, black against the moonlight. Everything was silent.

'Let's go.'

TIFFANY GLANCED up at the sky as they hurried along the sunken
lane towards the village. Amy Proudbody would probably still be
abed, but Tiffany could at least leave her a note. She wanted to
know that she was doing well, and she wanted Amy to send on
word of Henry as soon as she could.

'We will have to use a door at the inn,' said Esme. 'Really, it
would have been much more convenient to leave straight from
Dyrehaven.'

'Convenient, but not necessarily right,' said Tiffany.

Esme had grumbled that she couldn't open a door between
two places if she didn't know one of them, and had only managed

to get them out of the house by staring out of the window at a stable door. Tiffany didn't really understand how any of that worked, but given it would only take a few minutes to get to the village, she couldn't see it doing any harm.

Then she saw the light up on the hill.

'Do you—'

Esme squinted at it, and then she made a sort of gesture with her hands like she was stretching out the air in front of her to magnify the view.

'There are people up there. Men. Some sort of village ritual? We are well past Beltane and it is not yet the Solstice.'

'I can't think of anything,' Tiffany said. 'What are they doing?'

Esme peered, and then her face changed.

'They are pacing away from each other. Holding pistols.'

'A duel?' said Tiffany. Her stomach clenched. There was only one reason for a duel she could think of—and only two people who could be involved. She dropped her bag and began to run.

She was halfway up the hill when the shots rang out.

WILLIAM RUBBED his hands together as he returned from meeting with Cornforth's second, a brother he'd rustled up at short notice.

He shook his head.

'It's marriage or nothing,' he said. 'Mr Worthington says his lordship won't budge.'

And neither will Tiffany. She had been unequivocal.

He nodded, checking over his pistol. It had been supplied by Mr Worthington—apparently the one in the diplomatic service, who had probably hushed up many duels in the past.

'Do you intend to delope?' said William.

'Fire into the air? Yes. Of course. I have no reason to kill him.'

I am not my father.

'He might kill you.'

Santiago glanced up from his pistol to where Cornforth was standing ready. 'He might.' He took off his coat and handed it to his brother, then reached into the pocket and took out the necklace Tiffany had given him, winding its ribbon around the fingers of his left hand.

Then he moved to stand back-to-back with Cornforth.

'You will take care of Tiffany,' Santiago said quietly, over his shoulder. 'She is very special.'

'She is.' There was no discernable tone to Cornforth's voice.

'Ready?' called William.

'And you will apportion her no blame for this,' said Santiago urgently. 'She did nothing wrong at all.'

'Are you ready?' said Cornforth in reply.

Santiago squeezed the pendant in his fist. 'Ready.'

They paced the agreed fifteen steps and turned.

Santiago thought of Tiffany, glowing like moonlight as she created actual magic.

'Fire!'

He raised his arm in the air and fired straight up, eyes on Cornforth, as the other man aimed right at him and pulled the trigger.

～

TIFFANY SAW SANTIAGO FALL, and stumbled, her heart entirely stopping for a moment or two.

No no no no no!

Someone shouted, but Tiffany didn't even hear the words. She lurched up the hill, every step seeming to take an hour, as the other figures ran towards Santiago. Her breath wouldn't come. It was stuck on a sob in her throat. The hill was a hundred miles high. The air thick and impenetrable.

Finally, finally, she reached him, falling to her knees and clutching at his unmoving body. Mr Nettleship knelt there, tearing at Santiago's collar. Cornforth stood a few feet away, the pistol still in his hand.

Santiago's coat was already wet with blood. It spread across the chest and down his right arm.

'What have you done?' she cried, tearing at it. 'Send for the doctor!'

'I'll go,' said someone who might have been one of her other brothers.

'He's alive,' said Mr Nettleship, his fingers at Santiago's pulse.

'I aimed high! I aimed to miss!' cried Cornforth.

Santiago's eyelids fluttered, and relief flooded her. 'Can you hear me? Santiago? Wake up. Wake up, please. I'm sorry. Please don't die, I love you.'

His hand came up and she grabbed it, gazing down at his face as his eyes opened. 'Tiffany?'

'Yes! I'm here. I'm here, my love. You'll be all right,' she reassured him, based on no evidence whatsoever. She began tugging at his coat. She had to see what the damage was. 'Help me!' she snapped at Mr Nettleship.

Santiago cried out as they eased his coat down one arm, and she bit back her own horror as she saw the blood soaking his shirtsleeve and waistcoat. Her fingers shook. She needed to see where the damage was and if there was anything she could do.

'Tiffany! You cannot undress him,' hissed Cornforth, as she yanked at Santiago's waistcoat.

'You shut up,' she said, tears beginning to fall. 'You shot him. You just shut up.'

'You can undress me if you like,' Santiago murmured.

'Sound advice,' came Esme's voice from behind her, and relief flooded her. Esme would know what to do. 'Now.' She produced a knife and sliced his waistcoat open, flipping back the gory fabric and tearing at his shirt.

His golden skin was marked by black ink and dark hair, but no wounds. Tiffany blinked in confusion.

'The sleeve,' Esme said, and Tiffany tore at the fabric. He cried out again, and well he might, because the wound was on the inside of his right arm. And it looked awful, but it didn't look like it was going to kill him.

'Oh, thank God,' Tiffany sobbed, and threw her arms around Santiago. After a moment she felt his other arm clumsily pat her on the back.

'You didn't aim high enough,' said Esme drily.

'I am not going to die today?' he said, and she raised her head and pressed her lips to his.

'No, you're bloody well not,' she said, clutching him to her. 'But you are a ridiculous stupid man and I already regret marrying you.'

There was a hissed intake of breath from behind her.

'Marrying me?' said Santiago. 'No—' He tried to sit up and she pushed him back down. '*Querida*, you don't have to—'

'Are you dicked in the nob? Of course I have to.' It suddenly seemed very clear to her now.

She absolutely could not face losing him.

'Where did you hear a phrase like that?' asked Cornforth in a strangled tone.

'Nora,' said Tiffany distractedly. To Santiago, she explained, 'You clearly need someone to keep you out of trouble.' His blood was soaking into her clothes again. Why was she always soaking wet around this man?

'I cannot trap you,' he said. 'You said you wanted your independence.'

'Bit late for that now,' said Tiffany hysterically.

'But I thought—you said—you don't want to marry me...'

Tiffany drew back a little and looked down at his face. His stupid handsome face, with its scar and its golden skin and its dark beard stubble. His gold earring gleamed in the dawn light.

'I don't,' she said icily, 'recall you asking me.'

There was a short silence.

'Do you mean to tell me,' said Mr Nettleship slowly, 'that you two just decided to have a duel—to the *death*—over the honour of a woman, and neither of you actually *asked her what she wanted*?'

Santiago's gaze slid away. 'You had made it quite clear,' he muttered.

'I am capable of changing my mind!' she said. 'Did you really think it was better to die than to chance it?'

Another silence.

'I take it back,' she said in disgust. 'I can't marry you; you're clearly mentally incapable.'

'Too late,' said Esme cheerfully. 'Special licence?' she said to Cornforth.

'I'll … write to the bishop,' he said faintly.

'You don't have to,' Santiago said, and Tiffany wanted to let go of him but couldn't quite manage it.

'And get married by banns? Like anybody? I wouldn't dream of it. Come on, up you come, back to the house. We have a wedding to plan,' said Tiffany, and started to wonder if she'd gone mad.

CHAPTER 15

*T*iffany dreamed she was looking at herself, chained up in a tower.

Exiled from society, hidden away from everyone, cold and lonely and watched over at every second. Her jailers tossed pieces of bread and cheese on the floor, threw water over her, laughed.

'Let me help you,' Tiffany said to her nightmare self.

'No one can help me. This is of my own making,' she sobbed, and her jailers laughed and laughed.

Tiffany woke with a gasp. It was the fourth time she'd dreamt of it this week, and she was wrung out from it.

Well, not just from the dreams.

The whole of the last few weeks had felt like she had drunk too much Madeira. After they'd got Santiago back to the house, bleeding profusely all over Tiffany, the guests had stayed a day or two and then rushed back to London to share the exclusive news of the betrothal.

From then on, everything had been about the wedding.

Tiffany had moved her belongings from Dyrehaven straight to Esme's house and simply not asked Elinor's opinion on the subject. Santiago was established under Robinson's care, with daily visits from Madhu to administer whatever potions she cooked up in the kitchen. Tiffany barely saw him.

And now it was her wedding day, and all she felt was a sort of sick terror.

Once she was married, would that nightmare come true? Would she be shackled to him forever, kept prisoner by endless childbearing? Would she be locked away in his castle—according to the Peerage it was *actually a castle*—in the far reaches of Yorkshire?

Would she turn into Elinor, brittle and judgemental, desperate for the good opinion of others? Or ... worse. What if she turned into her mother, and simply ran?

She was to be married from her brother's house, and so for the sake of quieting the gossips, had agreed to travel there early in the morning to get ready. Esme dressed her, Madhu pressed soothing drinks into her hand, and Nora sat around exclaiming over the sheer decadence of the room.

Tiffany had chosen to be married in her silver tissue dress, the only one she'd ever really liked, and the one Santiago had first seen her in. Esme dressed her hair with flowers, and fastened on an exquisite opal necklace she had never seen before.

'Where did this come from?' she asked, touching the stones. They felt strangely warm to her touch.

'It is my gift to you,' said Esme. 'Beautiful, changeable, enigmatic. Fire and ice at the same time.' She paused, and added quietly, 'I gave your mother something very similar.'

Tiffany whirled around. 'You knew my mother?'

'Yes.' Esme exhaled sharply. 'I knew her and I loved her.'

'Do you know where she is?'

Her face shuttered. 'I only wish I did, child,' she said.

'But ... can you tell me about her? Nobody speaks of her—'

'No,' said Esme, and the sound was harsh. 'No,' she repeated, more softly. 'There is little I can say. Now, are you ready?'

Tiffany was not. She still didn't know if she was making a terrible mistake or if this was a wonderful opportunity.

Had the words she had uttered when she thought he was dying been true?

She could run. Could make herself invisible and escape the house. Go somewhere, anywhere, and never have to see him again.

Or she could make the best of the bed she had made for herself. Santiago was not a cruel man or a stupid one, duels not withstanding, and he was handsome and her heart beat faster when she looked at him.

And she was a witch, and Esme would probably help her put a curse on him if he turned out to really be dreadful.

'I am ready,' she said.

~

TIFFANY WAS LUMINOUS.

Santiago was fairly sure he'd seen stars shine less brightly. She wore her silver tissue dress—the one she'd worn when they first met!

Cornforth gave her away, as despite even Esme Blackmantle's best efforts, nobody had been able to contact Tiffany's father. He gave Santiago a polite nod, and in return Santiago's arm gave a twinge. Madhu's potions had worked wonders, but it had only been a few weeks since a bullet ripped through the underside of his bicep as he held his arm aloft, nobly shooting into the air.

Then Tiffany was there beside him. She turned to him, those mermaid eyes shining like the sea, and gave him the smallest of smiles.

Santiago beamed right back at her.

He remembered nothing of the ceremony, apart from when he slid the ring onto Tiffany's finger. It felt so … transformative. She was his now. Joined together in the eyes of God.

He walked her back down the aisle, and people cheered and wished them well. He sat down beside her at the wedding breakfast—which, this being the Ton, was served in the mid-afternoon. He allowed Esme Blackmantle and the other witches to bestow upon him terrifying curses should he ever think of distressing Tiffany in any way. He made small talk with any number of complete strangers whilst Tiffany went to get changed into her going-away dress, and he caught her in his arms in an unfashionable display of affection when she returned.

There had been a small part of him that thought she might have climbed out of the window.

'Ready to leave, Your Grace?' he asked her, and her pale face got paler.

'Yes, Your Grace,' she whispered, and he led her out to the waiting carriage.

And then finally, finally, they were alone.

'You are so very beautiful,' he told her, and she smiled tightly. Her throat worked. 'Are you all right, *mi amor*?'

'Perfectly well,' she replied, but she was not a good enough liar. 'Just a little tired. A busy day.'

It had been a busy day, and he was tired too, but that wasn't what was happening with Tiffany. With horror, he realised the truth.

They were travelling to his house on Grosvenor Square, which had been hastily staffed and cleaned and made ready for its new duchess, and then in the morning they would travel to Castle Aymers, a house that would be new to Santiago too.

But in between…

Tonight was their wedding night.

He thought about the way he'd had to coax her to share his

body heat that night at the ruins. Oh, she might have been tempted to kiss him the following morning, but no more than that. He wondered if she even knew what to expect. If anyone had talked to her about it. If her uptight sister-in-law had scared the life out of her.

'Tiffany—'

'It will be three days, will it not, to reach Aymers Chevres?'

He blew out a breath. 'I believe so. William assures me the finest rooms in the finest inns have been booked. We could even take the time to sightsee,' he offered, because he had seen little of the country himself.

'If you like,' she said politely.

Oh dear. Something was terribly wrong. Tiffany was never polite to him unless she was furious with him. And what more reason could she have to be furious than being forced to marry him against her will?

No matter that it had actually been her idea. Santiago had thought, for a brief moment, that she'd said she loved him that terrible morning at the ruins, but he must have imagined it. A woman in love would surely not be so quiet and polite on her wedding day.

But then why had she married him?

'*Mi amor*,' he began, and she gave him the sort of politely interested smile she might to a bore at a ball. 'I know it was not your wish to marry me. But I promise—'

'Haven't you learned it's dangerous to make a promise to a witch?' she said lightly.

'Evidently not. I swear to you, your fears of marriage are unfounded with me. I will never treat you as a possession. Your life will be your own.'

She looked down, and said quietly, 'Your vows said you would honour and keep me. Mine that I would obey and serve you.'

Had they? The whole ceremony had been a total blur. 'But

those are just … words,' he said. 'You do not belong to me,' he said, in defiance of his heart, which very much insisted that she did.

'In the eyes of the law, and of God, I do.'

'But in my eyes you are your own person. You are no one's possession. You belong to no one but yourself, Tiffany.'

She looked up at him then, shyly. 'Do you swear it?'

'I swear it,' he promised, and she gave a little smile.

'Your Grace,' she began, and he groaned.

'No. Not you. Don't do that. Don't ever do that.'

'Do what?'

'Call me Your Grace. I'm not a grace.' Santiago leaned back against the squabs and said moodily, 'I'm disgraceful.'

'Are you, though?' she said doubtfully.

He took his hat off and ran a hand through his hair. 'I have lied and stolen and cheated,' he said. 'I have been a pirate and smuggler. I have committed every wicked sin you could think of.'

'But you are not wicked,' she said.

And when she looked at him like that, he did not feel it. 'Am I not?'

'Your— San— Look, what should I call you?'

'Santiago,' he said firmly.

'The priest called you Edward.'

'Did he?'

'Yes!' She was smiling now. 'You just took your vows as Edward George William.'

'Did I?' he said in wonder. 'Well. To be honest, nobody has called me that in… well, ever, I think.'

She turned in her seat to look at him. 'Really? Why?'

He shrugged. 'My father named me after himself, but I don't recall him ever actually calling me anything. And my mother… None of those names mean anything to me. I have no claim to them. But Santiago... it is the city where I was born, and it is St James in Spanish, and so it is what I called myself. It is *my* name.'

Tiffany nodded as she thought about this. 'And I should call you that too?'

He nodded, and took her hand. She was gloved, but when they got home she wouldn't be, and he would just be able to feel her bare fingers against his. The thought was intensely erotic. 'And what should I call you, Your Grace?'

She paled a little. 'Well, not that. I don't know how I'm going to get used to being a duchess.'

He laughed. 'If my experience is anything to go by, it won't happen quickly.' He added hesitantly, 'Tiffany.'

She darted a smile at him. 'As long as you never call me Theophania.'

'Done.' He shook her hand and she laughed.

The staff, some of whom had been working for Santiago for barely a week, were lined up inside the hall of the ridiculous mansion that was now his home. The staff were introduced to Tiffany, and she gave every appearance of being interested to know their names and positions.

But of course, she had been trained to do this since birth.

Santiago wanted nothing more than to whisk her to his bedchamber and ravish her, but he had promised her he would wait until she came to him, and he meant to stick to that. Even if it killed him.

Later that night, as he lay staring at the canopy of his bed while imagining Tiffany lying naked in hers, he thought it very much might.

~

DINNER WAS SERVED at opposite ends of a very large table. Santiago declared this was absurd and invited himself to sit next to Tiffany, 'because I am a duke, and I can.'

There were footmen going in and out all the time, and so no chance for real intimacy, but she found herself yearning for it. Santiago was so handsome in the candlelight, his golden skin burnished to a deep copper, his eyes dancing, his strong hands flying as he talked. He kept picking up the wrong cutlery, swearing in Spanish, and trying again.

'It is a good job you did not make it to any ball suppers,' she teased.

'I will need my wife by my side to correct me,' he replied, his eyes on hers, and something leapt inside Tiffany.

His wife. She was his wife. And quite apart from the duties of a duchess and that huge array of servants—whose names she had attempted to memorise and failed—there were the duties of any wife.

Elinor had told her, before the Season even began, that she should submit to her husband in private matters. That it was her duty to bear him children. And that there was no point complaining about it because every woman had to go through it.

Privately, Tiffany thought that every woman having to go through it was not a good enough excuse for every woman having to go through it.

And so, no matter how charming Santiago was throughout dinner, how he smiled when he caught her hand and led her into the drawing room—'How can I drink port alone when my beautiful wife is in the next room?'—and how heated his expression was when he bid her a goodnight at the top of the stairs, she could not help the sick feeling in her stomach.

Aunt Esme's frank explanation hadn't helped in the slightest. Nor had Madhu's gift of a packet of powders that she assured Tiffany would allow her to 'plan your family'. Tiffany allowed her new maid to undress her and brush out her hair, while fixating on the details that simply couldn't be true. She lay in bed, trying to think about how it had felt to see Santiago dishevelled and sweaty, standing in the doorway of the saloon at Dyrehaven. If she could conjure that again, that desire, that desperation to be near him, then perhaps she could banish her fears.

She had more or less succeeded when she heard the clock strike, and realised she had been waiting for him for over an hour.

He wasn't coming.

As she washed and dressed the next morning, she told herself he was probably waiting until they reached Castle Aymers. Given the jolting of the carriage along the Great North Road, she thought privately that perhaps it was a good thing that he hadn't taken her virginity last night. Both Elinor and Esme, their approaches being quite different, had intimated that pain would be involved.

He did not visit her at either of the inns they stayed at along the way. Robinson had booked them into the finest inns the road book could recommend, and at each stop the proprietors were beside themselves at the prospect of serving a duke.

'It is ridiculous,' Santiago murmured, clearly embarrassed, as the tap room led a cheer to him and his new bride. 'I am merely a sailor.'

'A sailor with a castle,' Tiffany reminded him.

She wished Aunt Esme had let them use the magic door, but then again as Esme seemed to regard it as only for emergencies, she assumed it took something out of her to open. And besides, how would they explain to the servants that they'd arrived instantly?

When Castle Aymers finally did come into view, three days after they'd left London, Tiffany could only lean out of the window and stare.

'Is that it?' said Santiago, behind her, and she realised he'd never seen it, either.

'We have just driven through Aymers Chevres,' said Tiffany, who had been consulting the map tucked into the back of the Paterson's road book. 'It said Castle Aymers is on the left-hand side.'

'My house is on the map,' muttered Santiago.

He came up behind her, and Tiffany tried not to be affected by the proximity of his body to hers.

'But that is not a house! That is a … a…'

It was absurd. The wild, bleak landscape had been rising for a while, but now it thrust abruptly from the earth in a rocky heap, and from that heap a castle appeared to have grown.

The whole of it had a distinctly organic look, as if someone had planted castle seeds and a few hundred years later it was still growing. Buttresses and turrets sprouted from the rock, supporting a confused collection of keeps and walls. Roofs slanted in every direction. There were crenellations.

Tiffany giggled. She couldn't help it.

The road wound up the steep hillside, passing under an ancient, crumbling gateway that had holes in the top for pouring boiling oil on invaders. The outer walls of the castle had arrow slits in them.

'I had read your family have been here since the Conquest,' she said, looking around at the lowest of what appeared to be several courtyards. 'But I didn't quite realise they'd inhabited the same castle ever since.'

Beside her, Santiago looked a little nauseous.

The coachman, who had worked for the old duke, drove them around an ancient stone wall, through another gateway with boiling oil holes, and then suddenly they were curving around a neatly kept lawn bordered with rosebushes and lavender.

What seemed to be the entire staff of the castle had lined up outside what Tiffany was relieved to see seemed to be a more modern part of the castle—which was to say, probably only three hundred or so years old. Santiago stepped out, and offered her his hand.

'Here we go,' he murmured, a gleam in his eye.

The butler was an elderly man who had clearly served the old duke for many years; Tiffany guessed he was expecting to retire soon as he also introduced an under-butler to them. The house-keeper was a very sensible-looking woman who informed Tiffany that refreshments were on hand and so were hot baths if required, or perhaps a tour of the principal rooms? It could be a little tricky to navigate, she allowed, on account of the castle being made up of many additions and renovations that encompassed seven or eight hundred years of history...

Tiffany stared around at the great hall, which lived up to its name. Banners hung from its lofty ceiling, and there was a fireplace large enough to roast a cow.

'*Mi amor?*' said Santiago, touching her arm. 'Perhaps you would like to rest?'

She blinked at him. She was feeling somewhat faint. Castle Aymers was huge and so much more ancient than she had expected. It was probably haunted. And she was mistress of it.

She was shown to rooms that were perfectly spacious and elegant, and had lovely views through mullioned windows over a formal garden with more roses.

'His Grace's rooms are just through there,' said the house-keeper, Mrs Langham. She pointed to a door next to the dressing room. 'I shall leave you to get settled, ma'am.'

Tiffany took a nap, bathed and dressed for dinner in a new gown, which was blue and caught her eyes very prettily. A footman guided her down to the drawing room, where Santiago was fulsome in his praise of her loveliness. He was looking exceptionally handsome too, but Tiffany didn't know how to tell him that.

After dinner they took a branch of candles and a bottle of wine and went exploring through huge reception rooms and narrow stone corridors, frequently having to be rescued and redirected by footmen.

'This place is a maze,' Tiffany giggled. She never giggled. It must be the wine—and the proximity of her handsome husband who was surely going to come to her room tonight. 'We shall need to tie a piece of string to our doors.'

'String?'

'You know, like with Theseus and the Minotaur.'

He looked blank, but allowed her to lead him past ancient tapestries and through a heavy old door with a large latch.

'Oh!'

They were outside. A cold wind blew out most of the candles, and Santiago placed the branch on the ground, where it was sheltered by the battlements. The *battlements*.

'You have battlements,' Tiffany giggled, peering over the edge and wishing she hadn't. They were very high up.

'*We* have battlements,' Santiago corrected. 'All this is yours as much as mine.' He looked like he wanted to add something else there, but didn't.

'It is completely mad,' she said, turning to him and stumbling a little. 'A castle!'

He caught her in his arms, and for a moment she forgot how to breathe.

Moonlight illuminated his face, threw the contours into shadow and darkened the hollows. His hair blew around his face in a breeze that made her shiver. He pulled her closer, against his warm body, just as he had that night at the ruins.

'Tiffany,' he murmured, and she tilted her face up for him to kiss her.

And then he froze, and stepped back.

'I apologise,' he said.

She blinked at him, suddenly chilled. 'What for?'

'That was not appropriate. It is cold out here. Come, back inside, and maybe the kitchen can send up some chocolate.'

She had never been more baffled. Not even when Esme had told her she was a witch.

She was sure he'd been about to kiss her. And she'd been sure he'd come to her that night, now they were here at his ancestral home.

But as she lay awake in an unfamiliar bed for the fourth night in a row, the only thing to visit her was the nightmare.

She was locked in a tower, only now the tower looked cruelly like one of Castle Aymers's turrets, and she wasn't looking at herself but looking out of her own eyes at a bleak cell. Outside, a light swung and flashed. There was nothing in the cell but a straw pallet and a stone basin. When she stretched out to see inside it, a chain attached to her ankle clinked and chafed.

She was a prisoner. She had left everything behind and come to the other end of the country, to this fortress, with a man who was clearly repulsed by her. Was it because she was a witch? Was he frightened of her? Did he hate her? Perhaps he still thought she was the source of the creature that had attacked him and tried to assault Parliament.

He had blackmailed her, after all. Threatened to tell the world what she really was. A witch, in league with the devil, performing unnatural feats that would surely send her to hell.

Why on earth had he married her? He was a powerful man, and she a nobody, just a few parlour tricks to intrigue and entertain him. And he so handsome and commanding, a true hero and leader of men, with such sadness in his eyes. She had only wanted someone to love her, to show her the affection her family never had. In that strange febrile time, they had clung to each other, and now she was paying the price for it. While he enjoyed his freedom she was trapped, locked away, little more than a broodmare.

And then the demons came to take her. The old stories said that witches had compacted with the devil, but she never had, she had only tried to be right and good, but the evil inside her was too alluring and now the demons came to infect her mind and poison her child against her. She had to leave, if this baby was to have any chance at goodness and purity. Had to travel far away so her daughter could survive—

Tiffany woke on a breath so sharp it nearly choked her. Her hands went to her belly, but there was no baby there. How could there be?

Had she just dreamed of her own future?

SANTIAGO WAS WORRIED ABOUT TIFFANY.

Last night on the battlements he had come within an inch of kissing her, but he had made his vow—and for all he knew, a vow to a witch came with terrible punishments if it should ever be broken. He wanted her, quite desperately, but he could not slake his lust on an unwilling wife.

At breakfast she did not appear, and he was informed she had chosen to break her fast in her room. Apparently this was normal for married ladies, and nobody turned a hair, but Santiago had breakfasted with her for three mornings now, and he missed it.

William arrived, bringing Billy and some paperwork from his solicitors in York, and the two of them rode out to survey the land while Billy made a thorough investigation of the kitchens and selected himself an alcove in the servant's quarters. Santiago did not see Tiffany until just before dinner, and she seemed pale, distracted. She jumped when his hand brushed her arm.

'Is everything all right?' he asked, and she nodded, with a smile that didn't reach her eyes.

'Perfectly. Will Mr Nettleship be joining us?'

'No, he has rooms in the village.' Santiago was glad of this, because he wanted Tiffany to himself. 'Perhaps we can invite him for dinner another day?'

'It will be nice to get to know him,' she agreed.

A perfectly polite dinner passed, and she bid him goodnight before he could even ring for his cigars.

In fact, a week of perfectly polite dinners passed. Tiffany invited various local worthies to tea or to dinner, smiled and laughed and played a perfect Society hostess. She already seemed to know the names of all the upstairs servants and had found her way around the principal rooms. She made plans to decorate some of the more old-fashioned areas of the castle and renovate others.

She was, in short, the perfect duchess.

But he could not coax her to ask him to her bed.

Santiago had spent a lifetime relying on his wits and charm, and he had never had a problem getting a woman to agree to … well, anything. But here, in his own castle with his own wife, he found himself deliberately showing off.

As she took tea on the terrace with the wives of the local gentry, Santiago cantered past the edge of the formal gardens on his horse. It was a warm day, but that was not why he paused to strip off his coat and stretch. Feigning ignorance of the ladies watching him, he cantered on, clattering down one of the narrow cobbled passages to the outer keep.

Tiffany asked him if he had enjoyed his ride, and said no more of it.

He contrived to be in the stableyard when she came back from a trip to the village, and stripped off his shirt to wash under the pump. She walked straight past as if he was not there.

When he learned that a kitchen cat had kittens, he brought one up to show her, because what woman was unmoved by a kitten? She could come closer to stroke it and play with it, and their hands would touch, and—

'He doesn't like how you're holding him,' she said.

'What?'

'He thinks you're going to drop him. It's very high up there and he misses his mother.'

'How do you—'

She tilted her head and mouthed the word 'witch' at him.

Right. Of course. She could understand animals. Of course she could. And she preferred listening to the kitten than looking at him.

'Santiago?' she said, as he turned to go.

'Yes?'

'He is very sweet. Perhaps—'

His heart swelled with hope.

'—perhaps when they've been weaned, some of the litter can come up here? It would be nice to have companionship.'

He nodded and smiled and took the kitten back to its mother and managed not to scream that he was her companion, dammit.

He went to bed that night ready to cry. Tiffany had been especially beautiful that evening, her gown like the sky at twilight, her hair like moonlight, her eyes shining like stars. When she breathed, her bosom hypnotised him. When he gave her his arm to escort her up the stairs, the brush of her hip against his had him painfully aroused.

He dismissed Robinson and threw off his clothes in a rage of misery. Was this some punishment for his past sins? Was God testing him? He hurled himself into a chair and wondered if he should send for some whiskey.

He was so lost in his own misery that he almost missed the scratch at the door.

'I don't need you tonight, Robinson,' he called. 'You can sort it out in the morning.'

'It's not Robinson,' came his wife's voice.

He sprang to his feat in one movement. 'Tiffany?'

'Can I come in?'

'Yes!'

Hurriedly, he raked his fingers through his hair and stood, tugging his robe into place as the door between their chambers opened.

Tiffany stood there, in a robe that was little more than a froth of lace and artistry, her hair loose and tumbled about her shoulders, her cheeks pink and her eyes flashing.

'Are you ever going to come to my room?' she demanded, and Santiago abruptly forgot how to breathe.

CHAPTER 16

*H*e wore a banyan of scarlet silk embroidered with roses. Tiffany was sure she could smell them as he stood there gaping at her. For the longest time he said nothing, and simply stared as if all his wits had deserted him at once.

Her bravado seemed determined to go with them. She had to fight the urge to fidget. 'Well?' she said, as he continued to gawp.

'Well?' he repeated helplessly.

'Are you?'

'Am I'—he swallowed—'going to ... come to ... you ...'

'Santiago, are you quite well?' Concern replaced her annoyance, and she moved closer, her hand outstretched to feel at his forehead. He stared wildly at her as she did, but didn't stop her. 'Do you have a fever?' He had been behaving oddly this week. All that business with the horse and the stableyard pump.

He swallowed again, and shook his head.

'Is your arm paining you?'

He shook his head as if he didn't know what arms even were.

Tiffany let her hand drop. 'Then are you going to answer my

question?' she said, resisting the urge to wrap her arms defensively around herself.

She had dressed in her prettiest night rail and dressing gown, trimmed with lace and almost sheer. It was something Aunt Esme had told her she would need in her trousseau, but she wasn't sure if it was having the correct effect. Santiago looked like someone had just hit him with a mallet.

'Question?' he said faintly.

Tiffany wanted to stamp her feet in frustration. 'You have made me wait over a week now. Nearly a fortnight. Have I done something to offend you?'

'No,' he said, as if the idea was an offence in itself.

'Do I— Do I repulse you?' At this she did wrap her arms around herself.

'No! It is the very opposite of that,' he assured her. His eyes roved her figure, especially where her folded arms were pushing her bosom up. That was a mistake. Elinor had despaired of her unfashionable shape. Clothes did not sit well on such a bosom. Long stays had better be worn. Large breasts were for wet-nurses. Et cetera, et cetera.

All of a sudden tears welled in her eyes, as they had on all the nights he had not come to her. 'I know I am not accounted a beauty,' she said, as matter-of-fact as she could. 'I am an insipid, colourless little thing, but—'

'You are no such thing!' He stormed closer to her, fury darkening his face. 'Who has told you this? I will cut out their useless eyes.'

Well, that was quite a sensation. 'There is no need to be so dramatic,' Tiffany said, secretly pleased.

'There is. Tiffany, you are so beautiful. Exquisite. I cannot take my eyes off you.'

'You don't have to be kind—'

'I am not,' he said firmly, and he looked her up and down in a way that suggested he could see through her clothes, and very much liked what he found there.

Flustered, she said, 'I am merely asking why you have not come to me. I was led to expect—'

'Yes?'

She took in a deep breath, and it shuddered slightly with the force of her nerves. 'I believed you would come to me once we were married and we would ... consummate.' Her face burned. 'That it is my duty to ... to ... but you do not want me?'

He exhaled as he ran his hands through his hair, and it sounded almost like a laugh. Tiffany turned away, humiliated. But his words stopped her.

'You think I don't want you? Tiffany, *mi amor*—I want nothing *but* you.'

She turned back, eyeing him uncertainly. 'You do?'

He nodded, taking a step towards her, his hand outstretched. 'I think of nothing but you. My thoughts are filled with you. Did you not see me making a fool of myself this week? I cannot concentrate on estate business. I cannot hold a conversation. I have spent half my nights—well, you don't need to know what I've spent my nights doing,' he muttered, face flushing. 'But every moment has been about you.'

His eyes were dark as a storm. His voice shook. He took her hand, his bare fingers against hers, and thrill ran through her.

'Then why didn't you come to me?' she whispered.

'Because I made you a promise,' he said. 'At the ruins. I said I would never touch you unless you asked me to.'

'That promise?' she said. 'But— Oh, Aunt Esme warned you not to make promises! Or bargains! Mind you, if we had not made that bargain, we might well not be married,' she said, and the prospect of that—of having missed out on even this, of remaining unmarried while some other woman took him to her bed and shared his life—that was too terrible to think about.

'What bargain?' Santiago sounded distracted; he was looking at her breasts again.

Tiffany threw up her hands. '*What bargain?* You don't remember blackmailing me?' She scowled at him. Maybe she would keep the marriage unconsummated after all.

Santiago's eyes shot up at that. 'I never blackmailed you,' he said.

'Oh!' Tiffany nearly used one of Nora's words. 'You ... you did! You said if I didn't teach you how to be a gentleman, then you'd tell everyone I was a witch!'

'That...' he began, and shrugged awkwardly. 'Tiffany, *mi amor* —I never intended to tell anyone. Surely you must know that?'

'Then what was I teaching you for?'

But she knew, didn't she? She knew he hadn't really intended to tell anyone, and she knew why she'd wanted to spend time in his company. Because every time she looked at him, thought about him, closed her eyes and remembered the scent rising from his golden skin, her heart beat faster and heat rose in private places.

'But we sealed the bargain,' she whispered. 'Magically. I felt it.'

Santiago reached out and very gently brushed the backs of his fingers over her cheek. Tiffany shuddered.

'You felt that,' he murmured. 'I felt it too. Every time I have touched you. Tiffany.' He had moved very close to her now. 'I would never force you into anything. That bargain was no bargain. But the promise I made to you—magic or no magic, that was real. I will never touch you if you don't want me to.'

'But I do want you to,' she whispered, and he reached out, and — 'Wait a minute.'

Santiago exhaled sharply, his hand freezing. She stepped back and looked at him, at the darkness of his eyes, at the way his chest rose and fell, at the gleam of his golden skin in the candlelight.

Nearly two weeks she had lain alone, frustrated and desperate, loathing herself because he was repulsed by her, suffering nightmares of oppression and hopelessness, and all this time—

'You mean to say,' she said, 'that all this time, *all this time*, you have been waiting for me to come to you and I have been waiting for you to come to me?'

'You wanted me to come to you?'

'I thought you would! Isn't that what you're supposed to do?'

'I don't know, I have never been married before!'

In the next second laughter bubbled out of her. And in the second after that he was laughing too.

'Oh, we are both fools,' he said, and got no argument from Tiffany. He wrapped his bare fingers around hers and pulled her a little closer. 'Let me be absolutely clear,' he said, looking down at her with those dark, dark eyes of his. 'You want me to come to your bed?'

'Yes,' she breathed. Her pulse was pounding, all laughter forgotten.

'And I want you to come to mine?'

'You do?'

'I do,' he said fervently. 'Should we meet in the middle and make love in our dressing rooms?'

He had gathered her into his arms now, and his banyan was no barrier at all to the feel of his body pressed full length against hers.

'I think,' she managed, 'we should meet right here.'

'Excellent idea,' he breathed, and his mouth descended, and—
'Just to be clear,' he murmured, lips just brushing hers.

Tiffany wanted to scream with frustration. Her whole body arched towards him. 'I want you to kiss me, and make love to me, and do all the things husbands and wives do in bed,' she said. 'Is that clear enough?'

'Perfectly,' he said, and the last syllable had not left his lips before his mouth was on hers and oh—oh! This was what she'd wanted!

Tiffany had not only never been kissed, she'd never even seen a kiss. Polite pecks on the cheek were all that passed between Elinor and Cornforth. They showed no more affection to each other than they did to their children. But other girls whispered rumours, and even Tiffany had heard them.

She had never imagined it would be like this.

She felt almost feverish, her body trembling as his mouth took hers. His lips coaxed, caressed, and teased, and then his tongue was in her mouth and the intimacy of it shocked her. Her body knew what it wanted though, and pressed up against his, her arms twining around his neck and her hips arching shamelessly.

His hands were in her hair, and she'd never expected that to feel so good. His fingers caressed her scalp, her neck, and her skin tingled where he touched her. Then his arm went around her waist and pulled her hips in tight against his, and she felt—well, she had never felt anything like it before, but thanks to Aunt Esme she had a pretty good idea what it was.

And it terrified her, but she wanted it.

'Mi amor,' he breathed against her lips. His eyes were unfocused. 'Oh, Tiffany.' His fingers went to the lace at the front of her dressing gown. 'How do I—?'

She let go of him to unfasten it, and stumbled. He caught her, and used the opportunity to kiss her again. And he didn't move his mouth as his hands followed hers, and found the ties of her dressing gown and unfastened it, pushing the lacy fabric off her shoulders to fall unheeded to the floor. His banyan followed it, and beneath it he wore only his shirt and breeches, his feet bare.

Then he swept her back against him, her full body pressed against his with only her thin night rail and his shirt separating her breasts from his chest.

She wanted to touch him everywhere. Desire for him swept

through her like a fever, and her body arched against him without restraint. When his fingers caressed her bare arm she shivered with need.

She was so lost in him she barely felt him draw her down onto the bed, until he ran his hand up her bare leg and she gasped, sharply.

'I want to see all of you,' he said, and Tiffany nodded fervently.

'But only if I can see all of you,' she said, because the memory of his golden skin and dark hair and those black inked lines had been haunting her.

'Whatever my lady wants,' he promised, and drew back from her to stand, pulling his shirt off over his head as he did.

Tiffany could only stare. In the candlelight he truly was golden, like a statue. Only statues didn't have dark hair on their chests and arms, and they didn't have muscles that moved and flexed, and they certainly never had designs etched into their skin.

A turtle swam on his chest. A swallow flew on his arm. A serpentine dragon coiled its way over his ribs. Tiffany's mouth went dry. She wanted to trace those lines with her tongue.

On the underside of his right arm was a healing scar, livid red against the gold. He could have died that day, and instead he was hers.

'I know,' he said, following her gaze. 'I look like—'

'You're beautiful,' she gasped.

'—a common sailor.' He blinked, and a tiny frown appeared between his brows. 'What did you say?'

Tiffany knelt up on the bed. 'I said you're beautiful,' she said, and traced her fingers over the turtle's shell. Santiago shivered, just as she did when he touched her. She did it again, feeling his chest rise and fall beneath her fingertips. The hair there was coarser than any she had, and short, curling over his warm golden skin and tickling her in a way that she felt right down to the core of her.

Her breath came out in a ragged exhalation, and Santiago groaned.

'If you keep touching me like that,' he panted, and took her hand from his chest to kiss it. But not on the knuckles; on the palm, his tongue licking her in a way that made her gasp. He sucked one of her fingers, then a second, into his mouth, his eyes on hers.

She squirmed and shuddered, a sort of pressure beginning to build in her. When Santiago let go of her fingers and said, 'Take off your night rail,' she scrambled to comply.

She wanted—she needed—to feel his bare skin against hers. To press her body the length of his, see what that coarse hair felt like against the aching tips of her breasts, to feel the heat of him surrounding her.

He stepped back, unfastening the fall of his breeches, and by the time she'd pulled her night rail over her head he was naked.

Tiffany froze, night rail in one hand, and felt her eyes get wide.

Aunt Esme had warned her this process might hurt, and she had forgotten about that until now. But now she'd seen his ... er, his *himness*, she could quite see how.

'Oh Tiffany,' he said, somehow not noticing her shock. 'You are exquisite.' He reached out and cupped one heavy breast in his hand. 'I have had dreams about this bosom. Oh this bosom.' His thumb brushed her nipple. 'This bosom! It haunts me in the very best of ways.'

Tiffany whimpered. What was haunting her right now was the very frank advice Esme had given her about what was to transpire. She knew she was staring, and she couldn't stop.

Santiago moved in to kiss her, and stopped when she didn't

rise to meet him. 'Tiffany? Is everything...?' He followed her gaze. 'Oh.'

He straightened up, and Tiffany tried to calm her breathing. She was panicking. She thought the dragon on his chest was beginning to move.

'*Mi amor*, it is nothing to be scared of.'

'It—' began Tiffany, and swallowed again. 'It is just that I, um —that is—er, on statues—not that I look all that closely, of course, because what if they came to life? But they are not as... There is less ... um...'

Santiago put his hands on his hips and cocked his head. 'I think there was a compliment in there somewhere,' he said.

She dragged her gaze up to his and tried to smile.

He sighed. 'Tiffany. *Mi amor*.' He sat down beside her on the bed, all that lean muscle and golden skin right next to her. The hairs on his thigh tickled her leg as she sat back on her haunches as if this was all perfectly normal. 'If you have changed your mind, say so. We can stop.'

'I haven't changed my mind,' she said, darting a glance down to his groin.

'I won't mind,' he said.

Tiffany gave him an incredulous look. 'You won't? "Your bosom haunts me" and you *won't mind* if we stop?'

He let out a strangled laugh. 'Well—yes, I will mind, but I won't...' He shoved a hand through his hair. 'I won't be angry, or upset. I don't want you to do this if you're not ... comfortable.'

Tiffany gave him a sideways glance and said, 'I didn't think comfort was exactly the aim.'

'This is true, but being terrified isn't, either.'

She thought about denying she was frightened, then said, 'You can be scared and still want something, you know.'

He blew out a breath that sounded almost like a laugh. 'This is also true.' He touched her hand, caressed her fingers. 'Listen, I will promise you something.'

'Don't make it binding,' Tiffany said.

'I will.' He held their clasped hands to his bare chest. 'I will do everything I can to make this good for you. I promise I will bring you as much pleasure as I am capable of, and as little pain as possible. And remember, *mi amor*, it only hurts the first time.'

'Is that true?'

He shrugged awkwardly. 'Well, so I am told. I have never been with a virgin before.'

Tiffany felt she should respond to that. 'Neither have I,' she said, and he laughed.

'Come. Do you accept my promise?' She nodded. 'Do you trust me?'

She looked up into his handsome face, and remembered him windswept and soaked on that hilltop, asking her the same question.

'I do,' she said, and he kissed her softly.

At least, it started out soft. As he slid her naked body against his, passion swept through both of them. An ache grew in Tiffany that she prayed he could satisfy. His hands caressed her, learning the shape of her hips, her thighs, her breasts. He seemed particularly fascinated by her breasts. When he explored them with his mouth, she whimpered and trembled, but it was nothing to what was to come.

'I am not lying when I say your bosom haunts me,' he murmured, breath hot against her skin.

'I have never liked it,' she confessed.

He shook his head. 'It is magnificent. Perfect.'

'You wouldn't say that if you had to wear stays reinforced like the Iron Bridge.'

His fingers played on her thighs, and she shifted restlessly, because the ache was worst between her legs. 'Please,' she gasped, not knowing what she was asking for, and Santiago gave her a devilish look as he suckled on her nipple. His fingers slipped between her legs, and what he touched there made her cry out and clutch at him.

Her fingers were probably pulling his hair, but he didn't seem to mind. 'Good?' he enquired, and she nodded wordlessly, barely able to breathe. 'Mmm. There's more.'

'More?' gasped Tiffany, as he played with her. How could there be more than this? She arched towards his hand, silently begging him, and he kissed her mouth for a long, intoxicating moment.

Then he kissed his way down her body, settling himself between her legs and gazing at a part of her Tiffany hadn't even seen herself. And before she could ask what he meant by this, he put his mouth where his fingers had just been.

The sound she made was almost a shriek. Santiago froze, but when she gasped, 'More!' he grinned at her, and resumed his task.

Tiffany slid one hand into his thick, dark hair, rested her arm over her eyes and tried to remember to breathe. It was all too much and it still wasn't enough, because the pressure inside her was building to something and she needed him to show her how to get there. Her hips writhed on the bed as he licked and licked at her, and she was almost there, almost—

His fingers pushed inside her and without any warning, stars exploded inside her head.

Her fists beat against the mattress. Her hips twisted and arched, and inarticulate sounds came from her throat.

'Too much, too much,' she gasped eventually, and pushed his head away. As she lay there, gasping like a landed fish, he came to lie beside her, holding her gently in his arms until she thought she might be able to speak again.

'What,' she began, and got no further.

'It's good, isn't it?' Santiago seemed rather pleased with

himself. When he kissed her, she could taste herself on him, and that felt absolutely wicked. 'And there is more.' His hands stroked her hips, her thighs. She was still trembling.

'I'm not sure I can take more,' Tiffany whimpered.

'No?' He stopped stroking. 'Then we will stop—'

'Don't you dare,' she said, grabbing him by what she would politely call his hips, and shoving him against her. He throbbed hotly against her belly. 'I want everything.' She felt drunk. 'Please.'

He smiled, and kissed her sweetly. 'Whatever you want, *mi amor*.'

And it was uncomfortable, at first, but it didn't hurt. Perhaps everything else he'd done removed that possibility. Tiffany looked up at Santiago as he held himself above her, his jaw tight, and realised that she would never be more married than this.

'Are you all right?' he asked, through gritted teeth.

'Yes,' she said, and kissed his nose. That startled him into moving, and *that* felt good. Tiffany rocked her hips against him, and he groaned and pushed further into her.

'Yes. Oh Tiffany, yes.'

Her legs came up around his hips, because it seemed her body still knew what it wanted better than the rest of her. She moved with him, his chest straining as he arched and gasped above her. The hair on his chest tortured her nipples in the most delicious way. She felt the pressure building in her again.

The only words he seemed able to find were Spanish, but it seemed he spoke a torrent of endearments as he moved within her. His body was so large, so hard, so hairy and male. Tiffany grasped his shoulders and pressed her face to his neck and finally, finally licked his skin.

He made a whimpering sound and seemed to speed up. 'Touch yourself,' he gasped. 'Where I—'

Yes. Yes, that was what she needed. Shameless, desperate to reach that peak again, she slid her hand between them and touched herself there, where they were joined. Felt him going in and out of her. Gasped out his name—and then she was exploding again, shuddering and spasming, and Santiago was gasping too as if he'd reached the same place she had.

She held him to her, shaking, her arms wrapping around his shoulders and her fingers clutching at his neck, his hair. Santiago's heart hammered against hers, his breath coming fast and hard as he pressed his face against her neck. The world had ended and remade itself, and there were only the two of them left in it.

She breathed in his scent, and smelled … roses?

The carvings on the bed had sprouted into life. Roses twined around the posts and the canopy, a living bower of petals and thorns.

Well, it was a good job her husband knew she was a witch.

Eventually he lifted his head and smiled at her. '*Mi amor?*'

Tiffany patted his back clumsily. She had never been so wrung out in all her life. 'My love,' she replied.

He kissed her, a sweet, tender kiss that had her bones melting. Then he rolled onto his back, and while she felt the loss of his body it wasn't for long. He snuggled her into his arms, pulled the covers over them, and sighed happily.

'Are those roses?'

'Yes.'

'Did you do that?'

'I think we did.'

He laughed softly. Then he asked, 'Are you all right?'

'I can honestly say,' said Tiffany, her head on his shoulder, gazing at the turtle tattoo as it waved at her, 'I have never been better.'

～

SHE ASKED him about his tattoos, and he explained their significance to her. 'The turtle is because I crossed the equator. More than once, actually, but I don't need a whole colony of them.'

'The dragon? Is it Chinese?'

Disconcertingly, as her fingers traced the ink, it seemed to ripple and move, as if the dragon itself writhed across his ribs. 'Yes. After I ... ah, returned from Madam Zheng,' he indicated the scar on his cheek, 'the other traders were so impressed they declared I was honorary Chinese and must be marked as such.' He paused. 'These were European traders, you understand. The Chinese do not have quite the same attitude to tattooing.'

'How is it done?'

Painfully. 'With a sort of hollow needle, and black powder is rubbed into the marks it makes. It takes a long time. The dragon was weeks of work. But I was looking for a distraction, what with my face being ruined.'

'It isn't ruined. It's a very handsome face.'

She thought he was handsome. 'With a very prominent scar.'

'It makes you look dashing.' Tiffany kissed the scar, and Santiago felt like a king. 'There is a ... a chicken on your ankle?'

He laughed. 'Oh yes. It is a cockerel. De Groot and I got very drunk once. It... I think there was a bawdy joke involved. Anyway, we both woke up with them.'

Her fingers traced delicate patterns on his arm. He could swear he felt a flutter. 'The bird here? Is it a swallow?'

'Yes. I should have more of these, because they are meant to count miles travelled.'

'How many?'

'Five thousand each.'

'And how many should you have?'

He shrugged. 'Oh ... five? Six? One for the Pacific at least...'

He tried to do a calculation but his brain wasn't interested. 'Maybe more. I have never truly counted.'

She was quiet a moment. Santiago played with a bit of her moonlit hair. The fire was burning low in the grate, the curtains were drawn, and he had just made stupendous love to his beautiful wife. Life was very good indeed.

'This is the furthest I have ever travelled in my life,' she said. 'Before that, it was to Brighton.'

Brighton was a day's travel from London. Santiago kissed the top of her head and said, 'Then we shall travel. Anywhere in the world, I will take you.'

She made a small, sad noise against his skin.

'The pyramids,' he said. 'The Taj Mahal. Mountains. Jungles. Ice. Deserts. Where do you want to go?'

She traced the dragon's head with her fingertips. 'You can't leave the estate for so long.'

'Eh, William is very competent.'

'Or your business.'

'I have agents. Besides, we could set up new business in new ports.'

'And I... Will I be busy having babies?'

His arms tightened around her. 'Will you?' he said, his throat a bit tight.

'It is the duty of a duchess.'

She sounded so terribly sad. Santiago said as lightly as he could, 'Can a witch not control these things?'

'Well...' She looked up at him. 'Actually, Madhu did give me a powder I could take. To ... um, prevent that sort of thing from happening. But ... you are a duke, you need an heir.'

And he wanted one. He wanted a family with her. Some pale, some dark, all beautiful. 'We are young,' he said. 'We can wait. And listen, *mi amor*, children can travel. I did.'

'Did you like it?' Tiffany asked doubtfully.

'Well ... no, but that was because my father was a terrible man and my mother was miserable and they only had me to upset my grandfather with an unsuitable heir. But we will love each other, and our children.'

Tiffany twisted in his arms so that she lay facing him. 'Your mother and father did *what*?'

'Ah.' He hadn't meant to say it quite like that. 'Er, yes. My father was ... angry with his father for not getting him out of trouble. The duel, you know.' He might as well tell her. After all, history had nearly repeated itself. 'William's mother. My father abandoned her, and so her brother challenged him to a duel, and died as a consequence. Evidently my father expected his father, the Duke, to come to his rescue, but apparently it was the last in a long line of misbehaviours, and he refused to help. So my father fled abroad, and eventually ended up in the Spanish colonies, where he met my mother. Why he chose to marry her out of all the others, I will never know. Perhaps the prospect of a child who looked more like a savage than an Englishman.'

'You don't look like a savage,' she said, nobly ignoring his tattoos.

'Well, that is because I have an English wife to civilise me. Don't look like that, it's fine if I say it.'

'So...' Tiffany laid her head back down on his shoulder. 'He deliberately chose not to teach you how to be a gentleman, how to be a duke, just so your grandfather would be faced with an unsuitable heir?'

'That's about the size of it, yes.' Plus his father clearly wasn't very good at being a gentleman, and manners were probably quite hard to teach when you spent your life running from gamblers and angry husbands.

'What a ... a scaly, dunghill cove!'

Those words coming from her lovely lips in her neat and tidy voice made Santiago laugh. 'Billy?'

'Nora. But honestly, Santiago, I know one shouldn't speak ill of the dead, but what a nasty thing to do.' She cuddled into him. 'I am glad you are a better man than he made you to be.'

His heart swelled. 'You think I am a good man?'

She turned her head and kissed his shoulder. 'I think you are the best.'

She fell asleep there, curled in his arms, and Santiago lay counting his blessings as he drifted off. He slept peacefully, dreamlessly, until suddenly he was punched in the gut.

He did not swear out loud, because a man who'd had the kind of upbringing he had learned to assess threats very quickly on waking. He did shy away from his assailant, realising only after he had that he had fallen asleep with Tiffany. The room was dark. The attacker could be anywhere. He had to protect her!

He was about to try to wake her, to warn her of the threat, when he realised she was the threat. She was thrashing in her sleep, and as his eyes adjusted to the darkness he saw her pale limbs flailing in the sheets.

'Tiffany. Tiffany, *mi amor*. Wake up. It is a bad dream. Wake up.'

She lashed out as he tried to take her in his arms, but then her eyes opened, and she stared wildly at him.

'Who are you?' she said, and for an awful moment it was as if someone else was looking out from her eyes.

'Santiago. Your husband,' he said, and for a moment she was still. Then she blinked a few times, and looked up at him in confusion.

'Santiago? What is— Was I dreaming?'

'A nightmare, *mi amor*. Come here, lie with me. I will keep you safe.'

CHAPTER 17

*W*ere it not for the nightmares, the following week would have been the happiest of Tiffany's life.

She woke in Santiago's arms, breakfasted with him and went about the business of running a house that was half medieval castle. Then she would dress for dinner, taking extra care over her appearance, just to see his look of appreciation when she joined him. And all throughout dinner, as they told each other about their days, she anticipated the night ahead.

He did not disappoint her.

Tiffany wondered if this overwhelming physical joy was something all married ladies experienced, and then wondered why they would lie about it to unmarried girls. She wanted to shout about it from the rooftops.

Every night she fell asleep in his arms, satiated and happy, and every night she dreamed of the tower.

Of the chain chafing her ankle raw. Of the howling gale that screamed through the narrow window. Of the manger in the corner that held some unknown terror. Every night she fought and screamed, and woke up sobbing in Santiago's arms. He always soothed her back to sleep, but she knew it distressed him, and she thought the bruises forming on his body might be her work, too.

She took the powders Madhu had given her, terrified of the manger in her dream. She tried to stay awake, but Santiago's lovemaking was thorough and left her exhausted. She spent more time on her appearance, minimising the dark shadows under her eyes. But it wasn't enough.

'*Mi amor*,' said Santiago one evening, as they neared the top of the stairs. 'If you would like to sleep in your own bed, I will not mind. I know I am keeping you up at night.'

His kindness overwhelmed her. 'You know full well it is me keeping you up,' she said.

He cupped her cheek. 'The nightmares keep returning. Is it my presence?'

'No!' She felt so very safe and cherished in his arms. How could he be giving her nightmares? 'I don't know what it is. Perhaps I will see if there is a book of dreams in the library.'

There was not, the old duke having been an excessively rational man who did not believe in such folderol. It did not matter. This sort of dream was probably something all witches went through. If Aunt Esme were here...

Tiffany told herself that when she had a half hour to spare, she would write her a letter, but even that took some time. She had afternoon calls to make to anybody noteworthy in the area —to leave it too late would look like a snub—and various charities kept asking her to be their patron. Added to which, Billy was at a loss in the vastness of the countryside and had decided he would better serve his beloved guv'nor if he could learn to read and write, so she was arranging time at a local school for him.

She finally found time, on a rainy afternoon after the sleepless nights had begun extracting their toll in the form of a headache, to sit down in the small sitting room where she liked to deal with her correspondence, and began to write.

About three minutes later, the door opened, and Gwen stood there, looking somewhat startled.

Not half as startled as Tiffany herself, whose pen scratched a thick black line of ink across the paper. 'Gwen! What are you— I was just writing to Esme...'

'Are you? Bugger,' said Gwen, shutting the door and moving across to take the nearest seat. 'Esme ain't home, maid. I read your letter.'

Tiffany glanced at the paper, which bore Esme's name and nothing else. 'But I haven't written it yet.'

'I know,' said Gwen, as if this was a minor detail. 'I read it next week. That doesn't matter. Tiffany, your dreams ain't about you.'

'But— Yes, they are, I can see myself in them.'

'No. No witch ever has prophecies about herself. Not even me. You been dreaming about someone else.'

Tiffany stared wildly at her. 'But ... she looks like me. Do I have a sister?'

'I don't think so, maid. But you got a mother.'

At that point the door opened again and Santiago came in, attractively dishevelled from riding. He immediately said, 'I'm sorry, I didn't realise you had company.'

Tiffany gazed up at him, thunderstruck. 'Gwen says I'm dreaming about my mother.'

'Maybe,' Gwen said, making a rocking motion with her hand. 'But so is Esme, I reckon. Very quiet about it. But off she goes to France—'

'France? But ... we are at war with France.' Tiffany glanced at Santiago. They got the London papers a day or two late here, but at least she was allowed to read them now. 'We have just signed a treaty in Vienna, promising to force Bonaparte from his throne. They say a battle is imminent.'

'Or maybe Flanders. Begins with an F. Esme is the one with the knowing of places. But you are right about a battle, maid. 'Twill be the biggest seen for a hundred years. There will be songs about it.'

Tiffany didn't really like to think of what such a battle might entail, and made a mental note to pray for Henry Proudbody.

'But why is Mistress Blackmantle in Flanders?' said Santiago. 'Or France.'

'She seeks Amelia,' said Gwen.

Tiffany actually felt her face change at the mention of her mother's name. 'Aunt Esme said she knew her,' she said. 'But she would say nothing else.'

'No. There is little to be said,' said Gwen. 'But she has been agitated lately. Off to Kent and now overseas. And now she is in trouble.'

'Trouble?' Tiffany couldn't imagine her aunt in any sort of trouble. She seemed far too capable for that.

'Yes. 'Tis the beasty.' She looked at Santiago.

'The one that attacked me? And the Thames?'

'Aye. With the squirmers. You ain't the only one has dreams, my fine lady. I come to fetch you to help her.'

'Me?' said Tiffany. 'But—what can I do? I draw things. I make dresses look a bit nicer. How can I help?'

'You helped with Father Thames,' said Santiago.

'But we had Esme and Nora too,' Tiffany said, and trailed off as she realised they would probably be collecting Nora and Madhu too, now. 'I don't know what to—' She looked around helplessly. She had invitations to write and respond to. Mrs Langham's records to look over. Billy's schooling to arrange. 'I have things to do. I am a duchess now,' she wailed.

Gwen gave her a very old-fashioned look. 'You are a witch first,' she said. She stood. 'Come, maid. 'Twill take me time to work the door again, so get changed. Something practical.'

Tiffany had thought her day gown was practical, but she allowed Santiago to tow her from the room and up the stairs. 'I will help you,' he said. 'We cannot explain this to the staff.'

'Oh! No.' There was a maid and two footmen in hearing distance already. Tiffany thought fast, and then she swung herself into Santiago's embrace and giggled. 'Your Grace! In the middle of the day? How very wicked!'

His eyes darkened, and he muttered something in Spanish. 'Do not tempt me,' he said.

'It will explain why we are gone for a few hours,' said Tiffany, as she led him up the stairs.

'A few hours? My lady wife is ambitious,' said Santiago.

'Don't tempt *me*,' she replied.

He helped her change into the most practical gown she had, a dress she wore to walk in the gardens and inspect the roses, and put her sturdiest boots on. She did not have the time to change her stays for something that allowed easier movement, so the reinforced busk would have to remain. He fetched her his riding cloak while she filled her satchel with drawing materials, candles, and jewellery.

'The necklace you wore for our wedding?' he said, watching her slip the opals in.

'Esme gave it to me. It might help us find her.' She hesitated. 'You still have the pendant I gave you?'

'I will never lose it. It helped me find you,' Santiago said simply.

She slipped her arm around his neck and kissed him then. He was a good, kind and clever man, and if she had to be married to anyone, she was glad it was him.

'I will go then,' she said, and he frowned.

'We will go,' he corrected.

'No, I will go. I am the witch.'

'Tiffany, last time you went somewhere alone to do witching

things you ended up unconscious and nearly drowning. And I won't—' He broke off, and turned his head. 'I can't lose you,' he muttered. 'I can't.'

Her heart turned over. This man, who she'd only come to know because she thought he'd blackmailed her, and who she'd only married because Society had forced them to, this man—she couldn't lose him, either.

She touched his face, luxuriating in the feel of his skin against hers. 'All right,' she said, stepping back and picking up her satchel. 'You can come. But no heroics, you understand? This is witch business. You're coming purely as a … a…'

'Consider me your personal guard,' he said, and bowed with a flourish that made her smile.

They made it back downstairs with the help of Tiffany's invisibility spell, and found Gwen where they'd left her, staring at the door.

'Back to the house ain't the problem,' she said, staring at the iron key in her hand. 'It remembers home. It wants to go home. Getting to Esme, now…'

'One step at a time,' said Tiffany, and Gwen stepped forward and muttered something to the closed door. She inserted the key, turned it, and Tiffany held her breath.

The door opened into the upstairs hall of Esme's London townhouse, with the Queen Anne table and the painting that was probably a Reynolds. Gwen let out a small sigh of relief, and sniffed the air.

'Mutton curry,' she said. 'But Madhu does make that a lot.'

Before Tiffany could ask what that meant, Nora and Madhu's footsteps sounded on the stairs.

'Oh, there you are, Your Graces,' said Nora, sweeping into a curtsey.

'Barely half an hour has passed,' said Madhu. 'Are we ready?'

Both of them were dressed in sturdy outdoor clothing. Nora, Tiffany was shocked to see, wore breeches.

'Are we all going?'

'To rescue Esme? Of course.' Madhu flipped her hood up. 'We apologise for interrupting your honeymoon, Your Grace—'

'No, *you* apologise,' muttered Nora.

'Please don't Your Grace me,' said Tiffany. 'Esme says all witches are equal, so I am just Tiffany.'

'Right then, Just Tiffany,' said Nora. 'We need to get this door open, and find Esme. It took all three of us to get Gwen to you, and I reckon a fourth won't hurt. You'll need something of Esme's—'

'I have this,' said Tiffany, taking out the opal necklace.

'Of course you do, Your Grace.' Nora put her hand on the door, and said to Santiago, 'You can stay here, Your Grace. There's newspapers downstairs. Bonaparte has left Paris.'

Santiago looked outraged. 'Well, I will not be leaving my wife. I am coming with you. You may be in need of...'

Four female faces looked back at him with varying degrees of politeness.

'Er, sailing?' he said hopefully.

'We might as well take him,' said Tiffany. 'He'll only pine if we don't.'

He rolled his eyes at her, but stood back and let the witches work their magic.

'We wants the door to open to wherever Esme is,' said Gwen, as they each placed one hand on the door and held a token of Esme's in the other. A ribbon, a hatpin, a pocket watch, and the opals.

'Do we know where that is?' said Nora.

'Flanders. Or France.'

'You said there was a big battle coming,' said Tiffany. 'Would it help us to focus on that?'

'We don't want to come out in the middle of a battle!' said Nora.

'You won't,' said Santiago, from behind them. 'Battles don't usually feature doors.'

'He has a point,' said Tiffany. 'So. Esme, war ... oh, and a tower.'

'I seen the tower too,' said Gwen. She wrapped the pocket watch chain around her fingers and held the key ready.

'There was a bright light outside it,' said Tiffany. 'Flashing somewhat.'

'Esme, war, flashing light, tower,' repeated Nora impatiently. 'Now: concentrate.'

Tiffany did her best to, but her mind kept straying to her mother. Was it really her in the tower? Had Esme gone to rescue her and been captured? What was in that basin in the corner?

Concentrate, Tiffany. Esme war, flashing light, tower. Esme, war...

The door clicked open.

A torrent of noise assaulted them. The loudest Tiffany had ever heard. It was like the firing of the pistol that had shot Santiago, magnified by a thousand, and never-ending.

They were on a bleak spit of land extending into the sea, the land merely piles of shingle, and across that shingle raced men in strange clothing, carrying strange muskets. In the water floated craft the like of which she'd never seen before, huge and angular with no sails. As she stood staring, one of them beached itself and from it, more men began to run towards them.

Around them, a light flashed, and she looked up to see a lighthouse, red and white, shining a light brighter than she'd ever seen. The tower. The flashing light. And yet...

'What is this place?' Tiffany gasped. Santiago wrapped his arm around her and held her firm against him.

'Get inside,' said Nora, and opened the door they'd just come through, only now it led inside the lighthouse. Inside it was full of yet more men in those strange clothes, and lit more brightly than a summer's day.

'What the hell?' one of them shouted, and then the muskets were all pointed at them.

'Put your hands up,' suggested Santiago, as one of the soldiers—surely these were soldiers?—bawled at them to do the same.

'What the hell are civilians doing in here?' shouted one of them.

'Are you USO?' asked one.

'No, son, we're—' began Gwen, and Tiffany hurriedly spoke over her.

'Lost,' she said. 'Very lost.'

The soldier who had last spoken shook his head. 'I'll say. You British? You sound British.'

'Yes?' she said. They were speaking English, but with an accent she didn't recognise.

'British beaches are that-a-way.' He pointed. 'But what the hell you doing here? And … what the hell you *wearing*?'

He did not apologise for swearing in front of the ladies. Perhaps soldiers didn't.

Tiffany didn't know how to answer that, but thankfully Santiago stepped forward, his hands still raised.

'Gentlemen,' he said, smiling. 'There appears to have been some confusion here.'

'The hell you say. What the hell are you, Shakespeare in the Park? This is an invasion, buddy. You hear those guns?'

Those were *guns*? How could they fire so fast? How many of them were there?

'It is all I hear,' Santiago agreed.

'Well, you get hit by one of those, there ain't nothing to send home to your mama, you hear what I'm saying?' He shook his head. 'Corporal, get these people somewhere secure, huh? Away from operations. And pat 'em down. You armed?'

There was a pause. Santiago cleared his throat. 'I have a pistol,' he said.

They allowed him to reach for it, slowly, but when he brought it out the soldiers stared, and then laughed.

'Are you kidding?'

'That's an antique!'

Santiago looked hurt. 'I assure you, it is quite new. One of Manton's finest.'

'Who?'

Tiffany was taken aback. Everyone knew Manton was the finest gunsmith in London.

The soldier with the stripes on his arm took the pistol gingerly. 'You know, last time I saw something like that was on a grade school trip to Colonial Williamsburg.'

Tiffany glanced at her husband, who looked as blank as the rest of them.

'I see,' he said. 'Well, we are not intending to cause any harm; we are, as my wife says, merely lost. So, if you could hand that back to me, we will be on our way.'

He spoke very reasonably, but the soldier was shaking his head.

'Can't do that, buddy. Who else is armed? Hey, you, lady, what you got in that bag there?'

Tiffany clutched her satchel closer to her side. 'Nothing,' she said. 'Just drawing materials.'

Santiago winced.

'Drawing, huh? So you can make sketches of our defences?' He shook his head. 'I don't know who you're working for, but hand it over.'

'I'm afraid I shall have to decline your request,' said Tiffany, in her best duchess voice.

The soldier gave her a weary look. 'And I'm afraid I'm gonna have to bust a cap in your ass if you don't do what I say. Hand it over. Fellas, pat 'em down.'

To Tiffany's horror, the soldiers advanced, hands outstretched.

'I don't think so,' said Nora, squaring her shoulders.

'I do not permit this,' said Madhu nervously.

'I do,' said Gwen wistfully, eyeing the young soldiers.

Tiffany tried to move closer to Santiago, but the nearest soldier waved his gun between them. He grinned at Tiffany and held out his hands.

'You will not touch my wife,' Santiago hissed.

'Buddy, no disrespect but I gotta know what she's hiding in that corset.'

Tiffany's outraged gasp did nothing to stop him touching her. His hands ran lewdly over her body, beneath her cloak.

'What's this?' he said, finding the opals clutched in her hand. 'Hey, that's pretty.'

'You can't have it,' she said.

'Lady, I ain't a thief. Here, hands up while I search the rest of you.'

'Take your hands off me,' she said, backing away.

'Do not touch her!' growled Santiago.

'Sorry lady, gotta check you're not hiding anything.'

'I give you my word as a lady.' She had backed against the wall now.

'Unhand my wife,' snarled Santiago. When she glanced over, there were two soldiers holding on to him as he struggled towards her.

'I'd do as he says,' Nora said. 'He's known as a brawler.'

'She is mine,' he shouted, as the soldiers held him down. 'She belongs to me!'

Tiffany flinched, but not because of the soldier's touch.

She belongs to me.

With some detachment, she saw a soldier punch Santiago hard on the jaw, and he went down like a puppet with the strings cut.

She belongs to me.

She allowed the men to paw through her bag and take away the sketchbook and pencils, and watched as Nora easily lifted Santiago over her shoulder to carry up the narrow, winding stairs as they were directed.

She belongs to me.

He had promised her, mere hours after their marriage, that she belonged to no one but herself. That she would have her own life. That she was no possession.

She watched Nora set him down, not particularly gently, on the hard stone floor of the circular tower. The room was sparsely filled with some kind of machinery and equipment she didn't understand, and there was a rusted metal ring in the centre of the floor. The light coming from a strange lantern on the ceiling was so bright it was giving her a headache. There were men running up and down the narrow spiral stairs, shouting unintelligible things to each other, and all of them had those huge, terrifying guns. The witches were ordered to sit on the floor until the CO—whatever that was—could work out what to do with them.

Santiago began to wake, and Tiffany stared away from him as she sat on the cold, hard floor.

She'd been a fool.

He'd said all those things to reassure her, but had he actually meant them? Of course he wanted an obedient duchess who would bear him heirs. All that talk of travel—she knew perfectly well men didn't take their wives with them when they went off on their grand adventures. Look at her own father. Look at her mother, who she might never find now.

It was all an illusion, as real as one of her drawings.

Was this why her mother had run away? Was this why Elinor

and Cornforth had such a cold marriage? Was this all there could ever be? What a fool she had been to believe she could have anything else. What a jingle-brained, mutton-pated fool.

'Your Grace?' murmured Madhu, and Tiffany flinched. At least when she was Lady Tiffany she'd had her own name—even if no one ever used it. Now she was Your Grace, the Duchess of St James. No name. Just his wife.

She was her father's daughter. Her brother's sister. And now she was her husband's wife. She had lost her chance to ever be a person in her own right.

'I have some remedies in my pockets. I can help His Grace, but we may need to distract the soldiers.'

'He's fine,' said Tiffany, because Santiago was clearly awake now, massaging his jaw and wincing. She wanted to punch him again. Harder. Maybe get Nora to do it.

She wanted to cry. But crying would achieve nothing. Tiffany let fury build in its place.

'We need to work out how to get out of here,' said Nora.

Madhu considered. 'I could perhaps formulate an explosive,' she said.

'I could punch a lot of people,' said Nora, who looked as if this was her preferred option.

Starting with my husband. 'I could draw us a door,' Tiffany said. They had taken her satchel but she might have some chalk in her pockets.

'We're halfway up the tower. Must've climbed a hundred feet.'

'Oh. Yes.' There was a pain in her chest. It might be her heart breaking.

'And there are a great many men with guns,' Nora pointed out.

'And punching them will help?'

'Ladies—' began Santiago, and Tiffany turned cold fury on him.

'No. Not you. You've helped enough. This is witch business.'

KATE JOHNSON

He blinked at her in confusion. 'I... Yes. Of course.'

'Gwen, do you have any ideas?' Tiffany asked.

Gwen stared at nothing. 'The sergeant will die in a village crossed by a river,' she said.

'Well, that's helpful, thank you.'

Anger boiled in her. They were trapped here, in this tower, with these men carrying guns the like of which she'd never seen, and all Santiago had done to help was get himself punched in the face.

She tried to think. An explosion in so small a space would probably do more harm than good, and like her idea of drawing a door, still had the problem of being many feet above the ground. In fact, the lighthouse had been perched on a rocky promontory, so there was every chance they would fall into the sea and be dashed to death on the rocks.

If only Esme—

Wait. She wasn't thinking right at all!

'We only need a door,' she said.

322

CHAPTER 18

$\mathcal{N}$ora made an impatient sound. 'We're a hundred feet up,' she repeated.

'Not to the outside. To wherever Esme is. We got it wrong this time, but perhaps if we concentrate extra hard...'

'Extra hard?' scoffed Nora.

'Well, do you have any better ideas? We still have our tokens, yes? And Gwen has the key—' she broke off. 'Gwen, the token you chose. It was Esme's pocket watch?'

Gwen nodded. She still held it in one hand.

Tiffany slumped against the wall for a moment. 'Gwen,' she said patiently. 'You can see the past and the future, and you are holding a pocket watch, and you opened the door...'

Madhu groaned as she caught on. Nora said, 'She opened the door to the wrong... time?'

'Right place, wrong time,' said Tiffany. She pressed her hands to her face. 'Do you still have the key?'

'Yes,' said Gwen. She frowned, and felt at her bodice. 'No. Mayhap they took it?'

Tiffany made a noise of frustration. Nora swore. Madhu tried to soothe Gwen.

'Even if I had it, wouldn't guarantee we'd get to the right time,' Gwen said. She looked a bit ashamed. 'Esme did tell me not to tinker with it, after last time.'

'What happened last time?' Tiffany asked, morbidly fascinated.

But right then a commotion could be heard coming up the stairs. Tiffany saw Madhu reach into her pockets, and Nora square her shoulders. She felt in her pocket for some chalk.

She refused to look at Santiago.

'… let me see… Ah, yes, there you are.'

The door opened, and a woman stood at the top of the stairs, blocking them for anyone following. She was dressed in the most scandalous garments, all of a deep scarlet. It was almost like a riding habit, but with a skirt so short Tiffany could see her *knees*.

Her hat was quite dashing, though.

'Morning, chaps,' she said briskly. 'Seems you've been blown a bit off course.'

The witches got to their feet, Tiffany ignoring Santiago's outstretched hand. She noted that the other witches looked quite pleased to see this woman.

'Lot of that happening,' said the woman, and added to the soldier behind her. 'Like you chaps up at Utah beach, eh? A lot of confusion today. Well, up you come,' she said, and looked at them all squarely. 'I'll get you back where you need to be.'

To Tiffany's great annoyance, it was Santiago who spoke. 'Mistress Winterscale,' he said. 'We met at Mistress Blackmantle's soirée.'

'Can you believe these guys?' muttered one of the soldiers.

'We did, Your Grace, and I was sorry to see you leave so early. Mistress Buttars,' she nodded at Gwen. 'Miss Nayak. Miss Leatherheart. Miss…?'

Santiago cleared his throat. 'Mistress Winterscale; my wife, Her Grace the Duchess of St James.'

There was a slight hush amongst the soldiers behind Mistress Winterscale, who gave Tiffany a very thorough look over.

'An honour,' she said, but she did not curtsey. Tiffany gave her a nod. 'Now, Your Graces, my sisters, if you would perhaps follow me? Time and tide wait for no man.'

Tiffany glanced urgently at the others. They all seemed quite happy to follow this woman. Relieved, even. She was clearly a witch. Tiffany could not say exactly how she knew this, but Mistress Winterscale's poise and confidence probably had something to do with it.

'And you can take us where we need to be?' she said.

'Indeed I can. Sergeant, I shall need a briefing room. Spit spot!'

As they followed her down the narrow, winding stairs, Tiffany felt Santiago fall in behind her. 'Are you all right?' he asked.

I am a fool for marrying you. 'Quite,' she said haughtily, and shrugged away from him.

'So, who are these guys?' said one of the soldiers to Mistress Winterscale.

'Ah, top secret, I'm afraid.'

'Okay, but why are they dressed like they're in a play or something? Are they USO— I mean, what do you guys have?'

'ENSA. Not quite, but it'll do. Your CO will lend me his office,' she said, and it was a command, not a request.

In short order, they were bundled into what appeared to have been the lighthouse keeper's cottage, which had now been turned into an office that was being vacated by a rather put-out officer with a moustache.

'Goddamn Brits still think they rule the world,' he grumbled.

'Goddamn Brits kept the wolf from the door for two years on a worldwide front,' said Mistress Winterscale crisply, and closed the door behind the harrumphing officer.

A sort of silence fell, but only inside the room. Outside it, the rattle and crash of gunfire could still be heard, alongside other noises Tiffany could never identify.

'Now,' said Mistress Winterscale, taking off her hat and smoothing her jacket. 'Bit of a sticky wicket here. I do seem to spend half my time rescuing witches who are in the wrong time and place. Why is it so difficult to stay in your own time, hm?'

'When are we?' Tiffany ventured to ask.

'Probably best not to say. No spoilers. Now—briefly, please— what happened, and where and when do you need to be?'

Gwen was the senior of the witches, but Tiffany was the senior in social standing, and besides, Gwen didn't seem as if her head and her body were in the same week right now.

She cleared her throat, and tried to explain what had happened.

'We were considering trying to repeat the trick, but we don't have the key any more. And besides...' She bit her lip as she looked at Gwen, who was smiling faintly.

'What happened to the key?'

'The soldiers took it.'

'Along with my knuckle dusters,' said Nora.

'And my pistol,' said Santiago.

'Well, it shouldn't be hard to get those back. The problem is, I'm afraid, that while I can take you back to your own time, I can only do so in one specific place.'

'And where is that?'

'Essex.'

'And we are in...?'

Mistress Winterscale looked surprised. 'Normandy.'

'France,' said Gwen unexpectedly. 'Knew it was an F place.'

'Where did you mean to be?'

Tiffany shrugged helplessly. 'Wherever Mistress Blackmantle

is. She was supposed to be rescuing my mother, who is trapped in a tower somewhere.'

'You mother?' Mistress Winterscale's expression suddenly cleared. 'Of course! Amelia Davenport.' For some reason she glanced at Santiago. 'You are Lady Tiffany?'

Tiffany opened her mouth to explain that the 'lady' part had been superseded by the 'duchess' part, and shut it again. She nodded.

'Now it makes more sense. You are in the right place, I believe, but the wrong time. We could really use Esme's help here, but...'

Santiago cleared his throat. 'May I ask a question about this ... time ... journey business?'

'Of course, but don't expect to understand the answer. Quantum mechanics are quite complex.'

He smiled politely. Damn his eyes for being so handsome!

'You require a door in a specific place to take us home, correct? But we came here—now—using Mistress Blackmantle's key and Mistress Buttars's ability to see through time, aided by Mistress Blackmantle's pocket watch. Also correct?'

So he had been listening. And comprehending, far more than Tiffany really did.

'May I ask, Mistress Winterscale, if you can control the precise time to which you travel? The year—the day? The hour?'

'The year, certainly,' she said. 'The day, usually. The hour—not so precisely. But I need my door.'

Santiago glanced at Tiffany. 'My wife can draw,' he said.

Tiffany snapped. 'I have a name. I am more than your— Draw?' she said, as his meaning suddenly became clear.

Santiago didn't take his eyes off Tiffany as he spoke to Mistress Winterscale. 'If you had your door here, would it work?'

'Yes, but I don't—'

'Tell me what it looks like,' said Tiffany. 'And if you could retrieve my satchel, I would be most grateful.'

Mistress Winterscale seemed bemused, but she swept from the room and her voice was heard beyond, issuing orders.

'Tiffany,' said Santiago, moving closer. The room was too small to back away. 'What is wrong?'

His jaw was swollen on one side, the bruise already darkening. The skin around his eyes was tense, as if he was trying not to frown.

'Nothing is wrong,' she said. 'I shall draw the door and we can all go back to where—when—we should be.'

His eyes narrowed. 'What did you mean about having a name?'

She sighed. 'It doesn't matter,' she said. She closed her eyes. 'No, wait, it does. I don't have a name anymore, do I? I'm just your wife. The duchess.'

Santiago looked bemused. 'Of course you have a name. That did not change. Do you ... wish to be called Theophania now?'

'No!' She didn't know how to explain it to him. 'It's more that I ... I don't have an identity other than how I relate to you. For years the only connection that mattered was my father; now it is my husband. I am defined by men. One day, I will be the mother of a duke, and that is all.'

She looked over at the other witches, who were examining one of the strange devices in the cottage kitchen.

'I will never be my own woman. I will always be ... your woman.'

His brow creased. 'And I will be your man. That is how marriage works, no?'

He tried to take her hand and Tiffany shrugged him off. 'No! Because you do not belong to me, whereas I am merely a possession of yours. A belonging. Chattel. I fooled myself that you would give me the independence I wished for, and yet what has happened since our marriage? I have been a duchess, not a witch. I am only ever "Your Grace" to absolutely everybody. Even Billy! I couldn't even come here—now—on business that solely concerns witches, without you keeping an eye on me. I have given up everything I...'

Santiago looked very troubled, but he let her speak. Tiffany tried to organise her thoughts so she wasn't shrieking incoherently.

'That night. When you and my idiot brother shot at each other, do you know why I was there? I was running away. To go and live with Aunt Esme. And I was happy. I wanted it.'

He shook his head, uncomprehending. 'But you were the one who wanted to get married?'

'Yes! Because I thought you were dying! And I—' She broke off. It was too hard to explain. How could she want to be with him and yet yearn for her independence at the same time?

She tried to remember that feeling, how desperate she had been for him to live, how she loved him so much, how she would have given anything for him to survive. And now she had given everything, and she felt so ... hollow.

Then Santiago spoke. 'You wished to marry me solely because you thought I was going to die?'

There was a coldness in his voice she had not heard before.

'Yes,' she said wretchedly. She had suddenly realised her feelings for him and been stupidly rash.

'Ah. Becoming a duchess without a tiresome husband around to keep an eye on you. I see now.' He stepped back from her, and for the first time regarded her with contempt. 'I see now why you did not wish me to come to your bed, if I was to be solely a means to an end. Although an heir would cement your position in a way being widowed would not.'

'What do you—'

'And now you are stuck with a most troublesome husband who merely *requests*,' he spat the word, 'your presence in his bed. I have told you, you are free to decline at any time, but now you will not need bother as I will not trouble you any longer.'

'But—' Tiffany began, confused about how this had got away from her.

He turned away, then back again, and his face was dark with fury. 'There is the possibility that you are with child,' he said in a low, quick voice.

'I have been taking Madhu's powders.'

'Forgive me for not trusting the word of a witch.' He glanced down at her belly in a disparaging manner. 'If—' he began, but right then the door opened and Mistress Winterscale strode back in, followed by a soldier carrying their possessions.

'We will continue this later,' he said.

'Fine.'

'Fine.'

Tiffany snatched up her satchel and found her colouring crayons. She looked around for a section of blank wall, asked Nora to move a table, and addressed Mistress Winterscale for instructions.

As she drew, she rolled Santiago's words over and over in her head. She could not find the words to say that she loved him but also wanted her independence, and then she had said something that made him angry.

She did love him, that was the problem. She hadn't wanted to and she hadn't expected to, but the mere memory of him lying bleeding on the ground made her heart clench. She couldn't be without him. She couldn't be a witch with him.

It was impossible, and in her frustration she had made things worse.

'Don't cry, dear, there is always a solution,' said Mistress Winterscale with stiffness in her voice. 'We shall overcome and all that. No, the hourglass is a little larger...'

Eventually, she was happy, and Tiffany stood back to see a red door drawn on the wall, bearing an hourglass symbol and some hints of decoration. Mistress Winterscale had not been able to supply their full details.

'Is it close enough?' she said.

'Close enough for what?'

'Oh.' Tiffany realised she had not explained this part. She placed her hand upon the door and felt it come to life beneath her fingers.

'Remarkable!' breathed Mistress Winterscale. 'Can you do this with anything?'

'Anything that isn't living. Or food. But it doesn't last long.'

'Then we had better get moving. Do you all have everything? And you wish to be right here, at this lighthouse in Normandy?'

They nodded. Tiffany did not look at Santiago.

Mistress Winterscale produced a key from around her neck and paused. 'Your Grace,' she said, removing from her pocket a very small device that looked as if it might be a distant cousin of the Manton. 'Is your pistol loaded?'

'Does it need to be?'

'I don't know what will be on the other side of this door. France in 1815 is almost as bad as France now.'

Santiago nodded and loaded the pistol with shot and powder. 'Nora,' he said, 'you are good with your fists?'

'When I need to be,' she said.

'In the vanguard with me, please. Your Grace'—here he gave Tiffany a lightning glance—'to the back, please.'

What did that mean? That he cared about her? Or that he thought she might be carrying his child?

She was barely in place beside Gwen when the door opened onto a dark room that seemed very similar to the one they were in, but suddenly very much quieter.

'Same place, different time,' Mistress Winterscale whispered.

'The correct time?' Nora whispered back. Rain pattered on the roof, a blissful relief from the heavy gunfire.

'Well, only one way to find out.'

She curved her hand around the air and a ball of light appeared. A voice began, '*Qu-est ce—?*' and a shot rang out. It wasn't Santiago's pistol. Someone cried out and whimpered desperately in French.

The light grew large enough to illuminate the room, and Tiffany crowded in behind the others to see a man curled on the floor, clutching at his leg and swearing. To her great relief, he was wearing pantaloons and a grubby shirt, and the musket by his side was of a familiar type.

'*Quelle est la date?*' Mistress Winterscale demanded.

The injured man stammered out an answer. Santiago and Nora both slumped in relief but Tiffany had never learned French, and she really didn't have the energy to pull off the trick she had with Father Thames.

'He says it is the seventeenth of June, 1815,' Mistress Winterscale reported. 'Is that close enough?'

'It is the day after we left,' Tiffany said. She wanted to collapse with relief, too.

'The day before Waterloo,' Mistress Winterscale said. 'Cannot be a coincidence.'

'The day before what?'

'Oh … you'll find out soon enough.'

Mistress Winterscale rapped out a few more questions, but the Frenchman was sobbing in pain.

'Let me through,' said Madhu, and knelt by him, reaching into her bag and various pockets.

'I don't know why he's making such a fuss, it's a small calibre bullet and I only hit his calf,' sniffed Mistress Winterscale.

She made more demands in French, and this time got some answers. 'There are two women in the tower, he says. There are more guards in the base of the tower, three I think.' She shifted rapidly into French again, and then back when she got her answer. 'He does not know who is in charge. A foreigner. He is not here.'

'Then what are we waiting for?' said Tiffany. Aunt Esme and, possibly, her mother were up there.

The mother who had abandoned her when she was a mere babe. She ought to work out what she felt about that, but her head was full of Santiago telling her he didn't want her anymore.

But I love him.

And she loved him so much that the thought of being without him was like a physical pain. Could she survive if he decided to live a separate life from her, as so many couples did? Would she end up going to live with Esme, as she had originally planned?

It had once seemed like the only thing she wanted. And now it seemed a poor second choice.

A hand touched her arm. It was Nora. 'Are you ready?'

Tiffany squared her shoulders and forced herself not to look at her husband. 'Let's go.'

CHAPTER 19

*S*antiago watched his wife follow Mistress Winterscale up the narrow spiral staircase to the first floor and disappear out of sight.

Had she really only married him for his name and title?

For a moment, back there on that hill in Hertfordshire, he had thought he actually was dying. That he had finally succumbed to the bullet that all pirates and smugglers secretly expect, and he would never get to make love to Lady Tiffany and her magnificent bosom.

And then she had appeared above him, like an angel, and he suddenly hadn't been dying anymore, and she said she wanted to marry him, and now … was he misremembering? Had he got it wrong? Had all her talk of independence only lasted for as long as it took to get a ring on her finger? He could have died from that bullet, even though the wound hadn't seemed fatal. He had seen men bleed to death from simple wounds to the arm or leg, and he had seen gangrene set in more times than he wished to remember. Tiffany was a witch, she could probably have cursed him to death, or pushed him down the stairs, or—

But did he really believe that?

When they made love, she had looked at him with such love, such trust in her eyes. Could she have pretended that? Could it *all* have been a pretence? Out of all the people he'd met in London, especially the young ladies, Tiffany had been the only one not to fawn over him once she found out he was a duke. Exactly the opposite, in fact, which was one of the reasons he had fallen in love with her. But was all that a pretence, too? Had she merely been playing a very clever game?

He shook himself and gestured Gwen and Madhu ahead of him, taking up the rear with his pistol ready. They were here to effect a rescue, and she had made it painfully clear that she didn't want him here. Although it had been his idea that had got them to the right place…

From further up, he heard Mistress Winterscale say, 'Stand back,' and then there was the sound of a shot, and a door banged open. Feminine voices cried out, and he burned with frustration that he couldn't see what was happening. Ahead of him, Gwen moved with agonising slowness, and he thought he might die before he ever got there.

Then finally he stood in the doorway to the room they'd been held in earlier, and there was Esme Blackmantle, helping another woman to her feet from a filthy pallet bed.

For a moment his heart stopped, because she looked so very much like Tiffany, with pale, silvery hair and fine porcelain skin. But she was older, and looked terribly tired and pained. Her gown was ragged and stained, and around one bare ankle was a manacle and chain fastened to the metal ring in the floor he had seen last time. It gleamed horribly in the pale light from the witches' orbs.

She was staring at Tiffany as if she had seen a ghost, and the reaction was mutual. Tiffany stood frozen, gaping at the other woman in shock.

'It is you,' she whispered.

'Tiffany?' said the older woman. 'Is it really you?'

'Mama?' Her voice was almost inaudible, her eyes glossy with tears. Santiago wanted to go to her, sweep her into his arms and tell her it would all be all right.

He almost laughed at himself. Three minutes ago he'd been despising her as a fortune hunter, and now he wanted to hold her close and beg for her forgiveness. How could he have been so stupid?

Because you fear losing her. And he couldn't bear that. He loved her so much he was blind with it. He was clearly stupid with it. He must tell her he was wrong.

But now clearly was not the time. Tiffany was gazing at the woman who was unquestionably her mother, with such mixed emotions on her face.

'You have grown so,' said her mother. Amelia, that was her name. 'I knew you must have, but it is still a shock to see you now, a full-grown woman. The last I saw you were such a tiny babe.'

'And you left me,' said Tiffany quietly.

'I didn't want to! I had to!'

'Had to? What could have been so important you left your infant daughter? Your marriage to Papa was as awful as—' She broke off, not looking at Santiago, and ice stabbed into his heart. *As awful as ours?* 'So awful you left? And went who knows where!'

Amelia had tears rolling down her cheeks. Esme was practically holding her up. 'Anywhere,' she said. 'France, Italy, the Netherlands. Anywhere that was far from you—'

Tiffany's face crumpled and Santiago couldn't stand it anymore. He pushed past the other witches and put his arm around her, drawing her against his body. *I'm here. I'm here for you.*

Even if you don't love me.

Tiffany put her arm over his, squeezing it, and his heart swelled with hope.

'Why?' she whispered, and for a long moment the only sound was the crashing of waves outside. The mighty light from the tower above them cast its beam across the sea, but the night was otherwise dark and silent.

'So I couldn't hurt you!' cried Amelia, and Esme held her close, much as Santiago did with Tiffany.

Oh, he realised. *So that's how it is.*

'Amelia was afraid of her power,' Esme said, as Amelia sobbed in her arms. 'Afraid she would cause harm to those she loved. Like you, Tiffany.'

'And you,' said Amelia, looking up at Esme. 'I was so afraid of hurting people.' She glanced over to the far side of the room, and said bitterly, 'But that is all I have done.'

All of them looked where she indicated. Apart from Gwen, who was already there, standing over a sort of large basin and cooing. Beside the basin was a net on a pole, and a couple of toy boats. They were stained reddish brown. Around the basin, candles and heaps of wax stood, and eldritch symbols had been chalked on the floor.

On the basin itself was drawn a cockerel, curiously like the one on Santiago's ankle.

'Oh,' said Nora, her eyes going wide.

'It is afraid,' said Madhu.

'He's just hungry,' said Gwen, picking up a little toy boat.

'He hasn't eaten for days,' said Tiffany. 'He is considering eating your fingers, Gwen.'

Gwen pulled her hand back sharply, and there was a splashing sound as she dropped the boat.

'What is it?' Santiago ventured.

'The beasty with the squirmers,' cried Gwen. She seemed delighted.

'A squid,' said Amelia, wiping her eyes. 'They don't feed him for a few days when they want me to use him.'

'Use him?'

She turned her face away as if she was ashamed. 'To attack ships.'

The monstrous tentacles made of pure water that had grabbed him and hurled him from the sea; his ships that had vanished without trace; Mr Noakes's account of the vast arms of the sea that engulfed a vessel.

'That was you?' he gasped.

Tiffany broke away from him and approached the basin. Santiago forced himself to remain where he was. 'I have seen this,' she said. 'In puddles and ponds and lakes. I have seen it looking back at me. I thought I was losing my mind.'

'It was when I thought of you,' Amelia confessed. 'When they made me perform the spell. I thought of you.'

'But … why? When you were using this to kill people, you thought of me?' Tiffany looked appalled.

'Because that's why I did it! They threatened you. They said they knew where you lived; they even told me you were getting married…'

She glanced at Santiago, who gave her an awkward wave. This was one hell of a way to meet your mother-in-law.

'They lied, surely,' said Tiffany. 'Everyone knew I was getting married. It was quite the … um, event,' she muttered, cheeks turning pink. Probably not wanting to admit to her mother that she had been compromised into marriage.

'I couldn't take the risk,' said Amelia. 'How could I?'

Esme patted her shoulder. 'We should really get out of here,' she said. 'What did you do to the guards?'

'Knocked them out and tied them up,' said Nora. 'Esme, how did you get stuck up here anyway?'

'They took my key,' she said darkly. 'When I entered, they

were in here, feeding the squid, and they knocked me out and locked me up with Amelia. We were trying to formulate an escape plan.'

'Well, here it is,' said Tiffany. 'Gwen has your spare key, Esme, and—'

'I don't have a spare key,' Esme said, and Gwen looked a little shamefaced.

'I made a copy,' she said. 'Probably why it don't work so well.'

Esme looked as if she was about to remonstrate with Gwen for that, but changed her mind. 'Well, anyway. We can use that to get back.' She looked around the group and frowned. 'Lilith? What are you doing here?'

Mistress Winterscale gave a polite nod. Her clothing seemed even more at odds in this room.

'I just happened to be in the area,' she said. 'You know me, I do like a big world event. I felt a disturbance in the ether, people where they shouldn't be—or *when* they shouldn't be—so I came to investigate. I think I shall stay here for the now. Waterloo tomorrow. Don't want to miss that.'

'What is Waterloo?' asked Tiffany.

'Ah. Well, I might as well tell you. The papers will be full of it. Bonaparte and Wellington's allies will be facing off in the morning. In Belgium, I believe. Esme, I don't suppose I could…? No, well, I shall get there for the closing of it, and offer my assistance. What a pity you didn't end up at Dunkirk, eh?'

This was met with blank stares from all round.

'That will make sense in a century or so,' she said. 'Well then, I suppose I should find some clothes and a horse.'

'And we should all go,' said Madhu. 'I can't say how long those guards will stay knocked out for.'

'How do I get free?' Amelia asked, the chain at her ankle clinking. Santiago was about to suggest Tiffany draw some tools, when Nora bent down to inspect it.

She felt at the chain, where it was linked to the floor, and where it fastened onto Amelia's ankle. The skin was red and raw, chafed especially where the manacle had been welded into a circle. 'This might hurt a bit,' she said, and inserted her fingers between manacle and skin. Amelia hissed, but a second later Nora had pulled the metal apart with a snap at the weld.

Amelia gave a sob, and flexed her ankle. 'Thank you, Miss...?'

'Leatherheart. Nora, ma'am. Happy to help.'

'Now can we go?' said Tiffany, and Santiago ached to take her hand.

Esme nodded, and Gwen handed her the key.

'What about Squidbert?' said Amelia.

There was a slight pause while they all digested this.

'Squidbert, my love?' said Esme.

Amelia gestured to the basin. 'We can't leave him. He's been my only companion. Can't we release him into the sea?'

'He yearns for the sea,' said Tiffany. 'This basin is like a prison cell to him.'

'We are worrying about a squid,' muttered Santiago, as Nora rolled her eyes and marched over to the basin.

She hefted the heavy stone trough into her arms, and said, 'Fine. Let's go.'

They processed down the stairs, and Santiago really wanted to take Tiffany's hand, but she was preoccupied, staring at her mother as she was helped down the stairs by Esme. Right. That was going to take some coming around to.

Outside, rain was falling. The lighthouse rose above them, shining its light out into the night. Rain fell gently.

'He's not going to continue attacking ships, is he?' he said, peering into the basin where the squid, less than a foot across, peered back at him with its weird eyes. The pupils were oblong. 'I think it is an octopus,' he said, and Squidbert blinked at him.

'He says you are correct,' said Tiffany.

'You can really understand his thoughts?'

'Yes. He's very intelligent. He does not like being made to attack ships, but he doesn't blame my— Amelia for it. He understands they are both prisoners.'

Santiago gaped at his wife. Truly, she was astonishing.

He hoped to God she'd forgive him.

Amelia reached into the basin and touched the octopus's strange head. 'Goodbye, my friend,' she said. 'Enjoy the ocean.'

'He wants you to hurry up,' said Tiffany, still keeping her distance from her mother, who nodded, and Nora stepped away.

Then Gwen said, 'What's that?'

They all looked around, and then Tiffany said, 'Hoofbeats?'

'Oh no,' said Amelia. 'Quick, to the door—'

Santiago grabbed Tiffany's arm and sprinted. But it was too far. Even as they ran, shots rang out, and they all froze. He grabbed Tiffany to him, but her quick nod told him she was all right.

'Well, this is interesting,' said a voice, and Santiago thought he must be hearing things. 'Now there are two of you.'

He turned, dreading what he would see, but he was not mistaken. The beam of the lighthouse illuminated the giant bearded man as he swung down from his horse and strode towards them.

It was de Groot.

'Two witches at my disposal,' he said, striding over, a pistol in his hand and a French rifle slung across his back. 'Or maybe more?'

'You cannot hold me any longer,' said Amelia, defiant. From the corner of his eye, Santiago saw Mistress Winterscale reaching into her pocket, and wondered if he had time to reach for the pistol he'd holstered. But de Groot wouldn't shoot him, would he?

'I am the one with the guns,' said de Groot. 'And the guards.'

'We also have guns,' said Santiago, stepping forward, angling his body to protect Tiffany. 'The guards are unconscious. Hello, *mi amigo*.'

De Groot looked genuinely startled to see him there. '*Mijnheer* Santiago? But—what are you doing—?'

Santiago lifted his chin. 'You are responsible for imprisoning my mother-in-law,' he said.

De Groot threw back his head and laughed. 'I had not thought of it that way! Of course, I knew her child had married you. Even a mere trader hears that kind of Society gossip. Do you know your wife is a witch?'

'And a very good one,' said Santiago proudly. 'You have imprisoned her mother. And forced her to commit atrocities.'

De Groot shrugged. It was like a tree bending in the wind. 'Would we say atrocities?'

'Three of my ships went down with all hands,' Santiago spat, anger boiling to the surface again. This was no imagined betrayal. De Groot wasn't even denying it!

'Ships sink, *mijn vriend*.'

'Muller and Sons lost another one last week—that's a total of four. Pernice's lost two. Damsgaard has lost three now and you know how small his fleet is. Troop ships sailing home from the Americas have vanished. Packet boats across the Channel.' Santiago shook his head. 'Your own ships!'

De Groot shrugged again. 'Oh, I lied about those. They came in. They are protected, you see.'

'Protected by what?'

De Groot patted his own shoulder. 'Remember that cock on your ankle? A splendid joke, *ja*?' He nodded at the octopus in the basin Nora still held. 'That thing is repulsed by it. Part of the magic. It's clever, *ja*? All the French ships have them, carved in somewhere. And mine, obviously.'

The cockerel on his ankle. Was that why the creature had thrown Santiago to shore? The symbol had repulsed it?

And why he'd felt the magic, that night at Somerset House. That stupid tattoo de Groot had goaded him into. It had connected him to Amelia's dreadful spells.

'Did you know?' he said. 'Did you plan it?' Had his friend protected him, even while he was merrily drowning innocent sailors?

De Groot shrugged. 'I was pleased to think you wouldn't drown. You are my friend, *Mijnheer* Santiago. But the cock ... *nee*, it was some joke I will never remember.'

An accident. A drunken folly had protected him. Without it, Santiago could have gone down on any number of ships, and de Groot would have just let him drown.

Fury built in him.

'Tomorrow,' said de Groot, 'the French will attack. It has been raining heavily in Flanders. You saw to that, my little witch, didn't you?'

Amelia shrank back against Esme.

'And the water that has fallen will not only churn up the Allied cannon, it will rise. Rise as a hungry beast. He hasn't fed for a few days. He is starving.'

The true horror of that filled Santiago. That creature that had attacked him—it was going to come out of the mud and rain and devour the Allied armies. Wellington, and Tiffany's father, and even that boy from her village. They would be destroyed by the small octopus in the basin Nora carried.

And Bonaparte would continue his rampage across the continent, unchecked by any opposing forces. The magnitude of it overwhelmed him.

'But—why?' said Santiago. He regarded the blond giant he had come to consider a good friend. 'Why are you attacking the Allies? Aiding the French?'

De Groot's brow drew down. 'Because not all of us have the golden touch! Santiago the pirate and smuggler—so charming he walked out of Madam Zheng's lair with only a scar to show for it! The legend around you grew and grew. Money, women, all fell into your hands. And then you inherited a dukedom and married a beautiful witch! Meanwhile I lost ships to the Cape. I lost goods to the Revenue. I lost a child to the typhoid. I am no lover of Bonaparte but the money was too good, *mijn vriend*.'

'I am not your friend,' Santiago said.

'No. Indeed, you did not even invite me to your wedding! Not good enough for a feast attended by dukes and duchesses. Even royalty, I heard. The darling of the Society pages. Everything falls into your lap.'

Santiago could only laugh bitterly at that. He had told de Groot of his childhood, of his father's absences and his mother's religious fervour. Of the times he had to steal to eat, and slept in the street, and stowed away on ships.

'Maybe you will understand when you have a family,' said de Groot.

'He has one,' said Tiffany. She came to stand beside Santiago, and placed her hand on his shoulder. He swore warmth spread from it.

She stood beside him, his equal. His family. Something so precious he would fight to the death for it—and in his heart, he knew she would, too.

His wife faced the enemy with her head held high and said, 'We are his family. And we are witches, and there are seven of us. Plus a pirate.' She squeezed Santiago's shoulder and his heart nearly burst with pride.

'Pretty words, but what can you do?'

'I could punch your nose out through the back of your head,' said Nora, conversationally.

'I could blind you, or suffocate you, or make you see God,' said Madhu.

'I could send you into the middle of next week,' said Mistress Winterscale. 'Literally.'

'I could do this,' said Amelia, and suddenly Squidbert the octopus was flying from his basin and landing on de Groot's face. The octopus, who had after all been quite hungry, wrapped its arms around his head. Santiago knew that in the middle of those undulating limbs was a beak that could penetrate hard shells, and that it injected a toxin that could paralyse its prey.

De Groot screamed and flailed, and fired wildly with his pistol. Santiago was already turning away, back towards the lighthouse, when he felt Tiffany suddenly sag beside him.

She clutched at her chest, and he saw blood blooming there.

Cold horror swept him. 'Tiffany?' She was already sinking to the ground, taking him with her. 'Tiffany, no. *No.*'

She fell heavy against him as he knelt with her in his arms, her breath coming hard and uneven.

His hands shook. There was so much blood. His mind stuttered, helpless, useless. 'Tiffany. No. I love you. *Mi amor*, please don't die, I love you—'

She was gasping now. The others crowded around him, Madhu kneeling before him and tearing at Tiffany's bodice. 'Light,' she snapped, and several appeared above them.

'Tiffany?' gasped Amelia, beside him. 'My love, my baby— please. Not when I've just found you!'

Santiago knew he was trembling. He couldn't take his eyes from Tiffany's beloved face, pale in the moonlight. Her parted lips gasping for air, her sea storm eyes rolling back in their sockets, her silver hair falling from his pins and trailing on the wet ground.

I can't lose you, I can't, I can't—

If she died, he didn't know if he could survive it.

Everything they'd shared flashed before him. The way she'd leaned over him when he was injured, and her breast had brushed his arm. The way she conversed with the kitchen kittens when she thought he wasn't listening. The scent of her skin. Her resilience and strength. Her amazing magic. The way she gasped and clutched at him when he made love to her.

I love you.

'*Mi amor*,' he whispered, and tears blurred his vision of her. '*Te amo*, Tiffany.'

Then she gave a great gasp and coughed, and wheezed, 'Ow.'

And Madhu said, 'I have never seen that before.'

'What?' He tore his gaze from Tiffany's face to her chest, where Madhu had uncovered Tiffany's stays and was prising something from the central busk.

It was the lead bullet, flattened out like a ragged coin.

Santiago was quite sure his heart stopped. 'But—'

'They say silk stops a bullet,' said Esme doubtfully.

'I'd say it was less the silk, and more the quarter inch of solid maple,' said Madhu.

'I told you,' said Gwen, with some satisfaction. 'June.'

Santiago could only stare. Madhu carefully prised apart the shattered busk of Tiffany's stays, peered beneath it, and said, 'There are some nasty splinters. But the breastbone is intact. You have been very lucky, Tiffany.'

Amelia made a sound like laughter forcing its way through a sob. 'Thank God you weren't wearing those stupid light stays!'

Santiago wanted to sweep Tiffany against his body, but he was terrified of hurting her further. He bent over and kissed her face, over and over. She wasn't going to die. She was alive.

'I love you,' he whispered, over and over. 'I love you.'

Tiffany coughed again, and flinched. 'Getting shot in the chest,' she panted, 'really hurts.'

CHAPTER 20

'*I* assure you, I really am perfectly fine,' said Tiffany.

'*Mi amor*, you just took ten minutes to sit up.'

She dealt Santiago a cross look. 'But I am *able* to sit up.'

He smiled at her, in that way that made her heart turn over. 'Yes, you are.'

He had hardly left her side since they returned to London. The servants had been spun a tale about having to leave in some emergency involving Tiffany's mother, and then a fall from a horse was thrown in to explain her injuries. Although what sort of fall left a lady with splinters in her breasts, nobody asked.

Now that Madhu had pronounced her out of danger and in need of nothing more than rest, she was becoming somewhat bored. Not to mention that Santiago's constant concern was driving her slightly up the wall.

'Look,' she said, once she was comfortably settled with an excess of pillows. 'We really do need to talk about what happened at the lighthouse.' Her heart thumped uncomfortably, and it had nothing to do with her injury.

She and Santiago had said some terrible things to each other, and then since she'd been shot, neither of them had mentioned it.

Santiago nodded gravely. He was sitting, as he had for the last few days, in a chair right next to the bed, in the faded opulence of the duchess's suite in Grosvenor Square. The bruise on his jaw was quite brightly coloured now, since he had refused Madhu's treatment in favour of her treating Tiffany.

'William informs me that we can more than afford the price de Groot's widow is likely to offer for the business, and more besides. He has suggested a trust for the children.'

'Yes, and that's good,' said Tiffany, and then she felt a bit wretched because Santiago had just been betrayed by an old friend and watched him die in a somewhat unpleasant manner, and what she had to say seemed trivial by comparison.

But before she got there, a tap on the door heralded Billy, swiftly arrived from Castle Aymers in tow with Robinson.

'Guv,' he said. 'Er, Mrs Guv. I brung up the post for you.'

Tiffany knew she should have told him that was the butler's job, but she understood Billy was purely concerned for them both.

'Thank you, Billy. Would you take that plate down to the kitchen for me?' Tiffany asked, knowing full well that all the biscuits on it would have vanished by the time it arrived.

Included in the pile of letters were the day's papers, still trumpeting Wellington's victory over Bonaparte, and a letter addressed to Tiffany that bore the sign of an hourglass on the outside. She opened it, to find a missive from Mistress Winterscale.

History records that you are well, but you have my best wishes anyway. I thought I should let you know that I located your lord father, and he is well, but he has spent the entire campaign in Brussels. He is apparently indispensable to Wellington in the matter of

*supplying fine wines and meats, but nobody can remember him
going anywhere near a battlefield these last dozen years or more.*

Tiffany pressed her hand to her mouth, trying not to laugh, because laughing hurt. Her great and heroic father, little more than a quartermaster! She wondered if anybody had told the Peerage.

*I have also looked for a Henry Proudbody, who appears to be a
sergeant in the infantry. He is intending to return home to his sister,
but begs to inform she will need to make room as his wife is
increasing.*

'Henry! You dark horse,' she said out loud.

'My love?' said Santiago.

'Henry. My childhood friend. He has a wife and they are expecting a child. And he is a sergeant. I suppose I should stop thinking of him as a child.' She put down the letter and glanced at her husband, who seemed utterly bored by his own post. 'You know, I suppose we have Henry to thank for our marriage. In a roundabout way.'

'We do?'

'Yes.' Tiffany knew what they had to talk about, and she was trying to lead up to it gently. 'Speaking of which—' Another scratch at the door made her sigh. 'Yes?'

It was Hayrick, the under butler who had travelled down from Castle Aymers. 'The Countess of Chalkdown,' he announced.

'Who?' said Tiffany, bewildered for a moment.

Santiago coughed. 'Your mother?' he said, as that lady swept in, almost unrecognisable from the last time Tiffany had seen her.

That woman had been a shuffling, terrified wreck. This lady was elegantly attired and coiffured, her chapped hands hidden by gloves, her chafed ankle by neat half-boots. She held herself with poise, and waited until Hayrick had closed the door before she rushed forward.

'Tiffany! My love. How are you feeling? That Madhu is an excellent potion maker.'

'She is. And I am feeling quite well. As I keep telling my husband,' she added pointedly. Santiago shrugged unrepentantly.

'I still cannot believe you are married. My baby girl!'

Tiffany looked down at the letter still in her lap. *Your baby girl whom you abandoned.*

Granted, she had been abandoned in the care of her brother and his wife, in their large and comfortable country house, with a small army of servants. It wasn't quite being left at the church door.

But on the other hand, she had been left with *Elinor*, who—Tiffany could see now—was probably the worst person in the world to bring up a witch. Amelia had to know Tiffany would never fit neatly into the mould Society required, and Elinor was so absolutely terrified of being seen as different—lesser—by her peers that she'd been repressing Tiffany her whole life.

Perhaps she could find some kind of retribution against her sister-in-law for that. Or perhaps merely being ignored by a duchess was the worst thing that could happen to Elinor, and it had the distinct advantage of being terribly easy.

Amelia sighed, the hopeful smile fading from her face. 'I can see you're still angry about that. And I don't blame you. I would be, too.' She hesitated, still standing just inside the room. 'I have been talking things over with Esme, and she agrees: I owe you an explanation. It is not an excuse, but I hope it will help you to understand.'

Tiffany didn't want to hear it. But she knew that was childish. And she was, as her mother had pointed out, a married woman now. And a duchess to boot. She had no time to be childish.

I'd still quite like to curse Elinor with spots, though.

'Of course. Santiago, will you fetch a chair for—oh.'

Her mother glanced across the room and the chair by Tiffany's writing table slid across the floor to her.

Santiago whistled. Tiffany rolled her eyes at him.

Amelia Worthington seated herself elegantly, with no sign of the overwrought creature she had been in the lighthouse. But then she took off her gloves, and Tiffany saw that her hands were still healing from multiple cracks and bruises, her nails torn and bitten. This close Tiffany could see the skin under her eyes had been powdered to hide the dark circles, and that beneath her elegant day dress she was just a little too thin.

'I have thought about this,' said Amelia, 'and I think the best way is to start at the beginning.' She glanced at Santiago.

'Whatever you have to say, you can say in front of him,' Tiffany said.

Amelia nodded, and took a deep breath. Then she began speaking.

'My father was a religious zealot.'

This hadn't been what she was expecting. Tiffany knew almost nothing of her maternal grandparents. A baron, whose wife had died quite young. The baron himself had never tried to contact Tiffany, and she had a vague recollection of hearing of his death some time ago. Her mother had one brother, who did not trouble Society.

'Church wasn't enough for him. He delivered his own sermons, lectures—rants really—for hours at a time. Told us that we were wicked, told us of the devil, witches, fornication: all the reasons we were going to hell. And I was so unnatural. I could move things with my mind; I was—' Amelia hesitated, then continued, 'I was in love with a woman.'

She glanced at Tiffany and Santiago, neither of whom gave her any reaction. After the last few months, Tiffany found that this didn't shock her in the slightest.

'It was a strange, febrile time. The French king had been executed; the queen was in prison. There were even rumours that the royal children would face the guillotine. We feared the revolution would come here. We were trying to make the most of our lives while we still had them. But when I ran from Esme, it was into the arms of a man twice my age. A widower. I tried to comfort him, and ... well, one thing led to another.'

Tiffany deliberately didn't look at Santiago at that point.

'When we realised our actions had ... ah, consequences, he agreed to marry me. But by then I think we both knew it was a mistake. He was still grieving his first wife, and I was in love with Esme. I was desperately trying to repress everything about me that I thought was unnatural. I thought perhaps a baby would redeem me, something pure and good. That love would redeem me.'

She learned forward and took Tiffany's hand. Her eyes were bright. 'And I did love you, Tiffany. From the moment I saw you. You were so perfect, so beautiful. But I was so frightened that I would hurt you.'

'Why?' said Tiffany. 'If you loved me, why?'

Amelia let her go, and twisted her hands together. 'If ever I was possessed by demons, it was then. All I could think was that I would cause you harm.' She looked down at her lap. 'Sometimes the furniture in the room would rattle when I became upset. What if something fell on you? What if the ... the monster inside me took over? I didn't know what it was. Esme had tried to tell me I was a witch, but all I knew was that witches were brides of Satan. I was convinced I was wicked and defiled. And that I would contaminate you, too.'

Tiffany reluctantly supposed that made sense. The vicar at Dyrehaven was not one for ranting about the Devil, and neither was the priest at the church they attended in Town. But how many times had Tiffany repeated the line, 'Deliver us from evil'? If that was all one had been taught...

Amelia reached for her hand again, and by now there were tears in her eyes. 'I became so terrified I had to leave. For your sake. Because I loved you.'

And Tiffany found herself saying, very quietly, 'I understand.'

'You— You do?'

Tiffany looked down at their hands. Hers was smooth and neatly kept, even after days of bed rest. Her mother's was chapped and cracked, bruises showing at the wrists, the nails black.

'I repressed my gift, too. And I was raised by someone who,' she chose her words carefully, 'had little interest in understanding or appreciating me.' She glanced at Santiago. 'And I was afraid of loving the wrong person. But not because I was a witch.'

Because she had only seen one way to be, and it was Elinor's uncompromising conventionality. She had been told—she had been shown—that marriage was something that must be endured, something inevitable, something that came with endless rules and obligations. Something that confined a woman to the single role of 'wife' and gave her no other identity.

But that wasn't what Santiago had given her.

'But he accepts that you are a witch?' said her mother.

Tiffany glanced at Santiago, who had been listening silently all this time. *Also not a quality I expected in a husband, Tiffany thought drily.*

'I do,' he said, sincerely. 'I think Tiffany is magnificent.'

She smiled at him, just a little. And he smiled back.

'But how did you meet de Groot?' Santiago asked.

Amelia sat back in her chair. 'When I left, I went to the Continent. I travelled widely, with no real aim. And I thought of you every day. I tried to write to you, but I didn't know what to say. Eventually I met women who were like me. They made me realise that I had to embrace my gift, not repress it. That if I carried on in such a manner, it would destroy me.' She looked away. 'Esme had told me the same, but I was too indoctrinated in my father's ways to believe her. How different life might have been if I had!'

'Well, I wouldn't be here,' said Tiffany, and Amelia's gaze flew back to her.

'And I could never regret you, my love.' She took Tiffany's hand again. 'I made a small living travelling with carnivals and fairs, doing party tricks to entertain people.' She smiled. 'There was always someone looking to see how it was done. For invisible thread or some kind of accomplice.' She nodded at the basin and pitcher on the dresser, and they rose gently into the air before settling back down again. 'I was with one of these fairs when I met de Groot. You see, I had a trick. Has Esme told you about poppets yet?'

Tiffany shook her head.

'They are small dolls, used to represent a person. I would never use mine to control or influence a person, but I could use a small doll to influence a larger one.'

'Like you did with the squid?' Santiago said.

Amelia sighed. 'Exactly like I did with the squid,' she said heavily. 'I didn't know that's what he wanted, or why—not to begin with. Not until I was already locked in that tower.' She reached down, apparently without thinking, and rubbed at her ankle.

'I'm sorry,' whispered Tiffany.

'Why? You didn't do it.' She squeezed Tiffany's hand. 'You saved me.'

'Well, we had some help.' She smiled at Santiago, and he smiled back.

'I want to try to make some reparation for the things I did,' said Amelia. 'I thought—perhaps something for the widows and orphans of sailors? A refuge, perhaps. Somewhere they might learn useful skills with which to support themselves.'

'An excellent idea,' said Santiago warmly. 'If you require funds for this, I have far too many.'

Amelia laughed, and Tiffany realised it was the same way she laughed. This woman was more like her than any of the family she'd actually known.

'And perhaps something for soldiers?' said Tiffany. 'Henry Proudbody will need more than a footman's income if he is to support a family, and so will his sister. I thought to offer them employment at Castle Aymers, perhaps?' she added, to Santiago.

'Whatever you want,' he said.

Tiffany chatted with her mother about the people of Churlish Green, whom she had known for such a short time, and found herself relaxing. She had never expected this. To even meet her mother was something she had long ago given up on, but to find that they had a lot in common and could just ... get along, that seemed like a miracle.

After a while, Santiago excused himself to deal with some of his correspondence, and Tiffany rolled her eyes at her mother.

'I love him,' she said, 'but he has been here all day, every day since we got home. It is exhausting.'

Amelia smiled. 'That is because he loves you,' she said. 'I've never seen a man more smitten.'

Tiffany pleated the coverlet with her fingers. 'I did say some terrible things to him, just before we found you,' she said.

'It doesn't look to me like he cares.'

No, it didn't. And that cheered Tiffany hugely.

After her mother had gone, she called for her new maid and bathed, dressing in a fresh chemise and wrapper. Stays were not permitted at this point of her recovery, which was an inconvenience and kept her from dressing properly, but it was a pure relief to be out of bed and sitting in a chair. She wrote a letter to Amy Proudbody and enclosed a note for Henry, whenever he came home, and was just addressing it when Santiago came back in.

He hesitated by the door for a moment, twisting his hands.

'I thought you might appreciate some time alone with your mother,' he said eventually.

Tiffany felt warmth bloom in her. 'I did,' she said.

But now they had to talk. About the assumptions she had made, and he had made. Since she'd been injured, he hadn't left her side, but there were still things that needed to be said. Things she couldn't just leave lying there between them.

But she didn't know how to start. How to tell him she'd been so afraid, so frightened that she'd made a terrible mistake in trusting him, and squandered her one chance at independence. She'd let her old fears in, that he would trap her, treat her as a possession, and that all the love between them was a sham. Especially when she knew her feelings for him were so painfully real. The thought that she could love him so much and he might not care had obliterated the reality.

It was Santiago who spoke first. 'You said—back when we, uh … you said you still wished for independence and I realised…' He came fully into the room, and pulled his chair over to hers. He sat, and looked nervous for a moment. 'Tiffany. I have to be a duke and also a tradesman. I don't want to give one up for the other, and there are going to be times when one takes precedence. And I want to be your husband, but not spend every minute with you.'

She raised her eyebrows, and he looked a little embarrassed.

'Apart from when you have been recently *shot in the chest* and I am very concerned for your health,' he said meaningfully. He shoved his hand through his hair, which Robinson still hadn't persuaded him to cut. 'What I am trying to say is that I understand your concern. That sometimes you need to be a duchess and sometimes a witch.'

'Yes,' she said slowly. 'That's some of it.'

'Some?' He leaned forward eagerly. 'Tell me. I want to understand.'

And that was it, right there. He wanted to understand. He wasn't assuming he knew or not caring that he didn't.

She had been a fool to doubt him.

Tiffany smiled. 'I think you already do understand,' she said. 'I —I am not a thing to be owned, and shown off like a bauble.'

'No,' he agreed. 'Although you are very beautiful and spectacularly powerful, and I am incredibly proud to have you as my wife.'

She laughed, and winced. 'Keep that up and I'll be violating half of Madhu's orders,' she said. 'Look. I thought I didn't want to marry because I thought it would trap me. And with you … I think I had thought it was all going too well and there must be a catch, and then you said that about belonging to you and I just…'

Santiago opened his mouth, and she held up a hand to stop him.

'It's like in the Peerage. Mama is listed as the wife of the Earl of Chalkdown, and I don't even have a name. I didn't want to be a … a footnote. But I know I won't be, with you.'

'No,' he said. 'Didn't you notice how Mistress Winterscale had heard of you?'

Tiffany blinked. 'Had she?'

'Oh yes. She seemed very impressed. You will do great things, Tiffany. And I will be the proudest husband in the world when you do.'

She took his hand then, and he squeezed hers.

'And,' he said hesitantly. His face took on a hangdog look. 'The thing I said. To you. In retaliation. I didn't mean it. I was hurt and upset and I thought—'

'You thought what?'

He sighed. 'I thought I didn't deserve you. Why should a woman like you marry a man like me, who doesn't even know

359

that you don't wear green to an evening event? I am a ragamuffin street rat, and you…'

He looked her over, sitting there in her wrapper with no stays on, and it was if he saw her in her finest ballgown, wreathed in glamour.

'You are everything.'

'I think you are wonderful, too,' she said softly, and smiled as colour came into his cheeks.

'But when I thought I would lose you,' he began, and leaned even closer, their knees touching. 'When I thought I would lose you, Tiffany, I couldn't bear it. I realised I would do anything to keep you with me. Anything. I love you. With everything I am. I love you. And I always will. This I swear to you.'

Tiffany looked into his beloved face. He was so very handsome, but more than that he was so very dear to her.

She reached up with her free hand and brushed that errant curl from his face. 'I felt the same when I thought you might die,' she said. 'That's why I wanted to marry you. I realised I … I didn't want to be without you. That I love you, too.'

He leaned forward and softly kissed her lips.

'And,' she murmured against his mouth, 'you will recall that I demanded to marry you *after* I knew you would live?'

Santiago's face creased with chagrin. 'Forgive me for misremembering,' he said. 'I had just been shot.'

'I will forgive you,' she said, 'because I now know something about being shot myself. I don't like it. I will not be trying it again.'

He smiled at that, and kissed her again, and then he lifted her into his lap and kissed her some more, before reluctantly withdrawing.

'Madhu did say you were not to over-exert yourself,' he said.

'Madhu isn't here.'

'She might put a curse on me,' Santiago said, nuzzling at her neck as if he couldn't help himself.

'Then I will take it off. Because I am a witch, too.'

'Yes, you are. My duchess witch.' He kissed her mouth again.

'Perhaps,' said Tiffany, who didn't want him to stop at all, 'there are things we could do that wouldn't be an over exertion?'

He groaned, but then he grinned and stood up with her in his arms. 'I do love a challenge,' he said.

EPILOGUE

AUTUMN 1816

*T*here was no ballroom at Castle Aymers, as such, but the great hall was larger than most of the ballrooms Tiffany had been in, and with its ancient banners safely stored away and chandeliers rigged up, it looked quite magnificent. Outside, the weather was unseasonably cold, bringing Santiago's unenthusiastic plans for hunting and shooting to a merciful end.

Tiffany couldn't help the feeling that her mother might have had something to do with this.

The castle being huge enough to accommodate half of Society, they had decided to invite just the ones they liked. Among the great and the good mingled Esme's eclectic friends. The Misses Brockhurst had already cut a swathe with their strident opinions on the Grimm Brothers' fairytales, and Lord Hornwood had been seen eyeing up Percy Brougham, whose complexion had cleared up and who didn't seem to mind the attention at all.

Tiffany was just returning from her second surreptitious trip to the kitchens when she bumped into William Nettleship.

'You look very smart,' she said, because in his eveningwear he did.

'Thank you, Your—Tiffany,' he corrected himself. He glanced at the crumbs on her gloves and his face went carefully blank.

Hurriedly, she dusted them off and gave an unconvincing smile. 'Did you need something? Supper will be served soon, they tell me. I was just checking on the extra staff we brought up from the village,' she added as a rather lame excuse.

'Ah, yes. The vicar is telling everyone the poor relief scheme you and Santiago devised was his idea,' said William. Tiffany thought about being annoyed by that, and decided she had enough on her plate. 'And Mr Noakes is making a very detailed itinerary for your trip to Egypt.'

Tiffany rolled her eyes. 'I only said we might be thinking of a trip,' she said.

'He's very enthusiastic,' said William laconically. 'As it happens, I was looking for Billy. He's been reading a book of limericks and I can't shake the feeling he's going to start reciting them in front of polite company.'

Tiffany laughed. 'Oh, let him. We said we wanted the occasion to be memorable. Now, if you'll excuse me…'

She hurried back to the great hall, where a set was forming for a country dance. Smiling politely, she resumed her duties as hostess, introducing potentially interested parties to each other—Miss Brougham taking a shine to William that her mother did not know whether to approve of or not; Mr Noakes being fascinated by Miss Belmont's surprisingly detailed knowledge of the eruption of Mount Tambora—and making sure there were enough drinks and places to sit.

Speaking of… She spied a seat in one of the curtained window embrasures, empty probably because it was chilly, and took the weight off her feet for a moment.

Hosting a ball was hard work. She felt a little pink in the face, and reminded herself to adjust her appearance before she went back out there again.

The curtain twitched, and then Santiago was ducking into the alcove with her. 'Mi amor,' he said, quickly coming to sit on the bench beside her. 'Are you all right?"

'Oh yes, just taking a tiny rest. It is tiring, being a hostess.'

He looked troubled. 'We should have cancelled the weekend—'

'After all we've spent on it? There are people starving in this country, Santiago. We should never be so wasteful.'

'There are no people starving here,' he said. 'Thanks to you.'

She shrugged. 'The kitchens needed rebuilding and staffing. It only made sense to hire local people.'

Santiago slipped his arm around her and hugged her to him, careful not to disturb her hairstyle. 'And the crops that miraculously didn't fail in this wretched summer?'

'Luck.' She peeked up at his cynical face. 'And maybe a few ideas from Madhu. Why do you think I insisted on riding over all the fields at Beltane?'

'I thought you were seeking privacy for us,' said Santiago, pretending to look wounded.

'That was just the silver lining,' she told him, and he kissed her lips.

'My duchess witch,' he murmured, and his hand slid to her waist. 'Do you think our child will be a witch?'

Tiffany shuddered. 'Lord, I hope not. Babies are enough work without them accidentally making the tapestries come to life, or lifting their own cribs over their heads.'

Santiago looked stoically into the distance. 'I have survived the pirate queen of the South China Seas,' he said. 'I can survive this.'

'Do you think she would like to be the child's nurse?'

Santiago laughed. 'Have you told your mother?'

'No, but I can't believe she doesn't already know. Aunt Esme made a point of handing me a sarsaparilla earlier,' she explained gloomily.

She allowed herself to rest against him for a moment longer, then straightened with a sigh. 'Once more unto the breach. I have not yet greeted Cornforth and Elinor, and needs must, I suppose.'

'Why did you invite them?'

'Because I wanted Harriet to enjoy her first house party as an adult, and not be constantly at her mother's beck and call as she was at Dyrehaven.' She paused in straightening the skirts of her lovely deep green gown. 'Our party is superior to theirs, isn't it?'

Santiago grinned. 'Well, your brother hasn't shot me yet, so I can only say that is a significant improvement.'

They emerged back into the great hall, its noise and heat something of a shock, and Tiffany reminded herself to smooth out her figure before anyone noticed. Gwen, of course, would not be fooled, and she paused in her discussion of the tale of Snow White to look Tiffany over and say, 'I'm so glad you chose to call her Sylvia, dear. It goes so well with her colouring. Now, Miss Brockhurst, why did you choose dwarves and not cats, as in the Scottish tale?'

'I think we can safely say Gwen knows,' Santiago murmured drily as they moved away.

'Gwen could be talking about anything,' said Tiffany. 'She's rarely on the same week as the rest of us.'

'Whatever you say, *mi amor*. Ah, there is Esme...'

'It is a splendid ball, dear,' said Esme, as they reached her.

'Indeed. Billy's limericks are very funny, although I am not sure they are entirely suitable for ladies,' observed Amelia. Her gown was a deep, beautiful midnight blue, and opals shone at her throat.

Santiago shook his head in exasperation. 'Why did we teach that boy to read?'

'So that he can better himself and become apprenticed to William,' Tiffany reminded him. 'He has already identified three children at the village school who are not getting enough to eat. The teacher had no idea.'

'I saw young Henry Proudbody taking cloaks at the door,' said Amelia. 'He still seems quite shocked by the weather in Yorkshire.'

'It probably isn't always like this,' said Santiago, glancing out at the flakes of snow that were beginning to fall. 'Probably.'

'Hmm,' said Tiffany.

She saw her mother's eyes widen, and then she was saying very quickly, 'Gosh, I really must go and tell Madhu how well that shade suits her, my dear. Oh, and get some rest,' she added, with a darting glance at Tiffany's midsection.

She sighed, and turned, already knowing who she would see. She put on a brave face as Santiago greeted them.

'Ah, Lord Cornforth, Lady— but no, I must call you Chalk-down, now! Lady Harriet, how charming you look this evening.'

Harriet blushed and curtseyed and Tiffany wondered if she might have a little crush on Santiago. She couldn't blame her. He was looking quite irresponsibly handsome tonight, and extremely piratical.

Her brother wore a black mourning band over his already black evening coat and Elinor was in a grey dress, which did not suit her, and a black cap. Harriet had on a pretty white frock, trimmed with black ribbons, which was a lot more stylish than Elinor had probably been aiming for.

The Earl of Chalkdown had died following a fall from his horse outside a military encampment in occupied France earlier in the year. Tiffany received the news much as Santiago had spoken of his grandfather: a man she never knew, and was never likely to. Her mother had been somewhat less circumspect, and her cry of 'I'm free, Esme!' had echoed through Mayfair. They had both worn sombre clothing for a few months, and then forgot about him entirely.

'It is a splendid occasion,' said Chalkdown. 'The house is quite remarkable.'

'Yes, we must give you a tour some time. It may take until Michaelmas, though,' said Santiago, smiling.

'I really don't know how you go on with a house of such size,' Elinor said, gazing around at the lofty ceiling and diamond-paned windows. 'I should not like to live in a castle.'

'Then it is well that you don't,' said Tiffany pleasantly.

'We would not have come, but that we had to cancel our own house party after the sad news,' Elinor went on piously. 'But everyone has been most respectful, even going so far as to pretend we are not even here.'

Santiago nudged her, a smile tugging at his lips, and she fought to keep a straight face. It was petty, but it was vengeance of a sort. She wondered when Elinor would realise people were simply forgetting she existed.

'But he died doing what he loved,' Tiffany said, and her brother nodded thoughtfully.

'Serving the Iron Duke,' he agreed.

'Following him around like a little puppy,' Tiffany murmured under her breath, then louder. 'I say, Elinor, what a clever fan you have.'

The fan dangling from her wrist was not just edged in black, but painted that shade entirely, which Tiffany thought was going a little too far.

'And having already spared *the expense*,' Elinor whispered the last two words, 'of Harriet's new wardrobe, we thought it best to complete her Season. After all, the last young woman I launched into Society married a duke,' she added, with a laugh that verged on a simper.

Tiffany glanced up at Santiago, and felt her gaze soften. He had cut his hair, and the scar on his cheek was even more apparent now. His skin glowed golden in the candlelight. And his evening coat was green velvet.

'No,' she said, and leaned in to kiss his scarred cheek. 'I married a pirate.'

ACKNOWLEDGMENTS

Thanks must go to:

As ever, the magnificent, hilarious, frequently drunk women of the Naughty Kitchen. You are my people.

Jan Jones, for so much friendship and support, and this time especially for the historical advice.

Paul Couchman, the Regency Cook, for his excellent informative and entertaining classes on Regency food.

Louise Allen, whose fiction and non-fiction both helped me enormously with this book.

The Pride. You can't read this, because you're cats. But you're cats who are there for me, and I love you.

ACKNOWLEDGEMENTS

AUTHOR'S NOTE

This is my first historical novel! I've always loved reading historicals, but never wrote one until now. Therefore it's required more than my usual level of research (and more than my usual amount of poetic licence). Some of the stuff in this book is based in fact. Some, fairly obviously, isn't.

Theophania might not have been a terribly fashionable name in the Regency period, but it did exist, and had for hundreds of years. It was sometimes given to girls born on the Feast of Epiphany in January. Tiffany was a shortened version of it, which eventually eclipsed the original name. There's a whole historian's issue named after it: The Tiffany Problem, where something is historically true, but it sounds modern so no one believes it. My thanks to Terry Pratchett for opening my eyes to that one. I think our Tiffanies would have got on.

The chalk drawings on ballroom floors were a real thing. Not only did they look impressive, they also helped to give dancers some traction on a highly polished floor. Some artists became highly sought-after for their designs, which could include pretty much anything the client wanted, including things like coats of arms. They probably didn't come to life all that often, though.

It really did rain that heavily just before Waterloo, only—contrary to de Groot's plans—it was the French guns that got stuck in the mud. Whoops.

The statue of Father Thames in the courtyard of Somerset House is real: you can go and see it for free. Oh—and Foulness is a real place, too. You can't make up a name like that (my understanding is that it means something like 'bird headland'). Emphasis on the second syllable. It's actually harder to access now though: while there is a bridge leading to it, the land is owned by the Ministry of Defence, so it's not a good idea to go wandering around unless you want to get blown up.

Madam Zheng was a real pirate queen, and possibly the most powerful pirate the world has ever seen. Would someone please make a movie about her!

Kate

The author and One More Chapter would like to thank everyone
who contributed to the publication of this story...

Analytics
James Brackin
Abigail Fryer
Maria Osa

Audio
Fionnuala Barrett
Ciara Briggs

Contracts
Sasha Duszynska
Lewis

Design
Lucy Bennett
Fiona Greenway
Liane Payne
Dean Russell

Digital Sales
Lydia Grainge
Hannah Lismore
Emily Scorer

Editorial
Simon Fox
Arsalan Isa
Charlotte Ledger
Federica Leonardis
Bonnie Macleod
Jennie Rothwell
Caroline Scott-
Bowden

Harper360
Emily Gerbner
Jean Marie Kelly
emma sullivan
Sophia Wilhelm

International Sales
Peter Borcsok
Bethan Moore

Marketing & Publicity
Chloe Cummings
Emma Petfield

Operations
Melissa Okusanya
Hannah Stamp

Production
Denis Manson
Simon Moore
Francesca Tuzzeo

Rights
Vasiliki Machaira
Rachel McCarron
Hany Sheikh
Mohamed
Zoe Shine

**The HarperCollins
Distribution Team**

**The HarperCollins
Finance & Royalties
Team**

**The HarperCollins
Legal Team**

**The HarperCollins
Technology Team**

Trade Marketing
Ben Hurd

UK Sales
Laura Carpenter
Isabel Coburn
Jay Cochrane
Sabina Lewis
Holly Martin
Erin White
Harriet Williams
Leah Woods

**And every other
essential link in the
chain from delivery
drivers to booksellers
to librarians and
beyond!**

YOUR NUMBER ONE STOP

ONE MORE CHAPTER

FOR PAGETURNING BOOKS

**One More Chapter is an
award-winning global
division of HarperCollins.**

Sign up to our newsletter to get our
latest eBook deals and stay up to date
with our weekly Book Club!
<u>Subscribe here.</u>

Meet the team at
<u>www.onemorechapter.com</u>

Follow us!
🐦 <u>@OneMoreChapter_</u>
ⓕ <u>@OneMoreChapter</u>
📷 <u>@onemorechapterhc</u>

**Do you write unputdownable fiction?
We love to hear from new voices.
Find out how to submit your novel at
<u>www.onemorechapter.com/submissions</u>**